THE RISE AND FALL OF CONNER CODY

By the Author

Crossing Bridges

The Rise and Fall of Conner Cody

Visit us at www.boldstrokesbooks.com

The Rise and Fall of Conner Cody

by
Chelsey Lynford

2025

THE RISE AND FALL OF CONNER CODY
© 2025 By Chelsey Lynford. All Rights Reserved.

ISBN 13: 978-1-63679-739-7

This Trade Paperback Original Is Published By
Bold Strokes Books, Inc.
P.O. Box 249
Valley Falls, NY 12185

First Edition: July 2025

THIS IS A WORK OF FICTION. NAMES, CHARACTERS, PLACES, AND INCIDENTS ARE THE PRODUCT OF THE AUTHOR'S IMAGINATION OR ARE USED FICTITIOUSLY. ANY RESEMBLANCE TO ACTUAL PERSONS, LIVING OR DEAD, BUSINESS ESTABLISHMENTS, EVENTS, OR LOCALES IS ENTIRELY COINCIDENTAL.

THIS BOOK, OR PARTS THEREOF, MAY NOT BE REPRODUCED IN ANY FORM WITHOUT PERMISSION.

Credits
Editor: Shelley Thrasher
Production Design: Stacia Seaman
Cover Design by Tammy Seidick

Acknowledgments

Finishing this book was incredibly difficult. It coincided with a period in my life that took a tremendous toll on my mental health. Because of that, I relied on the support of others more than ever, so I have more thanks to give than I have room for.

A special thanks to the Bold Strokes Books crew—Rad, Sandy, Stacia, Cindy, Ruth, and everyone else—for their unwavering support and patience. I also owe a deep debt of gratitude to my editor, Shelley Thrasher, for getting me over the finish line and once again shaping my manuscript into something worthy of publishing.

To my parents, who love and support me even when they don't understand me, and my brothers, who think it's cool that I write books they'll never read: I love you.

To Loz, always the first to read my words: more thanks and love than I can express.

To my cats for teaching me there's no bad time to give love, especially when I'm on my laptop.

For Alexis, my friend, my sister, my partner in corporate misery. *Te amo mucho.*

For my favorites, Brie and Chelsie and Gray, I'm so deeply grateful for you.

Thank you to my family—Debbie, Peter, both Sheilas, and Amy, and my friends Dan, Heather, Erica, Brigid, Lauren, and my Freddo, for your unwavering support.

I'm so very thankful for my small (but growing!) group of author friends, especially my BSBestie, Jane.

And to you, dear readers! Last time I wasn't sure if I would have any of you, but your support gave me the motivation to keep going.

For anyone who ever felt unworthy of love.

RISE

Chapter One

The interview had been going so well.

Sure, Ned Scanlon asked too many questions of her and not enough of her bandmates, but she was Conner Cody, after all. She'd first appeared on this show as a toddler with her mother, back when Ned's hair was real, and though she had no memory of it, she had seen the footage too many times. Ned had bounced her on his knee, and she burst into tears that neither Ned nor her mother appeared willing or able to soothe.

Conner had always hated Ned Scanlon, his late-night talk show, and his bad toupee.

But she wasn't against using her fame to promote the band. For the most part he stuck to the script, and when he ventured outside the bounds, asking if she was giving up her acting career or still dating her on-again, off-again girlfriend, Vittoria, she used two decades of media training to guide the conversation back on track.

Until he had the nerve to ask about her fucking parents.

"I believe the term the kids use today is 'nepo baby,'" he said with only a slight sneer. "How do you respond to that?"

"I was a fetus on my first magazine cover. I'm the queen of nepo babies." Conner offered a practiced smirk to the whoops of the studio audience. "My family has opened doors for me that would never open for other people. But I hope my talent and hard work—*our* talent and hard work—will keep people coming back."

"Come on. Have you heard our girl sing?" Her best friend and the band's drummer, Maggie, squeezed Conner's shoulder with the muscled arm she had thrown around her.

Conner smirked as the audience cheered again. "It's a group effort, but thanks, Mags."

"What does your family think about this latest venture?"

She gave the usual canned answer that of course her family supported whatever she did, but he persisted.

"Surely your father had some words of wisdom for you, a guiding hand."

Maggie's hand on Conner's shoulder tightened. "Well, it's a different industry than when he got started back in the 80s, you know."

"All of our families are supportive," Emi, lead guitarist and, more recently, another of Conner's exes, said from the other end of the couch. Conner refused to be grateful to her for jumping in. "But they're not the ones who made the album. We are."

Ned nodded. "Let's go back to the album. Conner, you wrote numerous songs implying a, shall we say, less than ideal childhood. Have your parents indicated how they feel about being your muse?"

Conner's nostrils flared. "I don't give a damn what they think. Since you care so much, call them and ask. I'm sure you talk to them more than I do."

Behind the cameras, the producer drew a hand under his chin as the in-house band quickly began their commercial outro.

"And on that note, when we come back, for the very first time, Hestia Rising will perform 'Wicked Girl' from their debut album, *Broken Promises*!"

Conner leaned in. "Go fuck yourself," she said under cover of the audience's applause before stalking off the set.

Back in their dressing room, she waved off attempts to soothe her outrage.

"We were clear! We were *not* discussing my parents! You go let them know we'll never be back on his stupid show. Do you understand me? Never."

The band's manager, Kit, held up their hands. "He's a dick, Conner. Everyone knows that. I'll talk to them, I will, we'll make him apologize—"

"I don't want his fucking apology. I want him to walk off a cliff and land on a cactus."

"I'll work on that, too. Right now, I just need you to focus on the song."

Conner narrowed her eyes, glaring at them. She huffed one last time before she spun around. Not that focusing on this particular song helped calm her at all.

Around her, her bandmates went through their own pre-performance rituals. Maggie tapped out a rhythm on the coffee table, her bare arms flexing in the harsh light. Bellamy, their Southern belle bassist, short and sweet, threw M&M's into her mouth, humming to herself. And Emi…

Emi was lucky she was still in the band at all.

For her part, Conner paced back and forth. Fuck Ned Scanlon. Fuck her parents. And fuck Emi, too, for good measure. Slowly the tension slid from her shoulders and trickled down her body until she left it in a puddle on the floor. Everything else aside, Conner was a performer, and this album was her baby. She had poured her heart and soul into it, and she would continue to nurture it as it was released into the world.

She sped through her visualizations, fingering the notes she would strum, murmuring the lyrics, bouncing lightly on the balls of her feet to loosen up. Everything else aside, the rush she got from performing was as good as any drug she'd ever taken.

The light above the door flashed, indicating they were due back on set. The women gathered, their arms around each other. Conner made sure no part of Emi touched her.

"Keep it tight," Maggie said.
"Keep it cool," Emi added.
"Keep it right," Bellamy said.
"And keep it real," Conner finished.

They took their places on the dark stage. Conner picked up her Les Paul guitar and strode to the front, taking a stance in front of her microphone. When the cameras came on, Bellamy played the opening notes on bass before Emi joined in on her guitar, Maggie kicked up the beat, and the lights came to life, illuminating Conner as she opened her mouth.

Everything else melted away. Though they'd had some rocky rehearsals recently, Conner knew from the first note they were perfectly in sync. She tried her hardest to seduce the audience, vamping, flirting, caressing her guitar, moving suggestively against her bandmates. The song was about sex, inspired by sex, and she wanted to leave every single viewer desperate for exactly that.

She even made her way over to Emi's mic for the bridge, focusing on the space between her eyebrows so it appeared their gazes were locked on to each other. Their on-stage antics had become such a part of their performances that Kit had ordered them to keep it up regardless of the lack of off-stage relationship. Internet gossip boards burned up with speculation, and fans had even created a hashtag for the two of them.

The crowd shook the rafters with their cheers. Even as Connor and the others took a bow and waited while Ned announced his next upcoming guest (the poor soul), before they went anywhere near the internet, magazines, or social media, the band knew they had a hit.

The record label agreed.

Conner slammed her hands on the table, grimacing at the pain. "Absolutely not."

"Conner, be reasonable. The buzz is already there, and—"

"So we go on another show, play another song, and create more buzz. It's a damn good album. It won't be hard."

Three studio executives regarded her from across a broad mahogany table. Out the window, Conner could see Hollywood sprawled before her in all its complicated, pretentious, ruthless glory.

The band had debated for many long hours about signing with a label. Conner had the experience, the influence, and, perhaps most important, the capital for the band to go it alone. She had financed both of their EPs, using her contacts to bring in producers and a distributor. She could have done it again.

But Conner was busy enough, and as Maggie had sensibly pointed out, she was already writing their songs, singing them, and working closely with their producers. Dynamics in the group were precarious enough just with their personalities without giving her even more leverage. So they'd signed with an independent label that gave them more freedom than Conner had had in her adolescent girl-group days. More, but not complete.

"'Dark Streets' is the best song on there. Why not lead with that?"

"It's too dark," executive number one said.

"Well, duh, it's in the name. Besides, the entire album is dark. That's kind of the point."

Number two jumped in. "Which is why we would like to introduce you with one of your lighter songs."

"Why do you think that's what we suggested you play on *Ned at Night*?" Kit said gently.

That, too, had been against Conner's wishes. "Look how well that turned out," she said, although her heart wasn't in it. Too many people were already talking about the song. Glowering at each executive in turn, especially number three for no other reason than she reminded Conner of an ex, she told them to give the band a moment.

The four of them gathered next to the window. "Mags?"

Her gaze warmed Conner. "'Wicked Girl.' It's sexy as fuck, and it'll get attention."

"Bells?"

"Gotta be 'Wicked Girl,'" she replied immediately with a cheerful grin. "Everyone's talking about it already, Con. We're gonna be huge."

Conner grimaced, grinding her teeth before forcing herself to stop. Democracy could be overrated.

"I say 'Wicked Girl.'" Emi stared out the window, eyes narrowed at whatever her gaze landed on, with her hands shoved in her pockets.

"Nobody asked you, did they?"

"Conner!" Maggie pulled herself to her full height and crossed her arms.

Conner scowled. "Fine. Fine! It's 'Wicked Girl.' Call them back in and make everyone's day."

The studio heads were appropriately pleased, and Kit said nice things about the band's ability to hash things out amongst themselves. Plans were made for the video shoot, but Conner barely heard a word. All she could think about was how many times she was going to have to play the song in the months to come.

She really fucking hated that song.

Later, in the parking lot, Conner dropped into her beloved Porsche 911 and rested her head against the steering wheel. A tap on her shoulder nearly made her jump out of her skin.

"What do you want?"

Emi's tawny skin flushed, contrasting nicely with her dark-brown eyes. Conner looked away.

"I'm sorry, Conner. You have no idea how sorry I am."

"You keep saying that, but somehow it doesn't make me feel better."

"Tell me what I need to do. Please. I'll do anything."

"Oh, you'll do anything?" Conner lifted her sunglasses, finally meeting her gaze. "Go back in time and make a different decision. That'll do it."

Emi took a step back, sorrow etched all over her lovely face. Sorrow that Conner was sick and tired of seeing. Without another word she fired up the engine and peeled out of the parking lot, driving blindly until she found herself in the hills. Eventually she made her way back to the Pacific Coast Highway, at which point she pushed the twin turbos to their limits.

Maggie's car waited in her driveway. Sometimes she regretted giving her access to her gated Malibu neighborhood.

"Where the hell have you been?"

Conner grunted, closing the garage door behind Maggie's tall form. "And hello to you, too. I went for a drive."

"Get any speeding tickets today?"

"Not this time, but the night is young. I suppose I should ask you inside."

Maggie helped herself to a juice from Conner's refrigerator, sliding another one across the enormous kitchen island. "It's the polite thing to do."

She couldn't keep from chuckling. "All right. So why are you here and not home with your hunk of a boyfriend?"

"He told me if he sees you one more time, he won't be able to hold back and will probably ravish you on this very island right in front of my eyes."

Conner laughed outright. "I see. Well, there's a second time for everything."

"Ha. Very funny." Then Maggie narrowed her dark eyes. "Wait—"

"Calm down. I wasn't talking about Jamal. As if. I was talking about the island."

"Oh. *Oh*. Ew!" She backed up, and Conner laughed again.

"So, why have you darkened my doorstep?"

Maggie leaned forward, hands splayed on the besmirched (but sanitized) island. "Let's talk about Emi."

"Let's not."

Conner marched away, abandoning her juice. She refused to have this conversation again. Maggie followed, bringing up every old argument, but Conner ignored her. She'd heard them a hundred times.

"Just stop!"

"You stop. I'm not saying you don't deserve to be angry, but she's as much a part of the band as you or I. We're on the verge of something big here. Please don't screw it up. Just try."

Could she do that? Could she try to, if not forgive, then at least get along with Emi? They'd poured everything they had into this album, and all of them knew it could change their lives. Was it really worth giving that up for—

The pain, still so fresh, lanced her heart. She hadn't been worth it, either, at least not to Emi.

"You promised." Maggie's voice came low and full of warning. "You promised, Conner."

She had, and so had Emi. Conner pursed her lips. "I'll try. I really will."

"I knew you'd come around." Maggie threw a strong arm around her, knocking their heads together so hard Conner saw stars. "Now come on. You've been moping for a month. Let's go out tonight."

Conner nodded. She needed a night of debauchery. After all, what was the point of being rich and famous in a town like Los Angeles if she didn't do anything with it?

Chapter Two

The mezcal burned ever so slightly.

Conner took another sip, relishing the initial sting at the back of her throat before the smoky flavor followed in its path. For a Thursday night, Dorothy's was crammed wall to wall; with the diminishing nature of lesbian clubs, people had to take the opportunity while it still existed.

She stretched her legs in front of her, reclining on a black leather couch in the VIP enclave above the main dance floor. Maggie had rounded up a handful of friends, leaving Jamal at home in favor of a girls' night out.

Conner sauntered over to the balcony, resting her bare forearms on the cool black metal as she watched dancers grind below. Despite how often her fans pleaded with her, she never joined in the crush anymore.

She didn't belong in crowds. She *created* them.

People glanced her way, and a few pointed and waved, acknowledged by a flick of her fingers. They would remain mere hopefuls. Conner knew exactly why Maggie had brought her here, but she didn't intend to find company tonight.

A woman detached herself from the writhing mob and walked toward the staircase, piquing Conner's interest when security allowed her to pass. She watched, bemused, until the woman drew close enough for Conner to make out the blond pixie cut and toothy grin.

"Bree fucking Mathews. What's up, girl?"

"I heard I might find you here." Bree gave Conner a tight squeeze. "I haven't seen you out in a minute."

Conner shrugged nonchalantly. "Making an album and all that, you know. It's time-consuming."

Bree eyed her. "Is that so? Word on the street is that you were, well, off the street. I figured that Italian model had finally locked you down."

"Pfft." Conner threw back the last of her drink. "I told you to stay off the internet. Vittoria was…a lot, in good ways and in bad. But what about you? Has Bree Mathews finally figured out how to go on the prowl?"

Bree threw her head back and laughed loudly. "Not even a little bit. But I do okay."

"So I hear."

They fell silent. Conner didn't hold any ill will toward Bree these days and was happy her friend had figured her life out, but she was the subject of two of Hestia Rising's early songs for a reason.

"I saw your appearance on Ned Scanlon's show."

Conner groaned. Would she ever live that down? Her publicist had strict instructions to issue a no-comment on the many requests she'd received.

Bree squeezed her shoulder. "Don't worry about it. He's a jerk, and everyone is on your side."

"As if I give a fuck about that."

"Well, you never did. That was always the difference between us."

Conner smiled wryly. "I still can't get over seeing you at a lesbian bar like this."

"I can't get over the fact that you're up here alone and not down there surrounded by willing women."

Her earlier irritation surged back. "I'm allowed to not be a promiscuous slut for once, you know."

"Chill, Conner. It was just an observation." Bree studied her. "What's up with you? It's not the Ned Scanlon thing, is it?"

Conner shook her head. She felt like she was being asked what was wrong every fifteen seconds lately. She just wanted to wake up in six months and stop feeling miserable all the time. "I have a lot going on. The album and a Disney movie and now we have a music video to shoot, and I booked a spread for *Vogue*…I'm busy, you know?"

"Sure, but you've been busy since you were a baby. I've never known you to have less than three projects at a time." Bree eyed her again, and Conner returned the gaze steadily. They weren't as close as they could once claim, but Bree still knew her well, enough to change the subject without being told to. "I saw Maggie, but where's the rest of the band?"

"No idea." Bellamy was off doing whatever Bellamy did, and Maggie wasn't dumb enough to invite Emi.

They chatted for a few more minutes, discussing Bree's latest film and mutual friends, before Bree took off with her own group. Conner made her way back to Maggie's side and was reclining on their couch when the owner of the club approached, a bottle in hand.

"I heard someone was draining our supply of Rey Campero, so I knew you were here."

Conner tilted one corner of her mouth up in a grin. "You know you stock it just for me."

"On the house. You've been missing in action so long I was afraid it'd go bad."

Conner accepted with a quick thanks and hurried to say something else, not wanting yet another discussion about her state of being. "The place is packed. Your DJ's killing it tonight."

"She is, isn't she? You want to meet her and spin a few tracks?"

Conner was up before the offer was completed. Playing around with music was the perfect way to get her out of her funk, even if it wasn't what Maggie had intended.

They arrived at the DJ booth, where a diminutive, short-haired woman was nodding her head in time with the beat, capable hands moving quickly over a complex turntable. Conner watched her work. Recognition flared in the DJ's eyes at their introduction, but she didn't seem awed by her unexpected company or her boss, continuing to mix tracks.

"Do you spin?" Eva—that was her name—called over the music. Was that an Australian accent?

Conner offered a languid shrug. "Sometimes. I have a deck at home, and I usually do the music myself when I have a party."

"You want a go?"

Conner looked her up and down. "Absolutely I do."

Eva smirked and handed her a set of headphones before she pulled a microphone to her lips. "Hey there, shes, theys, and gays. Dorothy's has a very special surprise for you. Hold on to your panties and make sure you're extra thirsty, because joining me tonight is the one, the only, the stunning, that tall drink of water...Conner fucking Cody!"

The cheers and catcalls of thirsty sapphic persons washed over her like a tsunami. Conner gave them a cool wave, focusing on Eva's deck, nicer than hers but not unfamiliar.

She lost herself in the music, mixing track after track. She'd been so immersed in the entertainment industry since birth she couldn't comprehend doing anything else, but this wasn't a bad gig. Her hands and shoulder brushed Eva's several times, and Conner was surprised to find her dormant libido making a comeback. Maggie texted to say they were leaving, but Conner told her to go without her.

Closing time arrived before she was ready to call it a night. Despite the late hour, she was anything but tired, and she made a split decision. Maggie was going to be unbearably smug when she found out.

"You feel like continuing the party?" she said in a low voice to Eva, smiling and flicking her fingers at the remaining patrons calling her name as they headed for the exit.

"I thought you'd never ask. Just let me close up shop."

"I'll have a car out the back exit."

Conner summoned her driver. As soon as Eva slipped through the door, the black SUV pulled away.

"So."

"So."

Conner had picked up more women than she was willing to count. Her favorites were always the ones who seemed unfazed by her celebrity, on the surface anyway. Right now, Eva topped that list.

That would probably be the only thing she topped tonight.

"You're good. I can see why they hired you. Do you do private parties?"

"For my friends." She eyed Conner with a smirk. "Are we friends?"

"I think we will be soon."

Conner paid her drivers well, but not well enough to put up with a private show, so she kept her hands to herself for the drive, although the conversation was loaded with enough innuendo to make a Hollywood madam blush. Not that Conner knew any personally. She had *some* limits.

"Small matter," Conner said, deliberately keeping her tone light, "but I need you to sign an NDA."

"Excuse me?"

"It's nothing personal, but I'd rather not have my sex life splattered over Page Six. I learned that the hard way."

"Are you that kinky, darl?"

Conner licked her lips. "You'll have to find out for yourself. If it makes you uncomfortable, we'll take you home, no harm, no foul."

"Do you sign one as well?"

Bold, this one. No one had ever asked that before. Conner kind of liked it. She shrugged with a grin. "I will if you want me to."

Eva eyed her, and for a moment Conner thought the night was off. "You sure know how to romance a girl. Right, then. Where do I sign?"

Conner emailed the doc she kept on her phone, and all was squared away by the time they pulled up to the private entrance of her preferred hotel. Eva raised her eyebrows but said nothing.

She let out a low whistle when they entered the luxurious room. "I feel like Julia Roberts, but at least you spare no expense."

"No, I don't." Conner poured two measures of the whiskey that awaited them. "Though I won't be paying you $3000."

Eva took the proffered glass. "Damn. And here I thought I might come out ahead in this arrangement."

Conner's lip curled around her drink. "You will. Many times, if I have anything to say about it. How do you feel about hot tubs?"

"I'm not opposed."

"Good." Conner stalked toward her with a predatory grin. "You'll find one in the room behind you. I suggest you take off your clothes and join me. We didn't come here to talk, did we?"

Eva proved to be a wise woman and didn't respond with words.

By the time the sun rose, Conner was sated, sore, and sleepy. They'd eventually ended up on the king-sized bed, where she took one last opportunity to examine her lover. Eva dozed next to her with a satisfied smile. She'd surprised Conner, giving as good as she got, and all in all, Conner didn't regret the night.

She eased out of bed, gathering her scattered clothes.

"Skipping out?"

Eva pushed herself to a sitting position, letting the sheet slip away from her small breasts. Conner noted with some satisfaction the marks she'd left.

"I've got places to be. But take your time. I got a late checkout. Feel free to order room service, too."

Eva regarded her frankly. "I don't get you. You're an amazing lover, and you just fucked me six ways from Sunday, but I find you a bit cold otherwise. No offense."

"None taken." Why be offended by the truth? "But I had fun. I wouldn't mind a repeat if you're up to it someday."

"Well, you have my info," Eva said with a smile that relieved Conner. No hard feelings, then. She preferred to make her escape when her partners were still asleep.

Conner kissed her and flirted with the dangerous idea of lingering before she finished dressing and slipped away. As the elevator doors closed, the high of the last few hours began to ebb, and by the time they opened again, a numbed sense of emptiness replaced it.

Chapter Three

With the lead single selected, the label wasted no time preparing for the video shoot. Once it was ready, they'd release the song on the streaming services, do some promotion, and then release the entire album, at which point the band would go on tour. They'd never headlined a tour before, and Conner got tired just thinking about the upcoming year.

She'd previously worked with the director chosen for the video and generally approved of her work. The concept was simple—the song was about sex, so the video would be as well. Each member of the band would be paired with an actor and shoot four separate vignettes of seduction.

Conner arrived early at the studio. After reviewing the storyboards one final time, she consulted the wardrobe supervisor about her outfit.

"You need to think outside the box more." She put her hands on her hips before selecting a pair of high-waisted trousers. "Look at this. Pair this with a classic button-down, and you've got Katharine Hepburn."

The wardrobe supervisor pursed her lips. "Hmm. That won't do anything for your hips."

"What hips? Do you see any hips on this body?" Conner had not been blessed with her mother's notorious curves, and her hips would not be bearing any children. *Thank goodness.*

The supervisor continued to consider her suggestion. "You know, if I could find some suspenders…"

"Yes. Yes! That's the look." Someone called Conner's name. "I'll be back."

Her bandmates had arrived and were chatting with the director alongside four beautiful people. The talent. Rather crassly, Conner sized them up.

The first, a tall, broad-shouldered man, had sharp features and an impressive glare. His cheekbones could have cut glass, and his rippling pectorals threatened the seams of his shirt. The second was an attractive person with closely cropped hair and perfect umber skin. Their eyes caught Conner's critique, and they winked.

The third...Conner could have stared at her all day. Several inches shorter than Conner with curves made for caressing, she let her thick, glossy curls tumble across her shoulders, and her generous mouth was currently open wide in laughter, revealing an adorable gap in her two front teeth.

With some effort Conner tore her gaze away to the fourth, a man with boyish good looks often described with the outdated phrase "All-American," i.e., tan skin, blond hair, and blue eyes. Conner narrowed her eyes, tension building at the back of her neck. She recognized him, though less from the soap operas he used to star in and more for a period of her life that she'd rather forget. He greeted her by name, catching the attention of her bandmates.

"Want to clue the rest of us in?" asked Maggie. Having known Conner longer and better than the others, she likely suspected their connection.

"We ran in the same crowd years ago. Back when I was a dumb kid making dumb decisions. We lost touch after…"

Conner had written a song about the worst night of her life. That was enough. She noticed that Emi had sympathy written all over her face. She knew all the details of that night, even what had been kept secret from the public and the police. For the first time in a month, Conner wished she and Emi could talk like they used to.

The director saved her by introducing the actors and pairing them with the band members. Conner was pleasantly surprised to be matched with the beautiful girl, Melina. When she wasn't laughing, she had doe eyes the color of caramel.

"Hold on a minute," Conner said. "You're really pairing the Asians—" She pointed at Emi and Mr. Carved from Glass. "The Blacks." She indicated Maggie and the cheeky winker. "The White blonds." Bellamy and Conner's old acquaintance this time. "And the Hispanics."

"You're Hispanic?" Bellamy asked.

"My grandparents are from Argentina, Bells. You've met my mother."

"Oh, right."

"My point is, I appreciate the effort at diversity, but this is a bit on the nose, isn't it?"

Maggie nodded. "Conner's right, actually. Let's mix it up."

Everyone joined in, and after a few minutes of discussion, and a bit of do-si-do, everyone had swapped. That left Conner with the one person she didn't want, but Maggie lived up to her best-friend moniker by noticing and suggesting another switch, leaving Conner back where she started with Melina, who smiled excitedly.

Hours later, Conner was wondering if it was too late to change again. Blocking had been fine, but as they'd waited, scheduled after her bandmates' scenes were shot, Melina had clearly let her nerves get the better of her. The woman was very cute but seemingly also very green, and Conner yearned for experience.

"Cut! Cut, damn it." The director yanked her headphones off after they screwed up a take yet again. "Take fifteen, all right? Let's try to get this done today."

Conner stalked off to her dressing room, thankful the rest of the band had left when it was clear her scenes were taking longer. She twisted the plastic cap off a bottle of coconut water with such vigor it ricocheted off the mirror.

A soft knock nearly pushed her over the edge. She bit back a retort, not wanting to tear the head off some poor intern. "Yeah?"

"Hi, Conner." To her surprise, it was her costar, who didn't wait to be invited to come in and shut the door behind her, though she stopped there. "Can we talk about our scenes?"

"Sure." Conner waved a careless hand and dropped to the sofa, offering a water.

Melina declined, taking a seat next to her. "I just wondered—am I doing something wrong?"

Conner stared. Where should she start? The awkwardness, her tentative movements, the obvious nerves, the—

"It's only that you look at me like you hate me," Melina said in a rush.

"I—what?" Conner blinked. "I don't even know you."

"Right! Which is why I'm kinda confused. I mean, it's hard enough because you're *you* and I'm just me, and I really, really want this to work, but every time you look at me you just kinda glare, and you're intimidating enough as it is, and I—"

"Whoa, whoa, whoa." Conner held up a hand. Left unchecked, the girl might ramble into the night. "I don't hate you."

"You don't?"

Melina looked at her again, eyes huge and round, and Conner suddenly wanted to unburden herself to the stranger. How she hated not her scene partner but the song, how much it pained her to hear it as it played over and over and over in the studio, how desperately she wished she'd never written it.

She shook her head. *Stupid.* Melina seemed nice enough, but Conner was sure it would take about five minutes for her to spill Conner's secrets all over the internet.

"Of course not. I'm sorry. I'm just very stressed, and I'm letting it affect me, which is so unprofessional. I promise it has nothing to do with you." She shook her head again, pink-tipped tresses slapping her cheeks. "As for being intimidated, that's silly. I'm just a person. More experienced, obviously, but…"

A thought popped into her head, and she frowned at Melina. The kiss scene was where she kept messing up.

"Am I? More experienced, I mean. Have you ever kissed a woman?"

Melina flushed to her toes. "Well, um, no, but—I mean, I'm not opposed to it, the idea, I mean, in—in theory, but I haven't, um…no."

Conner hid a grin. *Adorable.* "It's different from kissing a man, but not so much."

"I just wish it wasn't on camera!"

Melina looked at Conner.

Conner looked at Melina.

Oh, no. Conner had seen that look on women before, and she'd acted on it more than once, but this…this felt wrong. As if she'd be taking advantage.

"Maybe we could practice in here?" Melina all but whispered. "Just once. Just to get it out of the way without two dozen people staring. Please, Conner."

How was she supposed to say no to that beseeching gaze? Was it taking advantage if Melina initiated the idea?

"Just—" Conner cleared her throat. "Just once."

They leaned close. Conner slid her hand onto Melina's knee and heard her gasp a split second before their mouths met. Then Conner had to swallow her own gasp. Soft and sweet, their lips moved against each other slowly, a curious test of a kiss. Conner hadn't kissed someone like this perhaps ever, so without guile or intention.

Melina gasped again when Conner's hand curved around her neck, and Conner broke off the kiss, uneasily aware that she was very tempted to chase this further. *Goddamn libido.* She hadn't so much as thought of sex for weeks, but after a single night of passion, apparently a simple kiss could now turn her on.

"So, um." She cleared her throat, trying to erase her aroused rasp. "Better, now?"

Melina held a hand to her red lips and nodded. "You were right. It is different," she murmured.

For a moment she appeared to be leaning in again, so Conner stood. "Right, well, let's…"

She paused, an idea shoving itself into her consciousness. A great idea. A brilliant idea.

"I've got it. Let's go."

She grabbed Melina's hand and dragged her along without an explanation. After discussing her idea with the director and intimacy coordinator, they closed the set, quickly went through the new blocking, and began to film again.

This time, whether their kiss really had broken the ice, or the lack of bystanders helped, Melina seemed much more focused, and Conner could now understand why she'd been cast. They sped through the small changes to their initial scenes, the foreplay before the seduction, and by the time they reached their actual sex scene, they were fully in sync.

"On this take, let's go all the way through," the director said. "I want you to run with your instincts and not worry about the cameras."

They were partially stripped of their outfits, and once the intimacy coordinator made sure both of them were comfortable, it was time.

"You good?" Conner asked quietly. Melina nodded, one corner of her mouth quirking up in a slight smile.

At the director's call, Conner picked Melina up and surged through a doorway, the fake door giving at the slightest touch. They devoured each other, hungry, yearning, desperate, Melina's plump breasts bouncing in her exposed bra as they landed on a bed. Conner paused. It was unscripted, but she gazed greedily at the woman beneath her. Then she sat up on her knees, jerking Melina back toward her by her thighs.

Melina widened her eyes, then shot her hand out, yanking Conner's head down, and they continued to make out furiously. With Conner's head buried between her breasts, Melina squeezed her ass, then raked one hand up her back. Conner captured her mouth in a bruising kiss, keeping Melina's lower lip trapped between hers as she pulled back. Then, slowly, gazes locked, she sat up, pulling her tank top over her head and revealing her bare torso.

"Cut!"

The director's voice dimly penetrated Conner's mental haze. She had filmed numerous sex scenes over the years, some more pleasant than others, so she was more than aware of the odd feelings they caused. She jerked her shirt down, offering Melina a hand up but letting go as soon as she stood.

The intimacy coordinator ran up, tossing each of them a robe. "Conner, I'll be there in a second."

Conner confirmed the director had everything she needed, accepting her effusive praise for how they'd finally brought it together, and headed to her dressing room, changing back into her own clothes. She fingered the suspenders. They'd come up with an interesting look for her, a far cry from her usual wardrobe of casual black on casual black, and she wanted to explore it.

"Hey, Con." The intimacy coordinator popped in with a friendly smile. They'd worked together on several films, so Conner had recommended her for the shoot. "Anything you need to talk about?"

"Nah. We were as comfortable as possible, girl, thanks. Melina okay?"

"She's fine."

"Cool. She made it easy."

"The way you ran out of the room made that obvious." So few people were willing to tease Conner.

"Don't be jealous, babe. I have plenty left for you." Conner winked, laughing when she rolled her eyes.

"As if. I'd never mix business with pleasure."

On that note, Conner departed, scowling as she slipped her Tom Ford aviators over her eyes outside. If only she had taken that vow.

The band and Kit gathered in the theater room at Conner's house to watch the final video. She always found something to nitpick when viewing herself on-screen, but she was used to it. The others, less jaded (in so many ways), exclaimed over their appearances.

She had to admit, the wretched song aside, it was a good video. Each pair was in a different setting—futuristic, modern, ancient times, and for Conner and Melina, 1940s noir—and the editing had been shaped around the song so that it reached its climax just as the players on-screen did.

Conner shifted in her seat whenever Emi and her partner appeared. Not only was it strange to see her kissing someone else, but their scenes also echoed her nightmares for the last month.

When it came to her final scene, which no one had seen before, everyone fell silent. She had to admit that it was fantastic. She and Melina totally looked every part of the lustful couple, tearing at each other's clothes, seeking kisses as necessary as oxygen. The video ended with her pulling her shirt over her head, cleverly framed so her breasts weren't visible, only Conner's bare back. The camera zoomed in as she leaned down, which she didn't remember doing, perfectly capturing Melina's look of awe. And then it ended.

Maggie whistled. "Damn, girl! You didn't hold back after we left, did you?"

"We were hot," Bellamy said, a grin stretching her cherubic cheeks. "I should film myself more often."

Kit jumped up with restless energy. "This was perfect. They're going to eat it up. I mean, shit, I'm sweating, actually sweating. Ladies, you better rest the next few weeks. Once this hits and the album drops, your lives will never be the same, and it's no holds barred on tour. We're going to be the biggest band in the world. Mark my words. The biggest band in the world."

Fueled by Kit's enthusiasm, they chatted late into the night, veering from tour strategy to what they would buy with their royalties to the interviews Kit was lining up. Conner offered them a place to sleep for the night, but everyone declined, and one by the one they left.

Emi was the last. Conner tried hard to keep Maggie's words in mind as they cleaned up the drinks and charcuterie in silence. Once finished, Conner gripped the sink, unwilling to turn around. She could feel those dark eyes on her back.

"Conner," Emi said quietly.

"What?"

"I hated seeing you kiss someone else, even if it was just for a video."

Conner finally looked at her. "Now you know how I felt."

Chapter Four

Conner curled up in the fetal position and groaned. Falling sick during the only real break she would get for months was brutally unfair. She could handle vomiting if it came after a night of partying, but throwing up for no discernable reason was uncalled for.

Deciding her stomach would let her live, she pushed herself to a sitting position on her marble bathroom floor. A spasm of pain shot through her abdomen, and she sank back against the jetted tub. She couldn't remember the last time she felt this awful.

Eventually the nausea subsided, and she dragged herself into the shower, feeling better once she was clean. The pain had been coming and going, but the vomiting was new, and she didn't like it one bit. Well, no more. She didn't have time to be sick.

Several hours later, she walked into a luxury senior-living home in Woodland Hills, her chin held high.

"Hello, ladies," she said to a group of white-haired women gathered in the home's garden. They looked at her expectantly, and she hefted a large container. "A dozen empanadas fresh from Nonna's, with extra chimichurri, of course."

Her tax accepted, they welcomed her with cheerful greetings, and she dodged half a dozen strong perfumes and wildly colored lipsticks as she walked over to a petite woman with dark features, her gray hair perfectly coiffed in a blunt bob.

"You look terrible."

"Lovely to see you, too, Abuelita." Conner pecked her grandmother's cheek.

"Walk with me," she said imperiously. "Bea. I see you eying the guava. You know those are my favorite."

The elderly woman snatched her hand back, and Conner chuckled as she offered her arm. "Good to see you're still ruling this place with an iron fist."

"Someone must. If you recall, I moved in here after your grandfather passed, God rest his soul, because I was lonely, not because I'm incapable of taking care of myself." As always, she crossed herself when speaking of Conner's departed grandfather. "But don't change the subject. Are you well?"

"I'm fine."

The hum her grandmother offered indicated anything but belief. "Are you on drugs, my girl?"

"Abuelita! Of course not. I can't believe you would ask me that."

"Why? It was true enough a few years ago. And look at you." She gestured with elegant hands. "So skinny."

"I've always been thin. Have you met my father?"

"Unfortunately, yes. And more's the pity, so did your mother."

Conner couldn't argue with that logic, although she winced at the unintentional dig at her existence. Then she winced again as the pain in her abdomen flared up. Fuck! Was she having the worst menstrual cramps of all time or something?

"Speaking of your mother, when was the last time you spoke with her?"

Conner frowned. "A few months? Whenever she was filming that movie in France. You?"

"Oh, we haven't talked since the last time she was in LA. She left in a huff."

"Shocking."

Conner's grandmother had been a cinema darling during the latter part of Hollywood's Golden Age, though she was unofficially retired these days, while Conner's mother's career ebbed and flowed between television and film. Conner herself had had two TV shows under her belt before moving on to movies and had little interest in going back to the small screen. One of the few things they all had in common, besides their dark-brown hair, was a penchant for familial drama.

Abuelita squeezed her arm. Conner was glad for the support as a wave of nausea swept her once more. "We come from a line of poor mothers, my girl. It simply can't be helped."

"Were you not close with your mother?"

"Oh, no. Mamá and I never saw eye to eye. She was very hard on all of us, and she never forgave me for running off to America. I thought going home to Argentina to marry would appease her, but it never did…not even the fourth time." She eyed Conner from the corner of one eye underneath heavy makeup. "I was curious if Camila reached out after your Ned Scanlon appearance."

"Oh, for fuck's sake, Abuelita. I'm so tired of hearing about that. And no. She didn't, though Seth texted me that I should have given him credit for taking me to my first concert."

Abuelita made a noise of dissatisfaction deep in her throat. "That man. I'll never forgive him for giving my beautiful Latina granddaughter such an Irish name."

"I'm as much Irish as I am Argentinian." Conner took wicked delight in stirring her up.

And it worked, for Abuelita ranted about Seth Cody, Conner's mother, and a variety of other subjects, including her third husband for some reason, leaving Conner to focus on keeping her stomach together. She wanted to curl up in the smallest ball possible. Oh, God. What if she had one of those kidney stones? They could just take out her entire kidney if this was how those felt.

"What?" She was suddenly aware they had stopped walking.

"Are you sure you're all right? You really don't look well."

"To be honest, I feel awful. I've got some weird stomach bug or something."

"Well, you never take care of yourself. All work and all play, existing on nothing but tea and liquor. Go home and rest. We'll see each other next month." She held Conner's face in her wrinkled hands, her fond smile quickly morphing into alarm. "You're burning up."

"I know. I think I'll take your advice."

Conner lurched to the side, giving a nearby shrub an unwelcome gift. When she stood, wiping her mouth, her grandmother regarded her frankly.

"Are you pregnant?"

"You know I'm not."

"Do I? Aren't all you kids liquid, or whatever you call it these days?"

Conner's irritation at her unwillingness to take her sexuality seriously overrode her amusement at her grandmother's awareness of sexual fluidity. All her Catholic grandparents had taken her coming-out in surprising stride, but she knew they hoped she'd at least swing both ways. No such luck there.

"Not this one. So no, I'm certainly not pregnant, and I never will be." *Only surefire way to end generational trauma.*

"Perhaps you should call your doctor, then."

"I will," Conner said, not intending to do so.

That intention stayed all the way home as she gripped her steering wheel tightly, through the evening when she skipped dinner in favor of as much Tylenol as the bottle recommended, and all night as she rolled in her bed, groaning and holding her right side. However, when she started her day by vomiting again, she gave up.

Conner groaned again when she hung up the phone, although this time out of frustration. Her GP had insisted that she get to the emergency room, but she absolutely refused to get an ambulance. It would be on TMZ before she arrived at the hospital. She called her personal assistant/driver/bodyguard. After a brush with a stalker, Conner had hired this acquaintance from her wilder days, and she was one of the few allowed to know some of Conner's inner workings.

"Appendicitis?"

"Quite acute. It needs to come out immediately before it bursts."

"Well, this sucks."

The doctor gave a surprised-sounding laugh. "I suppose it does, but that's better than the alternative. We can do it laparoscopically, so minimal scarring, if any, and if all goes well, you can go home tomorrow. In a couple of weeks, you'll be as good as new."

"My agent will be thrilled."

"Even superstars need breaks, Ms. Cody. Any questions? No? Then I'll send in a nurse with your consent forms and paperwork, and we'll get you scheduled for the OR."

Conner fumbled for her insurance card before the nurse arrived. Afterward, left alone with sweet narcotics dulling her senses, she picked up her phone. Then she paused. Who exactly did she plan to call? Her parents wouldn't care. Kit would have a nervous breakdown, so she wouldn't call them until she was home and recovered. Her manager Harlow was made of steel, but she couldn't do anything at this point. No need to worry her grandmother until it was over, either. She toyed with the idea of calling Maggie, but she might feel obligated to cut her trip with Jamal short.

Conner had made it twenty-three years going alone. She could do this.

A few days later, Conner was home, sore and medicated but on the mend. She'd had to reschedule a photoshoot, but otherwise, her appendicitis had come at a rare quiet time in her schedule. She smiled at the fact that even unexpected surgery bent to her will, though perhaps the pain medication helped her mood. She was sitting in her den, idly working with the beginnings of a song that wouldn't quit her head, when her phone buzzed.

The gate guard for her neighborhood said, "Ms. Cody, you have a visitor."

Once assured that Conner was fine, Abuelita had promised she wouldn't call a taxi and come over. She was nearly ninety years old and didn't need to take care of another person. No one else knew Conner had been sick, and she didn't have any meetings scheduled.

"I'm not expecting anyone. Who is it?"

He sounded skeptical. "Her driver's license says Sadie Cohen."

It was a good thing she was already sitting. Even her absentee mother would have been less surprising than this. It was a joke, right? Some crazy fan who had somehow found her address and was trying to trick their way in. It wouldn't be the first time. But the name…

"Ms. Cody?" The guard's voice sounded as if it came through a long tunnel. "Do you want me to send her away? Or I can call the police."

Conner took her time answering. "Let her in. She's my sister."

Chapter Five

The doorbell rang too quickly. Conner stared at the oversized wooden door for a long minute before she opened it.

Other than a few signs of aging, Sadie looked as she remembered from seven years ago. They didn't resemble each other much; Sadie lacked Conner's inches, and both her shoulder-length hair and her skin were several shades lighter. The eyes, though…they shared their father's green eyes, although Sadie's were surrounded by thin, black frames.

"Conner, hi. How are you?"

Conner blinked. "Um, okay."

They stared at each other. Then Sadie shifted. "Can I come in?"

"Sure."

They sat in the den in silence, Sadie on the loveseat and Conner in an armchair. Now that her initial confusion had faded, Conner grew annoyed. She hated surprises at the best of times, and this wasn't that. What kind of estranged sister showed up out of the blue and then didn't speak?

"Did you come over just to stare at me?"

Sadie's lips thinned. "This isn't easy for me either, you know. Your grandmother called me."

And the confusion returned. "My grandmother?"

"Yes."

"Short, demanding, Argentinian lady?"

"Sounds about right."

Conner sputtered, no real words managing to escape.

"She said you'd had surgery and gave me your address."

Conner reddened. "I don't need anyone to take care of me."

"I know you don't. Listen, Conner. We both know that the last time we tried this, it didn't go well."

What an understatement. Conner had done two lines in the bathroom beforehand, and their brief meeting had ended with Sadie telling Conner not to bother contacting her again. Which she hadn't.

"I shouldn't have said what I did," Sadie said. "You were just a kid, and obviously—"

"Hold on. Please don't condescend to me. I was—well, I was awful, and I guess, you know, I'm sorry."

"I'm sorry, too. I really am." Sadie smiled wryly. "Your grandmother also said that one of us had to stop being so stubborn, and it probably wouldn't be you."

Conner scoffed. "That definitely sounds like her."

She could have dwelt on how her mother's mother even knew about Sadie, much less managed to track down her phone number. However, the fact that Sadie actually came over interested her more. Their one brief meeting hadn't developed into a relationship, yet when asked, Sadie showed up.

Conner looked at her sister again. "An appendectomy isn't exactly brain surgery. I'm fine. So do you need money or something?"

Sadie's mouth fell open, and for a long moment no one spoke. Stirrings of regret poked at Conner.

"You're a real piece of work, you know that?" Sadie stood, grabbing a bag that Conner hadn't noticed until now. "I don't need your money, Conner. I've lived my entire life without it, and to be honest, I think I'm doing better than you."

When the door slammed, Conner flinched. The silence screamed at her. She was alone again. Like always.

Taking a shuddering breath, she moved as quickly as she could, wincing as she held a hand to her right side. Bursting out the door, she found Sadie reversing out of her driveway in a white Ford Explorer.

"Wait!" Conner slammed her hand on the hood. The tires screeched as Sadie jerked to a stop.

Conner held up her hands as Sadie rolled down the window. "I'm a bitch, okay? I know that. I'm trying. I really am. I'm sorry. Please come back inside."

Sadie studied her with a blank expression. "Do you still do drugs?"

She was tired of being asked that question but simply said, "No. I stopped a few years ago."

"Did you go to rehab?"

"No. I just quit."

"You just quit?" Sadie raised her eyebrows.

"Yes. I decided not to live that life any longer, so I didn't." She dropped her shoulders. "Come back inside, Sadie. Please."

A long, awkward moment, and then, "Okay."

Uncomfortably back in the den, they resumed their previous seats. Conner winced again, squeezing her hand into a fist. Her last round of pain relievers had worn off a while ago.

"Did you hurt yourself?"

Conner shook her head. "Just moved faster than I should have. It's fine."

"Let me see your incision." When Conner didn't budge, Sadie said, "I'm a nurse. C'mon." Reluctantly Conner stood and tugged her shirt up. Sadie frowned, peering at her three small incisions. "Sutures look good. You probably just irritated it. Are you on painkillers?"

"I'm switching between Tylenol and ibuprofen. They gave me something stronger, but I don't need it."

Sadie glanced at her over her glasses. "I'm not accusing you of anything, but is that wise?"

"I just told you I don't do drugs anymore." Conner gritted her teeth, yanking her shirt back down. "It's fine. Opioids were never my thing anyway unless I needed to sleep."

"Not your thing?" Sadie shook her head, muttering something else under her breath. "You're lucky to be alive. You know that?"

"I was there. I know that more than you do."

Just Conner's luck to get a second chance but her only sibling was a self-righteous know-it-all. Conner was no great prize, but maybe being alone was better than this.

"I was there, once, last time you were in the hospital."

Sadie spoke so softly Conner barely registered the sound. She jerked her head up.

"When you wrecked your car. It was all over the news, and I figured if my sister was dying, I didn't want to waste my last opportunity. You had security outside your room, but when I walked up, your grandmother came out. She took one look at me and said, 'You must be Seth's other kid.' You were unconscious, just lying there, all tubes and bandages." Her gaze lingered on the scar on Conner's temple.

Words escaped Conner. In a rare burst of parental acknowledgment, her father had gifted her a Bugatti for her sixteenth birthday. She'd repaid the favor less than a year later by wrapping it around a tree. Conner didn't remember the accident or much of her hospital stay, but she did recall waking up at one point to find only Maggie waiting for her. Her parents' schedules dictated their visits.

"I..." Did she wish she'd known? Would it have changed anything? She finally said, "That means a lot."

"Is that why you stopped the drugs?" Sadie asked gently. "Because of your accident?"

Conner shook her head. "I was sober when I crashed. I quit later."

"When your—"

"Why do you care so much?" Conner flexed her jaw.

Sadie pursed her lips before she answered. "We don't have to be anything, you and I. Shared parentage doesn't mean we have to have a relationship." She leaned forward, resting her elbows on her knees. "However, I'd really like to try. But before we do that, I need to know it won't be like last time. I have two daughters. My oldest idolizes you. I can't bring you into their lives if I think they'll be hurt."

Conner widened her eyes. She had nieces. For a moment, she considered lying. Sadie would leave again, which would hurt, but she was used to rejection. She didn't know anything about children. She'd barely had a childhood of her own. What kind of an aunt could she be?

"I don't use illegal drugs anymore," she finally said. "So you don't need to worry about that."

"Good. Because if you're up for it, I'd like for you to meet the girls sometime."

Conner nodded, swallowing hard. "Do you have pictures?"

Sadie pulled out her phone, scrolling through pictures of two cute kids.

Was Conner supposed to feel some sort of connection? Right now she was just overwhelmed.

"Do they know…?" She pointed at Sadie, then back at herself.

"No. As far as they're aware, my stepfather is my biological father. It seemed like an unnecessary conversation unless you and I ever reconnected." She smiled. "I wasn't kidding about Sarah, though. She's been obsessed with you since you started doing those superhero movies. She started begging to go to Comic-Con months ago."

"I could get you tickets. It's one of my last appearances before we go on tour."

"That's nice, but Asher and I think she's still too young for things like that."

"Asher is your husband?"

Sadie nodded.

"You have, like, an entire life. Wow. Would you tell me more about them?"

They chatted for another half hour, mostly in a stilted manner about Sadie's family and their lives in Santa Clarita. Conner slowly began to believe that the possibility of a relationship existed. But, inevitably, they ran out of things to say, and silence descended. Conner tapped a melody on her thigh.

"Is that one of your songs?"

"Huh? No. It's just something I was working on when you showed up. Do you want to hear it?"

Without waiting for an answer, Conner headed for the Steinway grand piano off to one side. Playing it was second nature to her. She took a moment to center herself and then began to play.

The song was incomplete, but as she played, inspiration struck, and she launched into a bridge, excitement flowing through her fingers. She could just imagine Emi tearing this up on her guitar. And with the slam of a door, the inspiration fled, and she stopped.

"Sorry. It's not finished."

"It's good. Does it have lyrics?"

"Uh-huh." Conner didn't look up from the notebook in which she scribbled the notes for the bridge.

"Maybe I could see them?"

Conner jumped as Sadie's voice came over her shoulder, and she clutched the notebook to her chest. "No! I don't show anyone my songs until they're finished."

Sadie stepped back, holding her palms out. "Sorry. I was just curious."

"It's a thing, okay?"

"Well, from what I heard, it was good. Very impressive. The most I create are notes for my kids' lunches." Sadie shifted on her feet. "I should probably go. Maybe we could get together for coffee soon? I know you're busy."

Conner nodded, trying to swallow the lump in her throat. "I can make time for that."

They swapped numbers, and Sadie headed for the door, stopping when Conner reminded her of her bag.

"I nearly forgot! I brought you some tea, and I made you chicken noodle soup...which is silly now that I think about it. For all I know, you might be vegetarian." She peered at Conner from behind her glasses, appearing bashful. "You don't have to eat it."

"I don't eat red meat very often, but chicken is fine. Thank you. I don't think anyone has ever made soup for me before."

"The girls and Asher love it." She handed Conner the bag. "Hannah drew you a picture, too. She didn't know it was for *you*, obviously, but I told them I was going to see a sick friend."

Conner lifted her head and gazed at her sister. They weren't friends, not yet, but perhaps they could be. The idea caught in her chest, both warming and strangling her.

She saw her to the door, terrified that Sadie would hug her, but instead they settled for an awkward wave.

As she watched her sister walk away, Conner suddenly blurted out, "Wait!"

Sadie turned, obviously curious.

"Do you want to come to a party?"

❖

Left alone, Conner poured some of her soup into a bowl and heated it in the microwave. Then, as she didn't own any magnets, she searched the kitchen drawers until she found tape and very carefully placed Hannah's drawing on her refrigerator.

Chapter Six

It should not have been this difficult for a celebrity to find a date.

Correction. Conner could have a dozen dates with nothing more than a one-sentence text. She could *find* a date easily. What she could not find was a date she really wanted.

She wasn't looking for a relationship at all. Been there, done that, bought the heartache. But she didn't want meaningless sex either. Been there, done that, bought the dental dams and regular testing because she was not about to catch anything. She just wanted a fun evening with someone she liked who wouldn't try to turn it into anything else.

Her ex-girlfriend Vittoria was in LA for a shoot, knew about the party, and texted several times that she was free, but Conner resisted. It was hard enough knowing they were in the same city.

In the end she took Lindsey Schafer with her. Lindsey played basketball for the Los Angeles Sparks, and they had met when Conner had courtside seats to a game. They had a few dates and more than a few rolls in the sack, but nothing beyond friendship ever developed. Not yet, anyway.

"I like this look on you," Lindsey said in the limo as they inched toward the venue. "It's new."

Inspired by the video, Conner had a new black suit tailored for her, complete with suspenders, although she left the white shirt unbuttoned to her navel and the bow tie hanging loose around her neck.

"I decided to try something different." She rested her hand on Lindsey's bare knee, admiring her little black dress. "I like this look, too, but it would be better on the floor."

Lindsey laughed and rolled her eyes at the same time. "You know you don't have to try so hard with me."

"Girl, I don't have to try hard with anyone, but I don't want to get rusty."

The world exploded in flashes as their limo pulled up and Conner climbed out, extending a hand to Lindsey. Posing both separately and together, she kept a practiced smile on her face as they slowly made their way through the line of screaming fans and slightly less aggressive press.

As she paused for the press scrum, her arm around Lindsey's waist, Conner idly wondered if they could end up together. They had enough in common, and they were certainly compatible in bed. Conner watched basketball; Lindsey played. They had plenty of fun when they hung out, even before they took their clothes off, and Lindsey could actually hold an intelligent conversation, which Conner couldn't say for all her hookups. Perhaps best of all, Lindsey understood what it was like to be in the spotlight.

Maybe someday. Even if Conner had felt something deeper than attraction, Lindsey seemed permanently hung up on someone from her hometown. But there were worse things than having a six-foot blonde on her arm. She allowed herself to appreciate Lindsey once more as they moved inside the warehouse venue, all thumping music and strobe lights. Maybe they would at least get a few orgasms out of the night.

She gazed right past Lindsey, squeezed her arm, and promised to be right back before slipping through the crowd.

"Hey, girl. Don't you look fantastic!"

Her partner from the video spun around, her face lighting up. She wore a boldly chosen gold number that clung to her curves. "Conner, hi! I mean, thanks! God, you look amazing. I mean, of course you do, but still, this is just..."

Conner, who hadn't missed Melina's noticeable swallow before she started rambling, chuckled. "Thanks." She held out her hand to Melina's date. "Hi. I'm Conner."

"I *know*!" A slim man in a startlingly shiny suit, he grasped Conner's hand between both of his. "I've waited on you at Ambrosia several times. All the waiters *love* having your table."

"Um, that's good?" Conner tried to extract her hand as Melina groaned.

"Conner, this is Eriq. He's my roommate and will not be accompanying me to any event ever again."

Her roommate? Conner perked up. "It's nice to meet you, Eriq. I love Ambrosia. You have the best chicken salad."

He wouldn't let go of her hand, blinding her with his smile. "I still cannot believe that my little roomie made out with *the* Conner fucking Cody!"

Conner raised her eyebrows at Melina, who turned the most attractive shade of pink. "You know, in the video."

"Have you watched it yet?" Melina shook her head. "I think they'll play it at some point tonight, up there on that projector screen."

Melina's cheeks darkened further. Really, she was the cutest thing. "Oh gosh. I hate watching myself."

Finally freeing her hand, Conner slid an arm over Melina's shoulders and leaned near, lowering her voice. "Well, I've seen it, and you and I, babe? On that giant screen? Smoking." She fanned herself with a wink.

Melina giggled, covering her mouth. "Stop it. I was such a nervous wreck that day."

"You couldn't tell," Conner lied glibly. "But I'm glad you'll get to see it. I didn't know you'd be here."

"They invited all of us from the shoot. Oh, look. There's Emi! I guess they came together."

Conner spun around, narrowing her eyes as the pair in question approached. Emi wore a tux—she wouldn't be caught dead in a dress—as did her date, her partner from the shoot, and they made a handsome couple. Something ugly churned in Conner's stomach.

Hands slid around Conner's waist. "I'm beginning to think you forgot about me," Lindsey murmured into her ear.

Conner kissed her, showing off just a bit. She made the rounds of introductions, ending with, "Emi, I'm sure you remember Lindsey."

The look Emi sent them would have soldered metal. The group settled into conversation, and perhaps no one else noticed that the temperature of the air between Conner and Emi rose several degrees.

Conner's attention ebbed and flowed. The label hadn't spared much expense for the party—silent waiters swooped in with platters of champagne and hors d'oeuvres, while the bar did a bustling service off to one side. The industrial space boomed with pop music, and the projector screen flashed through a slideshow of the band's various photoshoots and concerts. A dark stage awaited their performance later.

"Come with me," she said to Lindsey after a while.

Pulling her hand, she led her over to her sister Sadie and a man Conner assumed was her husband. Around the same height as Conner, he wore wire-framed glasses and had short hair the color of almonds.

Sadie looked like she might hug Conner when she greeted them but changed her mind at the last minute, to Conner's relief. They'd met for coffee once and chatted on the phone a few times, but they hadn't reached the hugging stage yet.

"Thanks for inviting us," Sadie said. "Conner, this is my husband, Asher."

Conner shook his hand before tugging Lindsey forward. "And this is my friend, Lindsey."

Sadie looked around the room. "This is pretty cool. Will you be playing?"

"Yeah. We plan to do a short set, but they want us out schmoozing the label execs and critics." Conner grimaced, running a hand through her chin-length hair. "And speaking of, our manager has been giving me the evil eye for a while, so I should probably make the rounds. But listen, I'm really glad you're here. Take advantage of the bar, all right? Let me know if you need anything."

Adorning her arm like proper eye candy, Lindsey bent her head to Conner's as they walked away. "Since when do you have a sister?"

"Since always, but we're just getting to know each other."

"Weird. I can't imagine growing up without any of my brothers."

By the time their set arrived, Conner's face hurt. She'd charmed the label's head honchos, gossiped with producers, given the same interview to reporters half a dozen times, and thanked so many people for coming that she had no idea who was actually there.

Kit took the mic, the spotlight on them as the band stood behind them in darkness. They looked particularly dapper in a Thom Browne gray seersucker jacket and pleated skirt.

"First of all, I want to thank you for coming. This night has been years in the making, and sometimes I thought we'd never get here." They glanced behind them, and Conner flipped them off. Kit went on far longer than Conner appreciated, thanking every single label exec, A&R rep, and producer, and by the time they reached the graphics team who had designed the album's cover art, Conner strummed the *Jeopardy* theme song on her guitar.

The crowd laughed. Kit held up one hand, chuckling. "Okay, okay. I can take a hint. Before I go, I have one final acknowledgment to make: to these four badasses standing behind me, who poured countless hours into making this album the fantastic piece of art that it is…enjoy every minute, my loves. You've earned it. As a gift, I have the pleasure of announcing that 'Wicked Girl' has cracked the top ten on the Billboard Hot One Hundred!" They started the announcement off nonchalantly but couldn't hide their excitement.

Conner vaguely heard Bellamy squeal while Maggie and Emi shouted something in triumph. Conner had a few hits back in her girl-group days, but this felt different. It wasn't manufactured and autotuned within an inch of its life. This was real.

She stood, somewhat stunned, as the stage lights came on and the crowd cheered. She saw Melina off to one side, who flashed that gap in her teeth in a grin, and Conner returned to herself, winking in reply as she strode forward to her mic.

"I guess we should give the people what they want!" she shouted, hyped off the energy.

Bellamy started the opening bass line, and they were off. It was easily their best performance of the song. For three minutes, Conner forgot how much she hated it and how much the composition had ultimately cost her. She even forgot to hate Emi, sauntering over to her mic during the bridge and whispering the lyrics in Spanish as she gazed into her coffee-colored eyes.

Barely taking a breath between songs, she launched into "Road Trip," a wild number with thinly veiled lyrics about being high. By the time it was over, Conner's white shirt clung to her with sweat.

The label president bounded to the stage, although *bound* was a strong term for a heavyset man in his sixties. He mopped his shiny bald head with a handkerchief as he droned on about the unprecedented faith the label had in the band—a bold claim given that other artists were there, signed to the same label—and finished by announcing their upcoming North American tour. The news was scheduled to drop on their respective social media at the same time, with ticket sales commencing soon.

Back in the crowd, Conner drained a glass of champagne while searching for her sister and brother-in-law, pulling her bandmates with her. "Sadie! Over here!"

"What did you think?" she asked after she made the introductions. She refused to feel nervous.

"You were great!" Sadie vibrated with enthusiasm. "Though I'm a little nervous to let Sarah listen if that's the sample of your album. Not exactly child-friendly."

Maggie snorted. "Conner hasn't done anything child-friendly since she *was* one."

"Even then it's questionable," Emi said.

Conner's nostrils flared, and she cut her eyes at Emi before speaking. How dare she feel like she had the right to tease her? "That's not true. I have that Disney movie coming out next year."

"Well, I enjoyed it," Asher said, giving Conner a nod. "You ladies are very talented."

"Thanks again for coming. I really, um…" Conner fidgeted with her hands. "I'm glad you're here."

"Are you kidding? A kid-free night getting to see my sister in her rock-star glory? This is fantastic!"

Conner beamed.

Sadie and Asher didn't stay late, which worked out for Conner as she was pulled in so many directions she didn't have a chance to talk to them again. She had enough champagne to put a lazy smile on her face but not enough to keep her from being annoyed by the empty flattery. She hated sucking up.

The singer who was their opening act for the first half of the tour, an up-and-comer named Lola, did a brief set. Conner didn't care for her pop style, but she had a pleasant voice and would rile up their crowds. She was more than easy on the eyes as well.

Full to the brim with champagne, Conner headed for the bathroom.

Halfway there, she spotted Melina cowering near the bar as some suit pontificated.

"Excuse me." She wedged herself between them and grabbed Melina's hand. "I need an escort to the ladies' room. You know us girls. Can't ever go alone." Despite her friendly words, she glared at the guy before pulling her away.

"Oh my gosh. Thank you! I thought he'd never stop talking, but I didn't want to be rude."

"Pfft. Rudeness is a currency in Hollywood. It's either that or sex."

Several minutes later, Conner glanced at Melina out of the corner of her eye as they washed their hands.

"How long have you been acting?"

"Six years. I moved to LA as soon as I finished high school, but I've only acted full-time for the last year and a half or so. Commercials, guest spots on shows, a few minor roles in films here and there."

"That's really impressive."

"Is it?" Melina turned those wide eyes to Conner, who caught her breath. "I mean, you know what it takes. You've been doing this your entire life."

"I know it takes hard work," Conner said slowly. "But I don't know the kind of hustle that you do. To keep grinding day after day like that…it's a lot." She nudged Melina with her shoulder as they exited the bathroom. "Just take the compliment, Meli."

"Meli, huh? No one's ever called me that."

"I'm sorry. I won't—"

Now it was Melina's turn to nudge. "I didn't say I minded."

Their gazes met. Melina's eyes were bright and dancing, and with a flutter in her stomach, Conner made a snap decision.

She pulled her to one side of the empty hallway, maneuvering Melina's back to the wall while wishing she had a better setting than fluorescent lighting and bare walls. "So I'm not alone in feeling a vibe between us?" she asked in a low voice, leaning forward. "Why don't we go out to dinner sometime and talk about it?"

For a moment, time hung suspended. Melina's mouth fell open slightly, revealing the charming gap between her front teeth. Conner swallowed but kept a grin on her face.

"Oh, I'm—I'm tempted—I mean flattered! So flattered. Like, the most flattered. But I think, um, I mean I definitely like you, obviously, but not like—it's just—well, um, I'm straight?"

Conner blinked, trying to parse through Melina's ramblings. "Is that a question?"

"Um, no. It's not a question. I think? I mean, no! It's—it's not." She pulled a hand over her face. "Oh, gosh. I'm making a fool of myself."

"No, you're not. If anyone is a fool here—"

"Please. As if you could ever be a fool. Look at you, all charming and gorgeous and sophisticated."

"You keep saying things like that, and I'll keep asking you out." She winked.

Melina blushed to the tips of her ears. "Oh, stop." Then she looked up, catching Conner's gaze again. "We can still be friends, right?"

"Of course. I could always use more friends."

"Awesome!"

Melina sprang toward her, crushing Conner in a tight hug, and she had no choice but to hug back. As they pulled apart, still smiling, the door to the hallway opened.

"Am I interrupting something?" Emi arched her eyebrows.

"Nothing at all. Meli, I'll see you out there."

After looking back and forth between the two of them, Melina left. Conner folded her arms and leaned against the wall.

"You don't waste any time, do you, Conner? Don't you have a date tonight?"

"Lindsey and I are just friends. Why? Are you jealous?"

Conner regretted the words as soon as they left her mouth and prayed Emi wouldn't answer. She got her wish, but Emi's wounded look as she brushed past her was answer enough.

No longer in the mood to party, Conner sought out Lindsey's blond head and found her at the bar next to Jamal and Maggie.

Conner slipped an arm over her shoulder and pulled her close enough to smell her perfume. "Do you feel like getting out of here?"

Lindsey grinned. Friends, they were…but no one said friends couldn't come with benefits. "My place?"

"Lead the way."

Conner waved at Melina as Lindsey led her toward the exit hand in hand. Melina briefly frowned before returning the wave with a wide smile.

Chapter Seven

"You look like crap."

"I've missed you, Harlow."

"I mean it. Are you taking care of yourself?"

"No. I figured I'd let things go just as my career hits a new level. It's not like my field of work depends on my appearance or anything." Her manager's look told Conner her sarcasm wasn't appreciated. "I'm fine. I promise. If you've forgotten my schedule, which would be gross negligence on your part, I've been very busy."

"You're about to be busier. Your publicist just emailed the press junket from now until your first concert." Before Conner could ask, she added, "I made sure she spoke to the label and mixed in the band's interviews. The ones in yellow are the outlets that specifically requested you."

They looked over the itinerary. Conner brushed her hair back from her forehead with a heavy sigh. Based on this schedule, she might be able to fit in a few hours of sleep next Tuesday.

When she glanced up, Harlow was watching her with an odd expression.

"What?"

"They've received numerous requests about 'Sixteen' in particular."

"Well, it was always going to get the most attention."

Harlow scoffed. "You're remarkably blasé for someone who's about to reveal a very traumatic and personal period of your life."

"It's not like much of my life has ever been secret. Might as well let go of one of the few."

Harlow gazed at her. A decade older, they had been together since Conner was emancipated at fifteen and had sought control of her own life. Although inexperienced at the time, Harlow represented youth and femininity in a world full of middle-aged men. Those traits had appealed to her, and Harlow had repaid her trust multiple times over.

"Is this you putting on an act like you always do, or are you actually okay with this move? She's not going to take it lying down, you know."

Conner swallowed a joke about exactly what the subject of her song *would* do lying down before leaning forward, her elbows on her knees. "I've wanted to expose her for years. You know that. Writing the song was therapeutic. I've come to terms with it, and now it's time for the world to know who she really is."

Harlow nodded slowly. Her short, platinum ponytail never moved, a feat Conner couldn't understand. "If you're sure."

"Aww, Harlow, are you going soft on me?"

Harlow's glare over her stylish black frames lowered the temperature in her office. "Please. I just don't want my biggest client to have a breakdown."

Conner relaxed, lacing her fingers behind her head. "But think of the headlines! Hollywood loves a good basket case. Don't worry. We both know my demise will be much more dramatic than a simple nervous breakdown."

Harlow looked at her again, the corners of her mouth barely dipping, but she didn't respond, instead shuffling several papers on her desk. "We have multiple offers." Conner flipped through the requests and immediately pushed one forward. When she read the name, Harlow almost chuckled. "I don't know why I bothered entertaining anyone else."

"I don't, either. She's the biggest and the best, and when have I ever settled for anything less?"

With very few exceptions, Conner had kept this period of her life to herself. An early draft of the song was among the first batch she ever wrote for Hestia Rising, but it took several rewrites before she was satisfied. When they decided to include it on *Broken Promises*, she had known this day was inevitable, and whatever nerves she might have had at one point were gone. This moment had been a long time coming.

They wanted to do the interview at her house, but she flatly refused. Some producer suggested the Beverly Hills mansion in which she'd grown up, still owned by her parents, although neither occupied it, but Harlow shot that idea down before Conner could compose her outrage into words. Finally, Harlow offered her own Santa Monica home.

Conner relaxed on one of Harlow's white couches. Though her decor was too industrial for Conner's taste, the familiarity was soothing. Across from her sat legendary television anchor Larissa Lamont, who had lived many lives—evening news, morning news, and daytime talk. Now middle-aged and respected across the board, she delivered specials that regularly topped the ratings. She was an easy choice, and Conner enjoyed working with her as much as any press.

"So, Conner, your band just released their first album," Larissa said after initial pleasantries. "And it's doing quite well."

"It's reached number five, so we're really happy."

"And you wrote all the songs?"

Conner nodded. "Emi co-wrote one, but for the most part, they all came from my life and my experiences."

"Let's talk about that point." Larissa brought her glasses up to her face to read from a notecard. Conner assumed the quote would appear in a graphic on the screen when the interview aired. "This is from *Rolling Stone*. 'Led by Conner Cody's velvet vocals, doused by whiskey and lust in equal measure, the album is sure to make the year-end list by many, but the true gem may lie in the depth of Cody's anger that seeps out of nearly every song.'" Larissa looked up again. "Would you describe yourself as angry?"

"I don't know about that, but I didn't have much love in my life growing up."

"You don't believe your parents love you?"

"They have a funny way of showing it," Conner said after a pause. "I mean, they weren't abusive or anything. I had food and clothing and any toys I wanted. But they were never interested in being parents. Nannies basically raised me."

Camila Morales had spread Seth Cody's misdeeds far and wide, like dandelion seeds, so they didn't need to discuss that point. Conner vividly remembered hiding in a closet and crying around the age of six while her mother screamed at her father and yet another twentysomething nanny after she caught them in the act, teaching young Conner quite a few new words in the process.

She returned her attention to Larissa, and they continued chatting about her parents. She had plenty to say about life with two people who so blatantly hated each other and seemed to resent her existence, as if she'd forced them together.

"Conner, I have to ask. If you dislike your parents so much, why did you follow in their footsteps so closely? The comparisons were inevitable."

Conner chuckled to hide a scoff. "I've been acting since I was less than a year old. It's all I know. And the music…I guess I come by it naturally or something. It's just in me. I can't stop people from comparing us, and I only hope they judge me on my own merits. But whatever. People can think what they want. I write my songs for me, you know?"

"Have your parents listened to the album?"

Conner pursed her lips. She could taste the answer on her tongue, bitter and sour, but it stuck behind her teeth. The silence increased, painfully awkward, and out of the corner of her eye, she saw Harlow approach the director.

"Let's take five!" he said.

Conner strode toward Harlow's bedroom, ignoring everyone in her path. She tried to slam the door behind her, but Harlow got in the way. Conner stared out the window at the pool. What would they do if she just jumped in, clothes and makeup and everything?

Harlow's voice floated her way, unusually muted. "Whatever your parents said to you—"

"They didn't."

"What?"

"They didn't say anything." Conner had always loved the water. Did she have any memories of swimming with her parents? "So I don't know if they listened to it."

Harlow didn't reply, which Conner appreciated. They'd wasted enough words on her parents already. When they returned to the living room, they agreed that Larissa should repeat her question, and Conner shrugged. Who cared, anyway?

Larissa removed her glasses and folded her hands in her lap. Her rich voice, warm and full of compassion, wrapped around Conner's shoulders like a faux fur stole. "So far we've discussed well-known events in your life. Now I want to talk about the song 'Sixteen.'"

Conner took a deep breath. "That song is about a brief relationship I had right after my sixteenth birthday."

"Some sort of power imbalance is implied."

"Very much so. Not only was she twice my age, but she was one of my producers."

Larissa leaned back. She already knew what Conner was about to reveal, but no viewer would be able to tell. "Everyone wants to know, Conner, who she is."

It was funny how easily someone could drop a bombshell. Just a few little words, and Conner wouldn't hear the end of it for months. "Britt Boyd."

Larissa paused for the viewers to absorb that revelation before dropping into Conner's history with the famed producer. Britt had been brought in to revamp the second season of *On the Bay*, Conner's television show that occupied most of her teenage years, when her breakout performance made the showrunners pivot the focus onto her. For months she had soaked up the attention Britt showered on her, but it wasn't until the wrap party that she turned flirtatious.

"I was sixteen. She was gorgeous and older, and at the time I didn't give a shit that she was married. She told me all the time how unhappy their marriage was and how she planned to leave him."

"And they're still married."

"Apparently."

"So it was consensual?"

Conner nodded. "Enthusiastically. The secrecy of it just added to the appeal."

"Did you ever…" Larissa paused for dramatic effect. "Did you ever stop to think that what you were doing was wrong?"

Conner weighed her words carefully. "No. Not at first, anyway. I knew people wouldn't understand, but when someone is telling you how mature you are, how you had to grow up fast because you were in the spotlight…it was easy to convince myself that the age difference didn't matter, that her husband didn't matter. To be honest, I thought I was hot shit."

"And the fact that she could have gone to jail?"

"You knew me during that time, Larissa. Do you think doing anything illegal bothered me?" The remark won her a smile and an accommodating head tilt. "Besides, not to be callous, but I wouldn't have been the one in trouble."

"But you waited until the statute of limitations passed before you ever said anything, and even now you—"

"I'm not protecting her. Don't get it twisted." Conner brushed her hair away from her face, shifting on the couch as she considered her next words. "After the affair ended, it took me a long time to understand what had happened. I was a kid, you know? She spent months filling my ears with how I was a great actress, how the show was mine now, what a career I would have with her by my side."

Larissa was nodding. "Which is how your song starts."

"Exactly. Some of the lyrics are her words verbatim. The song reflects the relationship." Conner abandoned her languid slouch and straightened, using her hands for emphasis. "Because soon it wasn't that I was a great actress, it was that *I* was great, that I was so pretty, so sexy, I could have any woman I wanted, she felt more comfortable with me than her husband, she wished I was her age…"

For a moment they waited, letting the words fill the space around them. The memory of how easily she'd been seduced and how grown-up she'd thought she was still shocked Conner.

"Was it sexual?" Larissa asked quietly. Conner nodded. "Was she your first?"

"Ah, no." Conner grinned. Larissa shook her head and smiled, which they'd definitely edit out.

"Who ended it?"

"Ohhh…" Conner gave a low whistle. "That depends on who you ask. Once the glitter wore off, being all secretive wasn't fun anymore. I was a teenager and wanted to go on dates. I wanted to brag to my friends. I wanted to stop playing coy in interviews."

She paused, thinking about the relationship that had followed Britt.

That girlfriend, a fellow actress, had been age-appropriate but deeply closeted at the time, which had eventually driven a wedge between them. *Damn. No wonder I have so much material for songs.*

"What was worse was the way she started to treat me. Saying all this shit about how I owed my career to her and how she was risking everything for me, telling me what movies I should do and which photoshoots I should book. Every time I pushed back, she gave me guilt trips over how miserable she was at home, and how I was the only good thing in her life." Conner scowled. "She has kids. Even back then, that made me uncomfortable."

Larissa nodded, making a noise of acknowledgment. "Do you—"

"I tried not to think too much about them." Conner was thinking aloud now. "It freaked me out that they weren't much younger than me. I felt like I should apologize, you know? To them. But I didn't do—I'm not saying I wasn't at fault, but I wasn't responsible for them."

"It sounds like you feel some sort of responsibility for the affair, though." Larissa frowned. "You were, as you said, a kid."

"In the eyes of the state of California, sure. But I knew she was married, I knew she had kids, I knew that no matter how consensual the sex was, she could get into real trouble. I knew. But…I just didn't care about any of the repercussions, for anyone. I knew what I wanted, which was her."

"Do you think that you were groomed?"

Conner's cheeks puffed out before she released her breath in a loud huff. She hated that term. Hated feeling like she had no agency. She had made a lot of dumb decisions in her life, but no one could ever claim she refused to accept responsibility.

"I don't know, Larissa. A lot of things were uneven in that relationship. It was confusing then, and it's confusing now."

"What made you decide to speak up?"

She took her time answering. As much as she'd prepared for this interview, verbalizing this part of her past had stirred up a cyclone of feelings. Residual anger crept up her back—at her parents, at Britt, at every person who saw the teenager climbing into the producer's car and didn't say a word. And at herself for being so fucking stupid.

"I don't want her to be able to do that to anyone else," she said firmly. "It took me a long time to sort out my feelings about what happened. At first I was just angry because I felt used, and then I was embarrassed—"

"Embarrassed? How so?"

"That I was so easily taken advantage of. Hell, half the time she had me thinking it was my idea. But I never would have pursued her. Never would have occurred to me."

"How do you feel now?"

She shrugged. "I just want it out there. I want people to know who she really is, and I want people to understand that not only men in this industry do bad things because of the power they hold. I don't want revenge. The only time I think about her now is when I sing the song, but it has to be sung."

Larissa didn't linger on the topic of Britt much longer, and Conner was grateful. Her emotions had been wrung out and were ready to dry. They finished the interview by discussing the overall revelatory nature of the album. Conner earned a laugh by commenting that writing an album was cheaper and faster than therapy, although a raised eyebrow from Harlow forced her to quickly mutter something about proper mental-health treatment. Conner's publicist kept her finger on the pulse of social media better than any high school queen bee, and Harlow often reminded Conner that she paid a lot of money for someone else to care about her reputation.

Larissa had one more thing to say after the interview ended and the cameras shut off. Conner gave her a grateful hug for her kind treatment.

"You're very brave, Conner," she said, squeezing her shoulder.

"Is it brave to tell the truth?"

"Yes," Larissa said frankly, although the question had been mostly rhetorical. "Give yourself a little bit of credit once in a while, honey."

Conner thought about that advice all the way home, where she stretched out on a pool float fully dressed and swigged from a bottle of tequila until she passed out.

Chapter Eight

Maggie

Maggie sipped her cranberry and vodka, surveying the party in front of her. Conner had thrown a going-away soirée before they went on tour. Always decadent and themed, with a carefully chosen guest list and borderline hedonistic, her blowouts were the stuff of enviously whispered Hollywood legend.

Maggie and Conner had met at an earlier version of these parties. The latter had been just fourteen, a brand-new freshman at their exclusive, private, Catholic high school, and Maggie a year older. A nominal student at best, Conner frequently missed classes when she was on set, so Maggie hadn't even seen her at that point, but the buzz on their new celebrity classmate was huge.

Maggie hadn't been sure what to expect when she walked into the Codys' Beverly Hills mansion with a friend, but it wasn't a complete lack of any adult figure or a wide-open liquor cabinet (the least of the temptations available that night). She met Conner on the deck when she offered Maggie her first-ever joint.

They clicked instantly. Maggie stood by her side during her emancipation process, through the drug years, all the way up to starting the band with the two of them while Maggie attended UCLA. Conner had taught her to drum, Conner had held her hand when Maggie's father died—

And Conner had introduced her to the love of her life. Maggie snuggled into Jamal's side under his strong arm as she stood next to him near the pool. He was a foley artist who had worked on one of Conner's films. She'd dragged a protesting Maggie across the room at one of these very parties, introduced them, and lit up like a beacon every time she walked past them the rest of the night.

Maggie leaned closer, burying her face in his chest. "What's wrong?" he asked.

"Just thinking of not seeing you until Thanksgiving. It's the longest we've ever been separated."

"Aww, don't worry. You're my girl, baby. You're always gonna be my girl. A few months apart can't hurt us." The soft bristle of his beard brushed her forehead. "You'll kick ass across the country, and when you get home, I'll be here waiting. Maybe then you can make an honest man of me."

His cheeks dimpled as he grinned down at her. Jamal had been dropping hints of taking the next step ever since they got their record deal. For a while Maggie just assumed he was freaking out at the thought that she might take off along with her career, but the hints kept coming, and she kept taking them in stride. Conner said Maggie ought to propose, but she was content to wait.

Speaking of the hostess...Maggie spotted her winding her way past the tiki bar toward the DJ, a notable deviation from the norm. Conner normally did the music herself. Maggie loved both the good and the bad in her best friend—though endlessly generous and loyal, she could also be entitled and self-centered, and she had control issues in spades.

"Conner!" She jogged to catch up.

Conner grinned as she turned her head. Maggie had seen all the many sides of her, but she loved Conner best in these moments, when she let her walls down, dropped whatever persona she'd adopted, and her smiles reached all the way to her eyes.

"Hey, girl. I thought you'd be glued to Jamal all night."

"Absence makes the heart grow fonder, or whatever." Her smile wilted. "And we're going to have plenty of that coming up."

"Don't think of it that way. Just imagine all the sex you'll have when we get back, all pent-up and desperate."

Maggie made a dissatisfied noise in her throat. Conner could paint it however she wanted, but it was still a long separation. The holiday break that split the tour in half was the only saving grace. Maybe Jamal would propose at Christmas.

"So, what's up with the DJ?" she asked, tired of thinking about being away from her boyfriend.

Conner glanced over, the corner of her mouth tugging up. "She's good, yeah?"

"She's familiar."

"The new DJ at Dorothy's, remember?"

Recognition dawned. "You're trying to hit that, aren't you?"

"You act like I haven't already."

"Jesus, Conner. How many people here have you slept with?" Maggie was more curious than judgmental. No stranger to casual sex, she didn't slut-shame anyone. If anything, Maggie was impressed at how deftly Conner managed her hookups. Never a hint of drama.

Conner looked around before shrugging. "Hard to say."

"Okay, Casanova. Am I pussy-blocking you right now?"

"Nope. First, you couldn't block me if you tried." She smirked, and Maggie smirked right back, mocking her. Conner had her issues, but her boundless confidence with women was not one of them. "Second of all, this drink isn't for her. It's for Meli."

"Who's Meli?"

Conner didn't answer, smoothly sidestepping Maggie, who watched her go. Conner passed a B-list movie star putting the moves on someone who wasn't his wife, then walked through an obviously intoxicated group of people Maggie were pretty sure were producers and up to a familiar woman with a wild mess of dark curls and a sundress Maggie immediately envied. What was her name? Melanie?

Intrigued, Maggie made her way over, wrinkling her nose at the same group of producers. They were definitely on something and loudly arguing about residuals.

The girl from the music video! *Interesting.* Maggie eyed Conner. After everything with Emi, it was nice to see her noticing someone else, even if it was ultimately nothing more than a rebound.

"Maggie! Hi! How are you? It's so good to see you!" The girl surprised Maggie by giving her a tight hug.

Conner looked amused. "Mags, you remember Melina, don't you?"

"Sure. How's it going?"

"I was just telling Conner how amazing her house is! I'd give anything to live on the beach like this. Where do you live?"

"My boyfriend and I have a place in Silver Lake. We've talked about moving somewhere like Pacific Palisades someday, once we have kids. I grew up in Santa Monica, and it would be nice to be closer to my mom. Where are you, Melina?"

"North Hollywood." She scrunched up her face. "I really like the area, but I'll be grateful for the day when I don't need to have three roommates."

"You're welcome to stay here whenever you need a break," Conner said. "I have plenty of room."

Maggie stared at Conner, astonished. They had briefly lived together before she bought this house, and Conner's intense need for privacy had nearly ended their friendship. She was generous with her extra rooms when anyone needed to crash after a party, but that was it. Never in her life had she extended an open-ended invitation.

Maggie listened as they discussed beach life. She'd watched Conner work her magic on countless women, but she didn't see any of those usual markers in this conversation. *Very interesting.*

"These drinks are going right through me." Melina giggled. "Conner, where's your bathroom? I keep seeing people go into the pool house. Is it—"

"No!" Maggie and Conner blurted out together.

"There's a powder room just past the kitchen," Conner said. "Another bathroom by the stairs and plenty on the second floor. Make yourself at home. Find me if you need anything. But, ah…" She glanced at Maggie.

"Don't go in the pool house," they said in unison.

"Why? What's—"

"Just don't." Maggie was surprised enough to see her at the party. The scenes in the pool house might have scarred her for life.

Maggie watched Conner watch Melina as she walked away, wishing she could see her friend's eyes through her mirrored sunglasses. A coconut bra and a grass skirt completed her commitment to the beach theme.

"You like her."

Conner grunted. "We're just friends."

"You like her, but you aren't flirting with her. Oh my God, she turned you down!"

"No, she didn't. She happens to be straight."

"She turned you down, *and* your gaydar is wrong for once!" Maggie crowed. "Well, well, well. How does it feel to be mortal like the rest of us?"

She really couldn't blame Conner for shoving her into the pool.

Maggie lost sight of both Conner and Melina as the night wore on. After she downed a few cocktails, she and Jamal danced close. The DJ was really good, whether or not Conner took her to bed tonight. She and Jamal got so worked up they snuck into the laundry room for a quickie blowjob.

After an enjoyable hour debating the hierarchy of female drummers with a world-famous diva, Maggie wound her way back to her boyfriend.

"Baby?" She wrapped her arms around Jamal's waist from behind. She loved feeling his abdominal muscles ripple under her touch. "I'm hungry."

He twisted his head to look at her, raising thick eyebrows. "Again? Already?"

"Not that, you horndog. Literally hungry. I'm going to hit up the buffet. Do you want me to make you a plate?"

He slid an arm over her shoulders, pulling her close. "Look at this woman. She's drop-dead gorgeous, she's about to blow up the world one snare roll at a time, AND she's offering to make me a plate! How lucky am I? But I'm good, baby. I ate earlier. Just grab me one of those pineapple things?" He kissed her cheek.

Maggie grinned at his group of companions, which included the newest villain from Conner's superhero films and an Oscar-winning director. Kissing him back, she spun away and headed for the kitchen. She was the lucky one.

Conner's back patio led directly into the kitchen, separated by a wall of large glass doors that could be, and currently were, slid aside so that the entire wall disappeared. Her chef had prepared a variety of Hawaiian dishes that were either on burners or ice, as needed. Maggie was filling a plate with pork laulau and sweet macaroni salad when someone stumbled into the room.

"Oh, hi!" Melina beamed and waved so wildly that Maggie looked behind herself to see if someone else was there.

"Hey. Having a good time?"

"The best! Except..." She giggled with an overly loud whisper. She had clearly hit up the bar more than a few times. "I was looking for a bathroom on the second floor, and I think I just walked into something I wasn't supposed to see."

"Did Conner explain to you how these parties work?"

"She said it was like Vegas." Melina frowned. "But no one's gambling. I've seen a *lot* of things tonight, but no gambling. Oh! Is that the pool house?"

"Definitely not the pool house," Maggie said hurriedly. "There's no gambling. Her parties are so popular because what happens here, stays here. That's what she meant by Vegas." It wasn't like Conner to be so blasé about confidentiality.

With an exaggerated wink, Melina pretended to zip her lips. Then her wide eyes lit up again. "Oh my God, food! I'm starving."

"Food is probably a good idea. And maybe some water to wash down however many drinks you've had?"

"I've only had two," Melina said, her mouth full of pastry. "But I hit up the candy bar. I have *such* a sweet tooth."

Maggie frowned. "Candy? There's not—oh, no. Oh, no, no, no. Melina, where was this candy bar?"

"That green table outside by the bar."

"That's not normal candy." Maggie could barely contain her laughter, holding her stomach. "Those are edibles. You're high as a fucking kite."

Melina stopped eating, bread still in her mouth. "Ooohhh. That makes so much sense. An *edible* bar! Or an edible *bar*."

She continued to talk to herself, but Maggie had lost the thread. Shrugging, she continued to fix her plate, grabbing extra pineapple for Jamal, and headed back toward the pool. The temperature had dropped with the sun, though it was still plenty warm, and she looked forward to cuddling with him. Melina followed, now going on about a show she'd filmed earlier that day.

"And I really think this could become a—Hi, Conner!"

Their hostess was climbing out of the hot tub and grinned at them. "Hey, Melina, Maggie. Food's good, yeah?"

Maggie nodded. "Really good. Tell your chef she knocked it out of the park."

"I will, thanks."

"And, uh, this one hit up the edible bar." Maggie inclined her head.

Conner's grin widened, and she cupped Melina's chin in her hand. "Is that so? You good, babe?"

"I'm great, baby!" Melina's smile stretched from ear to ear as she leaned into Conner.

"Awesome. Listen, I'm done for the night, but a car service is on call, so if you want to go home, just buzz the gate. Or feel free to stay here. Any open bedroom on the second floor is yours. Mags, keep an eye on her for me?"

She winked before spinning on her heel, draping an arm over each of the women waiting for her, models, by the look of them. They departed inside without another glance.

Maggie shook her head in disbelief. Conner's ability to find company with a snap of her fingers never ceased to amaze her, no matter how many times she saw her in action. That said, Maggie wished Conner could find someone special. A rotating door of strange women wasn't enough to douse her loneliness.

"She's just delightful, isn't she? So sweet and warm." Maggie blinked, side-eying Melina. She loved Conner, but were they talking about the same person? "And her eyes are so pretty, aren't they? The most gorgeous I've ever seen."

"Very pretty. Why don't you come hang out with us?" The last thing that girl needed was another round of edibles.

Maggie led her back over to Jamal's group, wondering how Hollywood hadn't devoured her yet. Then Melina fell from her mind as she wrapped herself around her boyfriend. He was the person with whom she wanted to spend her life. A pesky little thing like a tour would never come between them.

Chapter Nine

The weeks before the tour commenced flew by in a vortex of activity. Conner threw herself into band rehearsal, arguing about set lists and cover songs. She dug deep into her industry contacts to pull in cameos for almost every stop on the tour. Nearly every day saw yet another interview. Her workouts left her drenched in sweat as she added extra cardio to prepare for the grind of performing for hours night after night, and she squeezed in checkups with her doctor and dentist.

On the last night before the tour kicked off, Conner spread out in her king-sized bed, soaking up every bit of comfort and privacy, two things that would be scarce on the road. Her bedroom took up the entire third floor, with broad windows on all sides covered with remote-controlled blackout shades. Her bed and a large television dominated the main area, while a sitting alcove off to one side held a cushy armchair and a bookcase crammed to the limit with paperbacks. Her cedar-lined closet and oversized bathroom almost doubled the size of the floor.

Conner's bedroom was her sanctuary. She rarely hooked up with someone in her house, much less in her room. Only Emi and Vittoria had been allowed up here, and she regretted both instances.

Despite spending the day at the spa, massaged and exfoliated and pampered to the extreme, her mind raced far too quickly to get any rest. Were all her outfits packed? Had she gone over every instruction with her housekeeper? She'd pored over her schedule with Harlow, confident she hadn't overbooked herself, and her agent had clear instructions on when she'd be available to work again. Conner looked forward to reviewing scripts on the road so long as they wouldn't film in the next year.

She'd been in her early teens the last time she headlined a tour, so guardians had managed every minute. She'd only had to remember her lyrics and dance moves. This time, she'd been so involved in all aspects that Kit jokingly offered to quit. At least, she thought they were joking.

The weight of all the responsibility made her spine curve. Unable to bear it, she rolled over and grabbed her phone from her nightstand, waffling on who to call. She sent two quick texts, deciding to talk to whoever answered first.

Surprisingly, her sister's name popped up on her screen within minutes.

"Hi, Conner. Are you okay?"

"I can't sleep. You're up late."

"Sarah had a science project she conveniently forgot about until the last minute. So we did that, and then I had laundry, and well…" She uttered a half sigh, half laugh. "A mother's job is never done."

Conner couldn't relate. Nor, she was sure, could her own mother. She made a noncommittal noise in her throat.

"Why can't you sleep? You have a busy day tomorrow, don't you?"

"Yep. We have three interviews in the morning, then the show." They were kicking off the tour at the Troubadour, one of Conner's favorite venues, before heading out to Portland immediately afterward.

"Are you nervous?"

Conner blew out her breath. Talking to Sadie became easier each time, but she struggled to not show her sister any side that didn't have her shit together, whether it was fake or real.

"Yes, but also no. I know the band is ready, and I know the album is good."

"It's great. It's been on replay in our house constantly. Well, the clean version." She chuckled. "Hannah keeps getting the lyrics to 'Her Halo Has Horns' wrong, and it's the funniest thing."

Conner smiled, trying to identify her warm feeling at the thought that her sister liked her album. And that her nieces heard it often enough to—almost—know the lyrics.

"So what's making you nervous?"

"A tour involves a lot of moving pieces, you know?" Conner said after taking a moment to think. "We can do our part, but will the techs? The venue? The backing band? The opening act? The weather? The fans? What if one of us gets a stomach bug? I can make sure the girls are set, but that's it."

"Worrying about things you can't control won't get you anywhere."

"Maybe not, but it keeps me up at night. It's just…I want the band to be successful *so badly*, Sadie. More than anything I've ever wanted."

"Sweetie, it will be. It already is. You have a hit song and a great album, and the tour will be dank, or whatever it is Sarah and her friends are saying these days."

Conner guffawed. "Girl, please don't ever say *dank* again."

"I guess we can't all be as cool as you."

"I don't say *dank*. That's why I'm cool."

In moments like these, when they teased each other and the banter flew easily, Conner let herself believe that she and Sadie could build a lasting relationship. That she could have a sister, whatever that meant. That she might finally have someone permanently in her corner.

Sadie yawned. "I think I stopped being cool when I started struggling to stay awake past ten."

"You should go to sleep."

"So should you," Sadie retorted playfully. "Hey, Conner?"

"Yeah?"

"Don't be a stranger while you're gone, okay? Check in and let me know how things are."

Touched, Conner promised, and they hung up. Not a minute later, another face popped up on her screen.

Conner grinned, pushing herself up to a sitting position against the headboard. "Hey, girl."

"Hey, yourself," Melina said. She was sitting against a bare beige wall in what Conner guessed was her own bedroom. "I just saw your text. What's up?"

"Oh, nothing." She suddenly regretted reaching out to Melina when she was feeling vulnerable. She didn't want to ruin her new friend's high opinion of her. "Did I wake you?"

"Nope." Melina popped the word. "I was taking a shower. Very long day on set."

She was filming two episodes of a long-running crime procedural. Conner had run lines with her over fish tacos one night, forgoing much-needed sleep in the process. It was worth it to witness her exaltation over the role, her first multi-episode part.

"How was it?"

"Really good. We have strong chemistry, but tomorrow is our big kiss scene, which, ugh." Melina tilted her head back and let out a half sigh, half groan. "Do you ever get used to kissing strangers?"

"I made out with you when you were a stranger." Melina's flush gratified her teasing. "Honestly, though? Yes. That's not to say they've all been easy or fun, but remember, my very first kiss ever was broadcast for the world to see. It's normal to me."

"That makes sense. You've probably kissed as many people on screen as off."

Conner smirked. "I don't think that's true."

Melina laughed. "God, I wish I had half your confidence in, well, anything. I'm constantly worrying about what I'm doing with my hands and is my tongue behaving—"

"The difference between you and me is that I never expect my tongue to behave. In fact, I hope it misbehaves frequently."

Melina laughed, throwing her head back and exposing her tanned throat. For a moment Conner let her mind dwell on what it would be like to nip that neck with her teeth, and then she forced herself to focus on the joy that Melina's contagious laughter evoked.

"See? That's exactly what I'm talking about," Melina said once her giggles abated. "I love how you go through life like you know you're Conner freaking Cody and no one can ever touch you. Meanwhile, I'm busy wondering if I should get veneers and worrying about my weight."

Conner leaned her head back and considered that remark. Honestly, Hollywood's brutal, unrealistic standards would say Melina needed to drop a dress size or two. But even Hollywood was changing, albeit infinitesimally.

"Listen to your dentist on veneers, but leave that little gap between your front teeth alone. It's adorable and makes you stand out, and besides, I think that's in now."

Melina grinned, showing off that very gap. "You're very sweet. Do you have veneers?"

"No, but I had plenty of orthodontia when I was younger, and I get my teeth whitened."

"Have you had any kind of, you know, work?" Melina shifted on her bed, smiling sheepishly.

Conner pressed her lips together in a guilty grin. "Yeah...I got a breast enhancement as soon as I finished filming *On the Bay*. I was barely an A-cup, and it was clear my body had finished developing, so I just gave the girls a little boost."

"No way!" Melina's hand over her mouth did nothing to stop her giggles.

"Very way. And that's privileged information, Miss Velasco, so don't go spouting that off to anyone."

"Well, darn. I was planning to call TMZ as soon as we hung up." She stuck her tongue out.

"So your tongue does misbehave." Conner was unable (or unwilling) to fully erase a flirtatious tone.

Melina giggled again. Something about the melodious sound made Conner smile no matter how many times she heard it.

"I'm kidding, by the way. It's not a secret. I just don't want to talk about my breasts in every interview I do. In private conversation, however, they're fair game."

"I'll keep that in mind. I'm surprised, to be honest. You seem so comfortable in your own skin."

Conner shrugged. "I am. I didn't feel bad about myself or anything. I just wanted bigger boobs. I fill out my clothes better now, and in our line of work, it does nothing but help. It was as much a business decision as anything."

"That's very...pragmatic."

"You'd be surprised. I can be ruthless. Cold, I've been told."

"Yeah, right. I'll believe it when I see it."

A whisper at the back of Conner's mind suggested that someday, she would. She shook her head to disperse it. "So, tell me more about your day."

They talked for over an hour longer. Conner never did get around to mentioning her fears for the tour, mostly because she didn't need to do so anymore. She was more than happy to listen to Melina's cheerful chatter or gently tease her or offer pieces of career advice upon request instead.

But too soon, Melina was yawning. Conner pursed her lips as she made a quick decision.

"What you said about losing weight…you don't need to. Don't let someone else's beauty standards dictate something that's not right for your body, okay? You look perfect the way you are. Trust me."

"Hello, LA!" Conner grinned as five hundred people screamed back at her. Somewhere in that mass of humanity were Melina, her roommate Eriq, Maggie's boyfriend Jamal, and a few other friends.

Conner had played venues large and small, and while nothing beat the sheer noise of a stadium, she had a soft spot for these more intimate venues. The crowd so close she could smell them, making eye contact with individual people…these were the perfect vibes to kick off a successful tour. What worries?

"Some of you might have seen us before." Cheers went up from those who had. "But I think we have some fresh meat here tonight." Even more cheers arose. When a crowd was this stoked, she could read off the local weather station's news feed and still get a rise from them.

"For those of you who are new…"

The rest of the band started up an extended intro to "Her Halo Has Horns."

"Allow us to introduce ourselves. On the drums, our backbone, the sexiest set of arms you'll ever see…Maggie Jackson!" Maggie burst into a rousing solo.

"On bass, she's the belle of any ball, but be warned—she bites. Bellamy McCubbin!" Bellamy's dexterous fingers brought a moment of funk to the stage.

"And on lead guitar…she's small, she has gall, and her licks will have you in thrall." Conner waggled her eyebrows. "Emi Bhandari!" Emi launched into a wicked riff.

"On that note…you already know I'm Conner fucking Cody, and we are Hestia Rising!"

Chapter Ten

Touring was exhausting, isolating, and sometimes intensely boring, but it was an experience like no other. Conner loved it.

They'd outfitted three tour buses—one for the band, one for their opening act, Lola, and her entourage, and one for Kit and the rest of their staff. The band's bus held four small but private sleeping areas, two bathrooms, a kitchenette, and an open space where they could eat and relax.

Sometimes they did relax—playing cards, watching movies, and battling fiercely on the Mario Kart circuit, keeping track of their records on a whiteboard. Other times they worked—filming segments for social media, answering emails, or tweaking set lists and covers based on feedback from prior shows. Kit also had them record each other with a handheld camera for a possible documentary.

But sometimes...they referred to each other as four best friends, but damn, they could get on each other's nerves.

"Bellamy, *must* you slurp your cereal like that?" Emi snapped one morning.

"Leave her alone." Conner didn't look up from her morning social media scroll while eating her oatmeal.

"I beg your pardon, Your Majesty."

A second later Emi fired a blueberry muffin that bounced off Conner's temple. She popped her head up to find Emi cautiously smiling. After wavering between amusement and irritation, she threw a chocolate-chip muffin right back. They grinned at each other.

"Aww, look at y'all!" Bellamy squeezed each one's shoulders, beaming as she sat between them.

The sound of a door opening ended the moment, and Maggie shuffled into view, rubbing her eyes. "Why are you so fucking loud?"

"Good mo-orning," Emi and Conner sang in unison, glances catching once more as they laughed. Maggie muttered something unpleasant before dropping onto the bench seat.

The rest of breakfast passed uneventfully, although Emi continued to scowl at Bellamy every time she slurped, smiling beatifically whenever Conner raised her eyebrows at her. It was nice to be getting along with her again. Conner's stomach flipped, although maybe that was the bus.

"Where are we?" Maggie asked through a mouthful of waffle.

"Almost to Chicago, I think." They'd left St. Louis in the early morning hours after the band stumbled onto the bus in varying states of inebriation.

"Chi-town!"

Bellamy scrunched her button nose. "Why do they call it Chi-town? Are they shy?"

"It's from the name of the city, Bells. Chi-cago."

"But shouldn't it be pronounced differently?"

"Then it would sound too much like shit-town," Emi said with a snicker.

"We'll save that for Seattle." Conner waited for her to take the bait.

A Seattle native, Emi didn't disappoint. "I hate you. You know that?"

Conner shook her head, smirking. "No, you don't."

"Well, I—"

An extraordinarily loud burp from Maggie drowned out whatever she was about to say. The rest of them stared at her, clearly too stunned to speak.

"What?" She shrugged. "You know how coffee gets to me."

"Gross. I'm going to get dressed. We have that radio show after sound check."

Conner had nearly closed the door behind her when someone barreled through it and all but shoved her onto her bed.

"The fuck is wrong with you today?" She squirmed to right herself in the small space left.

Maggie shut the door and leaned against it, quirking her mouth. "That depends. What's up with you and Emi?"

"Nothing."

"You seem awfully friendly all of a sudden."

Conner took her time pulling clothes out. She had no urge to change out of her sweats until the concert, but she would probably be photographed, so she might as well make some sort of effort.

"I don't get you," she finally said, her ire growing with every word. "You want us to get along, but not too well, is that it?"

"I just don't want a repeat of history."

"Having a laugh together doesn't mean I'm going to fuck her."

"How am I supposed to know that? Last time you were normal one minute, and the next you were screwing like bunnies."

"Low blow, Mags."

Maggie reached forward, one hand on either of Conner's slim shoulders. "I only want to be sure you're focused. We're right in the middle of doing the damn thing here."

"I've been entertaining people literally my entire life, in case you forgot. I've got this. My focus is right where it needs to be." She shook off Maggie's tight grip. "Go focus on yourself and call Jamal."

"What the hell is that supposed to mean?"

"It means I think you should call your boyfriend and chill out. That's all. Geez. What's with you?"

"Nothing. I just wanted to make sure your head is in the right place. So, you know, be careful with Emi."

Maggie held her gaze, then jerked her head in a nod and departed. Conner flopped onto her bed. Had she told the truth? It *was* nice to be on good terms with Emi again. That was all.

Frustrated with both herself and Maggie, Conner finished dressing and did her makeup, tapping her foot as she waited for the rest of the band.

"It's a good thing we've got all day! Oh, wait. We don't!"

Bellamy popped her head out of her room. "Wow. We're there already?"

Conner didn't answer. Mostly because they weren't.

When they stopped at the venue, she took the opportunity for fresh air while they waited for Kit and the staff to confirm logistics.

"Hi, Conner."

She turned to find Lola standing at the door of her bus. Was all that long, black hair hers?

"Hey, girl. How'd you sleep?"

"Alone."

Conner nearly choked at her response.

"I thought a tour would be more…interesting. Especially with Conner Cody."

Conner stiffened. "The fuck does that mean?"

"It means your parties are legendary, and I'm waiting for you to live up to them." She sauntered forward. Conner could read her hips loud and clear, no lies detected. "I'm really, really fun, Conner. Come find out."

"Well, you know what they say?"

Lola leaned in. "What's that?"

Conner tucked one of Lola's long locks of hair behind her ear, letting her fingers linger against the soft skin she found. "Don't shit where you eat," she whispered, spinning around.

"I can be very persistent, Conner Cody!"

Conner glanced back. "As if I'm worth anything less."

Emi waited beside their bus, arms crossed. "Conner."

"What?" If Emi was about to act like a jealous ex, Conner would lose her mind.

"What did Maggie say to you earlier?"

Conner weighed the truth versus obfuscation. "She wanted to know if something was going on between us again."

"What did you say?"

Conner tightened her mouth. How dare Emi ask that question like she didn't know the answer? "I told her I don't make the same mistake twice." She pushed past her.

"So that's how it's going to be after all?"

"Yeah, Emi. That's how it's going to be!"

Maggie and Bellamy looked up as Conner stomped past them.

Emi followed half a second later. "You just couldn't leave it alone, could you, Maggie?"

Two doors slammed, but they were thin enough that Conner could hear Bellamy say, "Who needs TV shows when we have this band?"

Conner shed her irritation as she gazed longingly at Soldier Field while they passed it. Intimate venues held their own place in her heart, but something could be said for the overwhelming vibes of a screaming stadium crowd. Conner promised herself she'd bring the band back someday to play the largest venues in the country, and she'd let nothing and no one stand in their way. Not even themselves.

But right now, she'd take what they had. They breezed through sound check without issues and were soon pulling up to the radio station, where a squealing crowd awaited them. Conner raised her eyebrows at Kit.

"What? The bus has your logo all over it. It's recognizable," they said with an innocent expression she didn't trust one bit.

Conner pasted a smile on her face, the last to exit the bus. The crowd ratcheted up to another level. Who needed eardrums anyway?

"Hey, hi, how are you? How's it going? You'll be there tonight? That's great! I'll look for you. Of course I'll sign. What's your name? That's cute. Are you coming to the show? You better be there. I'll know if you aren't."

When they reached the door to the building, the four of them paused, throwing their arms around each other and posing for a quick photo. Emi leaned into her, her hand resting on Conner's stomach, and Conner knew their fans would pore over the image for days, trying to determine what it meant. The pair of them had generated so much gossip since day one that they even had their own hashtag portmanteau, Cemi.

"Chicago, you beautiful babes!" Conner shouted into her microphone that night. "Ladies, is it just me, or are they absolutely bringing it tonight?"

"Oh, they're killing it," Maggie said from her drum kit behind the other three. "What do you say we give them a little reward?"

Conner sighed dramatically. She loved winding up crowds. "I suppose. Let's see...I think it starts like this, no?"

The lights went dark before a spotlight shone down on Conner. She wore tight black jeans, black Doc Martens boots, and an oversized white V-neck hanging off one shoulder, soaked through with sweat.

She grinned broadly, wickedly, the crowd eating out of her hand. Lifting her pick, she waited until they were at her mercy, begging, and then she gave them what they wanted.

"Goddamn, that was a good show!" Maggie exclaimed as they strode off the stage.

She clenched Conner's shoulders from behind and jumped up and down. Bellamy crashed into her side, looping their arms together, and after a brief hesitation, Conner held out her free arm. Emi wasted no time tucking herself underneath it. Her hand tickled across Conner's back.

This was what she wanted, rocking out with her friends and giving their adoring fans everything they demanded. She couldn't deny that her interactions with Emi had left her a little mixed up, but that confusion would dissipate in time. Romantic complications were the last thing she wanted in her life.

"Awesome show tonight!"

Lola strode up to them, her black hair wild and free. Conner was reminded of how messy Meli's curls had been the last time they FaceTimed.

Conner lifted her arm off Emi's shoulders to offer a high-five. Lola squeezed her fingers briefly before releasing them. "Thanks, girl. You, too—the crowd was eating you up."

"Hmm. Only the crowd?" With that, Lola laughed, tossed her hair, and bounced away.

Conner kept her expression carefully neutral, though she couldn't stop herself from watching Lola leave. A soft snort from Bellamy broke through her concentration, and she laughed.

"Sheesh. That one is capital-T trouble," Maggie said. "Like Vittoria-level of trouble."

Emi growled in agreement. "*No one* is Vittoria-level trouble." Conner laughed again.

Kit met them backstage, rambling excitedly about how much the crowd loved "Her Halo Has Horns" and why the record label had already selected it as their next single. Conner let them talk themselves out as the band members separated to find drinks and change clothes. They had an extra day off, so they were staying put in Chicago, and the afterparty would no doubt go on for hours.

"Thanks, babe." A young venue staffer brought Conner her preferred post-show drink, ginger tea served room temperature with honey and hibiscus. She waited patiently until Kit finally looked her way again.

"Do you need something, Conner?"

She smiled sweetly. Too sweetly.

"Why, yes. I do. Why is the record label deciding our next single without any input from us?"

Kit ran a hand through their light-brown hair. "Before you get upset, just think about it for a second. It's the obvious choice. I know how much you want 'Dark Streets,' but we have to ride the momentum."

Conner narrowed her eyes. "Hmm. Okay. Then instead of getting upset right now, I'll save it for tomorrow, when you arrange a video conference with all of us." She leaned in, pointing a finger. "Before lunch, Kit. I don't care what their schedules say."

"Okay, okay. We'll discuss it." They held their hands up in surrender.

Conner stalked off in a trail of steam. These were *her* songs. She had written them, she had recorded them, and she played them for thousands night after night. They were *her* story, and the record label had no right to deny her the agency of choice.

The admission left a dent in her mood that ruined the afterparty for her. She lounged around for a while, drinking tea and offering one-word replies until everyone got the message to leave her alone. Finally she couldn't stand it anymore and tried to sneak away to the bus, intending to take a gummy and sleep.

Lola stood in her way. "I'm starting to think you're avoiding me," she said with an admittedly comely pout.

"I am."

Conner sidestepped the persistent singer, but she grabbed Conner's arm.

"You know, you're even sexier when you're brooding."

Before Conner could do anything, another voice broke in. "She does know. In fact, Conner's always aware of how sexy she is. Now please stop manhandling my lead singer. We require her arms in good working order so she can keep trying to steal my solos."

Emi pried Lola's hand off Conner's arm, sliding in the lightest of caresses down that same arm before taking her hand. Then Emi glared at Lola with thinned lips but didn't say anything else, merely pulling Conner with her. She didn't bother to look back.

Emi led her to their bus. Inside, Conner glanced at their still-entwined fingers.

"I don't need you to save me." Her voice lacked the edge of her words.
"I know." She, too, stared at their fingers.
They were alone. They would probably be alone for several more hours. Something warred inside Conner, a mixture of lust and pain, fear and loneliness.
"Emi..." she said without knowing what would come next.
"I'm sorry."
"What?"
"I'm sorry. I'm so, so sorry that I hurt you, baby." Her words tumbled out as her free hand found Conner's. "I don't even know why it happened, and I've regretted it ever since. Please, Conner, I—"
"Stop."
She froze. "Stop what?"
"Stop apologizing."
"But I really am—"
"I know!" Conner twisted away. "For fuck's sake, do you think I don't believe you? You've been apologizing since it happened. I know you're sorry, okay? I really do. You're sorry."
"Then why—"
Conner could barely look at her. One step forward, two steps back. "Because every time I think I'm over it, that we've moved past it, every time I can handle being in the same space as you, that I think we can go back to normal, you apologize again, and suddenly I'm right back in that doorway. I can't forget it if you keep bringing it up. So stop apologizing, please."
She stopped talking, but the words kept playing in her head, floating around in an all-too-familiar way.
Emi moved back, obvious hurt in her dark eyes, which didn't help Conner at all. "So what does this mean?"
"It means the past is in the past, Emi," she replied, already focusing on something else. "Let it stay there."
Emi apparently recognized the signs of inspiration and gave up. Conner shut herself in her room. Phrases rotated on a repeat loop in her mind. The song practically wrote itself, but she didn't stop until the sun came up.

❖

Relaxing in a rare hotel stay in Boston, Conner curled up on her bed with her e-reader and favorite hoodie. Just one show left, and they'd take a much-needed break for the holidays.
A banging interrupted her tranquility. Conner made a face at the door, but the person on the other side didn't stop. With a harrumph of annoyance,

she left her e-reader on the soft comforter. Hadn't she explicitly said she was to be left alone until showtime?

When she opened the door, she seized up as if doused with ice water. "Hello, Conner. It's been a long time, hasn't it?"

Chapter Eleven

"What the fuck are you doing here?"

Britt Boyd pushed her way inside. When Conner spun around, her mouth open to order the woman out of her room, Britt slammed the door shut, shoving Conner against it painfully. Dark shadows escaped copious amounts of concealer under her eyes.

"I'm asking the questions here. Who the fuck do you think you are, you little shit?" Her upper lip curled in a snarl. "Do you have any idea what kind of hell you've made my life these last few months?"

"Guess how many fucks I give about you."

Conner tried to free herself, but Britt simply squeezed her biceps harder. Whatever she'd been doing since they last saw each other must have included some hefty workouts.

"I was fired. My kids won't speak to me. And my husband is filing for divorce. You took everything from me, Conner."

This time Conner jerked free. She strode away, focusing on the skyline in the window as she tried to orient herself. Britt had issued a terse "no comment" when the interview aired, and Conner hadn't heard anything about her since. How in the world had she tracked her down to her hotel room? This had to be a nightmare, born out of too little sleep, too much stress, and a history of questionable decisions.

"Listen to me very carefully," she finally said, enunciating her words slowly. "I do not give a fuck about you. Why would I?"

"Oh, come off your high horse." Disdain dripped from Britt's mouth. "I knew you were a good actress, but I don't think I've seen anyone play the victim quite so well."

Conner sputtered several times before anything resembling the English language emerged. "Play the victim? Are you on something? I *was* the victim, you psychotic bitch."

"You wanted it! You were desperate for it. No one's ever begged for pussy like you did."

Conner shook her head. She'd taken a lot of drugs in her time—a few with the woman in front of her—but never any as powerful as delusion. "I said it was consensual. Never hinted otherwise."

Britt scoffed as she paced back and forth. Now in her forties, she was still a beautiful woman, but rage had twisted her good looks into something ugly and threatening. "You made me sound like some sort of scheming predator! Like I picked you out of a lineup and hunted you down! Do you know how it made me feel to watch that interview?"

"Oh, yeah? How did it make you feel? Uncomfortable? Guilty?" She moved closer and closer. "A little dirty, huh? Regretful, I bet. How about wrong? Did you feel like you did something wrong, Britt?"

"You knew what you were getting into when—"

"I was sixteen!" Conner was dimly aware of how loud their shouts had grown, but she didn't care. "I wasn't responsible for making the right call! You were! You were the fucking adult! Now grow up and accept the consequences like one."

"Take it back." Britt flung the words with such force that spittle landed on Conner's cheek.

The chuckle that escaped Conner's mouth creeped even herself out. "You really are crazy if you think I'm going to do that. Give me one goddamn reason."

"You cared for me, Conner." Her eyes flashed with lightning. "Whatever you feel now, you cared for me then. Just let it go."

Her hand landed on Conner's wrist. She shook it off. "I lusted after you. I wanted your attention. I didn't care about you any more than you cared about me. It was an affair, a mistake. Nothing more."

"You have no right—"

Conner's anger exploded like a star gone supernova. "I have no right? Go fuck yourself. I have every right! It's my life, too! You're the one who had no right—no right to come into my life and turn me upside down. I was a dumb kid, but *you* made a dumb decision. You had everything to lose. You knew it was wrong."

"Oh, and you didn't?"

"Like I said, you were the adult! It doesn't matter that I knew it was wrong. Why can't you understand that fact? If you had treated me like any other teenager on set, I wouldn't have touched you. Just a harmless crush. You opened that door and pushed me through it, and then you locked it behind me. You had the key! You were the only one who ever had a key."

She found herself staring Britt down, backed against the mirror. Conner glimpsed her reflection behind Britt's head, barely recognizing her pale, tight face. Someone yelled and rattled the door. She ignored them.

"You can't prove anything." Britt's voice had lost some of its fury, emerging in a shell of shaky defiance.

"Can't I?" Conner cocked her head. It was a bluff, but Britt seemed to buy it as her eyes widened. She pressed her advantage. "Or how about this? Your daughter's, what, nineteen now? I don't normally go for under twenty-ones, but I could make an exception. After all, unlike me those years ago, at least she's legal."

"You stay the hell away from her." Her snarl resembled that of a Doberman.

"You don't like that, do you? It would be easy. I've never met a woman I can't seduce. I learned that art from you, you know. I'll become friends with her, give her backstage passes to our shows, tell her how awesome she is. Then I'll invite her over to swim and compliment her bikini, telling her how much I miss having a body like that, so maybe she'll tell me what a great body I still have. I'll offer to put sunblock on her before I decide to sunbathe topless because no one else is around and we're both women. Does that sound familiar?"

Britt's voice trembled. "Stop it."

"Once I have her, I'll convince her that everyone else in her life is just in it for themselves. She won't need friends or family. She'll have me. When she tries to end it, I'll make sure she knows just how much sway I have over her. She won't want me to tell everyone about her drug habits, right? And it would be a shame if her sexual preferences were anonymously released onto the internet. Never mind that I'll teach her what she likes. Don't forget, I can destroy any chance she has at a future in the industry, because I'm all-powerful, and she's just a spoiled. Talentless. Brat." Conner's voice cracked even as it grew louder once more. "Does that sound fucking familiar, Britt?"

Britt grabbed her arm and wrenched it, shouting something unintelligible. Conner yanked free and shoved hard, sending Britt stumbling into the dresser. Conner had no idea what would happen next when the door to her room burst open, revealing security, Kit, the band, and a very bewildered-looking man in a suit.

"What the fuck?" Maggie lunged forward, the combined effort of Emi and Bellamy stopping her.

"Get her out of here." Conner pointed one shaking hand at Britt, who glowered at her until security dragged her out of sight. Then Conner turned to Kit and the hotel manager. "You two find out how she got my room number. Someone's ass better be fired by the end of the day."

"Just go, Kit," Maggie said when they opened their mouth to object.

Once left alone, her bandmates wrapped Conner in a tight, three-way hug as she backed up until she hit the bed, sliding to the floor. She hoped they squeezed until she couldn't feel anything anymore.

❖

By the time the concert rolled around, Conner had channeled her feelings into energy, and she was buzzing so hard that Maggie pulled her to one side and asked, entirely serious, if she was on cocaine again. She wasn't, though for a brief moment the temptation had flared, but she did take two shots of vodka before going onstage.

"Got 'em all worked up for you." Lola sauntered toward Conner, glistening with sweat after her set.

Conner's gaze tracked the bottle of water Lola drank from, her full lips pursing around the mouth. She couldn't deny the attraction. She was fit as hell, her body the perfect combination of lithe muscle, rounded hips, and perky breasts. But her relentless pursuit pushed Conner off-kilter. She was used to women (and men, regretfully) throwing themselves at her, but shameless desperation never appealed to her. She hadn't lied when she said she had learned the art of seduction, one she'd perfected over the years, although she practiced with a level of morality and restraint that Britt lacked. She loved playing that game, akin to foreplay for her.

"See something you like?" A satisfied smirk spread across Lola's olive-skin face.

Conner offered her half a grin as she pushed herself off the stack of empty equipment crates she was leaning against. "You'll know when I do."

"That better be a promise. After tonight, you won't see me for two months."

"Whatever will I do?" Conner used her best impression of Bellamy's Georgian drawl.

"Come to my room tonight, and I'll give you something to remember me by."

"Have you ever been told no?"

Lola snorted. "Have you?"

An image of the last woman to turn her down popped into Conner's head. She and Meli had gotten into the habit of texting while the other slept—Conner in the wee hours, Meli at a more reasonable time after Conner crashed. She liked having something—someone—to wake up to.

"Sure I have."

"I guess fools do exist. C'mon, Conner. This game has been fun and all, but we could be making this tour a lot more memorable."

Conner raised her eyebrows. "What do you want from me, Lola?"

"If I need to say it, then you're not living up to your reputation."

"See you later." Conner walked away with a roll of her eyes. She felt Lola's gaze on her but didn't turn around.

She couldn't keep herself from bouncing up and down on the balls of her feet as the band gathered for their pre-show ritual. Her bandmates' faces radiated concern, but she shook off their questions and bounded onto the stage to the cheers of their adoring legion of fans.

Boston went down as one of the best shows of the tour. Conner channeled all her feelings, her anger and aggression and pain and fear, into her performance, fueling the rest of the band, and the audience responded in kind, eating out of the palm of her hand. Her frenetic energy blitzed through all the markers on her watch's fitness app as she covered every inch of the stage, sometimes abandoning her guitar to work the crowd on the other side of the barriers. She decided last-minute to sing an acoustic version of "Sixteen," finally giving in to her fury when she reached the bridge and stretching her voice so far beyond its limit that Emi ended up singing lead on the final song of the night.

Only a shell of herself remained by the end of the performance, and she accepted the cheers and applause with as much of a smile and tired wave as she could muster.

"Conner," Maggie said once they were backstage, but Conner waved her off.

"Not now, please. I just want to go to bed."

Emi reached for her, but Conner shook her off, too, and headed for the dressing room without another word.

Later, in bed at the hotel, she looked at the clock and groaned. She was exhausted, both emotionally and physically, but sleep remained as elusive as pay equity for women. Despite the toll of the months touring, the stress of the day, and a flight to New York in less than twelve hours, she couldn't shut her mind off.

How had Britt tracked down her hotel room? Why had she reached out now? How had Conner never prepared herself to face her again? Why had she ever published that song or done that stupid interview? Why couldn't she just let it go? Why did she still remember how it felt, both the excitement at the beginning and the fear at the end? What about Conner made her such an easy target? Who, what, how, why…the questions swirled in the clogged drain of her mind.

"Fuck!"

She couldn't handle this. Conner lunged from her bed and tugged a sweatshirt over her head, making sure no one was in the hallway before she took the elevator down a floor. She refused to think about what she was doing.

Lola's sleepy eyes flew open when she found Conner in her doorway. "Wha-what are you doing here?"

"If I need to say it…"

The door was locked behind her before she finished the sentence. Lola dragged Conner to her bed before Conner pushed her away, creating some space.

"This is for tonight only, Lola. Don't read anything into this."

Conner recognized the look in her eyes. She would have promised

Conner the proceeds from her next five albums if she asked. A warning crept up her spine, but she shrugged it off. Making bad choices had led her to this place; maybe another one would get her out.

"Anything you say," Lola breathed, tugging the sweatshirt over Conner's head. "God, you're so gorgeous. I can't believe you're here."

Annoyed, Conner pushed her back again, then lowered herself into an indolent sprawl on the small loveseat. "I'm not here to talk. I think you can find something better to do with your mouth."

Lola followed her like an overeager shadow. "Don't tell me Conner fucking Cody is a pillow princess."

"Don't worry. You'll get yours and then some. Now, on your knees." Conner waited, eyebrows raised, until Lola obeyed. "I don't want to hear another word until I've come all over that pretty face of yours. Think you can handle that?"

Lola practically panted with anticipation as she nodded. Conner let her take her clothes off, but when she pushed her naked legs apart, Conner reached down to grab her long hair, enjoying the moan she received when she pulled Lola's head to one side.

"Oh, and Lola?" She licked the shell of her ear. "If you tell *anyone* about this, I'll destroy you."

Chapter Twelve

Conner's Porsche purred as she crept through a neat Santa Clarita neighborhood, scowling at the houses. After she made yet another turn inside the maze of suburbia, the disembodied voice of her navigation told her she'd arrived.

Conner parked next to a black sedan in the driveway of a two-story, Mediterranean-style home, just like all the others in sight. She'd stopped caring about the lack of character in the neighborhood, more concerned with what lay inside.

She hadn't known what to say when Sadie suggested it was time to meet her nieces and invited her for Thanksgiving, though she had no true reason to decline.

Conner's peers were among the most famous people on Earth. She'd curtsied to royalty and shaken hands with heads of state, not to mention what she had allegedly gotten up to with an English princess. She was most certainly *not* nervous about two children. Kids were easy. And if for some reason they didn't like her right away, she'd just give them stuff until they did. Conner had never met a friend she couldn't buy.

On that note, she forced herself out of the car, retrieved her carefully secured package, and rang the doorbell.

"Conner! Hi!" Sadie's excited greeting, accompanied by an equally enthusiastic hug, took Conner by surprise, but something inside her loosened as she returned the hug.

"How are you?" Sadie held her at arm's length in appraisal. "Your hair's gotten long."

Conner fingered one of her messy brown tresses, now brushing her shoulders. "I know. I had a photoshoot on Monday, and they were furious. As if I could just stop in the middle of the tour and fly back to LA to see my stylist. But she's taking care of it Saturday."

"I didn't say it looks bad, just longer. And you didn't answer my question."

She expected an answer. How unusual. "I'm…um…tired, I guess." Only a slight understatement. "How are you?"

"The same, actually. I worked a double on Tuesday so I could have today and tomorrow off, then spent all day yesterday cooking and cleaning. I told the girls to clean since they're out of school this week, but did they? Of course not."

Sadie's rapid delivery made Conner blink until it dawned on her that perhaps she was nervous, too. Was it a good sign or a bad one?

Sadie paused for breath, her eyes widening in dubious surprise as she looked at the object Conner held. "You brought a pie! I didn't know you cooked."

"I don't, but I pay good money for a wonderful chef." She held out the pastry. "It's pumpkin. Freshly baked last night, still warm when I got home from the airport around two."

"Geez. No wonder you're tired."

Sadie offered to take Conner's leather jacket, but she refused. Her jacket was her armor, as much a part of her persona as her heavily lidded eyes or close-mouthed smirk.

Despite the cacophony of voices and dishes from other parts of the house, Sadie led her to what appeared to be a playroom, with a small plastic kitchen to one side next to a table and chairs, and bins of toys lining the walls. So much color clashed in the room that she felt like she'd dived headfirst into a box of crayons. After explaining it would be easier to meet the girls without being surrounded by people, Sadie left, calling for her daughters as she went.

Conner had never had a designated playroom. She was usually left to her own devices in an entire wing of her own, her parents choosing the opposite side of the various houses they inhabited. Oddly, while she remembered *having* lots of toys, she had very few memories of *playing* with them.

"Mommy says you're my Aunt Conner."

The small voice startled Conner, but she recovered quickly, rearranging her features into practiced indolence as she leaned against the wall. "She says the same thing to me."

A young child watched her curiously, toying with one of her flaxen pigtails, her green eyes unblinking. Conner's green eyes. *Oof.* It had been one thing to see that she and her sister shared that trait; it was quite another to see it passed on to another generation.

"I'm Hannah." She marched forth until she stood directly in front of Conner. "You're really tall."

"You're really small."

"I'm only six, but I'll be bigger when I'm seven. Are you going to get bigger?"

"I hope not. How old do you think I am?"

She scrunched up her button nose. "Mommy says you're the little sister like me, but you're lots taller than Sarah, so you're probably…sixteen!"

Conner grinned. "A few years off. How high can you count, anyway?"

"A hundred. One, two, three, four…"

She kept going, but Conner was saved at thirty-two by the reappearance of Sadie in the doorway.

She looked at Conner, then at her daughter, before returning her gaze to Conner with a quizzical expression. "How's it going, Conner?"

"*Aunt* Conner," Hannah corrected loudly. "Fifty-nine, sixty…"

Geez. She was never going to get used to that. Conner had one aunt in Ireland, a severe, hard-drinking woman who projected her insecurities by frequently ridiculing everyone nearby.

"Seventy-two, seventy-three, seventy-four…"

Nearing insanity from the count, Conner knelt to Hannah's level. "What's in your hand?"

"Soccer pinball. I got it for Christmas last year. Eighty-nine, ninety, ninety-one…"

"I like soccer."

Hannah nodded but kept counting. "Ninety-nine, one hundred! See, Aunt Conner, see. I told ya I could! I can keep going! One hundred, um, one hundred, um…Mommy, what comes after a hundred? I can go backward! One hundred, um…ninety…"

"I have season tickets to Angel City FC. Have you been to a game?"

That finally got her to stop. Hannah's jaw dropped. "Do you know Paige? And Christen? And Katie? And…"

As she continued to list players (a couple that Conner knew far better than she'd ever tell a child), a glow rose on her face, and by the time she had run through the entire roster, she was all but vibrating with excitement.

"Mommy! Did you hear what Aunt Conner said?"

"Yes, I—"

"Can I go to a game? Can I get a jersey? Can I get *two* jerseys?"

Oh, God. She'd ended one monster simply to unleash a greater one.

"Do you think—do you think I can meet the players, too? Will they play with me? I'm really good. I can defend and score and play goalkeeper. Did you know they don't say goalie in soccer? Did you know…"

Conner tried to become one with the wall, sending her sister a silent plea for help. Though an old hat at screaming teenagers and eager women, she had no weapons in her arsenal to deal with a chatty kid. Hordes of Mongol warriors fled lesser barrages.

Sadie proved useless, merely chuckling and watching with a warm smile, traces of relief highlighted in her expression. Had she thought it wouldn't go well? Conner ground her teeth.

"Sarah!" When no one appeared at her call, Sadie shook her head. "Honestly, that girl. Conner, would you like to surprise her?"

Conner jumped at the chance to escape and followed directions up the stairs, the babble of the ankle-biter finally dwindling as she did so. When she knocked on the second door on the right, it swung open to reveal... herself?

A framed poster of Conner in her superhero garb dominated one wall, while enlarged pictures of Hestia Rising took up much of a bulletin board on another. Seated at a vanity, a preteen girl with long blond hair sang along with "Wicked Girl."

(Conner still hated that song, but in that moment, it didn't bother her quite as much as it used to.)

"Mom, I said I'll be down—Oh my gosh! You're Conner Cody."

"In the flesh." Conner relaxed, folding her arms as she leaned against the doorway. Her practiced half-smirk took its place on her face. This, she could handle. Fangirls were nothing new.

Sarah's mouth fell open, revealing braces as she gawked at Conner through her mirror. No one spoke until the song ended and silence filled the space. Sarah jumped, slapping her hand on a tablet before the next song cued up.

"I, um, I, um—you weren't—I didn't know you were coming to my room!"

"Should I leave?"

"No! I mean, uh, you can stay." She narrowed her brown eyes. "Are you *really* my aunt?"

Conner shrugged. "I have no reason to doubt it. Would you rather I wasn't?"

"No! But, well, you're *Conner Cody*—" The reverence with which she breathed Conner's name amused her no end. "And my mom is just my mom." The similar lack of reverence, delivered with a shrug, also had Conner laughing. On the inside, of course; contrary to the belief of some, she wasn't completely heartless, and she didn't want to hurt this earnest kid.

A kid who shared some of her DNA, a realization that was still so heady she preferred not to dwell on it. She hoped Sarah and Hannah got whatever good DNA Seth Cody provided.

Aware that Sarah was still staring at her, Conner nodded at the poster. "You're a fan?"

Her hair bounced as she nodded. "I like all the heroes, but Lyss is my favorite. Will there be more movies?"

"I have one left in my contract." Two, actually, but one was a secret, and it was worth more than her entire career to upset her studio overlords.

"And then what?"

"Then...I make other movies? Oh, you mean the series! It'll keep going with or without me, I'm sure."

Sarah frowned. "That would suck." Her hand flew to her mouth, and she whispered, "Please don't tell my mom I said 'suck.'"

Conner mimed zipping her lips and winked. Sarah's eyes grew impossibly wide before she recovered, winking back and grinning with a little wiggle.

"Aunt Conner!"

Conner jumped so high her WNBA friends would have been impressed. Hannah gazed up at her. "Mommy says it's time to eat, so you and Sarah gotta come downstairs."

When Conner strolled into the dining room, every head swiveled toward her. Vittoria used to affectionately refer to her, in Italian of course, as "my moon," for her ability to draw attention like the tides.

"Hey, everyone. I'm Conner," she said with a flick of her fingers.

A stream of introductions followed. A gaggle of wide-eyed kids and starstruck teenagers peered out from the kitchen, where Conner's nieces reluctantly headed for the kids' table.

"Skinny as a twig, green eyes, and the ability to reduce a grown woman to a babbling mess," an older woman said, narrowing her eyes in disapproval at Sadie's aunt, who had gushed for a solid two minutes about a movie Conner had filmed with her mother during a brief thaw in their relationship several years ago. Harlow had advised it would be good for her image, and, annoyingly, she had been right.

The woman continued. "You must be Seth Cody's kid." Conner scowled, and she laughed. "Now *that* must be from your mother. What a look!"

Sadie pursed her lips. "Mom! Be nice."

Conner looked up with new interest. So this was the woman who had fallen for the lines that had snared so many others and had her life changed because of it. Sadie shared only a faint resemblance with her mother, which filled Conner with envy. All anyone ever talked about was how much she was like her parents.

The woman's smile softened, radiating warmth. "I've been so eager to finally meet you, although not quite as much as my granddaughters."

A squeak of dismay emerged from the kitchen, followed by a wave of titters. All the adults chuckled, and everyone tucked in.

Conner sat between Sadie and one of her cousins, an attractive woman who Conner would have seduced by dessert in another setting. Today she was content to let everyone talk around her while she filled up on vegetables, stuffing, and a small slice of turkey that Sadie cajoled her into eating.

"So what do you normally do for Thanksgiving, Conner?" Asher asked as slices of pie and bowls of freshly whipped cream were handed out.

Conner accepted a fruit tartlet. Last Thanksgiving, she and Vittoria, during an on-again period, had spent a hedonistic week in Amsterdam. The year before that, she'd lounged around Saint-Tropez, brushing up on her French—the language, the kissing, and the women.

"I usually just spend it with friends," she said, before adding, as everyone stared at her, "Most of my family isn't American, you know, so they don't really do Thanksgiving. It's not a big deal for me. I guess my favorite Thanksgivings were the years I was in the Macy's parade."

"You were in the *parade*?!" Numerous small faces popped out from the kitchen until Hannah wriggled free of the group.

"Three times. I was around your age the first time, I think."

Hannah's mouth formed a perfect *O*, but her response was drowned out. Her appearance from the kitchen had unleashed the flood, and soon Conner was occupied taking selfies and videos with the older kids while Sarah pouted from her seat. Hannah led the younger set in peppering Conner with questions about meeting Santa, if she had ridden various attractions at Disneyland, and how soon they could come to her house (a question she repeatedly deferred).

Finally she escaped to the bathroom, returning to find only Sadie's younger brother David left in the dining room as he cleared the table. He grinned at her. "I think it's safe to say you boosted the popularity of every single kid here. They're all texting their friends now."

She followed his lead, gingerly stacking plates. "It comes with the territory."

"Don't do that."

She froze. "Sorry. Was I doing it wrong?"

"No. It's only that my dad has a rule that if Mom and Sadie cook, then he and Asher and I have to clean."

"But I didn't cook."

He laughed. "I think it's more of a gender thing. He's old-fashioned like that." David worked his way toward her, grinning again. "But I'm not. You can help."

Warily, for she recognized the look he was giving her, she continued picking up glasses and silverware. True to David's word, the men refused her offer to help clean.

He slipped into the dining room behind her when she left the kitchen. "Sadie says you're back in town for a little while. I have tickets to the Christmas symphony at the Hollywood Bowl in a few weeks. Would you like to go with me?"

Conner stared at him, tilting her head. "Are you asking me out? Your sister's sister?"

"You're not *my* sister."

"Ignoring the fact that I am a certified, card-carrying lesbian, I prefer a few more family trees between me and my partners."

"Ah, well." He shrugged, giving her a wry smile. "When the youngest-ever winner of *Maxim*'s Hot One Hundred walks in the door, a guy's gotta shoot his shot, you know?"

"I don't want to know what you do with your shots."

"His what?" Sadie walked in, her gaze flicking between her siblings.

"Nothing," David said at the same time Conner told her, "Your brother just asked your sister on a date."

She wrinkled her nose. "Ew, David. That's weird."

"We're not related." He retreated to the safety of the kitchen.

Sadie and Conner burst into laughter.

"Hey, girl."

"Hi! Are you on your way?"

Conner scuffed her boots as she held her phone to her ear outside Sadie's front door. "About that. The girls really want me to stay for dinner, so will you mind if I'm like an hour late?"

"Conner Cody, if your nieces want more time with you, you better stay as long as you can. Just come by tomorrow."

"Are you sure?" She pressed the phone tighter. "I want to see you. I miss you, or whatever."

Melina laughed. "I miss you or whatever, too. It's fine. I swear. Besides, I'm still stuffed, so I'll probably pass out soon. Text me when you're ready tomorrow. We'll hang out in our sweatpants, eat leftovers, and you can tell me every detail of the tour."

"We'll spend the whole day together, okay?"

"It's a plan. Can't wait!"

After they hung up, Conner returned inside. Everyone had left except Sadie's parents and David, who avoided her. They lounged around, picking at leftover pie and playing board games, interspersed with shouts at a football game in the background. Conner was vividly reminded of an episode she'd filmed during her sitcom years.

After Sadie's parents left, she pulled Conner into the kitchen. "Conner, I saw your interview with Larissa Lamont, about…"

"Oh. That."

"Yes, that. I just wondered if you're all right."

"Of course. Yeah. It's all good now. In the past." Conner shifted from foot to foot, the urge to run so strong it was as if someone had fired the starting gun at a track and field event.

Sadie's frown deepened. "If you're sure…"

"Yep. I am."

"Okay, but if you need to talk, I'm here. I hope you'll reach out if you do. To be honest, Conner, I wish more than anything that I'd been around during that time."

Conner scoffed. "No offense, but I wouldn't have listened to you any more than I did anyone else back then."

"Maybe. I spend a lot of time thinking about what life would have been like if we'd grown up together."

Conner swallowed, unable to admit she did the same thing. "You have a great family, you know? Don't wish it away."

"I don't. I just—well, you're here now, and we're all very happy about that." She smiled, and Conner had to swallow again.

"Me, too."

When they returned to the living room, Hannah was waiting in purple, polka-dot pajamas. "Aunt Conner?"

It took Conner a second to realize that was her. "Yeah, kid?"

"Will you read me a story?"

"Uh, sure."

Asher looked up from the coffee table, where he was playing cards with Sarah. "You don't—"

"It's cool. Besides, this is basically what I do for a living."

Hannah led Conner by the hand to her bedroom, a mishmash of princess and soccer themes. After some hesitation, Conner removed her boots and jacket, stretching out on the bottom bunk. Hannah scrambled up next to her and tucked herself under one arm. Conner froze, but when the girl rested her head on Conner's shoulder with a content little sigh, she made herself relax.

"You didn't get a book," Hannah said, her voice already slow with sleep.

"I don't need one. I have a story all in my head for you."

Conner began to recount the plot of her next animated film, figuring by the time it actually premiered, she wouldn't remember it.

"A long time ago, in a land far away, a young princess named Arlais lived in a beautiful, magical castle…"

Chapter Thirteen

"Harlow."

"Conner."

"*Harlow.*"

"Conner."

"Harlow!"

"You can keep saying my name, but we're not stopping until we're done."

Conner shoved away from Harlow's spotless desk and strode to the floor-to-ceiling glass panels that made up one wall. In the distance, the Hollywood sign taunted her. How much had she paid for Harlow to have this view?

"I need a break."

"I'll send for lattes. Mocha, to be seasonal?" Without waiting for an answer, Harlow ordered two through her intercom.

"I'll take it, but I meant a real-life break."

She peered at Conner over the top of her glasses. "You're going to Belfast for Christmas."

"First of all, spending any amount of time with either of my parents is not a break, and you know it. Plus, don't I have a photoshoot, an interview, and a signing on that trip?" She ticked off the itinerary on her fingers. "C'mon, Harlow. I'm running ragged here."

"We talked about this. Unless you're changing your priorities, this is what it'll take to have two successful careers." She softened a fraction of a degree, which was about as much as Conner ever got from her. "The tour will be over next summer, and things will get easier."

"For a month or so. Then I'm off to Germany to don my tights and cape once more."

"So book a vacation. Most of us don't get a month off, you know. And for the record, your character wears neither tights nor cape, thankfully."

"Lyss is more of a skintight leather catsuit kind of hero, isn't she? Glad you noticed." She delivered this remark with a wink, more out of habit than anything, which Harlow ignored, per usual. Conner wasn't sure what she would do if her manager ever actually responded to her flirtation.

"As I said, book now so we can plan around it. I can't work with you when you demand time off with no notice."

Conner scowled, grabbing her tablet and slouching in her seat as she scanned it. She was more booked than a Times Square hotel on New Year's Eve.

"Push *Entertainment Weekly* back a day, and move this shoot directly after Tom Ford."

"You know they hate that."

"I know I don't care." Conner returned Harlow's look directly back to her. "What? I don't. They'll bitch and moan, but then they'll do whatever I ask, because I'm the best, and so are you."

"With an ego like that, how do you get so many women to drop at your feet?"

"The perfect smolder, no inhibitions, dexterous fingers, and an even more dexterous tongue."

"Ugh. You annoy me. Three days."

"Try five."

"You're trying something, but it's not five. Three."

"Four, and I'll do this podcast while I'm away." When Harlow's lips thinned, Conner knew she had won and not to push it any farther.

"Fine. Where are you going?"

She decided in an instant. "Big Bear. Wanna come?"

"In your dreams."

"Usually I'm awake when I think of you like that."

"Go away, Conner."

The argument flew nearly as fast as Conner's G-Wagen did down the 210. She wouldn't dare subject her Porsche to snow and ice.

"I don't care how close it is to Christmas. We're not caroling all the way to Big Bear. You can fa-la-la fuck off."

"Who knew Conner Cody was such a Grinch?" In the seat next to her, Melina adopted a pleading pout, complete with puppy-dog eyes. Conner hoped she never realized how effective the look was. "C'mon, pleeease?"

"I'm not a Grinch! I just have taste."

Lindsey piped up from the backseat. "None of us will tell on you. Your street cred's safe with us."

"Don't let her fool you. I've heard Conner sing Christmas carols before."

Bellamy chortled as she caught Conner's glare in the rearview mirror. She and Lindsey were a study in contrasts next to each other—Lindsey, taller than even Conner and lean, and Bellamy, short and voluptuous.

"Et tu, Bells? That was one time, for a TV show. I had no choice. I just don't like them, okay?"

"Then you can do it just 'one time' for us, right?"

Lindsey and Bellamy continued to tag-team her from the backseat, but Melina remained quiet. When Conner glanced at her with raised eyebrows, she simply shrugged.

"I'm not going to make you do anything you don't want to."

Conner leaned toward her over the center console. "But wouldn't it be fun to try?" She risked taking her eyes off the road just in time to catch the hint of a blush on her cheeks. Try as she might, she enjoyed these little reactions too much to stop flirting with her.

As penance, she gave in. "Fine. One song. And I get veto rights!"

They ignored her disclaimers, and before she knew it, all four of them belted along with holiday classics from Bing to Mariah as they climbed the winding road into the San Bernadino Mountains. Conner didn't hide her displeasure, but neither did she hold back. Even among friends, she had standards to uphold.

Conner scowled at Lindsey and Bellamy's high-five as they climbed out of the car. "Thank God no one else witnessed that travesty."

Jamal's SUV pulled up next to them, and Maggie popped out, followed by his friend Harrison Fisher. Jamal hadn't wanted to be the only man on the trip, and Conner had acquiesced, mostly because he was the son of a famously prickly director Conner was dying to work with. She wasn't above pulling whatever strings were available to get what she desired.

"What travesty?" Maggie asked. "Your disregard for any laws of traffic?"

Lindsey smirked. "No. Just a full hour of Conner Claus and her merry band of elves."

"What?"

Conner interrupted before she could elaborate. "Nothing." As she led them inside, she elbowed Lindsey. "Tallest elf I've ever seen."

Nominally a cabin, Conner's vacation home sat on the water within a gated community, her only two real conditions when shopping. Beyond the primary suite and a converted studio, she hadn't done much to the house, turning her decorator loose instead. Her guests' appreciative murmurs reinforced that choice.

"Mags, you and Jamal are obviously in the suite above the garage. Everyone else, grab a room."

Lindsey caught Conner's gaze and licked her lips as they lugged their bags to their rooms. Conner suspected—and hoped—that Lindsey's bed would remain untouched.

While Jamal and Harrison grilled steak, chicken, and vegetables on the deck, warmed by a patio heater, Bellamy chopped ingredients for pico de gallo, Lindsey made a bowl of guacamole, and Melina worked on tortillas from scratch. Conner made the only thing she could—drinks, already buzzed by the time she started sneaking swipes of guacamole behind Lindsey's back.

Several hours later, the fajitas and tequila had lulled everyone into a sleepy inertia, so they draped about the living room in various poses of idleness. Conner stretched across the length of one couch, strumming her guitar with her feet in Bellamy's soft lap.

"Is that a new song?" Maggie asked, sitting on the floor between Jamal's legs.

"I don't know yet. Maybe it's an ode to Melina's tortillas."

"Now that's a song you should record." Harrison raised his glass. "I'd wife you up just for them, Mel, among other reasons."

She doesn't like being called Mel, dumbass. Conner's strumming morphed into a discordant screech. "I'm going to bed."

Everyone rose as if they'd been waiting for permission. Conner carefully returned her guitar to its case before halting Lindsey's progress.

"You know, I'm not that tired," she murmured into her neck, grasping her waist.

Lindsey arched into her touch. "What a coincidence! Neither am I. After I freshen up, do you want to talk…or whatever?"

"I like whatever, especially with you." Conner squeezed her butt before sending her on her way.

Conner brushed her teeth and contemplated changing into pajamas before deciding not to bother. When she heard a knock on her door, she grinned at herself in the mirror. "Come in! Give me just a sec."

After washing her face, she returned to her bedroom clad in only her underwear. "I figured I would save—"

"Oh my gosh, you're naked!"

Melina, who was decidedly not Lindsey, stared at Conner, specifically at one particular part of her body.

"You're not—"

"Why would I be naked? Why are you?"

"That wasn't—I'll be right back."

Conner ducked into her closet and emerged properly covered by a sweatshirt and shorts. With nearly any other available woman on the planet, she would have remained in the room, challenging her to get her fill of her nearly nude body while she charmed the woman into her bed. But she couldn't shake the unfamiliar sensation of embarrassment.

She half hoped her room would be empty, but Melina remained, fiddling with a bottle of perfume on Conner's dresser.

"You can try it if you want."

Melina nearly dropped the expensive glass bottle. "I'm so sorry. I shouldn't have—I couldn't sleep, and I saw your light was still on, and you've told me how you don't sleep much, so I thought…I mean, obviously you were still changing. So anyway I'll just—"

"Hey, hey, Meli? Chill, babe. If anyone is sorry, it's me."

"It's not like I haven't seen them before, anyway. I mean, who hasn't? Nooo! That's not what I meant! It's only, movies, and—and magazines, and, you know…"

Conner felt her eyebrows climb her forehead during the ramble before she relaxed. "I know what you meant. For the record, *one* magazine and *one* movie." She couldn't resist adding, "Good to know you've been paying attention."

Melina dragged a hand down her face. She was so cute when flustered. "I haven't been—oh, never mind. So what if I have?"

Conner's jaw nearly succumbed to gravity before she snapped it shut. Suddenly, flirting with Melina, previously a harmless game, now felt akin to walking a tightrope, and she refused to sacrifice a good friendship for a fruitless pursuit. "Then you would be in good company with the rest of the world," she said instead, flashing her reliable smirk that faded when something akin to disappointment washed over Melina's face.

They'd settled on Conner's bed, each under her own blanket as they discussed their respective upcoming film shoots, when her door opened again.

"Sorry. I had a phone…call." Lindsey's grin turned puzzled.

Conner sat upright. She prided herself on managing the women in and out of her arms with minimal-to-zero drama, but for some reason, she felt trapped in between these two, one of whom she would never sleep with and the other who never cared who else graced Conner's bed.

"Hey, girl. What about your phone call?"

"Um…I decided to take it down here so I wouldn't wake anyone, and when I saw your light on, I figured I'd say hi."

"Do you wanna hang out with us?" Melina asked. "We're just talking."

"Nah. I'm tired. See you in the morning."

Conner searched her face but found nothing but a cheerful smile.

After she left, Melina cleared her throat. "You thought I was her when I came in." Conner nodded. "What's the deal with you? I thought you were dating when I met her, but since then…I mean, it's none of my business."

"It's fine. You can ask me anything. Lindsey and I dated once, but we just don't have that thing, that spark, that whatever. But we have fun, so I guess you can call it friends with benefits."

"And I'm in the way." She started to rise, but Conner tugged her arm.

"Not at all. I can go without sex, Meli. I've practically been celibate on tour."

On cue, her phone lit up. One look at the screen had Conner selecting Do Not Disturb mode. Lola had texted her relentlessly since their night together, and ignoring her didn't seem to do any good.

"So you and Emi didn't...?"

Conner scoffed, rolling her head back along with her eyes. "No! Contrary to apparently popular belief, I can keep my pants on."

"I didn't mean that. Geez. I can't win tonight."

"It's all good. It's just that you aren't the only person to ask about her. And the answer is no. Emi and I are on our way to being friends again, but that's as far as it will ever go."

Melina picked at a cuticle. "Can I ask what the story is there?"

"I told you that you can ask me anything." Conner rolled onto her back, staring at the dark ceiling. Finally, she sighed. "To make a long story short, she liked me from the start, I knew it, and one day we ended up in bed. Actually, it was—well, not a bed. We were together about six months. Then, after a gig at a festival, I walked in on her with another woman."

Melina cringed. "That's awful."

"It sucked." Melina chuckled at her frank agreement, and she smiled. "But I'm over it. Really. I'd never let anything come before the band."

"How's the tour going so far?"

Melina seemed eager to move on from the topic of sex and relationships, and Conner followed her lead. The expected disappointment of her aborted romp with Lindsey never materialized. They talked for hours—about the tour, the band's dynamics, acting, audition tips, mutual acquaintances in the industry, and more. Melina confessed she'd been an extra in one of her movies, though their time on-set never overlapped, and Conner told her what it was like to grow up on sets.

She didn't remember saying good night or falling asleep. When she woke, the space next to her was empty and cold, which didn't bother her one bit. Conner didn't do sleepovers.

Maggie, Jamal, and Harrison went skiing for the day. Conner didn't feel like it, Bellamy had no interest, Lindsey was barred, thanks to her WNBA contract, and Melina didn't have the gear. Harrison tried his hardest to talk her into it, and Conner offered to pay for rentals and lessons, but she declined.

She found herself in her studio. Her conversation with Melina had stirred up something in her mind, and she needed it out. Bellamy drifted in at one point but left her alone, knowing her methodology, and Melina brought her a sandwich that slowly grew stale.

When she emerged, the skiers had returned, dusk had descended, and everyone was laughing uproariously at some story Harrison was telling over pizza.

Maggie cheered, pointing a bottle of beer at her. "I told you she'd come up for air at some point!"

"Do you have a new song?" Bellamy asked at the same time Melina said, "Sit down and have some pizza. You haven't eaten all day."

Conner rubbed her eyes as she sat between Melina and Lindsey, reaching for a piece of garlic bread. "Several, actually."

Melina leaned toward her, her eyes shining like pools of whiskey. "Will you play them for us today?"

Conner's bandmates laughed. "Conner doesn't let anyone hear her songs until they're perfect," Maggie said, to which Bellamy added, "Not even us."

"I refuse to give anyone an inferior product. That's why I'm so good in bed." She winked at Lindsey, but when she received only a slight smile in response, Conner knew she'd screwed up. She wasn't sure how, and for a moment she wasn't even sure she cared, but guilt won out. There really was a first time for everything.

After dinner, Conner caught Lindsey's sleeve and tugged her into the laundry room, another first as she'd never been in there.

"What's up?"

Conner folded her arms. "I should ask you that. You've barely talked to me all day. If this is about last night—"

"I just thought we were better friends than that."

"I…what?"

Lindsey sighed. "I don't care who you sleep with, but you could have given me a heads-up."

Conner blinked. "Once again, what?"

"You invited me up," Lindsey said as if by rote. "Twenty minutes later, Melina was on your bed. You really couldn't wait that long?"

"If I have to tell someone else one more time this weekend that I'm not some sort of sex addict…" Conner ran a hand through her shaggy tresses. "I've never slept with Meli. Not last night, not ever. She came by, and we started talking." *And I completely forgot you were coming.* "I should've just sent her on her way. I'm sorry. Are we cool?"

Lindsey regarded her for a second and nodded. "Okay. I just felt like a piece of meat for a minute."

"You're definitely not meat." Conner offered a grin, though she quickly dropped it. "I have to ask, though—were you jealous?"

Thankfully, Lindsey's reply seemed genuine. "Not at all. You know I'm totally in favor of you finding the love of your life."

"What about you? Don't you want to find the love of your life? You haven't dated anyone the entire time I've known you."

Lindsey's face fell into pensive, almost wounded, lines. Her gaze traveled a thousand miles away as she shrugged. "Of course I do."

Conner leaned against the washer (or dryer, she wasn't entirely sure which was which), trying to figure out her friend. Because they were friends, right? They didn't always hook up. But friends should know more about each other than she did of Lindsey, the sum total of which seemed to be that she had a large family in North Carolina, she loved sushi, and someone had broken her heart years before. And friends should definitely know how to comfort one another, something that made Conner extremely uncomfortable even with Maggie.

Lindsey glanced at her, light returning to her hazel eyes. "Wouldn't life be so much easier if we could just fall in love with each other?"

Conner agreed fervently, and they laughed. When Lindsey held out her arms, she didn't hesitate to return the embrace. That's what friends did. They could be friends, and Melina, too, for that matter, just like the band.

However, that didn't stop her from opening her door to Lindsey that night. Friends could still have benefits, after all.

Chapter Fourteen

Conner woke with a start somewhere over the Atlantic. The cabin of the Airbus remained as dark as the inky sky outside her window. She gave up on sleep and caught up on a fantasy show until the lights came on.

"Is there anything else I can bring you, Miss Cody?" The flight attendant peered through her eyelashes after delivering Conner's ricotta-and-truffle omelet and fruit spread.

Conner smiled. She'd once snuck a flight attendant into her first-class suite on an Emirates flight to Australia, but this one seemed more awestruck than flirtatious. "I'm good. Thank you. You've been wonderful."

"It's my pleasure. Please let me know if you need anything else." When she lingered, Conner knew what she wanted.

She ended up taking selfies with all the first-class staff, but she didn't mind, even though she didn't look her best after an eleven-hour overnight flight. Upon landing, she was whisked away by a private car as soon as she stepped on the air bridge. VIP service was worth every penny, even if every time she booked a flight, her financial advisor made the sign of the cross and raised his hands to heaven in despair.

Her grandmother's chauffeur, an institution who had disapproved of Conner for as long as she could remember, drove her in silence to her grandmother's equally silent Mayfair home. Her grandparents were in Belfast, where Conner would meet them in a week.

When in London, she always took advantage of the house, more private than a hotel but with both maid and chef service, though she used little of the latter except the odd breakfast. Conner's week disappeared as she filmed a glorified cameo in a movie, appeared on talk shows of both the morning and evening variety, spent an entire day in a photoshoot, sat for two press interviews, and appeared with Chelsea FC's men's and women's squads. Before she knew it, she was hopping across the Irish Sea, where her grandfather met her at Belfast City Airport.

"Happy Christmas, Granda," she said, receiving a grunt in reply.

She wasn't offended. He had never taken much notice of her, with one notable exception. An avid fan of both soccer and rugby (though he'd throw her out of the car without slowing for saying "soccer"), he spent long hours muttering obscenities at the television, a fact observed by Conner, who at the age of four shouted, "Bloody English pricks!" at the TV during one such game. He patted her head with one large hand and said, "Aye. Good girl."

Everyone was highly amused, at least until a few months later when she attended the World Cup with her father, and a reporter thought it would be cute to ask her who she was rooting for.

"Anyone but the bloody English pricks," she repeated blithely on a live feed.

She still had fans in England who held signs with the phrase at her concerts, considering it a badge of honor.

Her grandmother's greeting wasn't much better, as she surveyed Conner at arm's length. "Do they have food in Los Angeles? Or is heroin-chic back in fashion?"

"I never did heroin, but I do occasionally eat, Gran." She refrained from commenting on her grandmother's equally thin physique.

"Well, one never knows. I did wonder about your late nights in London this past week."

A chauffeur made a convenient cover for a spy. "I was eating on those nights. Just not food."

Her grandmother wrinkled her Grecian nose. "Don't be crude, darling girl. You are your father's child. At least you didn't bring them to my home."

"I have standards. Speaking of my father, where is he?"

"Upstairs somewhere, no doubt up to no good." She sent Conner a stern look. "You would do well not to imitate him so often, you know."

Conner ignored that remark. The Cody family were high priests in the art of overlooking. Her grandparents had remained married, seemingly content, despite months and years apart (and multiple affairs) as her grandmother's acting career took her to Hollywood, New York, and London, while her grandfather refused to step off Irish soil.

Conner tucked her hands into the pocket of her jacket as she trudged through the enormous, neoclassical-style manor. Built in the nineteenth century, it probably hadn't been updated since then, either, as dark and drafty as it was. Certain members of the family claimed it was haunted, which she attributed to a history of alcoholism.

She found her father on a balcony overlooking the back garden, holding a joint. As Seth finished a drag, she deftly snagged it, taking a long pull.

"Rude American," he muttered.

Conner settled on the cold bench next to her father, resting her boots on the stone balustrade in silence. Unfortunately, that wouldn't last forever.

Seth finished the joint and made to flick it over the edge before Conner intercepted it, scowling at him as she crushed it beneath her shoe. She'd dispose of it properly later without littering the grounds.

"I hear you bagged your producer, kid."

Conner's breath left her in an irritated huff. Why couldn't people just let it go? First Sadie, then Melina, Abuelita, Lindsey, and now Seth. "I think it was the other way around."

"Can't say I haven't done the same."

"Your producer or a teenage girl?"

He had the nerve to look offended. "Producers. My women have always been legal. I'm a philanderer, not a pedophile."

Conner relaxed, unaware she'd been tensed until then. She wasn't sure what she would have done if she'd discovered Seth's indiscretions went that far.

"Good to know that even you have limits."

"Christ, you sound like your ma when you get judgmental. Oh, don't be cross now—you look even more like her then, and I'm not high enough for that. Besides, your apple didn't fall far from my tree, did it?"

Conner bit the inside of her cheek. Why did she come here, often the only time she saw her father unless their paths crossed incidentally? Their relationship had never been as volatile as Conner's with her mother. Seth teased, and she retorted, but their truce was generally tolerable.

"Speaking of, how's that Italian model of yours? Feisty wee thing, I reckon."

She glared at him. "We're not together anymore."

"Damn shame. Suppose that leaves you free on tour, then."

She grumbled an assent.

"How's the tour been?"

She seized the common ground, and they swapped tales until their noses grew numb. Seth shared too much regarding his sexual conquests on tour, but he'd always treated her more like a casual acquaintance than a daughter. He'd given Conner her first sip of alcohol when she was eight, laughing until he fell over when she spit it out. But she'd take his benign indifference over her mother's outright disdain every time.

Christmas was pleasant enough. They exchanged overpriced gifts without a drop of sentimentality, just like the Christmases of Conner's childhood, before her grandparents went to mass at Saint Peter's with her uncle and his family. Seth mumbled something before scampering away, but Conner point-blank refused.

"When was your last confession?" Gran fixed her with an imperious stare.

Four years of Catholic high school had been more than enough for Conner. "If I tell you, you'll take the Lord's name in vain, and then you'll have something to confess. Better just to avoid that. You can say a prayer for me."

"Believe me, darling girl. I do."

Left to her own devices, Conner curled up in a chair next to a roaring fire in the library and texted Christmas greetings to her bandmates, managers, and a few others. Lindsey replied with a picture of her sprawling family, all in matching pajamas, which made Conner's skin itch. Then she called Melina.

"Merry Christmas, Conner!"

"Hey, girl. Merry Christmas. How's Texas?"

"It's seventy degrees here. Good thing climate change is a hoax, right? But it's great! My family won't get off my case about coming home more often or, better yet, moving home entirely, but that's nothing new." She ended with the heavy sigh of the long-suffering.

Conner stiffened. "Are you going to?"

"Of course not! Texas will always be my home, and I miss my family, but California is my home now, too. I love it there, and I've finally got my career to a place that lets me eat more than ramen noodles and cardboard pizza."

"Good." Conner tried not to let her relief show, but apparently her acting skills failed her for once.

Melina laughed. "Don't worry. You're not getting rid of me yet. I make friends for life, you know."

"Oh, we're friends, huh?"

"I thought we were…I mean, we talk all the time, and we hang out, and you even took me to your vacation home so I figured—"

"Meli, chill. I'm just teasing you."

"Oh." Then she giggled again. "It's hard to tell with you sometimes. But that's good! I'm not sure my family believes me anyway."

"You're telling your family about us? I'm not sure we're at that stage yet."

Melina paused, and Conner wished she could see her face. "Who knew you were such a tease?"

Conner lowered her voice. "Plenty of women could tell you that I'm not."

Did she imagine the catch in Melina's voice? "Yeah, well, I, um, I'll take your word for it. I should let you go. My mother's complaining that no one ever helps her cook, which is her way of telling me to get off the phone." Conner heard rapid Spanish in the background. "Mami! I'm talking to Conner in Ireland. Yes, that Conner. I *told* you—no, I'm not lying on Christmas!"

"Tell her that I asked you out and you rejected me."

"I didn't—Conner! That's not—I'm not—she'll throw her shoe at me if I say that. No, Mami. I know you never—I didn't do anything!"

"That's exactly right. You didn't do anything at all. That's why I'm all the way across the pond nursing my broken heart with a glass of whiskey."

Melina giggled. "Conner! Stop, please. You're so silly." Not a single person on Earth had ever called Conner Cody silly. "You behave, or I'll be the one throwing the shoe."

"As long as it's followed by the rest of your clothing."

Melina gasped, and the sound sent a bolt straight through Conner. "Okay, I'll stop. I'd like to leave your mother with a halfway decent impression of me."

"I still don't think she believes me."

"Hand her the phone."

"Absolutely not. You can't be trusted." Her tone was relaxed, playful, and definitely not flirtatious.

"Fine. When are you flying home?"

"The day after New Year's. Will you be home before you go back on tour?"

"Yes. I'll see you for sure."

"Fantastic. Bye, Conner. Merry Christmas."

"Same to you. Bye, Meli."

When they hung up, Conner glanced at the time and appreciated the serendipity. Another minute, and the alarm she had set would have gone off.

She FaceTimed her sister exactly at the agreed time so she could watch her nieces unwrap their presents. The girls had objected to Conner's absence at Christmas, only slightly mollified when she said she'd bring them souvenirs, something she still needed to buy. Conner had been coming to Ireland for so long she had no idea what a proper souvenir even was. Did they sell leprechauns at the corner shop?

"You really didn't need to spoil them so much." Sadie's complaints came halfhearted at best.

For Sarah, a faux leather jacket exactly like Conner's own beloved one. She had nearly fainted when she pulled it out. For both girls, two US Women's National Team soccer jerseys and a promise from Conner to take them to a game. And for Hannah, a four-foot-tall Barbie house. Her squeals deafened her family. Conner had also bought the family a Nintendo Switch and several games.

"Well, I had a lot of Christmases to make up for. Also, check your email."

She waited, catching herself biting her lip in anticipation. Harlow always chastened her for that. She had thought long and hard about what to buy for Sadie and Asher before Maggie suggested booking a weekend trip to Napa.

"Conner, this is too much."

"Have you ever been?"

"No, but—"

"The dates are flexible so you can wait until the weather is good and you have time off from work. Your mom said she would keep the girls."

Hannah, who Conner was realizing was always within earshot, perked up. "Why can't we stay at your house, Aunt Conner? Grandma doesn't have a pool." In the background, Sarah lifted her head with interest.

Sadie froze, and Conner didn't react much better. Hanging out with them was one thing, but babysitting? Overnight? They needed an adult for that. An adultier adult than Conner.

"We'll figure it out when the time comes," Sadie finally said. Paradoxically, hurt nudged Conner's heart.

They ended the call on that note, and Conner made her way to the grand piano in the drawing room. With its high ceilings, the manor had great acoustics. She didn't know how long she played, tweaking a song she'd written in Big Bear that worked through her feelings about Emi. Though the relationship had been ill-fated from the start, the manner of its demise didn't hurt any less.

Light applause caught her off-guard. Seth and Gran stood behind her with varying degrees of approval on their faces.

Seth nodded at her. "Not bad, kid. Interesting vamp."

"Just something I'm playing with."

Gran frowned. "Sit up straighter. Remember, one sings from one's diaphragm."

Conner exhaled. "I'm just messing around, Gran."

"Good practice habits breed great performances."

Seth sat next to Conner, nudging her to one side as he played a short glissando. "We're not all classically trained singers, Ma."

"But you were taught by me. Stand up, Conner, and sing."

The only thing Conner hated more than being ordered around was when she obeyed. She stood tall under her grandmother's watchful eye and her father's disinterested gaze and sang a Linda Ronstadt number without accompaniment.

"Excellent. I knew you could do better."

After a massive dinner where Conner overindulged in Christmas pudding, the family spent the rest of the day in a détente fueled by mulled wine and hot cider. Conner always enjoyed the contrast of her family's musical lilts with her flatter American tones and her grandmother's sharper timbre, her natural Irish softened by years of adopting posh English accents on stage. Although her cousins taunted her, and Seth and her uncle bickered, none of the repartee was cruel. The fact that her acidic aunt drunk herself into a snoring stupor in an armchair didn't hurt.

That night, as she headed upstairs, Conner passed their mammoth Christmas tree, postcard-perfect in front of a flickering fireplace, and paused. She couldn't say what prompted her, but she took a selfie in front of the scene and posted it to all her social media, something she rarely did. One of Harlow's interns usually handled her socials.

Later, Conner curled under a pile of thick quilts on a paneled, Tudor-style bed, her mind hazy and heavy with mead. She picked up her phone half a dozen times before finally cursing herself and pressing the call button. She didn't care at all that it went straight to voicemail.

"Hey, Camila, it's—it's Conner. Your daughter. Um, I just called to say Merry Christmas, so…yeah. Uh, bye."

Chapter Fifteen

"You look hot."

"That is *so* weird." Maggie applied eyeliner, staring at the mirror next to Conner. "You're one step away from talking in third person."

"Bellamy agrees." The words barely escaped before Bellamy dissolved into giggles, her long blond locks dancing wildly.

"When Conner looks hot, Conner won't wait for someone else to tell her. Conner believes in the value of self-confidence." She caught Emi's eye in the mirror and winked.

"Emi thinks Conner is absolutely correct: self-confidence is important, and she does look hot."

Maggie clearly tried hard to scowl through the grin spreading across her face. "You're all absolutely ridiculous. But yes, Conner, since your ego obviously doesn't get stroked enough, you look hot."

Conner admired herself once more. Her black short-sleeved crop top ended just below her breasts, revealing the long stretch of her bare abdomen before her wide-legged jeans began under her belly button. And as always, her trusty Docs on her feet.

"We're all hot. Look at these babes!"

She slung her arms over her bandmates and gathered them together. A year ago, they'd been elbow-deep in recording their first full-length album, only dreaming of the success to come. Conner had been fresh off yet another breakup with Vittoria and mere days away from tumbling into a mistake with Emi.

And now they had a sold-out tour, a Grammy nomination, and that mistake was a thing of the past. Hopefully. As was Vittoria. Definitely.

Soon enough Kit summoned them backstage to perform at a star-studded New Year's Eve party in Miami. It wasn't New Year's Rockin' Eve in New York City, but that was a relic anyway. Everyone who was anyone was in south Florida tonight.

"I read once that Miami has the hottest lesbians in the country." Conner nodded at familiar faces as she observed the mania around them while they waited to be announced.

"And what is your professional opinion?"

She grinned. "Miami doesn't disappoint, but I've never had trouble finding hot lesbians anywhere I go."

Kit's voice drowned out the mixture of incredulous snorts and laughter. "Ladies! You're up! Let's go. Bellamy, don't forget you're starting it off. Maggie, look up when the camera zooms in. Emi, you look great. Conner... please remember this is live."

She shot them a dirty look. As if she hadn't been on live television more than the rest of the group combined and then some. Kit was a great manager behind the scenes, but she wished they'd leave the performances to her.

She took the stage in a contrary mood, spurred by Kit's well-meaning instructions. *She* was the expert. *She* was the star. This was *her* band. When she faced the crowd, they screamed *her* name.

But she was also a professional, so she jumped around and raised her arms only far enough to make it clear she wasn't wearing a bra without putting the censors in overdrive. She also stuck to the lyrical changes that the network approved, cutting out a few swear words and two crude terms for body parts. Sadie had promised the girls could stay up to watch the performance, so it was just as well.

After riling everyone up with "Her Halo Has Horns," newly dubbed their latest single and rocketing up the charts, Conner was joined by two other sapphic singers, and the trio vamped and flirted to a medley of their songs, soon to be immortalized on social media in ten-second clips.

Backstage, she chatted up the pair for a while, contemplating if she wanted to take one or both back to her hotel for the night when a pair of arms encircled her waist.

"Who the—oh, shit."

A pair of plump, ruby-red lips pouted. "That's not a nice way to greet your opening act." Lola coolly turned her gaze to Conner's potential hookups. "You can go now."

The pair looked between Conner and Lola and nodded, retreating before she could get rid of the interloper.

"You better have a good reason for this."

"If you'd answered my texts, you'd know."

"The fact that I didn't should tell you something."

Lola folded her arms. "Why didn't you? We had a good time together, Conner."

Conner grabbed her wrist and yanked her to one side next to a stack of unused amps. Other artists, staff, and roadies looked at them curiously, but everyone was too busy to pay much attention. "I told you it was a one-time thing. If you can't handle that, it's on you."

"Yet here we are, New Year's Eve and neither of us with someone to kiss. Seems as good a time as any to bend the rules."

"I was working on that when you showed up." Conner narrowed her eyes. "What are you doing here, anyway? You're not in the lineup."

"I know other people besides you," she replied with a coy glance, toying with her long hair.

"Then kiss one of them."

Lola huffed but remained annoyingly persistent. Half the reason Conner was in this conversation to begin with. "You know, you don't have to be a bitch. You could try other personas."

"This one works well enough for me, thanks. But please, keep insulting me. That'll get my attention."

"I didn't think you took 'bitch' as an insult. Some women wear it as a badge of honor."

"Then you don't know me at all. I've never been 'some women.'"

Her derisive snort made Conner want to grind her teeth.

"Please don't start telling me how you're not like other women. That is so overdone."

Conner's sigh weighed ten pounds. "What do you want, Lola?"

"You. You're the hottest person on the planet, and you know it. Sex on a stick. We still have months on tour together, so we might as well get some fun out of it." Lola lowered her voice. "You had fun with me, right, Conner?"

"I have fun with a lot of people. You and I aren't the beginning of something special, so just let it go."

Conner held her gaze, lifting her chin when Lola squared her shoulders. She probably should have felt bad about rejecting her, but she didn't. She'd been completely clear about no encore performance. If Lola couldn't accept that fact, it was her problem.

"I'll see you on tour." A threat flavored Lola's words.

Conner leaned forward, holding Lola's chin in her hand. The proximity was a shallow reenactment of their hookup. "Don't fuck with me, babe. Got it?"

She tried to enjoy the rest of the night. The entire lineup returned to stage for the countdown, and as cheers erupted at midnight, the band exchanged chaste kisses. Conner's gaze locked with Emi for several seconds when they parted, a moment destined to be dissected by their fans for the next three months. They had been a mistake, but maybe—

Arms landed on Conner's shoulders as her fellow musicians began to sing "Auld Lang Syne," and her line of thought crashed to a halt. She arched her eyebrows and winked as a cameraman focused on her, ever on brand.

"Hey, girl," Conner said to Bellamy later. Though the crowd had departed, the party continued behind the scenes. She nursed a vodka tonic as she slipped through the mass of bodies, trying to decide if it was worthwhile to stay. She hadn't spent a New Year's Eve alone in a decade, but tonight she felt unmoored, restless, discontent.

"Having fun?"

She shrugged. "Sure. You?"

"I was having a great conversation with this drummer, but they just asked me back to their room, so…"

Conner nodded in understanding. "Want to go back to the hotel with me? Not like that, obviously."

Bellamy laughed. Conner's bond with Bellamy lacked the intensity of her relationships with Maggie and Emi, but that very absence made Bellamy easy to be around.

"Good timing. Your stalker is around here, you know."

Conner cringed. "Which one?"

Bellamy laughed again. "That's a question no one should ever have to ask. Tonight, it's Lola."

"Ugh. I know. She talked to me after our set."

"What are you going to do about her?"

"Deal with her until the tour is over, I guess." Her bandmates would kill her if they knew Conner had slept with her. She tended to regret relationships, not hookups, but Lola was proving the exception.

In the hotel elevator, Bellamy hooked their arms together, and Conner leaned her head against her shoulder, inexplicably weary. New Year's Eve was supposed to be fun. Performing was supposed to fill her with adrenaline. She was Conner fucking Cody, and she was rich and famous and young and pretty. She had everything.

"What's wrong, honey?"

"I don't know, Bells. Do you ever feel like something is missing?"

"No, but I'm not looking for the same thing you are."

Conner pursed her lips. "I'm not talking about sex."

"Neither am I," Bellamy replied gently.

The doors chimed, and she hurried out, muttering something that might or might not have passed for good-bye, not really caring either way. She hated introspection. Stress was just dragging her down, that was all, and once she got back on the road, she'd be too busy to dip into maudlin territory.

She had just started running water and undressing for a shower when someone knocked on her door. Conner frowned into the mirror and contemplated ignoring it before shutting off the water and grabbing her robe. It wouldn't take long to get rid of Bellamy.

"Listen. I'm not really in the mood for—"

She choked, aware of nothing but her own rapid breathing and the striking ghost from her past in the doorway.

Vittoria smiled. "Hello, gorgeous. Have you missed me?"

Chapter Sixteen

Vittoria walked in like she owned the luxurious hotel suite and sat on the small sofa in the sitting area, crossing her long legs and gazing at Conner expectantly. Confidence, thy name was Vittoria.

Conner finally gulped in a deep breath, not sure if oxygen had made its way to her lungs in the last five minutes. "Vittoria."

"Ah, she speaks. I thought perhaps you'd sung yourself...oh, what is the word? Voiceless?"

"Mute," Conner said before she could stop herself.

"Yes, thank you, *mia luna*."

My moon. Conner hadn't heard those words slip like a caress from Vittoria's pillowy lips in over a year.

She shook her head. "I really need to get better security. How did you find my room?"

"I know you. I know which hotels you prefer. The front desk staff would never stop a famous model from surprising her girlfriend."

"You're not my girlfriend."

"Not currently, but they don't know that."

"Not curr—Jesus, Vittoria, are we doing this again? I'm tired."

She pulled a bottle of water out of the minifridge, eyeing the tiny shots of liquor. She needed to be either really sober or really hammered for this conversation.

"Of course we are. We're always going to do this. I've decided we belong together."

"Oh, you decided? Well, gee, Vi. Thanks for clueing me in." When Vittoria's forehead betrayed a tiny crease, Conner sighed. "Letting me know."

"You're quite welcome."

She leveled a look at her over the top of her water. "I know you understand sarcasm."

"So much that I've mastered it in three languages."

Conner shook her head. She'd thought she was finally free of Vittoria. She was as potent as a drug, and quitting her had been like quitting cocaine, complete with withdrawal and cravings.

"Stop glaring at me all the way over there and sit."

"I'm fine here."

"Then I shall come to you."

Before Vittoria could rise, Conner marched to an armchair and plopped down, kicking her feet onto the table. Vittoria's clear amusement at her petulance just aggravated her further.

"If you ruin your posture by sitting like that, you'll never model again."

Conner slouched even lower in response, and Vittoria laughed. The sound, like ringing bells, brought back countless memories. When they weren't in bed together, they'd spent half their time laughing.

And spent the other half arguing.

"Always such a child." Vittoria tsked with a fond smile.

"What *do* you want, Vittoria?"

"You, obviously."

"A lot of people want me."

She laughed again. "Your ego! You have not changed a bit. I've missed you, Con." She leaned toward Conner, her short skirt inching up her thigh. "Yet, you are alone tonight. Where are all these people who want you?"

"Everywhere I go. I just wanted to be by myself."

Vittoria tilted her head and watched her, letting out the slightest sigh. Conner didn't back down from her gaze, and as they sat in silence, her thoughts inevitably strayed to their previous relationship.

They'd met backstage at the Paris Fashion Week three years prior, both walking for Givenchy. Conner caught her eye as they passed each other backstage, and her smirk earned a flash of a smile from the notoriously stone-faced supermodel. Vittoria sought her out later, and what began as a quick romp in a dressing room turned into a weeklong stay on the Adriatic coast. Conner had been enthralled, Vittoria infatuated, and they followed their passions, which led them up and down a rocky path, strewn with bliss and blowups.

"Well?"

Conner narrowed her eyes. "Well, what?"

"Take me back, *mia luna*. I need you. No one makes me smile like you do."

"I'm pretty sure the last time we saw each other, you told me that I always ruin everything."

Vittoria shook her head, sending ripples through her mahogany hair. Conner would never deny that Vittoria was the single most attractive person she had ever met. "I was angry. You know I don't mean those things, just as I know you don't mean what you say when we argue."

"Actually, I did mean what I said." She sat back and folded her arms. "You're never satisfied, not with me or anyone else."

"I've changed. I thought about what I want, and it's you. That's all. Only you."

Conner's scoff emerged less forcefully than desired. "You can't change who you are."

"Con-*ner*." Vittoria's nostrils flared, and she slid closer on the sofa. Conner pulled her legs away. "Stop fighting this. Think about how good we are together. We are queens, are we not? What is that term your magazines love so much?"

"Queen of the nepo babies," Conner replied, biting the inside of her cheek to hide a traitorous grin.

For all her faults, Vittoria understood Conner in ways no one else did. The eldest daughter of rich, disinterested parents—a Monégasque Formula One driver and an Italian model turned Fendi designer—Vittoria knew exactly what it was like to be dogged by accusations of nepotism and how to use that to her advantage.

"Yes, yes. We are both those queens, and queens must never mingle with the plebians. That was your mistake after me, you know."

Conner jerked her head up. "Excuse me?"

"I know all about your romance with your guitar player. I'm not upset, of course. I would hardly expect either of us to remain celibate. Emi is lovely, but she's not on our level."

"You're such a fucking snob! You don't know her at all."

Vittoria's almond-shaped eyes widened. "So protective. Perhaps you two are not finished after all? I am not opposite to that."

"Opposed." Correcting Vittoria came annoyingly natural to her. She glared at her former paramour. "And you're not, but I am. You know that. I'm not going to change."

Vittoria's lovely mouth tightened. A casual observer would have missed the reaction. "I am aware of your preferences, though still they confuse me."

"It's easy. A one-off threesome is one thing. Sharing a girlfriend is another." Conner pointed at her. "You prefer consensual non-monogamy." Then she pointed at herself. "I don't, and I'm not going to change."

Vittoria rose so suddenly that Conner lurched back in her seat. "I'm not asking you to change. I'm telling you that I have."

"I don't want—"

"But I do." Then Vittoria's lips were on hers, taking the kiss with such certainty that Conner couldn't do anything but grip the velvet under her hands. When she pulled away, she sagged into her chair, her head spinning. She didn't need alcohol after all.

"I won't see anyone else. Only you. Isn't that what you wanted all along?"

What did she want? Vittoria had always been too intoxicating, with her beauty and unblinking, singular focus on the object of her desire. She spoke of her wishes as if they were foregone conclusions and the steps to get there, merely foreplay. The modern-day incarnation of a Salem witch, weaving spells not with eyes of newt and rhyming chants but with a silver tongue and generous praise.

Vittoria's favorite Dior perfume weaved tendrils throughout her mind. "Think of it," she whispered into Conner's ear, all but straddling her lap. "We'll rule this little kingdom of Hollywood together. Every magazine cover, every walkway, every camera will be ours with the snap of our fingers. Helen and Paris will have nothing on us."

"They launched a war," Conner managed to say. She could barely think with Vittoria this close.

"Antony and Cleopatra, then."

"Killed themselves."

"Louis the Fifteenth and Madame de Pompadour."

"She died of tuberculosis."

Vittoria murmured an Italian curse, but her gaze never left Conner's. "You read too much. Quit putting me off and accept that we are inevitable."

Perhaps it was Vittoria after all. Conner couldn't imagine her body responding like this to just anyone. This was what she did best, anyway: follow her lust. Her mind and her heart would catch up.

Vittoria's breath tickled her neck. "I know you remember what it was like between us. You wrote that song about it."

"Wha—what song?"

"The one that says 'I die a little every time she comes undone on my tongue.'"

A snort of laughter escaped her, and Vittoria leaned back, the corners of her mouth tugging in a frown.

"'Wicked Girl' isn't about you."

"Of course it is. Who else could it be about?"

Perversely, Conner wanted to lie and taunt her a bit, but she resisted. "No one. Or maybe everyone. It's just a song."

"Then which one is about me? Or are there more than one?"

"Now who has the ego?" Conner refused to feed it and kept her mouth shut.

Vittoria did no such thing.

"So this is how we're going to play?"

She pressed kisses down Conner's neck to her chest until she reached the top of her robe, pausing before grinning so sinful, even Satan would have gulped. But she stopped there, pulling back and smirking when Conner's hips twitched toward her. Then, in a completely uncharacteristic move, she knelt, gazing up at her in supplication.

"Must I beg? You always tried to top me, Con. Here I am, on my knees for you—and I kneel for no one."

Conner's lips parted as she watched Vittoria wait for her. This was a first, and more beguiling than she wanted to admit. She almost bought it, too, except that Vittoria was a model, not an actress, and her beautiful face remained confident, almost cocksure with her eyes slightly narrowed and her mouth pulled into a half-smile. So damn sure that Conner was putty in her hands regardless of seating positions.

The worst part was that it was true.

"Your song is 'Her Halo Has Horns,' okay?" Conner wondered if the air in her room had been laced with a hallucinogenic, responsible for her dizziness.

Vittoria laughed softly. "I should take that as a compliment, yes?"

"Take it however you want."

"What about 'Sixteen'?"

"'Sixteen'?" She blinked as Vittoria's abrupt change in tone dissipated the fog in her mind. "That's not about you."

"No. It's not. Why did you never tell me of Britt Boyd?"

"I don't know." Conner shifted in her seat. "It's none of your business."

Vittoria leaned back, umbrage taking over her face. "None of my business? You gave the entire world a song and Larissa Lamont an interview, but it's none of *my* business?"

"Right, Vittoria. It's none of your business. I didn't tell you because I didn't want to talk to you about it. If I decided after we broke up that I wanted to announce it to the world, that's my call."

She crossed her arms. Vittoria frowned at her for a long moment before her expression relaxed. She pressed against Conner's legs again, reaching up to intertwine their hands.

"What are you doing? Fifteen minutes together and we're already arguing."

"I know. Isn't it wonderful?"

"No, it's not."

"Yes, it is. We argue, and then, *mia luna*, then we make up."

She pulled Conner's hands, one to each side, and pinned them to the armchair. Conner didn't resist, letting her head loll to one side as Vittoria's mouth became reacquainted with her neck, her jaw, her ear. Conner sighed, giving in to the arousal flooding her. She'd never been able to deny her. Surely that meant something. It felt so good to let someone else take control, even if the thought made her tremble.

"See? Your body remembers me. Say yes, Conner. Give me six months to prove that it's only you for me."

"Six months?"

Vittoria repeated the phrase in Italian.

"Six months." Conner rolled the words in her mouth. "I'll be on tour for the next six months."

"It's perfect, no? Then you will see that I do not want anyone else, even when you aren't around. You will tour, and I have London, New York, Milan, Paris, all of that. You can take me to your awards shows, I will walk the runways for you, and everyone will be jealous of us."

"You just want to go to the Oscars, is that it?"

Vittoria tossed her head. "I can go to the Oscars if I want. But I look better with you."

"You should know I already have a date for the Grammys."

"Who?"

"A friend."

"Who is your friend?"

"No one you know."

"Tell this friend that you have a girlfriend."

"I don't have a girlfriend."

"You will by the time you leave this room." Her mouth resumed its exploration. "Does your friend do this?"

I wish. She brushed the unbidden thought away. She had promised herself that she would stop thinking of Meli that way. Getting back together with Vittoria would definitely end the futile fantasizing about her straight friend.

"I'm not taking you to the Grammys." She barely succeeded at keeping a gasp out of her voice as Vittoria found a particularly sensitive spot. Her hands began creeping up Conner's thighs.

"I don't care. Give me my six months, and you won't ever take anyone else out again."

With difficulty, Conner pushed Vittoria away until she got some breathing room. She was breathless, woozy, aroused, confused. Seduced.

"Six months?"

"Six months."

"And you're sure monogamy is what you want?"

"I'm sure that you are what I want. If monogamy is the price to pay, so be it."

Not exactly the most romantic declaration of feelings, but nothing else in Conner's life had ever lived up to fairy-tale expectations. The supermodel and the superstar, at least, had something of storybook fate about it.

She dipped her chin in the slightest of nods, and they tumbled to the floor, where Conner soon stopped thinking at all.

Chapter Seventeen

Screams shattered Conner's eardrums as she stepped out of the limousine. She stretched her lips across her teeth in a practiced smile, breaking into a real one when she heard Melina's exclamations behind her.

"Oh my God. This is the craziest thing I've ever seen!"

"You've had roles in some big films. Didn't you go to their premieres?"

She slipped her hand through Conner's arm. Her pink Michael Kors dress accentuated both her caramel skin and certain other assets that Conner absolutely did not notice. She had a girlfriend, albeit one she'd kept hidden. A beautiful, fun, secret girlfriend.

"Sure, but when you have a bit part, you don't get invited to walk the red carpet, and even if I did, I wouldn't have one of the world's most famous faces at my side."

"Someday you'll walk a red carpet all on your own, and every camera will be dialed in on you no matter who your date is." Something ugly reared its head in Conner's stomach at the thought of Melina's faceless date, and she squashed it with expediency.

"Maybe, maybe not. I don't care. I just want to act."

Their arrival at the press scrum prevented Conner from following up that answer. Awards shows were odd events. While she appreciated the urge for recognition, she loathed the fanfare. It was all so unnecessary. Pasting a fake smile on her face, inching through long lines as people shouted her name over and over, answering inane questions about what she was wearing and who she was with, pretending to care about ninety percent of the people who ran up to hug her like long-lost friends...and that was before she sat through several hours of ceremony.

That said, she certainly didn't mind when she won.

"So you really don't care if you ever make it big?" she asked once they were seated.

"I'm making a living doing what I love. Why do I need to be famous on top of that? I get all the satisfaction I need when I win a role and do a good job." She finally dragged her attention away from the star-studded crowd to look Conner in the eyes. "Would you still act if you weren't a celebrity?"

"I think so."

Maggie snorted, and Conner elbowed her. "Rude."

"You forget I know you better than most. You pretend to hate all of this, but you thrive on fans screaming your name."

"I can get that from—" Maggie's hand cut her off at the source, and Conner resorted to shooting daggers with her eyes until she was released. How could she be so strong? "I cannot believe you just did that, you vile woman. Why are we friends?"

"Because I'm the only person on this planet who doesn't kiss your famous little ass." She dipped her head at Melina. "No offense."

She giggled. "You two are so cute. Just like sisters."

"My sister is nicer than her," they replied in sync before catching themselves and cracking up.

Conner caught Maggie's hand and squeezed it. "You love me in all my conceited glory."

"And you love me at my bluntest." Maggie returned the squeeze with a wink. Down the row, Emi looked as if she would retch, while Bellamy faked choking. Sisters, indeed.

Once they calmed down, Conner returned her attention to Melina. "I enjoy the craft of acting. I like to dig into a character, understand her, mold her. I want to feel as if I've changed someone or at least made them think, and when I'm gone, I want to leave something behind, something beautiful."

"You do that every day."

Her sardonic chuckle melted into a cough as she absorbed Melina's sincerity. She made her nervous sometimes, for reasons she couldn't define. As the lights dimmed, the beginning of the ceremony saved her from having to reply, though it wasn't dark enough for her to avoid a long, searching look from Maggie.

The band had been nominated for Best New Artist, which to her irritation wasn't the first category. She adopted a nonchalant smile when it finally came up, entirely at odds with the roller coaster in her stomach. Melina squeezed her arm when their name was announced, but all Conner could do was raise her eyebrows in acknowledgment. She'd poured years of her life into this band, and more than a small part of herself. If the band wasn't successful, what did that say about her?

"And the winner is...Hestia Rising!"

The air in Conner's lungs whooshed out. She blinked once, twice, and then her senses roared back. At some point she had risen to her feet. Kit hugged her from behind, whispering how proud they were. She turned to Melina, and the glow from her face made everything else dim.

"I knew you would win! I knew it!"

She cupped Conner's face in her hands, and Conner smiled so softly, she barely recognized herself each time she saw the image plastered over social media and tabloid covers for weeks to come.

Onstage, the rest of the band took turns thanking various loved ones, leaving Conner for last. She'd won a few awards over her career, some bigger than others, and her habit of never preparing a speech had morphed into a superstition, though she'd never admit it.

She hefted the statue in her hands when she approached the microphone. "A few years ago, my friend Maggie and I decided it would be fun to find a few more people to play with and see where it went. That journey has been fun, hard, and the best thing I've ever done, and we're just getting started. I'd like to thank our manager, Kit, the biggest and best pain in my butt, and..." She made sure she included the producers and the record label, threw Harlow a shout-out, and thanked her grandmother for teaching her to sing properly. Unlike the rest of the band, she didn't mention her parents, who had contributed nothing more to her upbringing than DNA, a bank account, and a therapist's wet dream.

"I know I need to wrap it up. I want to give a shout-out to my favorite family out in Santa Clarita, and"—she noticed Melina in the audience, clasping her hands under her chin with such affection that her heart played a rhythm Maggie could never duplicate—"to a very special friend, who I hope knows how important she is to me. And to my girls!" They crowded together, arms thrown around shoulders, squeezing tightly. She lofted the statue again. "Only the first of many!"

Backstage was a whirlwind of camera flashes and tight hugs, shouts of congratulations and grins that, for once, she didn't fake. Emi kissed her right on the lips, and Conner never knew if that was intentional or not. She didn't care. She could ride this wave of euphoria all the way to the end of their tour and into their second album, whenever she wrote it. This was worth every single bit of missed sleep, every harsh word, every painful memory her songs dredged up, every drop of sweat when they performed. Even the heartache.

Stumbling home completely hammered long past midnight, holding hands with an equally drunk Melina, Conner tripped right out of her shoes and into her refrigerator, where she managed to snag two bottles of water through her peals of laughter. Afterparties were a lot more tolerable when she'd won an award, as well as when she drank her weight in vodka.

While Melina searched for the bathroom, Conner hoisted herself onto the kitchen island, stretching out on her back on the cool granite. She fumbled for her phone, blinking several times to focus as she scrolled past dozens of texts.

> **Vittoria:** Brava, mia luna. Thank you for including your very special friend in your speech. I shall have to find a way to show you how important you are to me, too.

She ended with a winking emoji.

Conner exhaled sharply as she dropped her phone on her chest.

Oh, fuck.

Screams shattered Conner's eardrums as she stepped out of the limousine. She stretched her lips across her teeth in a practiced smile, but inwardly she took a metaphorical deep breath. She maintained a policy of never commenting on her relationships—a rule Vittoria promised not to break, again—but it wouldn't take Isaac Newton to figure out they were back together when they walked the red carpet at the Oscars.

Vittoria emerged in a slinky crimson number cut to show off her impressively long legs, and Conner's mouth ran as dry as the Mojave. She still carried trepidations about the viability of their relationship, but physically, the chemistry was as alive as ever. The bits and pieces of time they snatched together had her walking sideways.

The crowd of onlookers ratcheted to an even higher decibel as the pair of them joined the queue of celebrities waiting their turn. A thousand flashes captured the moment Vittoria slipped her hand into Conner's.

"I'm going to murder you after this," Maggie muttered through her smile, following them with Jamal. Emi, Bellamy, and their dates were in the next limo.

Perhaps keeping her reunion with Vittoria secret until that night hadn't been Conner's brightest plan. It wasn't her fault they all hated her and had threatened to have Conner committed if she ever talked to her again.

Well, maybe it was *slightly* her fault.

Conner wasn't up for any acting awards this year, but Hestia Rising was booked to play, a nod to their current buzz. Her mother wasn't nominated either, which Conner hoped meant she wasn't attending. Abuelita didn't feel up to a public attendance, which worried Conner, but she promised to watch from home, as did Sadie.

"Conner Cody and Vittoria Lorenzi!" The Entertainment channel's red-carpet reporter vibrated with glee. "When did this happen?"

"I climbed out of the limo and there she was. Wild coincidence."

The reporter cackled and turned to Vittoria, who merely offered her a frosty smile. A few pointless questions later—for the record, Conner was wearing Victoria Beckham, Vittoria in Armani—they moved on to the cameras, who had them pose together, apart, and the band alone. Conner's eyeballs already stung from the flashes.

Hestia Rising performed "Wicked Girl," and Conner ratcheted up her flirtatious interactions with Emi during the performance. Their fans went rabid over it, and Vittoria, the exact opposite of a jealous lover, would eat it up.

She didn't have a chance to check her phone until they were at the afterparty at the Beverly Hilton. Waiting for Vittoria to bring her a drink, she read through a multitude of texts. Harlow advised her that Camila had attended after all, which had Conner on edge until she decided that her mother wasn't at this particular party. She also had a few choice words about Vittoria, which Conner ignored. Her publicist wanted to capitalize on the relationship, and Conner considered firing her. Her sister and both grandmothers praised their performance and questioned Vittoria's presence with varying degrees of politeness.

Conner wondered what was taking so long. She made her way through the crowd, smiling and chatting with people she never cared to see again, until she reached the bar. No Italian supermodels in sight, although an Australian actress gave her the once-over. Annoyed but refusing to be suspicious, Conner again waded through a sea of people until she emerged in a quiet hallway and dialed.

"Conner! Hi! Are you having fun?"

She smiled at the excitement in Melina's voice, even though she watched from her living room in pajamas, which sounded so nice.

"I guess. These days tend to be very long."

"I bet. I'm sure your feet are killing you. I saw you on the red carpet, by the way. You look so pretty, just stunning."

Conner's breath hitched. "Thanks, girl."

"And on stage, too. I mean, the band. You all look great. And, um, so does Vittoria." Her voice ended on a high note.

"Yeah, she—they—everyone is gorgeous."

The pause was so long that Conner pulled the phone from her ear, wondering if the connection had been broken. "I'm really happy for you, Conner. How long have you been back together?"

"We've been kinda figuring things out for a couple of months or so. With the tour, we've haven't spent much time together."

"Right. That must be hard...Is that why you kept it quiet? Or did everyone else know about it?"

Oh, no. The band was upset, but Melina was actually hurt. Conner needed to fix this faster than a magic spell.

"No, no, no. We didn't tell anyone at first, because...what if it didn't work out? It wasn't just you. Ask Maggie. She's furious with me."

Melina's laugh rang hollow. "I've realized that's how you two work. Anyway, if Vittoria makes you happy, then it's great."

"Thanks, Meli."

They chatted for a few more minutes, and then Conner returned to the party, trying to figure out why the conversation bothered her. Vittoria found her quickly and interrupted her ruminations.

"I've been looking for you. Where have you been?" Without waiting for an answer, she pushed a glass of mezcal into Conner's hand and nodded her head across the room, pulling Conner close. "I made a new friend, and she wants to play."

The liquor crashed hard into her stomach as Conner followed her gesture. A familiar actress in her mid-forties caught her eye and raised an eyebrow. Gorgeous, officially straight but clearly at least curious, unattached as far as anyone knew, and not the oldest woman Conner would have slept with (that title belonged to a friend of her mother). A year ago, she would have been all over her without a second thought.

"Do not give me that look." Vittoria wrapped her arms around Conner and kissed a special part of her neck. "I'm asking you, and if you say no, you and I will go home alone. She's not for me. She's for us."

It was an important distinction, one that didn't exist the last time they dated. All she had to do was say no. "Would it make you happy?"

"*Molto felice.*" Very happy.

It wasn't even some great hardship for Conner. Sapphics all around the world salivated over the mere idea that this particular actress might be queer. Really, she owed it to the sapphic community. It wasn't in any way a comment on Vittoria's satisfaction with their relationship. She bit back a moan as Vittoria's mouth worked its magic on her collarbone.

Conner smiled. "Lead the way, babe."

Chapter Eighteen

Stage. Party. Airport. Runway. Hotel. Airport. Bus. Rinse and repeat.

When Conner looked back on the latter half of the *Broken Promises* tour, the memories blurred together in one rushed clip, as if they had made a movie but she saw only the trailer. Her career necessitated distance from anyone she dated, but she had to give Vittoria a true chance. There was a reason their off-on relationship never stayed off, right?

She didn't bother complaining to the band. Maggie all but snarled at the mention of her name, Bellamy made a face suggesting a bad odor, and Emi…

Her apologetic-puppy-dog persona had disappeared, as had their tenuously reestablished friendship. Only a shell of the Emi she knew remained, a polite and professional, yet distant, Emi. A coworker, nothing more nor less. Not the Emi she wanted in her life. Clearly the news of the relationship hurt her, but Conner didn't have the patience to talk to her about it. Her romances were none of Emi's business.

And then there was Lola. Fucking Lola.

After the tour resumed, Lola cornered Conner in a bathroom during sound check, sidling up behind her while she washed her hands.

"Did you miss me?" Her purr slithered around Conner's neck, choking her.

"No."

Conner turned off the water and shouldered her aside with no consideration for her comfort, reaching for the air dryer. She should have remembered that Lola liked it rough.

"We have months of long rides and lonely nights ahead of us. Let me make it a little easier for both of us. I've been craving that sweet pussy of yours."

Conner bit the inside of her cheek so hard that copper rested on her tongue. Her pivot was a study in control, as was her low voice.

"I'm giving you one more warning, Lola. This is sexual harassment, and if you want to continue—"

Conner's mouth ran dry. She'd heard the words about to spew from her mouth before.

"If you want to continue in this industry, you'll keep those talented lips of yours shut, babe. Don't make me be the bad guy. You were all too willing to spread your legs for me. Why stop now?"

Conner dug her nails into her palms. She was *not* Britt Boyd. She and Lola were both consenting adults. She'd done nothing wrong except fuck around in a moment of weakness, and now she was learning the consequences.

She swallowed hard. "If you want to continue on this tour, you need to leave me alone. I am the headliner. You are my opening act. We had a one-night stand. Nothing more, nothing less."

Lola's eyes narrowed to dark slits. "I have a contract."

"Yes, you do. I suggest you reread it. Carefully."

Lola eased up after that, though she continued to flirt and make suggestive comments, which Conner simply ignored. After the Oscars, Lola did a complete one-eighty and was openly hostile. Conner was tempted to lock Lola and Emi in a room and see if they could screw the anger out of each other.

If things with Vittoria didn't work out, she was seriously considering celibacy.

But things with Vittoria were…okay. Good, perhaps. They might even progress to great if Conner could stop holding her breath and waiting for the real Vittoria to emerge from behind this impersonator who was not quite as selfish, not quite as demanding, not quite as consuming as before.

No one could accuse Conner of not giving it her all. She met her girlfriend every time she could cram it into her limited timeframe, taking advantage of time zones to squeeze a few extra hours into the clock. Kit and the band reeked of disapproval, but she paid them little attention. Conner's candle had been dual-tipped her entire life, and she was at her best when she burned it at both ends. Only when she grew bored did trouble brew.

Every time she appeared in the crowd at a fashion show, her distracted countenance popped up on gossip sites. She posed for photographs with people she didn't care about and allowed brief interviews every time her publicist twisted her arm, all in the name of a supportive girlfriend. After the shows, Vittoria detailed her appreciation in a myriad of inventive ways in their hotel room, and then Conner was gone again.

The tour ended with a bang to a sold-out crowd at the Kia Forum. Conner poured her heart out, frequently abandoning her guitar to cover every square inch of the stage, tossing her guitar picks to some lucky fan after every song, and finally peeling off her soaked shirt as a gift for the most inventive sign she read, finishing the show in a black Tom Ford bra. She even did something she swore never to do: reuniting with her old girl group to sing one of their hits. They'd assembled a whole slew of guest stars but kept that particular performance a closely guarded secret.

During "Dark Streets" the band fell silent, letting the crowd sing the chorus to them. Despite the pain and fear behind the song, Conner stood in awe, feeling like a succubus as she fed off their energy. Short of sex, she was sure there wasn't a better feeling in the world.

They finished with "Road Trip" and took a bow, sweaty arms around each other, panting and beaming in equal measure. Conner soaked in the cheers like sun after an Alaskan winter, the adulation making her high.

"Los Angeles, you are fucking glorious! For the last time on the *Broken Promises* tour, we are…" She paused to grin at her bandmates and pull them a little closer.

"Hestia Rising!"

Backstage, they met their friends and loved ones—Jamal, Maggie's mother, Emi's family, Kit's friends, even Bellamy's father all the way from Savannah. Conner had her own group, warming her in a way she couldn't label: Harlow, Lindsey, Melina, Eriq, Sadie, and Sarah, who had joined forces with Conner to wear down her mother until she reluctantly caved. Abuelita had declined the invitation, citing her age.

And Vittoria. Conner was pleased, she truly was, but the idea of Vittoria mixing with her friends and family in a box for several hours without Conner to chaperone had anxiety hovering at the back of her mind all night.

"Aunt Conner!"

Sarah met her with an exuberant hug, though she quickly fell back, her cheeks turning rosy. "That was awesome! Thank you so much for letting me come!"

"You can always come to my shows…as long as your mom agrees." Conner winked at Sadie, who smiled ruefully.

"It really was a great show, Conner."

"Aunt Conner, um, do you think maybe we could take a selfie?" Sarah twisted her feet. "Kaylen McGee told the whole school that I was lying about you being my aunt because Wikipedia says you don't have any siblings."

Now Conner had beef with a twelve-year-old.

They took several pictures and a video just in case any middle-schooler tried to claim the pictures were fake. Then Sarah glanced up at her several times, quickly redirecting her gaze every time Conner caught her.

"Sarah? What's up, babe?"

"Um, I was wondering if, um, you would want to, um, come to my birthday party, maybe?" She twisted one foot, mumbling toward the ground. "Only if you aren't busy. It's not a big deal. You probably have better things to do. I don't think it's going to be very fun, anyway."

"Hey, kid?" She nudged Sarah's chin with a finger, grinning when her niece finally looked up. "Of course I'll come. It's cool."

Sarah's brown eyes widened to an almost impossible size before she caught herself. "Really?! I mean, um, yeah, it's cool."

"Does that invitation extend to me?"

Slender arms encircled Conner's waist as soft lips descended on her neck. She squirmed away. "Did you like the show?"

"Of course I did. You're so sexy onstage." Vittoria pulled her closer, nuzzling her neck again, though Conner couldn't let herself lean into the embrace, feeling all kinds of eyes on her. "And I had such *fun* with your friends."

The hair on the back of her neck rose. She recognized that tone. She tried to pull away, but Vittoria resisted, and Conner succeeded only in awkwardly shuffling to one side.

"Wha—Vi, stop! My niece and sister are right there."

"When did you become such a prune, *mia luna*?"

"Prude. It's prude. And I'm not. I just don't want to give a free show to a preteen."

Vittoria finally released her, blinking incredulously. "My Conner never cared of such things."

Maybe I'm no longer your Conner. The words sprang to Conner's lips, and she recoiled, shaking her head as if the thought would fall out of her ear. She and Vittoria had to work out. They were perfect for each other, the exact type of person Conner was supposed to end up with—sexy, sophisticated, well-traveled. If she couldn't make it work with Vittoria, who kept coming back to her, what did that say about her? Maybe she was simply destined to be alone. After all, she was so good at it.

Conner brooded through the afterparty, watching her friends dance while she sipped a hot toddy after her regular post-performance tea. At one point she idly counted how many people in attendance she'd slept with but stopped when she reached two hands. Then she brooded some more. Lola and Vittoria were far too friendly for her taste, moving together in ways that would incite a jealous rage in a more insecure woman. Or one who cared more.

"Conner!" Melina plopped down beside her, wild caramel ringlets bouncing everywhere. "Why aren't you dancing?"

"I don't dance."

"Sure, you do. C'mon." She tugged at Conner's hand, laughing when she failed to budge her an inch.

"I don't. Have I ever danced at any party we've gone to?"

"Well, I...but you...I'm sure...geez. Maybe not. Why don't you dance?"

"I just don't. Please drop it."

She did, tilting her head to one side like an adorable puppy as she scrunched up her nose. "You look sad."

Conner took a moment to compose a reply. "Just the normal post-tour letdown, I suppose," she said, realizing the truth as she spoke it, with some relief. It wasn't just Vittoria. "I'd forgotten what it feels like. You work so long, but it feels like it's over in an instant. Then it's like, what do I do now?"

Melina took her hand, squeezing it. "You spend some time with your friend Melina who missed you very much while you were away. And I overheard something about a birthday party?"

Conner smiled. The faint beat of Melina's pulse traveled through their still-clasped hands. "Apparently so. What do thirteen-year-old girls like? Asher and Sadie are getting her a phone. Maybe some earbuds and a watch to go with it?"

"You know what you should do? Write her a song. Anyone can buy gadgets, but very few can write a song. She'd love it. Sweet kid, by the way. I talked to her and your sister for a while before the show started."

"Yeah. She's cool." Conner rolled the idea of a song around her mind. "A song is a great idea. Thanks, Meli. Hopefully I can come up with something in time."

"Of course you can. I've never known anyone as talented as you." Melina's fond smile, the tiny gap between her teeth shining through, made Conner's own pulse flutter. She wondered if Meli could feel it.

"Wanna come to the party and hear it in person?"

If possible, Melina's smile widened. "I'd love to. I hope your other niece is there, too. You talk about them so much, I feel as if I already know them."

"Great. I can't show up without a date, you know. I have middle-schoolers to impress."

Melina threw her head back and laughed. "We certainly can't have that. We must maintain Conner Cody's street cred at all times."

Conner forced a chuckle. "I'm that shallow, I guess."

"No, you're not." The seriousness of her tone snatched Conner's attention. "I think you believe that because you've been told that you are, but these glimpses I get of the real Conner more and more often? She's not shallow. The real Conner cares enough to attend a kid's birthday party and worry about the gift. She writes songs that make people think and feel so deeply. She calls people out for their wrongs on national television even though doing that brings up her own trauma."

Conner's throat worked overtime, and she swallowed the last of her drink to postpone her reply. She felt stripped naked more than she'd ever been in front of a camera, and she shivered, chafing from the vulnerability. The Conner that Melina spoke of didn't exist. She couldn't exist. She didn't have a chance to exist, not in the real world. That Conner would be torn to bits.

"You're too kind for Hollywood, Meli Velasco. Please don't let it ruin you."

Meli smiled gently, bringing up her other hand to cup Conner's face, and Conner bit her tongue to stop herself from turning to brush her palm with a kiss.

"Girl, this is our song!" Eriq burst out of nowhere, screeching to a halt as he looked between the two. "If I'm interrupting—"

"You're not. Go." Conner gave Melina a friendly shove. "Have fun. Get a drink or three! Dance your ass off."

She watched them race away, dancing with more exuberance than grace, before another figure detached itself from the writhing crowd. Vittoria stalked toward her, gaze as focused as a jungle predator, and Conner leaned back into the loveseat she occupied, lifting her chin. She couldn't fight the tendrils of arousal winding their way up. Vittoria's attention was a double-edged sword, capable of both slicing and ravishing the object of her focus.

She straddled Conner in full view of the partiers, not that Vittoria cared one lick about audiences. "You looked quite comfortable."

"It's a soft couch."

"Being obtuse doesn't suit you. I'm not speaking of the furniture."

Conner made a noise in her throat. "We're just friends."

Vittoria regarded her, one corner of her mouth tugging up. "I wouldn't care if—"

"We're just friends."

"Repetition does not equal truth. But keep your secrets. I've been hearing some very interesting stories about you and Lola."

"Excuse me?" Conner struggled to rise, pinned by Vittoria's long limbs. "What did she say?"

"That only your admirable faithfulness to me kept you away from her, which is—"

"Not true."

"Oh?" An intrigued eyebrow slowly arched. "You were not faithful?"

Conner glowered, first at her girlfriend and then in the direction of the dance floor where she knew her (thankfully former) opening act to be. Goddamn Lola. "Of course I was. We slept together once, before the holidays. That's it. She's fucking crazy, so don't believe anything she says."

"But crazy can be so delightful." She ran her fingers through Conner's hair, scratching her neck with short nails. Conner bit down on a sigh of pleasure.

"You would know."

She was rewarded with a bark of laughter. "Such cheek. You're lucky I find you so irresistible. But back to this Lola. If you want—"

"I don't."

"But—"

"No, Vi."

"I am merely trying to make you happy." She cupped Conner's cheeks in her hands, bringing their gazes together, amusement and affection warring on her lovely face. "Please let me."

"I—I am. But Lola won't make me happy. The opposite, actually."

Vittoria hummed. "Fine. And your little actress friend that watches you with puppy eyes?"

Conner's frustrated groan was probably loud enough to be heard by the subjects of their conversation. She didn't even know where to start with that sentence. "Just give it up, okay? If I want to be with someone else, I'll let you know. You can do the same."

"I will." Her voice whipped through the air.

The tension hovered for a moment longer before Vittoria's shoulders relaxed. She toyed with Conner's locks again, tugging just enough on the pink tips to reawaken her slumbering libido.

"Come back to Milano with me. No more of these, what do you call them, flying visits."

"I have a birthday party. You practically invited yourself, remember?"

Vittoria pulled back, allowing a hint of a sneer to wrinkle her otherwise unlined visage. "I was being nice. You weren't serious? A child's birthday party instead of me?"

"She's my niece. Of course I'm going. You have a nephew."

"Yes, and I send him many lovely gifts. Buy the girl a toy and be done with it."

"She's twelve."

"A car, then."

"She's twelve!"

Vittoria harrumphed. "You are so contrary tonight. I might be annoyed if I didn't know how to turn it to my advantage."

She stole a kiss, her tongue demanding attention, and Conner surrendered after only token resistance, allowing her hands to creep onto Vittoria's vegan-leather-clad ass. This was what it meant to be with Vittoria, sparring and amorousness in equal measure. She understood what she was getting into. This was how she knew to be in a relationship. The only way she knew.

Chapter Nineteen

"I can't believe I let you drag me into this."

"Oh, shut up." Conner didn't bother to look up from her guitar strings. "You dragged yourself. Bellamy asked to come because she's nice, and you two just couldn't bear to be left out."

In the background, Bellamy preened, Maggie rolled her eyes, and Emi continued to grouse. Conner tried to tune her out. Sure, it wasn't very rock-and-roll to be playing at an event center in Santa Clarita—most bands started out in these places, then won Grammys and went on country-wide tours, not the other way around—but it was a special occasion. The most special.

The weirdest part was, although she wasn't sure how her attendance at Sarah's party had evolved into a full-blown performance, she was actually excited about it. So uncool.

"Oh my God, Emi. Would you give it a rest? Just leave! We can survive with one guitar."

"I'm sorry if after a year on the road, the last thing I want to do is play a free show for a bunch of kids!" She shoved her guitar none too gently into its case and stomped out of the room.

Conner's string vibrated with a jarring twang. She stared after Emi, biting the inside of her cheek. Maybe they really did need a break. God knew they'd all been up each other's asses for too long.

Maggie met her gaze with a shrug. Bellamy jerked her thumb. "I'll go get her."

"No. Finish setting up. It's me. With Emi, it's always me."

She found her in the back alley where they had parked, taking a drag on her vape pen.

"What the hell is your problem? I'm trying to do a nice thing for my niece. If you don't want to be a part of it, that's fine. No need to stick around if all you're going to do is bitch. Also, I thought you quit that shit."

"It takes a lot of nerve for a stoner to lecture me about vaping."

"First of all, I'm not a stoner. I just need help relaxing. Second, you know I rarely smoke. Third, that's not marijuana in your cartridge. Fourth, you didn't answer my question."

Her dark, narrowed eyes bored holes into Conner as she continued to smoke. Pursing her lips, Conner tried again.

"I know you don't like Vittoria—"

"I don't give a fuck about Vittoria." Conner rocked back before the heat of the words singed her. "But YOU…you, I—was I just a diversion while you waited for her to come crawling back? Or was it worse than that? Was I supposed to make her jealous?"

Conner stepped farther away, wishing she'd never spoken. There was no good way to tackle Emi's questions, because while her particular accusations were wrong, Conner couldn't honestly say that the relationships weren't related. The longer she waited to answer, the guiltier she looked.

"It's not like that," she finally said, chickening out of the full truth and opting for partial honesty instead. "Vittoria and I getting back together had nothing to do with our relationship."

"That's hard to believe, given that she dumped you, you got with me, we split up, and suddenly you're back with her again."

"Suddenly? Suddenly?" Conner had never wanted so badly to shake someone. "You and I have been over for nearly a year! It was months before Vittoria and I got back together."

"Yeah, but—"

"And need I remind you that we broke up because you fucked SOMEONE ELSE!"

Emi's mouth worked as she stared at Conner for several long seconds. "Well, at least it got your attention."

Conner's jaw unhinged at that comment. What the hell did that even mean? Before her brain caught up enough to formulate a retort, the door to the event center creaked open.

"As much as everyone is enjoying the sounds of you two screaming obscenities at each other, fifty kids are inside waiting for the surprise they've been promised." The set of Sadie's jaw foreshadowed trouble.

Emi brushed past without a word, but Conner hung back, fiddling with the sleeves of her plaid button-down shirt.

When Sadie cleared her throat, Conner forced herself to meet her gaze, straightening her shoulders.

"If this is a problem—"

"It's not. We're professionals. Don't worry."

"It's my daughter's birthday—"

"I won't mess this up for her. I know you and I are very different, and I'm not who you envisioned as a sister, but I would really love it if you could give me a chance without expecting me to screw up."

Lips pressed tight, Sadie tilted her head to one side. When Conner imitated her, she relaxed, nodding. "You're right."

"Cool. Let's go. I'm about to give the cleanest performance of my life."

The squeals of fifty-odd tweens and teens deafened them. The band had survived exponentially larger crowds, but the proximity and high pitch of this one left an impression. Nothing was more eardrum-shattering than the exhilarated shrieks of teenage girls.

"As I'm sure everyone knows," Conner said, wondering which was Kaylen McGee. "I am *The* Conner Cody." More cheers. "But what *some* of you might not know is I'm also Sarah's aunt, so Hestia Rising"—she waited for the cheers to die down, sharing a grin with Bellamy—"is here to celebrate her. Happy thirteenth, babe. First request is all yours."

Blushing furiously, Sarah surprised her by requesting a song off their first EP. They launched into it, and although it took some coaxing, the kids eventually began to dance.

Conner had more fun than she'd expected. They let the kids request songs but threw in covers as they wished, goofing around, not caring if they messed up a riff or lyric. The night reminded her of the jam sessions they'd had before their record deal. When was the last time one of them had simply started playing and let the others jump in when they caught on, or the last time she and Emi had challenged each other to dueling solos? They were overdue for some time apart, sure, but when she came back from shooting, they needed to rediscover why they had become a band in the first place.

After an hour or so, the rest of the band took a break while Conner played the song she wrote for Sarah, a humorous yet sweet number that had been surprisingly easy to compose. As Emi and Maggie took over for a few songs, Sarah approached her by the refreshments, where the adults tried to be unobtrusive yet observant.

"Thanks for the song, Aunt Conner, and for, you know, everything. You're the best."

She threw her arms around her, and Conner freed one arm to pat her back. "No problem, kid. Are you having fun?"

"Yeah, mostly. My friends, um…" She ducked her head, mumbling incoherently until Conner leaned down. "My friends want me to dance with this boy, but I don't want to."

"Then don't. Is it because he's a boy, or because you don't like him?"

She twisted one foot, glancing at her classmates, most of whom gathered in small groups with only occasional mingling. "Both, I guess?"

Conner held her by the shoulders. "Listen to me. Don't ever do anything with anyone that you don't want to, okay? And if you're uncomfortable, then you call me, and I'll come get you, no questions asked."

"Okay." Sarah hugged her again. "I'm really glad you're my aunt, even if I didn't believe Mom at first."

"Well, I'm really glad you're my niece."

Some of her friends sidled up, asking for selfies, which Conner obliged, pulling Sarah into all of them. It was her birthday, after all. When she noticed Sarah lingering, she raised her eyebrows.

"You don't want to join your friends?"

"I will, but I was wondering, um, do you think you could teach me to play guitar?"

Sarah delivered the request so rapidly Conner had to take a minute to parse it out before she could answer. "Uh, sure. My filming dates got pushed back a month, so I should be home for the rest of the summer. I'll talk to your mom."

Sarah beamed, her braces shining brightly. "Awesome! I mean, cool."

Conner smiled as she watched Sarah skip back to her friends. *Cool.*

Chapter Twenty

The first half of the summer was one for Conner and her nieces to remember. Soon after Sarah's birthday, she and Melina took both girls to Disneyland for two days, an event birthed when Hannah took a throwaway "Sure, babe" as a sworn oath. Sadie agreed only after Asher and Conner persuaded her, and she insisted that Melina attend as well. Annoyed at Sadie's lack of trust, Conner had determined to make it a flawless outing.

Without Melina, it might have all gone very wrong from the start. She remembered sunblock, made sure everyone drank enough water, and recognized when Hannah's crankiness meant they needed to ride the railroad or visit the Animation Academy while Conner took Sarah on the Matterhorn and Grizzly River Run.

For her part, Conner made sure everyone got the rides they wanted and bought the girls so much merchandise their hotel room at the Grand Californian looked like Christmas morning. If she was going to do Disney, she would do it right, which meant a day apiece for Disneyland and California Adventures, with a night on the property to maximize their time.

"Mommy wants to talk to you 'cause I hafta take a bath." Hannah marched into the sitting area of their suite and handed Conner's phone back to her.

"Okay. Do you need help or anything?"

Sarah followed her out. "I'll watch Hannah before I shower."

"Thanks, kid. You're great." Conner winked, and Sarah puffed up with pride before schooling her features.

"The girls seem to be having a good time." Conner glanced at Sadie's face on the screen but couldn't detect any sarcasm or surprise.

"We all are. We'll sleep well tonight, though. I think we walked ten miles, and Hannah wanted piggyback rides for half of that." She laughed, recalling how much the girls had dragged by dinnertime. They'd revived with the fireworks, but Conner hoped they'd crash soon. She sure wanted to.

"Thank you for doing this, Conner. You're going to be their hero forever."

"I'll settle for hip aunt. I've had fun, too. Only a few people outside the hotel recognized me, and I haven't been to Disney since..." Perhaps she shouldn't mention that trip. Eighteen and plastered, she'd been asked to leave when she and a group of other young Hollywood miscreants sang (to use the word lightly) the theme song on It's a Small World for the duration of the ride, substituting a few choice words here and there. "In several years," she said, hoping the incident hadn't been as widely publicized as she remembered. She'd been in the news so often during that period.

"Well, you better rest up. Another day tomorrow! I hope the girls go to sleep soon."

"As soon as they're clean, and then so will Meli and I."

"Meli and I will what?"

Conner looked up and forgot how to speak. Meli emerged in a fluffy towel, curls as untamed as ever, clean and fresh-faced and far too beguiling with her straight-from-the-shower look. Conner could not imagine her showering. Nope. That was dangerous territory.

Hearing two voices repeating her name stirred her from her stupor. Melina watched her with concern, while Sadie grinned. "Everything okay?" Melina asked.

"Tired."

"Is that all?"

Conner narrowed her eyes at her sister, fairly certain she sensed teasing. "Yep. So I'll text you when we leave tomorrow?"

Before she could hang up, Melina leaned over Conner's shoulder to peer at the screen. "Good night, Sadie!"

This was just unfair. All kinds of soft parts pressed against her while her nose took an olfactory journey down something sweet and clean. She closed her eyes and counted the back of her teeth with her tongue until Meli left. Then she beelined to the shower. A cold one.

When she emerged, ruffling her hair with a towel, upbeat music echoed through the door. She trailed the sound with a frown, opening the bedroom to...a party?

Melina and the girls bounced around the sitting area to ridiculously upbeat pop music, the volume rivaled only by their giggles. Conner assumed they were dancing, although the moves resembled nothing she'd ever seen.

"Aunt Conner, we're having a dance party!" Hannah's gleeful voice bounced off the walls and ricocheted among the furniture with her tiny body.

Sarah screeched to a halt, balls of pink blossoming on her cheeks.

"Come on, join us!" Meli danced past her.

Conner watched her jump around with Hannah, both with more

enthusiasm than grace, neither seeming to care. She caught Sarah observing her, uncomfortable awareness creeping up her neck that she would follow whatever Conner did.

Melina approached, seizing both of Conner's hands, her palms soft and warm. "It's only us, Conner. No one's going to see you."

"That's not..."

Three pairs of beseeching eyes rested on her. Any one of them, from the wide-eyed innocence of Hannah to the hero worship of Sarah to the softness of Meli that Conner didn't dare linger on, would have worn her down. All at once made the result simply unstoppable.

No one was going to see. No paparazzi would crowd so close she could smell their body odor, no tabloids would spread rumors, no managers would hound her about going to rehab, no smug middle-aged men on late-night talk shows would bring up unwanted nicknames, no sketch comedy shows would use her problems as fodder for laughs.

She pulled away from Melina, whose smile trended downward before blooming once more when Conner accessed music on her own phone.

"If you're going to have a dance party, you need the right soundtrack."

At first her limbs didn't feel like her own—heavy and clumsy as her body tried to remember how to move. She hadn't danced like this since she was a teenager, even in the privacy of her own home. Onstage, she stalked, jumped, vamped, or even writhed, as the song demanded, but she never danced.

Hannah seized her hands and jumped around with a frenzy determined by her own whims rather than the beat. Conner couldn't help but laugh. Had she ever done anything so silly, purely for the fun of it? Sarah showed off moves presumably from social media, which she gamely copied, before Hannah pulled her in dizzying circles. When she released her, Conner stumbled right into Melina's embrace.

"Oops!" Meli straightened her with a giggle but didn't let go. They gazed at each other, and before Conner could talk herself out of it, she tightened her grasp and pulled Meli with her. They orbited the room, demonstrating exaggerated moves to the cheering girls. Conner would have danced forever just to bask in the glow of Meli's smile.

After the song ended, they held hands a beat too long. Conner blinked just in time to stop herself from drowning in Meli's amber eyes. Averting her gaze, she pivoted to Hannah, picking her up and flying her to the bed she was sharing with Sarah. Dancing never got her anywhere but trouble.

Her patience didn't last as she settled the girls, overtired and whiny. She stretched across the foot of the bed, scrolling through her phone, while they bickered with each other for no apparent reason. All of them could have fit in the king-sized bed. Finally, she snapped.

"That's it. No story, no tucking-in, nothing. Go to sleep."

A space alien could probably hear Hannah's wailing. Head in her hands, she looked for help from Melina, standing in the doorway.

"It's really sad," Melina said in a raised voice, waiting until the girls quieted to continue, "that you two can't get along. Because I happen to know that your aunt had a super-good story prepared." That was news to Conner, who always pulled her stories from her films.

Hannah immediately quieted and scurried under the covers, while Sarah settled on the opposite side of the bed, buried in her phone. Satisfied, Conner lay between them and concentrated for a second.

"A long time ago, there was a land called Prydain, and in this land lived a boy named Taran, a girl named Eilonwy, and a pig named Hen Wen."

Surprisingly, Hannah stayed awake, riveted, until Hen Wen was rescued and Conner called time.

"I want a pig," she said at the conclusion, rolling onto her stomach. "But what happened to the Horned King?"

"That's for next time."

"Okay. Aunt Conner, is Melina your girlfriend?"

"No," Conner said too loudly. "She's not. We're just friends."

"Do you have a girlfriend?"

"No. I mean yes! I do."

Her head dropped along with her stomach. What was wrong with her? Vittoria had been a significant part of her life for several years. She was a total smoke show, and anyone would be lucky to have her as a girlfriend. Their six-month deadline had come and gone, and the fact that Conner let it pass without saying anything had to mean something. She was just tired; that was all.

"I wish Melina was your girlfriend."

Conner was past mistress in the art of giving in to temptation, but even she refused to go down the path that remark opened up. "She's my friend, and yours, and sometimes that's better. Good night, kid."

She encountered the temptation outside the door.

"Thanks for the assist earlier." She held up her hand for a high-five.

"We made a pretty good team today."

Conner watched her walk into the bedroom they'd be sharing. Maybe she should sleep on the couch. "Yeah. We did."

A muffled giggle diverted her attention. Sarah's eyes widened as she peeked from her door before another giggle escaped the hand over her mouth.

"Find something funny, do you?"

Sarah glanced at the door Melina had closed behind her, then smiled. "Conner and Melina, sitting in a tree," she said in a quiet, sing-song voice. "K-I-S—"

"Finish that word, and you're dead."

Sarah didn't, although a cheeky grin revealed her thoughts on the subject.

In their shared bedroom, Conner adopted a blank face. She'd never been a praying sort of person, even in Catholic school, but she seriously considered the prospect as she slid into her bed. Melina, stretched out on her own bed in shorts nearly covered by her oversized T-shirt, combined adorable and sexy in a way that Conner didn't know how to handle.

In fact, she didn't know how to do anything in this situation. She'd never had to deal with an unattainable attraction. Also feeling guilty about her unfaithful thoughts, she floated adrift in a sea of uncertainty.

Ironically, Vittoria wouldn't care in the slightest. She'd adopt an oh-so-sexy smirk that said, "I told you so," without verbalizing a word, and then she'd tell Conner to go for it, with details to follow. Or, better yet, she'd suggest that Conner should bring Melina into their bedroom, an idea that infuriated and nauseated her. No. Conner was staunchly monogamous in her romantic relationships and wildly hypocritical for denying Vittoria the open relationship she wanted while Conner chased another woman in her dreams.

She had friends who never drifted from the platonic realm. She had a long-term girlfriend. She'd had plenty of purely sexual encounters. Conner understood the various forms attraction could take and the differences between them. But Meli…she was everything, all at once, and it was almost too much. She didn't understand it.

In the mostly dark room, a sliver of moonlight through the curtains providing an ethereal glow, she could just make out Melina's face as she slept peacefully. She caught herself smiling. Why did it hurt so much?

Chapter Twenty-one

Behind her mirrored sunglasses, Conner silently observed the crowd around her, well aware that they observed her right back, most not even bothering to hide their gawking. After Sarah's birthday party and their Disney outing, the word was out about the Cohen girls' famous aunt.

She opened a group chat on her phone. Emi still wasn't talking to her, which suited her just fine, so she left her out.

Conner: Imagine the damage I could do to these uptight suburban soccer moms. The HOA would never recover.
Melina: LMAO you are so bad!!
Maggie: Do it.
Bellamy: She doesn't need encouragement.
Maggie: DO IT.
Bellamy: I can't handle y'all.
Lindsey: Don't knock it till you try it.

Conner chuckled as she shoved her phone in the back pocket of her jeans. She could think of a few better things to do with her Saturday morning, but cheering on Hannah during her soccer game wasn't so bad. Not that Conner cheered aloud, of course. She had her limits, even for the girls.

"She's pretty good."

Sadie didn't take her eyes off the field. "Yes, she is. This is the first year she's played up an age group, which makes me nervous, but Asher said she was ready, and so did her old coach." Then she snorted. "Hannah said she was too good for her old team anyway. She must have gotten her humility from you."

Conner smirked. "That's my girl."

"I play basketball." Sarah finally looked up from the new phone permanently glued to her hands. "I'm pretty good, right, Mom?"

"Of course you are, sweetie. Great tackle, Hannah!"

"I'll come watch you play when I get back from filming."

Sarah nodded and copied Conner's pose by shoving her hands in her leather jacket. "Cool."

"Aren't you two hot in those jackets?" Sadie asked.

"It's about the look, not the temperature."

"Duh, Mom. It's about the look."

The onlookers left Conner alone until the end of the match, when some unspoken signal sent the hordes rushing in. She barely managed to push Sarah to Sadie before she was engulfed.

She scribbled autographs blindly, pasting a smile on her face for the ever-present cell phones. The soccer field was one of many in the complex, and word must have spread faster than the balls were kicked. Conner's peripheral vision filled with hands thrusting phones, pens, and a plethora of objects with unknown aims. What was she supposed to do with someone's water bottle? The same hands stroked and groped whatever they could reach, until someone snatched her baseball cap right off her head.

"Hey!" She spun around, but her scathing bark died on her lips. The person had vanished, her favorite Angel City FC hat along with them.

Conner held her hands in the air and refused to smile for any more pictures, not that anyone in the increasingly frenzied crowd stopped. Her heart pounded as people pushed closer and closer, choking her with their demands and proximity and disregard for anything other than their wants. Meat markets were treated with more respect.

She couldn't move. She could barely breathe. She was no mob virgin, but tendrils of panic popped up like shoots of grass, stabbing her with fear that this might be the one that got out of control. Had Sadie been able to get the girls away?

"Let's go." A familiar voice in her ear prepared her for the hand that wrapped around her bicep.

Imposing and fearless, her bodyguard pulled Conner along as she brushed people aside with as much regard for them as they had demonstrated for Conner. As soon as the sea of bodies parted, Asher met them, wrapping a paternal arm over her shoulders. She stiffened. It was one thing for a paid bodyguard, but Conner had no need for fatherly actions from anyone else.

She shrugged him off as soon as they reached their cars, where Sadie and the girls were safely secured. Sadie rolled down her window.

"That was scary."

"Yes, it was. I don't know what to say." Her bodyguard honked. "I should go."

"I'll call you later?"

Conner nodded, smiled at the girls, and slid into the passenger side of a blacked-out Porsche Cayenne.

"I told you this was a bad idea," her bodyguard said.

"Come on. You can count on one hand the number of times this—stop. Stop the car."

She was out the door before the tires quit rolling. Not bothering to school her expression, she strode over to the grove of trees bunched at the edge of the parking lot, in view of the field Hannah had played on.

"You have a lot of fucking nerve." She whipped off her sunglasses to properly glare at the paparazzi clustered together. Their lenses shuttered furiously, but she didn't care.

"Conner, who are the kids?"

"Do you have a secret family?"

"Are any of them yours?"

"Conner, is it true your father has other children? Are those kids some of them?"

That one hit too close to home, for she and Sadie had discussed the likelihood of other half siblings scattered around the globe.

"We have a deal, and this?" She waved her hand around. "Isn't it. If I ever see any of you around these kids again, you'll never get another tip."

"Who are they?"

"None of your business. I signed up for this. They didn't. I'm serious. I will hide in my house for the rest of my goddamn life if you don't leave them alone."

One of the photographers scoffed. "Yeah, right."

"Try me. And here's a photo for you." She held up her middle finger, waiting until every single one got several shots before walking away.

Back in the car, she fumed. She had hated the paparazzi for as long as she'd been aware of them, dogging her every move since her first steps, but as an adult, she acknowledged they were a part of the life she had chosen, whether she wanted it or not. Like most celebrities, she had an unofficial agreement with them: occasionally, her publicist tipped them off to her location, and in return, sometimes they left her alone. Sometimes.

After a terse conversation with her publicist, Conner typed an email to her lawyer and smashed "Send" so hard she nearly dropped her phone.

"I don't want to go home."

They continued to exit the 405. "Since when do you prefer anywhere but your house?"

"It's not the house. It's the—" She closed her eyes. The person. It was the person. She didn't want to be alone, and as much as she liked her bodyguard, she wasn't who Conner wanted. "Can you take me to NoHo?"

Conner had been to Melina's apartment a few times to pick her up, but she'd never been inside beyond the front door. She hadn't thought of texting ahead, relieved when she saw her navy Honda Accord parked on the street outside.

"Oh my God, it's Conner fucking Cody!" Eriq opened the door and gasped, a hand to his chest. How were his teeth that white?

"You don't have to do that every time you see me."

"Girl, please. I will never get over the fact that you have a thing for my lil' roomie."

She rolled her eyes and swallowed, choosing not to let that remark get to her. "Is Meli here?"

"Oh, *Meli!*"

Now that got to her. That was her nickname, not anyone else's.

Melina emerged from a hallway, her quizzical expression blooming into an ear-to-ear smile. "Conner? I wasn't expecting you…was I? Not that I would forget you, obviously, I'm just—"

"Hey, girl. Are you busy?"

Relief washed over her with the force of a Pacific wave when Melina answered in the negative. What a fool she would have looked by her assumption if that hadn't been the case.

They retired to her room, chased by vaguely suggestive murmurs from Eriq that flamed Meli's cheeks and warmed Conner's heart. Slowly, she told the tale of the afternoon, finding herself stretched on the bed with her head in Melina's lap.

"She's going to keep the kids away from me. I know it. She's freaked out."

Meli stroked stray hair away from Conner's face. "No, she won't. You said yourself this doesn't happen often."

"The crowds, maybe. But the press…you know what they're like. That picture of us when I won the Grammy still hasn't gone away."

"Aww, are you that embarrassed to be seen with me?"

"Anything but. I just wish everyone didn't immediately jump to something salacious every fucking time I'm seen with a woman. You don't need that crap in your life."

"I'm a big girl. Don't worry about me."

Conner fell silent, concentrating on the fingers running through her hair until they stilled.

"Unless it caused a problem for you. Maybe your—um, Vittoria was mad about it? After all, it did seem kinda…well, obviously it wasn't what it looked…I'm not saying anything was—"

Conner laughed. "Meli, chill. It was just a picture, and she doesn't get jealous."

Understatement of the century.

A part of her wished Vittoria was jealous, just a little. That she wasn't so willing to share. That the thought of Conner with anyone else drove her crazy, just like the idea of Vittoria with someone else used to make Conner sick. And somehow, in her mind, if Vittoria was jealous of Meli, her guilt over her feelings for Meli would be justified.

She didn't need to be told her logic was flawed.

She spent the rest of the day hanging out with Melina and her roommates, blowing off the fact that she'd previously committed the afternoon to learning her lines. Sitting on a futon in the cramped living room of a beige, three-bedroom apartment in North Hollywood with someone untouchable, her awestruck roommate, and two more strangers had never been her idea of a good time, but it was…pleasant. Fun, even. She entertained them with tales of outrageous parties and scandalous gossip, and they reciprocated with stories of the trials and tribulations of struggling creatives, a world entirely new to Conner.

Her appreciation for Melina deepened upon learning that she'd held three jobs simultaneously when she first moved to California, and that she was the only one of the four roommates who supported herself entirely in her chosen profession. She verified some of Eriq's anecdotes of celebrities he'd served and gasped at others. Her reenactment of growing up on the set of sitcoms evoked tears of laughter, and her admission of how terrified she'd been at fifteen, alone in her first place after being emancipated, left everyone in silence. Eriq saved the moment by revealing that Melina had worked as Mirabel at Disneyland for a year, something she had withheld from Conner while they were at the amusement park.

"You let me make a fool of myself trying to dodge the same superhero that I play on screen so that my seven-year-old niece wouldn't figure out they're not real, and you've actually been one of those characters? I'm questioning our entire friendship, Melina."

"No, you're not."

Conner turned her head, adopting her most wounded expression.

"Conner…"

She ducked Melina's questing hand, refusing to look at her.

"Conner, come on! Ugh, fine."

Conner waited a moment, and when Melina's attention didn't return, she quickly glanced at her, only to meet her mischievous gaze.

"I knew you weren't mad!"

Melina pushed her shoulder playfully, and Conner seized her hand, tightening her grip when Melina tugged. They ended up in a tussling match, pulling back and forth and loudly chortling, which died off when Melina suddenly rolled onto her back, Conner kneeling atop her.

Conner could count every delicate eyelash, every tiny freckle, every star that shone from her whiskey-colored eyes. Someone's pulse thudded, but she couldn't tell whose. Were they alone? A tiny puff of air escaped Meli's plump lips. Conner caught her breath before exhaling deeply.

"I'm not mad," she said in a hoarse voice that belonged behind a smoky bar. "Never at you."

She sat up, pulling Meli with her. Meli tucked her chin almost demurely, and when her eyelashes fluttered, Conner's heart lost a beat it would never get back.

"I'll remember that."

"I hope you do."

Loud whispers brought them back to the present. Two of the roommates disappeared into the hall, leaving only Eriq and his beatific grin stretching ear to ear.

He clapped his hands. "So! In-N-Out?"

Once there, she let herself get talked into a hamburger wrapped in lettuce, although she drew the line at a shake and settled for stealing some of Melina's French fries, an act some fan caught on their phone and spread all over social media before she made it home. Her six a.m. appointment with her trainer would be brutal enough, though she might appreciate the protein in the burger, given that Conner was expected to add ten to fifteen pounds of muscle every time she put on the superhero bodysuit.

But six a.m. beckoned, regardless of her protein intake, so afterward she asked Melina to drive her home.

"Still worried about Sadie?"

"Hmm?" Conner lifted her head as they crept through the omnipresent traffic. "What did you say?"

"I asked if you're still worried about Sadie. You've sighed three times."

"Oh. I guess so. It's just...I don't know how to do family." She waited for Melina to laugh or scoff or mock, but she saw only raised eyebrows inviting her to elaborate. "I spent more time with my television families than I ever have with my actual family. Tell me about yours."

"We're normal, I guess. Not to imply you're not normal, of course. Maybe, um, average is the better word for mine. Boring, even. Or—"

"Meli? You're not going to offend me. My family is far from normal, average, boring, and any other word you might come up with."

"Okay. Um...you already know about my sister and my brothers. My sister and I shared a room until she moved out, which wasn't great, if I'm being honest." She laughed. "In middle school we had a line of tape running through across the floor, and God help you if you crossed it. My brothers were the same way, fighting constantly."

"Do you get along now?"

"Yeah. We're really close. My brothers still compete over everything, but not enough to be in mortal peril at any given time anymore. My oldest brother, Samuel, really calmed down once he became a dad. And I've told you about my niece and nephew."

Conner smiled in the darkness. Melina's affection shone through every word. "What about your parents? Do they still think you're lying about me?"

She burst out laughing. "I think my mom does. Growing up, I thought she was hard to please, and maybe she is, but she just worries a lot, and she doesn't always understand that I don't want to copy her life and be a wife and mom."

"You don't?"

Melina glanced at her. "That always surprises everyone. I wouldn't mind getting married someday, but I never wanted to have children. All I've wanted to do since I was a kid is act."

"Not exactly compatible with raising children, speaking as one of those children."

"Some people seem to have it figured out."

"I guess. I don't want kids, either."

Meli smiled. "We'll just be the cool aunts together."

Conner returned the smile, annoyed with her heart for thumping extra hard.

Thankfully, her face didn't betray her attraction, for Melina continued. "My dad wasn't very affectionate when I was a kid, although he's mellowed out, but he was always there when I needed him, you know? He turns sixty next month."

"Are you having a big party?"

"My brothers and sister are, but I can't go." She sighed.

Conner nodded in sympathy. "You don't have much say about your schedule once you book a role. Can't they move the party?"

"It's not that. It's, well, I don't have the money for the plane ticket, Conner. You've seen my apartment—four people in three bedrooms, which is the only way we can afford it. I save up to go home once a year at Christmas, and that's it."

Lindsey, who hadn't come from much before becoming a basketball superstar, had once claimed that money was a foreign concept to Conner, and she wasn't entirely wrong. She'd grown up enough in the last few years to have a decent idea of her net worth and the amount of cash in her bank account, unlike her uncontrolled spending as a teenager, but she still never gave much thought to any purchase except real estate.

She supposed most people would be embarrassed at the income disparity, but the solution seemed as obvious as a thunderstorm.

"Are you booked around the day of the party?"

"No, but—"

"Let me buy your ticket."

"Conner! You can't…I couldn't…you don't have to…I didn't mean…"

"Why shouldn't I? You need a plane ticket. I have the money. What? Why are you shaking your head at me?"

"Because it's very generous, but I don't want it to become a thing between us."

"That only happens if we let it. I have more money than you. It's simply a fact, just like you're nicer than me."

Meli laughed so hard that Conner wondered if they'd veer off the road. She didn't stop until they came to a red light, finally wiping one eye. "I don't have a single response to that remark."

Conner shrugged. "Merely stating the truth. C'mon, Meli. Just let me do this. I'd do anything if it would make you happy."

With any other woman, Conner would have read the world in the half gasp, half sigh her words evoked. But she'd rarely done something simply to make someone happy. Buying their affection or attention, sure. Because they had asked, plenty of times. To get something in return, often. To put a smile on their face? Not so much.

"You're sweeter than my aunt's horchata," Meli finally said after a silent mile broken only by the clicking of her blinker. "And a very good friend. I would appreciate a plane ticket very much, but only on one condition."

"Name it."

"Come with me."

"To Texas?"

"No, to Antarctica. Of course to Texas, you dork. My family will love you."

Conner grinned, unable to help herself. "I don't know if we're ready for that step."

They came to another stop. "You made a fatal mistake, you know that? You revealed your weakness. It would make me very happy to take you home to Texas, so now you have to."

She reached toward Conner suddenly but withdrew her hand just as quickly, as if she'd changed her mind halfway there. Conner found herself leaning forward, begging for her touch, anywhere, it didn't matter, just the barest brush of skin against skin.

"I guess I do." Her voice sounded husky and hoarse.

Meli nodded, her gap-toothed smile making her appear shy yet knowing. "You do."

Conner gazed at her, wondering how she would ever get her heart back from someone who could never be hers.

Chapter Twenty-Two

"Would I lie to you?"

Sarah watched her out of the corner of her narrowed eyes. "You might."

"When?" Conner's outrage was only half-manufactured.

"Like when you told Hannah you loved how she styled your hair even though it was worse than when Dad tries to do our hair."

"She's seven. I couldn't hurt her feelings."

"Would you hurt mine?"

Conner shifted gears, speeding up to pass someone. If she said yes, Sarah would be hurt. If she said no, Sarah would think she was lying and be hurt. Women, even teenage nieces, could be so damned difficult.

"I wouldn't, but you're thirteen now. Basically an adult. You're old enough to handle the truth, and the truth is exactly what I said: You're doing great. You're working on open chords, and you've learned the 4:4 time signature. It takes a long time to master guitar."

"How long did it take you?"

She shifted on the leather seat. "I was more self-taught, just from watching my—other people play when I was growing up. My grandmother, though, taught me to read music and to sing, and I started piano lessons when I was Hannah's age."

"Hmm." Sarah sank into thought, and Conner relaxed, hoping she was out of the danger zone that was the topic of Seth Cody. "Hey, Aunt Conner?"

"Yeah, kid?"

"Did you learn guitar from watching your dad play?"

"Um…yeah. Him and others. A bunch of people were always around."

"I know who he is. I looked him up on Google. He was in a band a really long time ago." She scrunched her nose. "They all had long hair and wore flannel."

Conner laughed. Seth Cody, rock god and notorious Lothario, would die if he knew how the current generation perceived him.

"You wear a lot of flannel, too."

She stopped laughing. "I don't wear that much."

"Yes, you do. And lots of black. Don't you get hot?"

"It's fashion, babe."

Sarah straightened up, nodding. "Oh, yeah. It's about the look."

Conner tried to tone down the amusement in her smile. Brands around the globe frequently offered her handsome sums of money to endorse their products, knowing their return on investment would be exponential, given her loyal fans would move to the moon if she looked at it twice. Having her own little mini-me was something else. Something frightening, if she dwelled on it.

Thankfully, a moment later, Sarah gave her something else to contemplate.

"Why doesn't he want to meet us?"

Conner nearly drove off the road. She could have handled the sex talk or the gay talk. Hell. She'd rather have the dead-pet talk. Surely this was a question for someone more adult than her. She barely understood her own relationship with her father, much less Sadie's.

"It's not that. To be honest, I'm not sure he even knows you and your sister exist."

Sarah's tiny "oh" pierced Conner's heart.

"Babe, it's not about you at all. He met your grandma for one night and never knew your mom. They decided it would be better if your grandpa raised her with your grandma, and they were right. He's not a very good dad. You're not missing anything."

Sarah fidgeted with her seat belt. Finally she nodded and looked at her. "You know what? At first I was glad you're my aunt 'cause you're Conner Cody and you're, like, awesome. Now I'm glad because I think you needed a new family."

A nuclear bomb could not have rendered her more speechless. Her eyes began to burn, and she wondered what she was allergic to until she realized they had filled with tears. She swallowed hard and blinked until she was certain she was in control. The next time she had to cry on camera, she had the material.

"Aunt Conner, you missed the exit."

"Oh, shit. I'll get the next one." She sounded like she'd swallowed gravel and cleared her throat again. "You know what, kid? I'm glad, too." She reached out and ruffled Sarah's blond hair, laughing when she squirmed away.

"Stop! You're messing up my look!"

Nieces were a trip. For the first time ever, Conner could think of family without getting a bad taste in her mouth.

The Rise and Fall of Conner Cody

❖

As summer reached its zenith, Conner found herself relatively content, for once. She gave Sarah guitar lessons once a week, ending with dinner at the Cohen house, and Sadie started letting the girls visit her in Malibu to swim. She dragged her friends to Sparks games to watch Lindsey play and hosted a three-day bash for the Fourth of July that ended one relationship, started two more, and caused Conner to swear off parties forever.

Or at least for a few months.

One day in late July, Conner stared at her closet before scrunching her nose and dropping into an overstuffed armchair in her reading nook. She hated packing. Texas in August was capital-H Hot, and not in the sexy kind of way. Four pairs of shorts lay in her suitcase, and she was seriously considering leaving it at that. Maybe an extra set of leggings for the return flight.

Shrugging, she picked up her copy of Nancy Mitford's *The Pursuit of Love*. She'd been on a Mitford kick ever since she read a biography of the sisters and was currently obsessed with the idea of portraying Decca Mitford in a film adaptation.

When her phone vibrated, she glared at it for a second and contemplated ignoring it, but curiosity won out. She wrinkled her forehead when the gate guard told her who was waiting there.

I'll open the garage for you. I'm in my bedroom.

After she sent the text, she returned to her book, feigning indifference, but the words floated off the pages into thin air without traversing her brain. Instead, she tracked the closing of a door downstairs, the soft tread of approaching footsteps, and her increasing anxiety over this unannounced visit from abroad.

"There you are, *mia luna*. Aren't you going to greet me?"

Conner placed a bookmark on the page and closed her book, taking as much time as possible. Only then did she meet the expectant gaze of her girlfriend. "Hello, Vittoria. What are you doing here?"

Vittoria's plump lips formed a perfect pout. Usually the sight made Conner want to tug on her lower lip with her teeth. "I'm visiting my girlfriend. Am I not allowed to do that without permission?"

"I'm just surprised."

"Since you have been so reluctant to come to me, I decided to come to you."

Conner scowled. "I'm about to be living in Europe for the rest of the year. I refuse to feel guilty for wanting to spend time at home."

Vittoria's eyebrows twitched up. "Who said you should feel guilty? I understand how much you love your house, which is why I've decided to move in."

Conner blinked. She'd been deep into her book before Vittoria arrived, and she shook her head to refocus. She was starting to hear things. "Move in where?"

"Here. With you," Vittoria said slowly, as if speaking to someone with limited knowledge of the English language.

"In this house?"

"In your pool house." Conner must have gotten under her skin for her to resort to sarcasm. "Although your pool house can be quite fun at times. Yes, in this house, in this room, in this bed." She pulled Conner to her feet before murmuring into her ear, "In the shower, on the dining-room table, that one time on the diving board of the pool."

She kissed her, and Conner returned the motion with perfunctory attention. She suddenly wanted to grab her suitcase and run to LAX a day early. It wouldn't be the first time she'd slept in an airport.

"We shall have to decide the bathroom and closet situation. I suppose one of us can use the closet in here, and the other can use one downstairs, and the same for the bathroom." Vittoria rubbed her hands up and down Conner's arms, occasionally pausing to kiss her neck. "I'll let you keep your precious closet up here if you'll give up the bathroom. We'll turn one of the guest rooms into my closet: the blue one, I think. It's the largest."

"That's the girls' room."

Vittoria chuckled. "Conner, you're a lesbian. Every room in your house is a girls' room. Although does that mean you have realized we are not made for monogamy? I can't tell you how much of a relief that is. I knew you'd give in eventually, but you are so stubborn. What a long seven months this has been!"

"No, no, no." She didn't know which misconception to address first. She decided on the easier path. "The blue room is for my nieces. For when they stay over."

Vittoria looked at her, a barely perceptible tightening of her lips the only sign of her displeasure. "You didn't tell me the children stay here."

"They don't, yet. But they want to, so someday…"

She was pathetic. Redecorating a room on the nonexistent chance that Sadie would ever trust her kids here overnight.

"We can discuss that later. Right now, I haven't been touched in weeks, and I came a very long way to see you." She tightened her hold on Conner, licking the shell of her ear. Conner twitched. "And I'm not wearing any panties."

Conner had been panting after Vittoria since she was twenty. Senses heightened at the mention of her name, pulse racing at the hint of her scent, underwear soaked at the brush of her skin. Even when she couldn't stand her, she wanted her. Yet here she was, all but literally on her doorstep, and

Conner felt...annoyed. At the interruption, at the brazen declaration of a major life decision, and, mostly, at herself.

What had changed? Not Vittoria. She was the same person Conner had met at the fashion show all those years ago. Still jaw-droppingly gorgeous, still sex on legs. Still mahogany of hair and blue of eye. Still a touch selfish, a little manipulative, a bit conceited. Still unapologetic about all those attributes. And, most important, she, who had the world waiting breathlessly at the tips of her perfectly-manicured fingers, still wanted Conner.

"I think we should break up."

At first, Vittoria didn't react. She simply held Conner in her arms, watching her with a smile playing on her lips until it bloomed fully. "No, you don't."

Conner twisted away. "Yes, I do. I want to break up."

"You've been grouchy since I walked in the door." She appropriated Conner's former seat in the armchair and crossed one slim leg over the other. "So go on, get it out. What are you upset about now?"

Conner used to think condescension was a game. Vittoria would pretend to be superior, amused by her moods, humoring her until Conner would get so irritated and wound up that she exploded, and Vittoria would calm her down with laughter and kisses. It was their thing, and it worked. Or so she thought.

"It's not that I'm upset about something, although I am. It's just—"

"Are you or are you not upset?" This time, the edges of her amusement sounded frosted and cool.

Conner lifted her chin. "Yes. What do you mean, you're moving in?"

"It means I'm going to live here with you, *mia luna*. Being in LA will be good for my career. Even I won't be able to model forever, and my agent wants me to start breaking into movies."

Conner couldn't halt her derisive snort. "Just like that, huh?"

"No different than a child actress who decided she wanted to be a rock star, so she did." Vittoria had never smirked like this before. "Elle, Rosie, Rebecca...they did it, so why can't I?"

"And I don't get a say on who lives in my house?"

Vittoria tsked. Her amusement had evaporated. "I'll get a place of my own. Is that what you want to hear? My God, you are obsessive about your privacy. It simply seems ridiculous when I'll be spending my time here anyway."

Conner threw her hands into the air. "Are you even listening to me? I don't want you to move in!"

She felt the chill of Vittoria's glare on her cheeks. "I can hear you perfectly well. No need to shout. Don't you think it's time you outgrew these tantrums?"

Conner bit so hard on the inside of her cheek that she tasted copper, trying to avoid accepting the accusation of temper tantrums. She spoke carefully. "I don't care if you live in LA, or Milan, or Timbuktu. Wherever you are, it won't be with me. I. Want. To. Break. Up."

Vittoria continued to regard her silently, almost dispassionately save for the telltale tightening of her lips. Conner stared right back, trying not to give in, although it went against her nature. People were supposed to argue during arguments. It was in the word itself!

Finally she couldn't stand it any longer. "I need to finish packing."

She pulled a variety of V-neck shirts out of her closet, chucking them at her suitcase. Throw in some flip-flops and undergarments, and she'd be set for the weekend, though perhaps she should include one evening outfit.

Vittoria harrumphed. "You see, you need me around, to save you from your fashion choices if nothing else. Tell me that is not what you plan on wearing in Europe."

"That's not what I plan on wearing in Europe."

"Thank goodness. That might do for lounging in your trailer, but your reputation would never recover if you wore such things out."

"I'm going to wear them in Texas this weekend."

Her nose crinkled. "What is in Texas?"

Conner's shoulders heaved with a sigh. Why was she still here? "I'm going to Texas with Meli to visit her family."

For a moment only silence filled the air, and then, implausibly, Vittoria began to laugh. Actual, one hundred percent amused laughter. Usually it took a combination of some intoxicating substance and Conner at her most relaxed to evoke this sort of mirth.

She brushed at the corner of her eyes. "So that is what this is all about."

"I don't get it." Conner's phone vibrated, but she ignored it.

"I can see why you think you want to break up now."

"I don't 'think.' I—"

"I knew you were attracted to the woman, but I didn't realize it was this deep. You like her. You want her, and to have her, you believe that you can't be with me. How many times do I have—"

"No! Goddamn it, Vi. How many times do *I* have to tell *you*? I don't want an open relationship! I want to be with one person at a time, and it's not you. I'm sor—no, I'm not sorry. I don't want to hurt you, but that's how I feel." She ran a hand through her hair, leaving it an unruly mess. "We never should have gotten back together."

Vittoria remained maddeningly amused. "All right, Conner. Go meet her family and seduce your little straight girl, and when you've made your conquest and you're bored, you know where I will be. In fact, I ought to move in while you're gone and save us both some time."

Was she always this infuriating? Deep down, Conner knew the answer, and she didn't like what it said about her. Every previous time they had broken up, it had been in anger, usually instigated by Vittoria, who was equally always the one who summoned Conner back with a snap of her fingers. A summons that Conner had never been able to ignore, until now.

"First of all, no, you're not moving in, for many reasons, one of which is that Meli is going to be staying here while I'm gone." She chose to ignore the knowing laugh that her words evoked. She also ignored her phone as it vibrated again. "Second of all, she and I are friends, nothing more. This breakup has nothing to do with her."

"Yes, it does. You cannot stand the fact that she doesn't want you, that the great Conner Cody has found the one woman she can't have. It's quite hilarious, to be honest."

Conner twisted the tank top in her hands until it was probably ruined for good, wishing it was Vittoria's neck. God, she was just like—and the realization hit her so hard she fell forward with her palms on the bed.

Vittoria was just like Britt.

Both women always telling her how she felt, who she was, what she was going to do. Both ignoring her words and feelings. Both so maddeningly condescending. And both able to get at Conner's true fears.

You have no talent. You get by on your name and your face.

You only want what you can't have.

Suddenly, she understood what had changed. It wasn't Vittoria—it was Conner herself. And she wasn't putting up with that kind of bullshit anymore.

She straightened up. "You need to go. We're over, Vittoria."

Vittoria scrutinized her for a long moment with stormy eyes. Finally she set her jaw and stood. "Fine. I'll go. But listen to my words, Conner. When you get your straight girl out of your system, you *will* come back to me. You always do. And shouldn't you answer that?"

She picked up her vibrating phone, intending to silence the damn thing, until she saw the name on the screen. Abuelita's nurse.

"Hello?"

She never recalled the actual conversation. When she hung up, Vittoria was still there, eyebrows knitted in rare concern.

"What happened?"

Conner sat on her bed, cradling the phone in her hands. She looked up, suddenly glad she wasn't alone, even if she was with her freshly dumped ex-girlfriend. "My abuelita passed away."

FALL

Chapter Twenty-three

Silence could be so loud.

Technically, it wasn't silent. The Gulfstream, as luxurious as it was, roared through the air, and the occasional murmur of the bored flight attendants filtered out from the rear. Conner had a TV show playing in front of her, though her earbuds were at low volume, and she hadn't a clue what had happened on the screen in the last hour.

She glanced at her mother again. Camila never had much to say to her, but she'd spoken so little on this trip that Conner was starting to become alarmed. Her father said that she had taken the news stoically, for Conner hadn't been able to make herself deliver it.

"C'mon, Seth. Unless you've pissed her off recently, it's better coming from you."

"Your ma doesn't like me even when I've done nothing."

"She tolerates you more than me, anyway." He grunted, which Conner took as acquiescence, but she couldn't keep herself from adding, "Be a father for once."

"Jesus, Mary, and Joseph, but you're an ungrateful brat. Fine, fine. I'll call her."

As her grandmother's emergency contact and, apparently, the executor of her estate, she had spread the news and overseen the extremely detailed funeral plans. For Abuelita had left nothing out, down to the black dress Conner was expected to wear during her LA memorial service, in which she was also to sing Schubert's "Ave Maria" in Spanish. Never mind that Conner didn't like dresses, didn't know the lyrics to "Ave Maria" in any language, and was a rock star, not a classical musician. Typical Abuelita, dictating from beyond.

Conner smiled sadly and leaned back in her seat, abandoning her movie entirely. Her grief came and went; she was sad, of course, but Abuelita had been very old and passed peacefully with a stroke in her sleep. But until Conner met Sadie and the girls, Abuelita had been her most significant relationship within her family. She had rarely approved of Conner, but she had always supported her.

She looked at Camila again. She didn't know many of the details of their relationship, other than Abuelita and Camila hadn't gotten along any better than Camila and herself did. But surely her silence was due to her sorrow. Abuelita had still been her mother.

She briefly wondered how she would feel when Camila or Seth passed, but she immediately shut down that line of thought. Nothing good awaited there.

"Do you have something to say?"

She jumped. "No."

"Then why do you keep staring at me?"

"I—" She chickened out. "Are you ready for dinner?"

Camila waved her hand, so Conner summoned the flight attendants, who delivered chicken piccata with linguine and roasted asparagus. She was against chartered flights on principle, but Camila had insisted, so she figured she might as well go with her. At least she didn't have to deal with anyone else on the twelve-hour flight to Buenos Aires, although she'd have liked the buffer.

Camila spoke once during dinner, to complain about the pasta, as if they hadn't had their choice of meals when scheduling the charter. Conner's parents had been in their forties when she was born, so for as long as she could remember, Camila had been fighting the middle-aged spread as her notorious curves caught up to her.

"I don't think you need to worry about a few carbs," Conner said, for Camila looked good, as voluptuous as ever.

"You'll learn soon enough that you always need to worry about carbs." She cast a critical eye over Conner. "You ought to worry about your trainer. Are you joining the military?"

"It's for a movie. They like their superheroes ripped."

She sniffed. "Oh. Those things."

"Those things" paid more than Camila had ever commanded and were fun to make to boot, but Conner didn't pursue the argument. If she were elected Pope, Camila would criticize her prayers.

She had only been to Argentina a few times, so her relatives were more like strangers and treated her as such. Some polite, others suspicious, and a sundry few wildly curious about her Hollywood life. After several enormous family meals where she enjoyed the food more than the company, they had to participate in an overblown public memorial, the keystone of the three days of national mourning decreed by the Argentine government. Isabela Morales had been the nation's sweetheart in her day, even if most people Conner's age barely knew who she was. Still, the appreciation and genuine grief she observed from the crowd touched her, and she felt a lump in her throat more than once.

Then, Mass. Though she'd been forced to attend during school, Mass remained a foreign concept that bored and annoyed her. She spent more time admiring the rococo altarpiece and nineteenth-century frescoes than paying attention to the service. It was a nice distraction.

Back on the plane to repeat the rituals in Los Angeles, she reflected that she had never been so immersed in that side of her culture. Speaking only Spanish for several days and eating her weight in carbonado and empanadas made her wonder what else she had missed out by her mother's utter rejection of her Argentine heritage. Harlow once told her that Camila had tried to change her name to Cami Morgan when she first began acting, but producers wanted to capitalize on Abuelita's fame.

Back on the plane, she decided there was never a better time to ask.

"Why aren't you fluent in Spanish?"

Camila's unamused glower took its time crossing the aisle. "Because I'm American. I speak English."

"Don't be ridiculous."

"Don't ask stupid questions."

"It's not stupid! Abuelita speaks—spoke—Spanish, and so did Abuelo. Therefore, common sense would dictate that you would learn it unless you refused."

She arched one dark eyebrow. "Since you're so desperate to know, my father moved back to Argentina when I was six and didn't return until I was an adult, and my mother was busy filming movies."

"That's a story I know all too well." She knew the instant she spoke that she should have kept her mouth shut.

Camila's brown eyes flashed with lightning and anger. "You and the rest of the world. You made damn sure of that."

"What was I supposed to do, Camila? Lie and declare you and Seth parents of the year? Give me a fucking break."

"Why don't you give me a fucking break! Parenting doesn't come with a manual, and you certainly weren't an easy child. Always whining, so desperate for attention." She swallowed what remained of her gin and tonic. "I suppose some things never change."

"Fuck off. I have the right to tell the truth about my life."

Camila's retort died at her back. She had years of practice in deflecting her mother's barbs, though she was not as immune to them as she wished to be.

In the airplane's small bathroom, she splashed water on her face, staring at herself in the mirror. People liked to say she resembled Seth, which was mostly true, but she always feared how much of Camila lurked under the surface. She didn't want to become the angry, bitter woman sharing the plane, but at twenty-four, had the prospect already been set in motion?

She returned to her seat, intent on passing the time with a book until she fell asleep. Hopefully Camila would continue to down gin and tonics and drift off, too. They were safe together only when they were unconscious.

Her mother obviously had other ideas. With a refilled glass, she allowed Conner less than half an hour of peace.

"Do you know what your problem is?"

Conner groaned as she put her book down. She should have gone with a movie. "If I say yes, will you let it go?"

"That's precisely your problem. You don't let anything go. You're an adult, Conner. Whatever you think that you lacked as a child—never mind that we gave you anything you ever asked for—whatever mistreatment you think you suffered as a teenager, just grow up and move on."

The sputtering that emerged from Conner's indignant mouth resembled no sound ever heard on Earth, although it might have been capable of summoning distant aliens. Regardless, it did nothing to deter her mother.

"Do you see me going around talking about how much my mother neglected me?"

"Well, she just died, so that would be a bad look on your part."

Camila's mouth opened before slamming shut so hard Conner swore she heard her teeth clack. Her jaw worked several times as if she were literally swallowing her words. Conner's shoulders tensed as she prepared for the assault. She knew from experience that Camila's fury could flog her far worse than a belt or a hand could.

An eternity passed before Camila spoke. Her voice emerged distant and quiet, and Conner tensed further. "I would've thought you'd be more upset about this. She always preferred you to me."

What a strange way to describe their relationship. Conner picked at the remains of chocotorta, her favorite dessert, on her plate. She bought some from a restaurant in Pasadena every year for Abuelita's birthday. Well, she used to.

"People say it's normal for grandparents to treat their grandchildren differently from their children," she replied, treading with care.

"I barely knew my grandparents. For all you think your father and I failed you, at least we didn't keep you from your family."

Except the sister I didn't know I had.

Conner tried to remember one of the prayers from Mass. At this point, she was willing to give anything a shot to keep from losing her temper. "Sorry to say you'll never find out about grandparents. I'm not having children."

"A rare good call on your part."

Even God couldn't have kept her mouth shut. "What the hell is that supposed to mean?"

"Being a parent isn't for the selfish." The ice in Camila's glass rattled. The truth often hurt more than lies. "You would know."

"Yes. I would."

God, she was insufferable. Mean and self-righteous and petulant and only unbothered precisely when Conner meant to get under her skin.

She tried again. "Abuelita said we come from a line of bad mothers."

Camila made a noise in her throat. "She wasn't wrong about that. She should never have been a mother." She took a sip. "I knew I shouldn't have, but everyone makes mistakes."

Conner bit the inside of her cheek. She didn't care for being referred to as a mistake, but she was used to it. Almost.

Camila stared into the distance. "It's your father's fault. I had already made the appointment. All I had to do was go."

Something inside Conner hardened, a hand slowly clenching her insides. This was new, and it was going to hurt.

"I had done it once already, you know. A year or so before I got pregnant with you. It was easy…only took an hour, and I never said a word."

"Seth's?"

The haughty look her mother sent her was almost enough to make her laugh. "Who else? But he asked why I was sick, and I told him, for some reason. Let's keep it, he said. Let's keep it and we'll get married. We can't have a baby out of wedlock." She laughed. It wasn't funny. "I should've known better. He had never said anything about marriage until then. That Catholic guilt is something, or so I thought. I didn't know about his other kid for years."

"Sadie," Conner whispered.

"What?"

"Sadie. My sister's name is Sadie."

Camila laughed again. Had it always been so bitterly flavored? "Right. Your precious sister." She made the word sound like something she'd found on the floor. "He didn't have so much of a problem with a bastard kid then. But I canceled my appointment, and we got married, and then you came along." She shook her head. "You're right not to want children."

"I know."

"Do you know how much your life changes when you become a mother? That's all anyone sees you as. Forget getting offered any good roles. I went from a leading lady to a background player overnight. I was named the sexiest woman alive a few years before you were born, for Christ's sake, and I couldn't buy a second glance afterward. And your body—your tits sag and you get stretch marks, and you're never desirable again. Your father made sure of that. The goddamn nannies...I guess we got a two-for-one deal: childcare *and* whore. At least he can never deny you. You got his eyes and his appetite."

Conner stood. Her fingernails dug into her palms. "You're calling me a slut? Fuck you, Camila."

She stood, too. In her heels, they were the same height. "No. Fuck you! I didn't want to be a mother. I've always hated being a mother. I'm Camila Morales, goddamn it! I have three Emmy awards and two Golden Globes. I worked all my life to be known as someone other than Isabela Morales's daughter, so imagine how it feels to constantly be referred to as Conner Cody's mother! Everyone, even my own fucking mother, cares more about you."

"Why do you blame ME?" Their shouts were surely heard in the cockpit over the engine. She didn't care. "I didn't ask to be born! And I certainly wouldn't have chosen you!"

"Even your father—"

Conner was either going to laugh, cry, or scream. Maybe all at once. "Seth doesn't give a fuck about me! Don't you dare blame me because you couldn't keep him happy!"

Camila's hand shot up. Conner jerked back, her own arm rising. Her face stung already.

"You don't want to do that."

Their chests heaved. She didn't know what would happen if her mother ignored her warning and slapped her anyway. She didn't want to know.

Finally Camila's hand lowered, infinitesimally but just enough. "If it hadn't been for you, Seth would have left for good a long time ago. I'm tied to him forever, even though I will never have him." Camila's gaze spat vitriol all over Conner. "I should have aborted you when I had the chance."

Conner had to work around the cotton in her mouth before words escaped. "Yes, you should have."

Harlow picked her up at the Van Nuys airport, the blood draining from her face when she took one look at Conner. "What did she do?"

"Take me to Meli's."

"Conner—"

"Now."

She didn't remember the trip to North Hollywood. She was barely aware of her surroundings when she charged up the stairs. By the time she pounded on the door, she was in a cold sweat, ready to claw her own skin off.

Eriq answered, the surprise in his expression blooming into bewilderment. "Conner? What—"

Conner shoved past him. "I need Meli."

She didn't even knock this time, just burst into her room. Meli jumped up from her bed, her forehead creasing.

"Conner?"

She fell into Meli's open arms, her sobs engulfing both of them.

Chapter Twenty-four

At the Hollywood memorial and private burial, Conner spoke exactly once to her mother.

"Don't talk to me."

Camila seemed more than happy to comply. Seth took one look between the pair and shook his scruffy head. Conner had been surprised to see her father and grandmother at Abuelita's funeral, aware no love was lost between them.

"We're here for you, darling girl," Gran said, briefly cupping her cheek. "He's here for her, too, I suppose. God knows why." She nodded toward Conner's parents, who appeared to be in one of their sporadic détentes.

Good. Grand. Fantastic. Great. Terrific. She couldn't have cared less if the devil himself appeared to support Camila. They were welcome to each other.

"I'm also here to fulfill an old debt."

Conner turned her steel glare to Gran. "I know you had some ancient beef with Abuelita you won't tell me about, but did you really come out of spite?"

She patted Conner's cheek again, this time in clear condescension. "Don't be so crass. It's a poor look for you. And the answer is no. Your grandmother and I did not always agree, but she was a worthy opponent, and I always keep my promises. Now stand up straight and lift your chin. Cameras are around."

The memorial passed in a blur. She sang in a fog, completely unaware of her quality, though Gran gave an approving nod. During the string of tributes by a variety of Hollywood legends, which were surely heartfelt although she didn't hear a word, she stared at the crowd through her sunglasses, since Los Angeles had the nerve to be sunny.

Harlow, her assistant, her agent, her publicist, her lawyer, her accountant. All on her payroll. Her damn gynecologist was probably out there somewhere. Kit, sitting with some label execs trying to suck up.

Maggie with Jamal, her mother, Emi, and Bellamy. Vittoria, sitting up front, who had surprised her with her support from the moment she got the call. Asher and Sadie in the very back. And Meli, with Lindsey on one side and Harrison Fisher on the other.

Conner scowled.

After the private burial, she retreated to Malibu, where she had been coerced into allowing Maggie's mother to host dinner. She blinked at the food that covered nearly every surface in her oversized kitchen.

"I made a squash casserole," Bellamy said with an incongruously cheerful smile.

Squash. Casserole. She understood the words but not the meaning, and glancing at the dish, she planned to leave it that way.

"I brought a pie." Harlow arched an eyebrow at Conner. "I'm from the Midwest, after all."

"You're not from California?"

"Correct. I had a life before you barged into it, you know."

Lindsey nudged Bellamy. "And I brought my mama's homemade macaroni and cheese. We're from the South. We grieve with full bellies." She held her arms out to Conner. "Come here, sweetie. How are you?"

"A little nauseated by all this food, to be honest. But thank you."

"You can freeze most of it," said Maggie's mother, the next in line for her hug. She always smelled of Charlie perfume and something extra that Conner associated with homecooked meals and dinner-table conversation.

Before releasing her, Mrs. Jackson kissed her cheek and rubbed her lipstick off with a smile, her signature move. Though she'd given Conner more than a few lectures about her behavior over the years, she always accepted her presence as Maggie's friend for reasons Conner could never determine. She hadn't exactly been a good influence.

"But whether you eat or not, you shouldn't be alone," she said.

Why not? If she wanted to be alone—which she did—she should be left alone. She was a grown woman, and she could grieve however she liked, even if grief wasn't taking the form she'd have guessed. She *was* sad; of course she was. The idea of never seeing Abuelita again made her chest tight and her throat close, and if she dwelled on the unhappy thought, she wanted to throw something. Her death just didn't feel real.

Instead, she kept returning to her mother's words, fighting back a shudder every time they replayed in her head like a reel. Camila Morales was the reason therapists stayed in business. Conner didn't understand why her existence set her mother off so fully. She hadn't asked to be born. She hadn't asked for Camila and Seth as her parents; no sane infant would. She hadn't asked Seth to sniff after every skirt that passed. She hadn't asked for any of it. She'd just gotten away from them as quickly as possible, but apparently she hadn't gone far enough.

"Conner..."

"Huh?"

Even Melina's sympathetic smile grated on her nerves, but she forced herself to return it. She had slept in Meli's bed for three days after returning from Argentina, barely rising to drink or shower, and through it all Meli had just held her and stroked her hair. Their closeness made her ache in an entirely different way than Abuelita's death did.

"I asked if you wanted us to leave. Poor thing, you're a thousand miles away."

Conner shook her head. "Everyone can eat and hang out. It's fine."

"Are you sure?" She leaned into Conner, brushing shaggy locks out of her eyes with clear affection before hugging her tightly. Over her shoulder, Vittoria acknowledged the pair with a knowing tilt of her head, and Conner pulled back.

The day had bloomed into one of the unusually hot days Malibu experienced occasionally, so everyone remained under the air conditioning, rotating between her kitchen and living room. Mrs. Jackson forced a plate into her hands, so she took a bite of macaroni, developed lactose intolerance from the sheer volume of cheese, and abandoned the plate on the dining-room table she never used.

She found a safe haven in the empty den, where she lost herself in her Martin guitar, the first one she'd ever played. Conner usually composed on the piano before moving to other instruments to craft a song, but today she simply closed her eyes and let her fingers roam as they wished.

When she opened them again, she had an audience.

Conner let her hand fall, strumming her guitar pick against her thigh. "What?" Her voice ricocheted off the high ceiling, louder than she'd intended. "What?"

Kit held their hands out in supplication. "Just enjoying the talent. That's all."

"If you want to watch me perform, buy a ticket."

They laughed, although it wasn't a joke. But if they wanted a show... she slid to the piano and began to play. Harsh, furious chords conjured a storm cloud over her head as she struck keys so hard that her fingers hurt. She played and played and played, but nothing could drown out the voice that continued to occupy her mind.

When a hand landed on her shoulder, she nearly snarled. Harlow's impenetrable mask gazed down on her. "I think that's enough for now," she said quietly.

Conner knew, in the deep recesses of her brain, that everyone was here because, on some level, they cared about her. Or, at least, they cared about what she could do for them. Harlow, Kit, and the band relied on her for income. Mrs. Jackson viewed her as a charity case. Sadie felt guilt over their lack of a relationship during Conner's troubled years, and Asher was here for Sadie. Lindsey and Vittoria desired her ability to give them endless orgasms. And Melina…

She hadn't figured her out yet, but something was there. She probably wanted Conner to launch her career. Hadn't she mentioned a few weeks ago how much her follower count on social media had risen since they'd attended the Grammys together?

A persistent buzzing in her ears whispered that she was being unfair, but she brushed it off. Everyone always revealed themselves eventually, so they might as well skip the games. She was growing weary of them. That was one thing she had to give her mother, she mused, burning with resentment. At least Camila never hid how she felt about her. She had always suspected her mother hated her, and now she knew. It was good. Out in the air. Bandage ripped off. Abuelita would have been so pleased that they'd finally talked openly.

The words burst out like water in a lake with a faulty dam. "Everyone needs to go. Get out." She stood, whirling around. "Why are you all standing there? I said leave! Get the fuck out of my house! Just go, just go, just go, and leave me alone!" Her voice rose until it crashed into the rafters, and everyone but Harlow and Maggie flinched.

Melina tried to say something, but Maggie stopped her. She knew. She was Conner's best friend, whatever that meant, and she knew when to leave.

By the time Conner's house emptied out, her jaw hurt from clenching it. Or she thought they'd left, until she stalked through the foyer and crashed into Sadie.

"What part of 'get out' didn't you understand?"

Sadie pursed her mouth. "I understood all of it, and I'm going. Asher's waiting in the car. I just wanted to say that I'll be here when you need someone."

"I made it twenty-three years without you in my life. I'll be fine."

"You know…" Sadie sighed. "Someday you'll realize that I'm just trying to love you."

Conner turned her head, feeling like the words had struck her cheek. "Someday you'll realize it's not worth it."

She didn't wait to see if Sadie left. Conner shut herself in her theater room, cued up Abuelita's films, and curled up under the thickest blanket she could find.

Chapter Twenty-five

In later years, Conner referred to it as the summer that wouldn't end. And not in a "lazy-hazy-crazy days" kind of way.

With a week to go before she departed for Europe, performing at a festival in the Netherlands the night before she was due in Berlin, she was packing once again, but this time it was for cooler weather with less-desirable company. Her Texas weekend had been replaced by the Argentina trip, although she'd insisted Meli still use the ticket.

"You'll just have to meet my family another time," Meli had said, refusing to leave until Conner promised.

She had spent the last few days alone at home, ignoring most of her texts and phone calls. When her phone vibrated once more, she gave up trying to remember how many shoes she had fit into her largest suitcase the last time she filmed abroad. The pool beckoned.

A glass of mezcal in her hand, she floated on a lounger, both feet trailing in the cool water as she admired the sky in those ethereal minutes post-sunset. Waves crashed on the beach below. Moments like this made it easy to forget everything else. Conner liked to forget.

She relaxed, stretching to the tips of her toes as she took a long sip. She could stay like this for hours if she let herself, ignoring her troubles. She might even fall—

The door from her kitchen opened. She screamed and flailed, losing her drink as she plunged into the water. For a split second she wondered if the water was safer than an intruder, but the need for oxygen won out, and she emerged, coughing and sputtering, to find Maggie squatting at the edge of the pool.

"Thank God you're not drowning. This shirt is dry-clean only."

Wiping water from her eyes, scowling, Conner splashed water toward her. Maggie squealed and jumped back.

"You bitch!"

"Me? Jesus, Mags, have you ever heard of knocking?"

"I haven't knocked in years. Didn't your gate guard tell you I was coming?"

"My phone is upstairs."

Maggie waited as Conner hoisted herself out of the pool. Wringing out her short hair, she squinted at the water, finally shrugging when she spotted her empty glass at the bottom. A problem for the pool guy.

She took her time drying off, unsure about this visit. Maggie hadn't been exempt from Conner's isolation. She'd spoken only to Sadie, briefly, giving in to her guilt over kicking her out after Abuelita's funeral.

Conner's longest relationship was with solitude. Growing up on a set with no siblings and no cousins on the same continent hadn't created an environment for organic friendships, and her parents didn't know what playdates were. By age ten her nannies were gone, and she didn't attend a physical school until age twelve. When her back was against the wall, she sought the comfort and familiarity that only seclusion provided.

The sole exception had been running to Meli after her confrontation with Camila, a craving so strong she'd felt as if she were an avatar under the control of another, and she feared too much introspection into those three days. She feared many things relating to Meli.

But Meli was a concern for another day. Right now, she had to deal with Maggie, who had apparently decided, not for the first time, that Conner's alone time had reached an unhealthy level. Maybe she was correct—likely she was correct—but Conner had the right to decide that for herself. She wrapped the towel around her body, preparing to tell her just that, when her annoyance morphed into confusion.

She was nowhere to be seen.

The annoyance roared back to life. The stress and pain had only just begun to ease from her shoulders when she was flung into the water by Maggie's abrupt arrival, and now she had the impudence to disappear.

Conner squared her shoulders, the tight set of her jaw promising nothing good for her friend. She marched into the kitchen. No Maggie. The den. No Maggie. Finally, the darkened living room, where they rarely spent time unless she had a large gathering. There she found her, sitting on the couch with her knees to her chest. Conner's annoyance dissipated as she watched her, concern pooling in her stomach.

"What's going on, Mags?"

Two words. Life-changing. "I'm pregnant."

The air left Conner's lungs in a whoosh as she dropped onto the nearest chair. Her gut roiled until she reminded herself that Maggie was pregnant, not her. For some people, this was good news, albeit good news that could derail the future of her band.

But the band wasn't important right now. After taking a moment to chase down her voice and swallowing hard, once, then twice, she moved next to Maggie.

"So, are we happy about this?"

She answered without words, and the conflict swirling in her dark eyes was a shard to Conner's heart. She slid closer, wrapping an arm around Maggie's tense shoulders.

"Okay. Um. What do you—"

"I'm getting an abortion."

Conner's fragile emotions flinched at the term, such a recent source of pain for her. But wasn't Maggie doing what Camila should have done a quarter of a century ago? If she and Jamal truly didn't want a baby right now, then they were saving a child, and themselves, from a lifetime of hurt. Conner would know. But Jamal—

"Is Jamal taking you?"

This time Maggie didn't meet her gaze. She picked at one of her fingernails for several moments before answering. "He's on a trip with his brothers, and he doesn't know."

"Oh." Conner urged herself to tread with care. "Are you planning to tell him?"

"My body, my choice, remember?"

If Conner had been a turtle, she would have pulled her head back into her shell to avoid getting it snapped off. Since she wasn't, she just tried again. "I agree. You know that. I just wondered because he's going to find out someday, and he—"

"He's only going to find out if you tell him, and you're not going to tell him." Her glare drilled into Conner. "Are you?"

"Of course not. It's not my business."

"Exactly."

"So you're never...?"

Maggie dropped her face into her hands, elbows on her knees. Conner rubbed her back. "I can't tell him. He would want to keep it, and I—I can't."

Conner opened her mouth, then shut it, and opened it, then shut it. She had so many questions yet was entitled to none of the answers. But she could be supportive. She had been there when Maggie's father died, and when her high school boyfriend dumped her, and that really awful haircut at nineteen. Conner was totally supportive.

Harlow got Maggie into Conner's extremely discreet gynecologist with her usual efficiency, and it was all over and done in a matter of days. Despite Maggie's protestations, Conner insisted that she stay over until Jamal returned.

Maggie spoke of the abortion only once. "Swear to me that we'll never discuss this day again."

She shouldn't. Even Conner knew that keeping issues locked inside invited trouble. But to say so would make her a hypocrite, and Maggie wouldn't listen to her anyway.

"I promise, babe."

The band went their separate ways for the fall—Maggie to Asia, part of the backing band for the tour of a young K-pop star; Bellamy giving lessons back home in Georgia; and Emi in LA, working as a studio musician. All waiting on Conner to write their second album. Not that it was a great priority for her in Berlin, where she found plenty of distractions.

"Oh, *God*!"

The woman's arched back collapsed to the leather couch. Conner rolled onto her elbow, wiping her smug grin on her shoulder.

"How in the world did you do that?"

"I pay attention." Conner walked her fingers up the woman's soft stomach before tweaking one of her puckered nipples, laughing at the squeak she provoked. Before she could see what else she could provoke, a knock rattled the flimsy door of Conner's trailer.

"Ah, shit. Give me five minutes!" She returned to her guest with a forced smile. "Back to work, I suppose."

The woman dressed, although Conner didn't bother with anything more than a robe. She wasn't due in makeup for another hour, and she needed to shower. After sending her on her way with a kiss and a promise for more tomorrow, she was filling a glass of water when the knock returned.

"I don't suppose you know anything about that woman limping away from your trailer?" her costar asked upon entering, making himself at home.

Conner smirked. "I know many things, like that she works in Craft Services and she's a big fan of my talents."

"It didn't take you long to get back on the saddle...or the German. What do you have against American women, anyway?"

She sat across from him. She'd met Teddy Maguire three movies ago, her partner in saving the world one alien bad guy at a time. Their characters' will-they, won't-they flirtation was due to come to fruition the day after tomorrow in a steamy make-out session, but off-screen they were more like partners in partying.

"What's that supposed to mean? I appreciate all women equally."

"Well, word is you were hot and heavy again with a certain Italian supermodel until very recently."

She scrunched her nose. "Whatever. Ancient history as far as I'm concerned."

"We'll see."

As much as she liked Teddy, she wanted to wipe the knowing smirk right off his chiseled face. "You will see. I'm telling you we're done for good."

He held up his hands in supplication. "Down, girl. I believe you. At any rate you bounced back quickly in a number of ways. I figured I'd be walking into a tempest in here."

"A tempest? Because I dumped Vittoria? Please."

"More like Lola, but pick your poison, I guess."

"Lola? Went-on-tour-with-me Lola?" She scoffed. "Why in the world would I devote any brain cells to her?"

He stared, and the inklings of unease stirred in her chest. "You really don't know?"

She set her water down so hard it sloshed over the top, splashing the faux granite. "Teddy, I'm gonna give you one chance to explain, because you've been cryptic since you walked in."

His cheeks puffed up before he blew his breath out in a heave. "You better check your phone. Your girl Lola just came out with a new song, and, uh, you're not going to like it."

Conner found her phone under a heap of clothing. When she took it off Do Not Disturb mode, it exploded with notifications that she ignored, instead searching for said song.

Three minutes later, she clenched her phone so hard, she was surprised the plastic case didn't crack.

"Teddy, you better find someone else to fill my costume, because I'm going to kill her."

"What the hell do I pay you for?"

"Not the impossible."

It was a good thing a screen, an ocean, and a continent separated Conner from Harlow. Otherwise she might have been tempted to strangle her.

"Nothing is impossible if you have enough money. Maybe I should find someone who can do what I ask."

One of Harlow's perfectly sculpted eyebrows inched up. "You can throw more money at people and find someone who will tell you whatever you want to hear, but you'll never find anyone who does half of what I do for you."

"Yet you can't make some stupid song go away."

"So stupid you're sweating over it?"

Conner ground her teeth. "I'm not sweating."

"Then why are you yelling at me to make your lawyer find some nonexistent precedent on which to force her to issue a retraction?"

"I'm not yelling!" She moderated her tone. "I'm not. I just don't understand how she can run her mouth about how terrible a person I am, and your only advice is to not comment on it?"

"Conner, I'm a lawyer, too, in case you forgot. You have no case for defamation here. She's not saying anything you haven't said about your parents or Britt Boyd, both of whom you actually named. She's only insinuated."

Conner's outrage grew until it threatened to burst the seams of her trailer. She was forced to take several deep breaths before she could form a word.

"How dare you! I'm nothing like her. I would never do something like she did. Ever. The fact that you would even think of comparing—"

"I wasn't comparing you with her. Calm down." Her words, more order than request, did nothing to help Conner's temper. "If you would think clearly for two seconds, you'll realize that I've always had your back. All I'm saying is that you know what it's like to write a song about a subject who doesn't appreciate it, but your dislike does not equal a lawsuit. Just accept it, ignore it, and it will die down. God knows someone else is always creating controversy in this town."

Conner folded her arms and slouched in her seat. She wasn't Camila, she wasn't Seth, and she sure as hell wasn't Britt. It was one thing for Lola to live in some delusional realm in her own head; it was quite another to present those delusions to the real world as fact. Conner had enough people who didn't take her seriously, who believed she was just another troubled child star turned screwed-up adult, who drooled over every salacious bit of rumor.

She let her head fall onto the back of the couch, shoving her hands into her unruly hair. She never had taken that shower. "It just makes me sound like a—like a—"

"Like a woman who sleeps around without a care for the trail of destruction she leaves behind?"

Her head snapped up in astonishment before her chin slowly slunk to her chest. She felt like somebody had stolen the wind right out of her. "Is that what you think of me?"

Her dread grew as Harlow took her time answering. She had known her longer and better than anyone else besides Maggie. If even she thought Conner was a piece of shit…

"I think you believe that if you put up barriers and tell people not to get attached, then you're safe from repercussions. But while you might be protected, others aren't. An NDA doesn't regulate emotions."

"But I told her it was a one-time thing! I told her it didn't mean anything."

Harlow tilted her head. "Managing expectations is excellent in theory. In practice, it's not always realistic. Otherwise, you would have stopped getting hurt by your parents a decade ago."

Conner's fury roared up from the back burner on which it had been simmering. "Fuck you, Harlow. What the hell do you know, anyway? You're a fucking robot."

She wanted to reach through the screen and shake her. Anything to get a reaction. Whatever it took to crack her blank expression.

"If that's how you feel—"

"It's just what I said, isn't it? For fuck's sake, won't someone take me at face value?"

"Fine." Her clipped words were the closest she'd ever come to snapping at Conner. "I've bent over backwards for you for a decade, and I thought we—never mind. If I'm no longer satisfying your needs as your manager, then perhaps you should do as you say and pay someone else more money."

"Maybe I should." She glared hard enough for both of them.

"One last piece of professional advice, then, while I'm still on your payroll: grow up, Conner."

The screen went blank.

Chapter Twenty-six

Except for the ever-loyal Sarah, Conner couldn't buy sympathy. Sadie informed her that Sarah had promptly trashed her signed poster of Lola when the song came out.

"She insisted that you would never treat someone like that, and Lola must be lying." Sadie chuckled. "Then, of course, she told us how she never really liked Lola or her music all along."

Conner smiled. Sweet kid. It would be a shame once she figured out what kind of person Conner really was. "At least someone out there gives me some credit."

"Hey. Who said I believed her? I just wasn't as dramatic as my teenager."

"Well, thanks."

"Can't you do anything?"

"Not according to my manager." Conner's smile turned into a scowl at the thought of Harlow. They hadn't spoken once since their falling-out. Well, good riddance. Talent managers were a dime a dozen in Hollywood, and a hundred would salivate at the thought of representing Conner Cody. "Everyone advises me not to comment, but it's so frustrating. I didn't do anything to her except boost her record sales." Well, that and a few orgasms, but Sadie didn't need to know that. One night did not equal a tour-long relationship.

"That stinks. She's probably right, though. It'll die down. It always has before, right?"

Right. Because courting controversy was Conner's thing. No wonder everyone believed Lola.

She stomped around on set for days, daring anyone to say a word to her. Her fight scenes were never better as she poured her aggression into her character. Lyss was a badass, a half-human, half-alien assassin who had finally come to terms with her heritage and would confront her mentor in this film after unveiling his betrayal. At the moment, Conner felt like she could easily work with that.

"I trusted you. I told you everything!"

"And you're helping to save the world, my dear, even if it isn't the world you envisioned." He rested his hands on the arm of the chair she was bound to, leaning close enough she could smell his minty breath. She appreciated the mouthwash. "I never would have gotten this far without you."

She spat in his face.

It wasn't in the script. They'd never rehearsed that way, and all previous takes had her in stony silence. She had no logic for her decision other than it felt right at the time.

For some reason the director didn't cut the scene. The actor playing her mentor blinked, wiped the spittle off with his sleeve, and sneered. "You're going to regret that," he said softly before raising his voice. "I truly had higher hopes for you."

The scene went back on track, and when they were finished, Conner rushed to his side. "I'm so sorry. I have no idea what came over me."

"It's quite all right. It was a good call, although some warning would have been nice."

The director walked up. "He's right. Lyss isn't known for being stoic. I liked it, Conner. We'll keep it in."

Standing off to one side, her party-partner Teddy pretended to wipe his face down, and Conner flipped him off. In the distance she saw the woman from Craft Services, who had ended their fling as quickly as it began with some lame excuse about staying professional. Only Conner's ego was hurt.

When a day off arrived, she dragged Teddy out an hour after they finished their last scene. They went to a gay bar in Schöneberg, escaping the press camped out around their Bebelplatz hotel via a private parking garage.

"What's your plan if you pull?" she asked Teddy, brushing lint off his shoulder.

"Go back to his place, I suppose. I'm not trying to sneak someone out from under the nose of the entire cast."

"Ugh, Teddy. That's so dangerous."

He cocked his head at her. "Oh? And what's your plan?"

"To get happily drunk without speaking to a single woman. This shop is closed. No room for anymore crazy."

He blew a raspberry right in her face. Conner made a show of wiping her cheek in disgust. "I got a hundred bucks that says you have your hands up some fraulein's skirt in the bathroom before I'm done with my drink."

"The bathroom? Please. I have standards."

"That didn't stop you at the People's Choice Awards."

Her mouth dropped in outrage as she held a hand over her chest. "Teddy! Have some respect. It was the SAG Awards. Get it right."

He laughed, and Conner's mood improved enough for her to smile as their banter continued until the taxi pulled up outside the bar. The place was packed, but a flash of Conner's ID got them hustled inside to a clean booth and glasses full of liquor before she could say "famous."

The crowd leaned far more toward Teddy's tastes than Conner's, but that was fine with her. She had meant what she said in the taxi. She was done with women, at least until Lola faded into obscurity.

Despite his professed intentions, Teddy hung around once they got drinks.

"What are you doing? Plenty of cute guys here." She waved a careless hand.

"I don't know if I should leave you alone. I kinda feel bad."

Conner rolled her eyes. "Nothing is going to happen to me. I doubt anyone even recognizes me, and if they do, it'll be fine." When he didn't respond, she leaned forward, pressing her abdomen against the tabletop. "Go talk to someone. You're relatively anonymous here, so have fun. Meet someone crazy."

He cracked a grin. "The crazy ones are the best in bed, but you would be the expert on that subject."

Conner squinted at him. "Not sure if you're criticizing the amount or the quality of the women I sleep with."

"Con, there's an entire song currently blowing up the internet that suggests it's the quality."

"Oh my God, fuck all the way off." Conner groaned, dropping her head to the table with a thud. "Ouch."

Eventually he drifted away, and Conner was left alone. She kept her back to the bar, so she wasn't spotted or bothered, just as she wanted. Though she'd encouraged Teddy in his pursuit, she couldn't ignore a twinge of abandonment. She stared at her empty glass, annoyed with herself. Why was she like this? One of the most privileged people on the planet, yet she was never satisfied. She wanted to bang her head on the table again, but the producers probably wouldn't appreciate their female lead showing up with a concussion.

As she circled the rim of her glass with her index finger, a shadow fell over the table. "You're either a very fast worker, or you have no game at all."

"Perhaps I am simply bringing you a drink."

Conner stiffened before relaxing. Just a bartender. "Sorry, and thanks. I wasn't aware you provided table service."

"We don't, but when I have Conner Cody in my bar, I must do the most, no?"

Conner dipped her head. "You don't, but I appreciate that."

"You are alone?" She gestured at Teddy's vacated seat. "May I sit?"

No. Don't do it. Stop entertaining strange women. "Sure. Why not?"

They eyed each other in relative silence. She was older than Conner, though not yet middle-aged, with slicked-back black hair about the same length as Conner's recently trimmed locks, hovering around her chin. Warm, intelligent green eyes regarded her, the laugh lines around them suggesting a friendly nature.

"I have a question or something," Conner said eventually. When the bartender nodded, she went on. "Forgive me for making an assumption, but you don't appear to be who I would expect to find working at this bar."

"Because I am a woman?"

"I assumed, but if I'm wrong, I'm very sorry."

She smiled, revealing a deep dimple. "Don't be. You are right, and yes, it is unusual, but I am one of the owners. I like to see what is happening."

"And your bouncer told you tonight would be a good night for that?" When her companion tilted her head with a furrowed brow, Conner clarified. "The man checking IDs at the door. We call them bouncers."

"Ach. Yes, he did mention something. Someone, perhaps. But only to me. We are very discreet, or we would not be in business."

Conner didn't let her attention drift Teddy's way, not wanting to draw attention regardless of how discreet they were. "That's good to know."

"I could tell you the same thing."

"Good to know?"

Uh-oh, they were flirting now, just a little. "Yes, good to know," she replied with a chuckle. "But also, it is unusual to see someone like you, with your tastes, in my bar."

Conner's smile was laced with vinegar. "Sometimes it's nice to be left alone. No, no. I didn't mean you," she said in a rush when the woman began to stand. "I just meant a different kind of attention. You might have heard I'm a cold-hearted bitch who sleeps around."

"Are you?"

Conner nearly drenched the owner with her own product, managing to swallow it all before giving in to her coughing fit. "Wow. You don't mince words. Um, probably? Yes. I can definitely be a bitch, I've been told I'm cold before, and what can I say? I enjoy the company of women, and they enjoy me."

"I am sure that they do." Definitely flirting, but still light, almost unintentional. "So why are you angry about it if it is true?"

"Who said I was angry?"

"Your voice."

Conner stretched her neck before deciding to answer. "Just because individual facts are accurate doesn't mean the story is true. Let me give you a hypothetical. Say you and I go home together tonight, and I tell you before anything happens that it's only one night, it doesn't mean anything, don't read into it. If I give you all the warnings, and you still get your feelings hurt the next day, who is to blame?"

"You very much want me to say that I would be to blame, yes?"

"You don't agree?" She was nearly ready to give up on women entirely.

"Nobody can prevent feelings from occurring, even a cold-hearted bitch." Conner knew that much was true. If she could, she'd stop having dreams about gap-toothed actresses who texted her every single morning from their bed in LA. "Did this person give you a reason to believe you might not agree on what the night meant?"

Conner wiggled her foot under the table. She scratched her nose. With one of her hands, she tapped a beat on the sticky table. No matter what she did, she couldn't ignore the truth. "Maybe. A little."

"There can be two truths, you know."

She let Conner finish her drink in silence. What was the truth? Conner was a cold-hearted bitch who slept around, yes. Lola was a borderline obsessed psycho, also yes. Lola was well off the mark and over the line in her song, yes. Conner had led her on and played with her heart…no. She couldn't see the truth in that part. Sleeping with Lola had been a terrible idea from the start, but she had been blatantly clear to the point of rudeness about what that night was and what it wasn't. Afterward, she had gone beyond clear in her disinterest.

As she played with her emptied glass, the woman spoke again. "You and I going home together tonight, that was a story, yes? A fake?"

Conner nodded, the corner of her mouth pulling in a reluctant grin.

"Would you like to make it true?"

She laughed softly. "I would like to, but I'm trying to behave. For now. But thank you."

"I understand. When you finish your filming and your behaving, you come back to my bar, and perhaps we will make a different story."

"I just might do that."

"And tonight, your drinks are free of charge."

"That's kind but unnecessary."

"Conner Cody comes into my bar and rejects me, but at least I can say I bought her a drink."

Conner laughed again. How refreshing this exchange was! It reminded her of Meli's persistently upbeat presence, in a way. Then she faltered. She had talked to Meli very little since the song came out, and neither had brought it up, conspicuous in its absence. She wasn't sure she could bear hearing that the illusions Meli carried about Conner's character had been finally shattered. Maybe the timing was for the best. She'd be gone for months, and when she returned to LA, they could go back to their own circles. Meli would be fine; she would always draw people to her like a friendly little lamp to fireflies. And Conner would, someday, stop wanting to tangle her hands in Meli's messy curls.

When Conner's bodyguard came by to check on her, the bar's owner offered her a drink on the house.

"Thank you, but I'm on duty tonight, after all. Gotta keep this one out of trouble." She jerked her head at Conner, who rolled her eyes.

"Yeah. We know I can't make my own decisions. I'm ready to go, anyway."

"Thank you for choosing my bar, Conner Cody. You will remember what I said about making a different story after your movie is finished, yes?"

(Spoiler alert: they did.)

Teddy ended up getting lucky that night, so after extracting multiple promises to be safe, Conner left him and stepped outside to meet their taxi.

A pack of paparazzi awaited them, launching a verbal assault at Conner in English, German, and various combinations as soon as she stepped outside.

She cursed too loudly. Someone in the bar must have spotted her and blasted it on social media. At least Teddy wasn't with her. His closet was hanging on for dear life as it was.

"Conner! Have you spoken to Lola?"

"Over here! Conner! What do you have to say about the song?"

"How do you feel about being the subject of a song like you wrote about Britt Boyd?"

She gritted her teeth while her bodyguard pulled her along, one strong arm over her shoulders, brushing the paparazzi aside with the other with little care for their comfort.

"Surely you have something to say. Come on!"

"Hey, Conner! What are you doing at a gay bar?"

"Conner, have you heard the rumors about Lola and Vittoria?"

She faltered at that question before ducking into the waiting car. Flashes continued to bombard them as they drove off, causing spots in her eyes long after they left the cameras behind.

Conner rubbed her temple. One night. All she had wanted was one night away from bullshit. Times like this made her consider if it was all truly worth it. She didn't need the money, and while the adoration could be gratifying at times, it was fleeting, halfway based on her physical attraction and dependent on constant production.

But the pride she felt when landing a role she worked so hard for, the rush of sinking her teeth into a character and bringing it to life, the therapy of writing songs and creating a coherent story of an album, and, above all, the intense thrill when someone told her one of her movies or songs had affected them—that was when she knew she was doing what she was meant to do. For better or worse, Conner was an entertainer.

Right now was definitely the worse side of the equation. She desperately needed to be alone. Only then could she find some equilibrium and abolish the rage that filled her as Lola's lies continued to spread like a novel virus.

Back at the hotel, she ran the hottest bath she could stand and lingered until her skin was pink and pruned. Then she gave in to curiosity and opened an internet search.

Neither Lola nor Vittoria had outright confirmed anything, although both had issued coy statements with just enough ambiguity to indicate they were definitely together, or at least wanted people to think so. Knowing both of them, Conner guessed the former. An obviously staged photo of the pair mid-embrace on some beach flamed the gossip.

Good riddance. They deserved each other, and Conner couldn't have cared less except she was the obvious connection—was, in fact, the reason they met—and this was yet another excuse for paparazzi to bother her.

She fired off a request for a call to the band's group chat, took a gummy, and eventually fell into a restless sleep.

"Is it true?"

Conner's eyes narrowed to slits as she stared at the image of her best friend in one corner of her tablet. "I can't believe you're actually asking me that."

"It's a fair question." Maggie examined her cuticles. "You've made some questionable choices in who you sleep with, Con. Be honest."

"Like you've always had spectacular taste," she muttered rebelliously. "Remember the gamer from UCLA? I'm surprised he hasn't been on *Dateline* yet."

"This isn't about me. It's about you and whether you banged the crazy chick. So, did you?"

When she paused, all three of them groaned in unison. Conner let her head fall back, knowing she was in for it now and resigned to her fate.

"It was one time!" she said, over their grousing. "After the Boston show. Not a tour-long affair like she's saying, and certainly not any leading on or breaking of hearts. I was really fucking honest that it was one night only. I was with Vittoria for the entire second half of the tour!"

None of them appeared to be moved. Emi shook her head, dark eyes narrowed in obvious judgment. "What the hell were you thinking? You really could have screwed up the tour."

"But I didn't, did I? She didn't harass any of you. She didn't spread lies about you. She didn't write an entire song about how you wronged her. She didn't start dating your ex because she has some sort of weird obsession with you." The last one was a little bit of conjecture, but she was sure she wasn't far off the mark.

When Bellamy, normally her last line of defense, opened her mouth, Conner understood just how pissed they were. "But it could have. Come on, Conner. What if she had left? What if she'd publicized her version—I know she's lying, calm down—what if she had done that during the tour? It really could have hurt ticket sales. You don't need the money, but we do. You know that."

She did know, especially in Bellamy's case. Guilt warred with anger in Conner's heart. She just wanted one person always on her side. One moment of unconditional support. There had to be somebody in this world she wasn't going to let down.

When she looked up again, Bellamy and Emi continued to stare at her with downturned expressions, while Maggie fiddled with something off-camera.

"What do you want me to say? 'I'm sorry. I'll never sleep with Lola again'? Done."

"How about 'I accept that my actions can have unintended consequences, and I will consider how they may affect myself and others in the future.' Sound good?"

She folded her arms. "Sounds condescending as fuck, but sure, fine, whatever you say, Mags. You know, I don't need another mo—" She caught herself just in time.

"You don't need another what?" Maggie's voice was quiet, barely above a whisper. Dangerously soft.

"Nothing."

"You were going to say something. What is it?"

Conner's eyes bored a hole into Maggie, who still wouldn't look up. Finally she said, "Monitor. I don't need another monitor."

"Right. A monitor."

"Maggie, I didn't…"

While Bellamy and Emi held their own conversation trying to figure out what they were talking about, Conner silently pleaded with Maggie to meet her gaze. To say something. To be her best friend and realize Conner hadn't meant to allude to the event they were never going to mention.

She gave up. "I'm sorry that I've disappointed you once again." She disconnected while Emi was mid-sentence.

Rolling onto her back, she glowered at the white ceiling of her hotel. Then she grabbed her phone and dialed Maggie. No answer. She dialed again, and it went straight to voicemail. Her phone landed with a telltale crunch somewhere near the bathroom.

"Well, fuck."

Chapter Twenty-seven

Conner never put much stock in the holiday season. Her only experience trick-or-treating at Halloween was an episode of television when she was eight. Thanksgivings were nonexistent. And though Christmas meant presents, it sometimes meant presents opened with only her nanny and presents Seth forgot to bring on their trips to Ireland and presents her parents never bothered to open.

As a teenager she had hardened herself, which worked great until this year when her wounded feelings leaked all over the place. Now at Halloween she was struck with sadness when Sadie texted her a picture of the girls all dressed up, and at Thanksgiving she burned with envy as Meli rambled on joyfully about her Friendsgiving celebration, and at Christmas she was consumed with loneliness despite being with family.

She spent the last two weeks of the year at Belfast, partially out of habit and partially out of a desire to see her remaining grandparents, flawed though they were. Christmases with Abuelita had been rare, but for some reason Conner missed her more than ever. She wanted to eat empanadas and see Abuelita's eyes light up when she spoke Spanish and listen to Old Hollywood gossip.

"You look exhausted, darling girl," Gran said in greeting. "Long hours on set, or long nights?"

"Long nights on set, for the record. Much of the film takes place after dark, so no one's going to be able to see a damn thing in theaters."

"One of the benefits of being onstage is that lighting remains an art."

"Maybe I should give the stage a try," Conner said as casually as possible.

Gran studied her. "You're my grandchild. There's no reason you could not, although not this iteration of you."

"This iteration?" Conner jutted her chin out.

"Yes, this iteration. No need to be cross when it's the truth. Stage acting is a different skill set, one that you do not currently possess. But with practice, I've no doubt that you would do just fine."

Conner took a deep breath and swallowed, not quite willing to admit her deepest wishes just yet. "Thanks, Gran. That's—"

"Besides, you already made your stage debut."

"I did what?" She was not prepared to deal with Gran's mind starting to wander.

Her grandmother leveled her with a stern expression. Conner straightened. "I brought you onstage with me for the summer run of *Annie* when you were just a wain. You were in the chorus. Don't tell me you forgot. The things I had—well, it's a good thing the director owed me a few favors."

Oh, good God. Conner could read between the lines, and if her grandmother started reminiscing about her affairs, she was staying at the Hilton. She could only stand one oversharing Cody at a time.

And speak of the devil himself, there he came, strolling in with a whistle, rakish as always.

"Happy Christmas, kid. Did you bring your drama with you or leave it on the Continent?"

Her father, ladies and gentlemen. A version of Conner in an alternate universe probably explored her daddy issues through a string of disappointing men instead of being a lesbian. She shuddered.

"Fuck off, please, Seth."

Gran picked up the spoon she was stirring her tea with and waved it in her direction. Conner winced as droplets of boiling liquid struck her hand. "So disrespectful, the pair of you. He is your da, Conner, even if not a good one." The comment would have offended many people, but Seth continued to pour liquor into his coffee as if he hadn't heard. "You shouldn't refer to him by his first name."

She couldn't remember deciding to stop calling them Mom and Dad. It had simply happened, a year or two before she was emancipated. Seth and Camila felt right for two people who had never attempted proper parenthood.

"I'm going to lie down," she said instead of arguing. "Call me when it's time for tea."

Halfway up the stairs, Seth called her. Not by name, avoided as much as she avoided his title, but "kid," which he had used as long as she could remember.

"Have you talked to Camila?"

She slowed but forced her suddenly wooden feet to keep moving. "Not since this summer. Why would I bother?"

"I just reckoned—a girl goes through hard times, she needs her ma."

He caught up to her. Apparently she had stopped after all. "My times are just fine, and I wouldn't reach out to her if I had terminal cancer."

"Just fine? Look at the state o' ya. You couldn't stay out of the news if you moved to Tibet."

"I can't control the media, Seth. If you and Camila taught me anything, it was that. Now please excuse me. I'll jump off the balcony if I have one more minute of quality family time."

Curled up in the center of her Tudor bed, she ignored the pricking of her eyes. Let the press circle jerk to her until they ran dry. She didn't care. Not about Lola or Vittoria running their mouths about her, not about Maggie pushing her away, not about Harlow's continued silence, and certainly not about Camila fucking Morales. She didn't care at all.

It didn't occur to her until she was about to drift away that perhaps Seth's bumbling words meant he cared just a bit.

Conner brooded her way through Christmas. If anyone noticed, they didn't remark on it. She brought up her email half a dozen times to draft a formal termination to her contract with Harlow, but no words came. The same held true when she attempted to write a song.

"How's the football?" she asked her grandfather on Boxing Day, dropping into the armchair next to his.

Swigging a beer, he grunted as the crowd roared. She peered at the screen. Liverpool at Chelsea, who had just scored.

"Tied up now. Are we rooting for Chelsea?" Slowly his head turned toward her, with a look like she had just beamed down from an alien ship. She shrugged. "Sorry. Liverpool, then?"

He made some sort of growly noise that she couldn't interpret. Oh, well. She'd tried. With no interest in the game, she departed.

She found Seth in the kitchen, assembling a sausage sandwich. "You want one?" he asked, holding out the bread.

She wrinkled her nose. "Gross. No thanks."

"Your loss." He drizzled ketchup over the sausages, making it even worse.

She snatched the bag of crisps. "But I will take these."

"Hey! Those are my favorite! Give it here."

"Mmm, cheese and onion." She took a second one before allowing him to retrieve the bag. He grumbled under his breath. "You sound just like Granda when you do that."

"He's my da. You can't deny genetics, as much as you try."

She stole another crisp. "What's that supposed to mean?"

"Don't play daft. You know what I mean. You and your ma are icing each other out again, and I'm stuck in the middle."

"What are you talking about?" Conner threw her hands in the air. "I don't get you two. I really don't. You've been separated for years, but you're not divorced. You do nothing but argue when you're together, but you talk enough for you to feel as if you're in the middle."

"It's complicated. Your ma—"

"Is crazy, yeah, I know. Why do you indulge her? Why did you even get married in the first place?"

He rubbed the back of his neck. "I don't know...you know your Gran. She reckons if you get a girl pregnant, you have to marry her. And your other grandmother agreed. So we figured we'd do it and get them off our backs."

Conner absorbed that explanation without any immediate response coming to mind. That certainly wasn't the impression she'd received from Camila. Seth would roll over to avoid conflict, but it was tough to picture Camila giving in so easily, although it provided a convenient excuse to get Seth to comply if she'd actually wanted it. Still, Camila had implied that Seth had persuaded her.

"So you married Camila because Gran and Abuelita forced you?"

"Something like that. I suppose they weren't keen on the idea of bastard grandchildren."

She bit her bottom lip before reminding herself to stop. "But...you already had a kid. You didn't marry Sadie's mother. So what was different?"

He took a large bite of his sandwich while Conner's impatience grew. She grabbed the bag of crisps and ate a handful, glaring as they chewed in unison.

"If I married every woman who claimed I fathered her child, I'd have been in jail for bigamy years ago. It's the price a man pays when he's famous. Be glad no one can accuse you of it."

The crisps sat uneasily in her stomach. She wavered on whether to ask the question before deciding she'd go insane if she didn't. "Are you saying that Sadie isn't yours? Why didn't you take a paternity—"

"I don't have time for all that, do I? You meet a girl on tour, you take her back to your room and have a good time, and you send her on her way." He took a drink, raising his unkempt eyebrows at her over the rim. "Sound familiar?"

She harrumphed, wishing he would just get on with it.

"These women...you know what they're like. Half the time they go from one room to the next. Hell, sometimes we're all in the same room."

"Too much information, Seth. I just want to know: is Sadie yours?"

"You've been in the business too long not to realize that everyone wants a piece of you. Did I take her ma for a ride? Yeah, I reckon I probably did. I don't remember every woman I've fucked. That doesn't make the kid mine. It's real easy to claim that once I've left town."

She let him finish his sandwich in silence, even surrendering the crisps for good. Her appetite had vanished. Believing her parents was always a toss-up; they lied as needed to serve themselves. Seth could be fibbing to make himself look better. He probably was.

But...what if he wasn't? It didn't change how she felt about Sadie and the girls. And it didn't make sense anyway. Sadie had gone out of her way to avoid anything resembling taking her money, and she was as wary of the attention that dogged Conner like a shadow as Conner herself was. She got nothing out of claiming a familial tie except the relationship.

Back in her room much later, after tossing and turning for hours, she pulled up the Halloween picture Sadie had texted. At first it had made her smile and her stomach roil. Hannah was adorable as a mini Princess Arlais, beaming from under a tiara that Conner had sent her from the Berlin premiere of her new animated movie. But while she had Conner's character, Sarah was Conner herself, complete with black boots, ripped jeans, a loose button-down, and, of course, her leather jacket. Sadie had even let her (temporarily) dye her hair brown with electric-pink tips.

She peered at the picture, trying to see any resemblance. When she looked past the costumes, it became murky. Hannah's eyes were the same color, but that didn't mean anything. Their faces weren't the same. Their hair was different. And while Sarah had burgeoning musical talent, that was probably due to Conner's teaching and innate ability as much as anything genetic.

It was hard to look past the costumes, though, especially Sarah. The likeness startled her, but the hero worship freaked her out. She was no role model. Sarah could do better than a heartless, promiscuous loner who let people down at every turn. The sooner everyone realized that, the better.

She glanced at the time. Hopefully not too late in California.

Sadie answered on the third ring with a frown. "Hi, Conner. What are you doing up so late? Or is it early?"

"I couldn't sleep."

"Is everything all right?"

"Yeah. I just..." She couldn't say it. What good would it do? "I really miss you and the girls. I want to come home."

She thought Sadie would laugh at her childish tone, but she didn't. "Oh, sweetie. We miss you, too. Sarah has a countdown on her calendar to the day you're supposed to come back, so if that changes, you have to be the one to tell her."

Conner forced a laugh. If Seth was telling the truth, she would never, ever tell the girls. "Are they still up?" she asked, suddenly desperate to hear their voices.

"Yes, they are, and if you're up for it, they can talk as long as you want. No school anyway, and how often do they get to video-chat with their favorite aunt all the way from Ireland?" She paused, furrowing her brow. "Before I get them, are you sure you're okay? You seem...sad."

"I'm fine. Really."

Conner's stomach flipped for the entire time it took Sarah to appear and grab the phone. She was their aunt. She was their *favorite* aunt. Maybe there could be more to family than blood.

"Aunt Conner!" Sarah grabbed the phone with such vigor that Conner's stomach did an extra roll. "Why aren't you asleep? What time is it there?"

"It's time for me to talk to my nieces. How are you?"

Sarah launched into a rapid-fire recap of the latest middle-school gossip and what resident mean girl Kaylen McGee had said now. That girl really had it coming to her. Conner blinked as she tried to keep up, interjecting words of agreement every so often.

Hannah didn't allow Sarah to monopolize the phone for long, tussling over it until Conner closed her eyes to prevent motion sickness and enforced sharing with a five-minute rule.

"Aunt Conner, when are you coming home?" Hannah asked with a yawn. "Will you be back before soccer starts?"

"I will, and I already have a suite booked for the Angel City FC opener. Do you know anyone who would want to come with me?"

"Me! I would!"

"Oh, good. I thought I would have to go by myself, and where's the fun in that?"

"And can we stay"—her mouth opened in another enormous yawn—"at your house?"

"Kiddo, you can stay all weekend if your mom and dad say yes."

"I'll go ask them!"

And she was off, ignoring both Sarah and Conner's calls that she didn't need to ask immediately.

Sarah shook her head. "She's going to ask about that every single day until it happens. Thanks."

"Hey, you're invited, too. Unless you're too cool to hang out with your sister and aunt now."

"Hannah's annoying, but you're pretty cool."

"I am cool. Thanks for noticing." Their gazes caught, and when she winked, they both laughed. Conner needed that more than she could explain. "What else is new with you?"

"I finished learning 'Wonderwall' but I'm having trouble with 'Zombie.'"

"That's awesome. Are you still hitting the B fret?" Sarah nodded. "That's okay. Just keep working on it, and we'll go over it during our next lesson. You're doing fantastic. I think you'll be ready for your first show by the time I get back."

Sarah's eyes nearly popped out. "No way! I can't play in front of people."

"You play in front of me."

"You're not people. You're my aunt."

If she could bottle the feeling of hearing those words and sell it, she'd double her fortune. "That's right. Well, you should probably go to bed. Thanks for staying up and talking to me. I really, really miss you."

"I really miss you, too. I wish you weren't gone so much."

"Me too, kid. Me too."

They continued to chat despite Conner's attempt to end the conversation, until neither of them could keep their eyelids open, and Asher carried Hannah to bed.

Sarah looked away instead of saying good-bye, so Conner waited until she peeked back again, something she always did when she was uncomfortable.

"I have a question before I go."

"Shoot."

"Um, you know that song that, er, Lola did?"

Conner kept her face neutral. "Yes."

"I guess I was just wondering...why didn't you say anything about it? Like you haven't done any interviews to tell people the truth."

Because the manager I can't seem to completely fire said not to and for some reason I listened. She blew her breath out. "Well, people that I pay to advise me said that it's in my best interests to ignore it. Sometimes when people deny something, it just makes them look guiltier." The sentence stuck in her head, nagging at her, but she couldn't figure out why.

"That doesn't make sense."

"Not really, but it's her word versus mine. Someone has to take the high road, I guess. For the record, it's not true."

"Well, duh," came Sarah's immediate and staunch response. "Obviously."

Conner grinned. "I'm glad you feel that way."

When they finally hung up, Conner flipped her pillow to the cool side and lay down with a sigh. Seth was full of crap. She had a special bond with her nieces, and nobody was going to take that away from her.

CHAPTER TWENTY-EIGHT

Bellamy

Bellamy tugged at her cropped shirt, extremely aware of her bare midriff. She never understood how Conner or anyone else was comfortable in these things. Of course, they were all slender and gorgeous, and she was, well, less so.

She gave up and made her way to the bar, holding her hands over her stomach. There she found Emi, clad in Tommy Hilfiger overalls, nursing a beer.

"Hey, Bells. Having fun?"

"I guess so. I wish I hadn't let Conner dress me."

"You look great."

"I feel…exposed." She pulled on the hem of her shirt again.

"Grab one of Conner's button-downs. They fit the dress code." She chuckled. "I'm pretty sure she chose a nineties theme just so she could dress like she always does."

Bellamy laughed. Probably so. Where was their host? She hadn't seen Conner since she arrived. Though it wasn't unusual for her to disappear upstairs with a female friend or two at some point during her parties, she usually put in more face time than this.

She wasn't the only one missing her. Kit strolled up, looking every bit the part in a Chandler Bing–inspired sweater vest and khaki cargo pants. "Where's Conner?"

"Do we look like her keeper?"

"Well, you—" Bellamy said before Emi smacked her arm. "Ow. No, we don't know where she is."

"If you see her, let her know I'm looking for her." They paced back and forth. "We need to discuss the album."

"What album?" Bellamy asked, wondering what she'd missed. That happened a lot.

Kit's lips thinned in a narrow line. "Exactly. The label is breathing down my neck, and I think she's been avoiding me since she came home."

"It's only been a week."

"I understand, but she's had plenty of time. If she wants this dual life, she needs to keep up her end of the deal. I'm just doing my job."

Emi and Bellamy exchanged a look. This didn't sound good for anyone. Conner hated being backed into a corner, and Kit hated anything requiring patience.

Emi jerked her head, taking one for the team. "I've got some ideas." She slipped her arm through Kit's and pulled them with her. "Let's sit by the pool and talk about them."

She sent a look over her shoulder, and Bellamy's marching orders were clear. She waved at the Australian DJ dancing alone at her deck, passed by a curiously subdued Maggie engrossed in her phone and Jamal laughing with a bunch of guys, circled a group of professional athletes whose fitness made her feel chubbier than ever, and steered clear of the pool house. If Conner was in there, someone else could get her. She wasn't interested in the sordid happenings inside.

On a whim, she went into the kitchen, where she barely made out a faint sound over the music. She traced it to the darkened den, where she finally cornered her host.

"What are you doing in here? Everyone's outside, and Kit's looking for you."

Conner barely lifted her head from the sofa. "They don't need me to party. I provide the location, the drinks, the music, the food, and the places to sleep. My job is done." Her head lowered. "Kit can keep looking. I have no patience for their nagging right now."

Bellamy lifted Conner's feet to slide under them. "I guess that means you haven't written our second album."

With one arm over her eyes, Conner cast about with the other until she landed on one of the dozen dog-eared composition books scattered about the room and waved it in the air. "I have enough songs for three albums."

"What's the problem?"

Conner made an odd sort of gurgling growl in her throat. "I have songs, Bells, but not an album."

She didn't really understand the difference, but that was why Conner was the songwriter, not her. Rubbing Conner's shins through her ripped jeans, she tried a different route.

"What's wrong, honey? I don't understand why you'd throw a party if you're not interested in attending."

Conner's head lolled to one side, and her chest heaved in a sigh. "It's what I'm expected to do. I can't let people down, can I? I sleep around, I complain about my parents, and I throw parties."

Ah. So it was one of those nights. "Right. I'll leave you to it."

"Leave me to what?"

Bellamy waffled. Conner in any mood, but especially this kind of mood, was mercurial at best, and the wrong word could end in sarcastic disaster. Finally she sucked it up. "Don't bite my head off, but sometimes when you're feeling sorry for yourself, you're not very much fun to be around. So if that's what's going on, I'd rather be outside."

Conner shot up, and Bellamy flinched. She was in for it now. But after a moment of silence she peeked through her fingers to find Conner peering at her with a quizzical expression.

"Am I really that bad?"

"Sometimes, yeah."

"Hmm." Conner rolled her bottom lip between her teeth before peeking up at Bellamy, one corner of her mouth quirking up. "Maybe I should join gen pop for a little while. Give me a hand, will you?"

Despite their six-inch height difference, she pulled Conner to her feet, casting a look over her Adidas sneakers, baggy jeans, and crop top similar to Bellamy's, except her jeans were so low-slung that a good inch of her Calvin Klein underwear was visible below her belly-button piercing.

"How are you comfortable in that? Never mind. Don't answer."

"You're not? Why didn't you say something?" Before she could answer, Conner darted toward the stairs. "One sec!" She reappeared in no time at all, thrusting an oversized, white, button-down shirt at Bellamy. "This is more your style. I should have known."

Bellamy quickly pulled it on, grinning once she was fully covered. Much better. Conner fussed about her for a few minutes, rolling the sleeves to her wrists and messing with the collar.

"You know what you really need? Penny loafers. So hot-nineties mom."

"Aw, shucks. You know what? You're not so bad after all."

Conner chuckled. "Is that so? You make it sound like news. Do you think I'm a bad person? Be honest."

Her tone was light, teasing, but it left an aftertaste that made Bellamy slow to a stop and pull away so she could look her friend in the eye. "I'm always honest."

"I know. That's why I'm asking you."

"Oh. You're serious."

Bellamy took her time, thinking all the way back to meeting Conner. She'd enlisted in the military to escape small-town Georgia, which had gotten her all the way to Los Angeles Air Force Base, and she didn't intend to go back. One day after her four-year stint ended, she had been at a local retailer, messing around with a bass guitar she could only dream of affording, when a shadow fell over her, carrying a familiar voice complimenting her playing. Within half an hour, the seeds of a friendship had taken root, along with an invitation to play with Conner's band.

"Yes, you are."

"Took you long enough to answer," Conner said with what sounded like a forced laugh.

"I wanted to be sure." She shrugged. "You can be self-absorbed and controlling, sure, but you have a better heart than you give yourself credit for. Look at everything you've done for me."

Conner slung an arm over her shoulders. "I'd do it all again. I'm good for a few things."

"You're good for more than sex and money, you know."

"Obviously." They emerged into the backyard, and Conner waved her free hand. "Who else would throw such killer parties?"

They settled in chairs near the pool with Melina, Emi, and a few other friends, including Harrison Fisher, Jamal's friend who'd been hanging around since Conner had invited him to Big Bear last year. With the mild weather typical of late winter in Southern California, it was still fairly comfortable outside, although steam rose from the heated pool.

Bellamy amused herself by watching Harrison attempt to flirt with an oblivious Melina, while Conner glowered in the background for some reason. She really was in a mood tonight. She kept glancing toward Maggie as well, who refused to catch her eye.

Something was off there. Bellamy would be the first to admit she didn't always pick up on social cues or nuance in any situation, but normally the pair were like sisters, frequently bickering but with an unbreakable bond that made everyone else—namely, her and Emi—often feel like outsiders. It had been a lonely six months for Bellamy when Conner and Emi dated.

When Conner rose to get another drink, Bellamy saw her chance and lunged to catch her long strides, nearly tripping up Jamal in her haste. "Conner!"

"Yeah, babe?"

"What's going on with you and Maggie?"

Conner sent her a look so sharp it sliced across Bellamy's cheekbones. "What did she say? I didn't do anything wrong. I was a good friend!"

The force of her words sent Bellamy stumbling backward. "Whoa. Chill! I didn't accuse you of anything."

Conner shook her head, shaggy tresses flying. "I just—I can't talk about it, okay?"

She continued to the bar alone, while Bellamy stared after her, scrunching up her face in confusion. She had assumed the pair had just had an argument, but clearly something more had happened. Unease stirred in her stomach.

Everyone in the band had their strengths, their roles. Though all could and did sing, Conner and Emi had the true voices. Bellamy herself was generally the peacemaker. Conner was their leader, but Maggie was the glue, keeping everyone (including Conner's ego) in check. If that was disrupted, what would become of Hestia Rising? She loved the band. They were the family she'd never had, unearthing creativity within herself that no teacher had ever bothered to pursue. The Air Force hadn't taught her much beyond how to kiss ass and properly make a bed, and she had nothing back in Georgia besides her father's medical bills, his single-wide mobile home, and the Dairy Queen she'd worked at in high school that kids called the Dirty Queen.

Spinning on her heel, she marched to Maggie, who was still curled up in a chair, scrolling through her phone. "Mags, what happened with you and Conner?"

Maggie jumped, her phone bouncing from hand to hand like a cartoon before she caught it inches above the ground, glaring at Bellamy as if she was the one who dropped it. "Nothing. What did she tell you?"

"She didn't tell me anything except that she was a good friend and couldn't talk about it. What's going on?"

Maggie eyed her for another long minute before the fight left her, letting her defined shoulders slump. "She *is* a good friend, and I don't want to talk about it either, okay?"

Bellamy watched her, perplexed. Now that she thought about it, Maggie had been off ever since returning from her Asian tour. What if she wanted to quit the band and pursue full-time touring? Surely that wasn't it. She was so worried about being apart from Jamal. Then why did she sign up for another tour? And she wasn't snuggled up to him like she normally was. But Bellamy couldn't imagine Conner being caught up in drama between Maggie and Jamal, nor any person and a man...

She shrugged. Nothing she could do regardless. After getting another drink, she joined the group of dancers on the deck, enjoying throwbacks from the Spice Girls, Quad City DJ's, and Robyn, until some producer got a little handsy, so she excused herself to the bathroom. On the way back, she bumped into Conner, staring at the table of edibles.

"Trying to decide what you want?" Bellamy selected a brownie bite.

Conner offered her a lazy smile. "You say that like I haven't already."

Excellent. A chill Conner was the best Conner. They followed a meandering path around the pool with no real destination, chatting about Conner's final role as superhero Lyss.

"I know they had this idea that she'd be one of the faces of the new generation of heroes for the next decade, but I did three movies, two cameos, and a limited series. She grew up, and so did I. It was time to move on."

"At least they didn't kill her off. Staying in another dimension to keep them safe is a noble exit, and you can always come back."

Conner shrugged. "Maybe someday."

"So what do you have lined up now? After our album and tour, of course."

She groaned. "Not you, too. I promise I'm—did you hear that?"

"Hear what?" Bellamy looked around, but everyone seemed normal.

"Someone—" Conner stiffened, and this time Bellamy heard it, too.

The woman's voice telling someone to stop sounded once more, louder, and Conner bounded off like a hound that had picked up the scent, Bellamy on her heels. Around the corner of the house, in a small side yard with a gate to the front of the house, they found Melina and Harrison, she with her back against the house and he too close to her, holding one arm.

"C'mon. You came back here with me for a reason. Don't be like—"

Harrison had a split second of warning as Conner yanked him away from Melina before her fist connected squarely with his nose. He howled, bent in half, and when he straightened, dark-red blood slipped past the hands over his face.

"You fucking bitch! What the hell is wrong with you?"

"What the hell is wrong with *you*, pencil dick? If I heard her say stop, so did you."

"This is none of your business. Shit! I think you broke my nose."

"I'll break more than that if you don't shut up."

Bellamy had always been aware of how tall Conner was, but she seemed to grow an extra inch as she stepped closer to Harrison.

"Listen to me. You don't touch her. You don't talk to her. You don't look at her. You don't even think about her. Do you hear me? If you so much as breathe the same air as her again, I'll rip your pathetic balls out through your throat."

"Conner, I—" Melina said.

"You're never going to work in this town again, you dumb bitch," he said to Conner, spitting blood on her shoes.

She laughed. "Do you think I'm afraid of your father? At any given time, a dozen A-list producers and directors like your father will cream their pants if I sign on to their film. I make more money in interest alone than your sad little trust fund ever dreamed of having. I'd rather beg on the streets and sell my body than see her hurt."

He sneered. "You'd know a few things about selling your body."

"That's enough, asshole." Maggie lunged toward him before Emi held her back.

"It's okay, Mags. We're done here. Jamal!" Conner called without moving her gaze from Harrison. Jamal materialized from the crowd that Bellamy only now realized had formed. "Harrison has had too much to drink. Please make sure he gets home safely. Oh, and Jamal?" She grabbed his bicep. "Let him know he's no longer welcome here."

"Sure thing." Judging by the look on Jamal's face, the conversation would not be pleasant for Harrison.

Melina's gaze had never wavered from Conner, and her dark eyes continued to track her as she moved closer, murmuring words Bellamy couldn't make out. Melina lifted Conner's hand with such care that Bellamy wondered if she'd hurt it. Feeling like an interloper, Bellamy backed away with everyone else, jumping when the music started again. She hadn't noticed it had stopped.

Maggie's thunderous expression made her pause. Maybe Conner and Melina's obvious closeness had caused their rift. No one liked being replaced. Not for the first time, Bellamy wished she was better at picking up on unspoken cues.

Eventually Conner and Melina rejoined the group, both with flushed cheeks. Kit popped up with a small towel and a bowl of ice.

"Hand in towel, towel in ice." They thrust the bowl at Conner. "Chivalry is wonderful, but we have a show in a week."

Conner accepted it with a roll of her eyes, grimacing as her hand settled into the ice. "I know how to throw a punch. Relax."

Kit began to swell up with a lecture, so Bellamy hurried to ask, "How *do* you know how to punch like that?"

"Six years of stunt training when I played Lyss. The director said, 'No superhero should punch like a girl.'" She scrunched her nose.

"It was very stupid and very gallant." Next to her, Melina fussed over Conner's hand. It seemed as if she wavered between leaving it in the ice or holding it in hers.

Conner shrugged, though she grinned before she changed the subject to Emi's studio sessions. They chatted about the industry for a while, and Bellamy relaxed. The talk seemed to calm Kit, and she liked conversations in which she could contribute.

The subjects ebbed and flowed, and they were in the middle of a debate on the best music festivals when the DJ started up Tupac's "California Love."

Conner stopped mid-rant about Bonnaroo and raised her glass. "Yes! It's about time!" Maggie echoed her with a cheer.

Emi snorted. "Oh, please. I've never met people so obsessed with a place as Californians."

"That didn't stop you from moving here. Don't be jealous because no one writes songs about Seattle."

"We don't need songs written about us. We've produced some of the most iconic musicians. Nirvana, Brandi Carlile, Heart, Jimi Hendrix…do any of them ring a bell?"

"Heart started in Canada, and none of those artists felt strongly enough about Seattle to write songs about it, whereas I bet I could name at least one song from every decade back to the sixties with California in the title."

Melina shook her head, laughing. "No way."

Bellamy leaned over. "Don't take that bet. She's a walking music library."

"You're on." Emi bent forward, resting her elbows on her knees. "When you can't, you have to let me write my own solos on the next album."

"Maybe then, it'll get written," Kit said so quietly Bellamy barely heard them.

But Conner did. "Shut up, Kit. You're on, Emi, and when I win, I get to play lead guitar for every song in our next show. Okay. Let me think for a second."

"And you can't use 'California Love.'"

Conner scowled. "You can't set the rules after we agree, but fine. 'California Gurls' by Katy Perry, 'California' by Phantom Planet, 'California' by Belinda Carlisle, 'Going Back to Cali' by LL Cool J, 'Hotel California' by the Eagles, 'California Dreamin'' by the Mamas and the Papas..."

"You missed—"

"I'm thinking! Hold on... 'California' by Lorde! So there." Smugness radiated off her like extra-strong perfume.

Emi groaned, throwing her hands in the air. "I don't know why I try. But Seattle is still better."

"Better at rain, maybe." Conner laughed and high-fived Bellamy.

"I don't know why you try, either. Bow down to California superiority. Right, Mags?"

"Yeah." Maggie spoke without emotion, picking at one of her nails.

Conner narrowed her eyes, and Bellamy opened her mouth to ward off whatever scene was about to unfold, but Melina interrupted them. As always, Bellamy struggled to follow the speed of her delivery.

"Y'all are so funny. We all moved here for a reason, right? Why are you arguing that one place is better than another if you left that place to move here?"

"Because it's easier to make it in the music industry here. That's it." Bellamy nodded in agreement with Emi, at least until she continued speaking. "As if you're any better, Texas. You guys are obsessed with yourselves."

Conner smirked. "She's right about that. Name one other state that makes waffles in the shape of their state."

"Name one other state that has better tacos, barbecue, or Blue Bell ice cream."

"We have way better tacos. Name one other state that has worse politics."

"Florida," Kit, Emi, and Melina said in unison.

Bellamy raised her hand. "To be fair, Blue Bell ice cream is the best. At least y'all have something to be proud of in your hometown. What does Georgia have?"

Conner nudged her knee. "Peaches, babe. You have peaches."

Melina laughed. "I like fruit as much as the next person, but is that the best you can come up with?"

Conner smirked. "Have you ever had a really, really good peach?" Bellamy thought she heard Maggie groan, but she was focused on Conner, leaning closer and closer to Melina. "A very ripe peach, round and soft, so plump you can dig your fingers into it and squeeze." Her voice dropped. "When you bite into it, it's the sweetest juice you've ever tasted, with the slightest tang, and it's just dripping down your face. I can't think of anything I want more."

Bellamy saw Melina's throat work in a swallow, while Emi bit her lower lip. She was just confused. "Are we still talking about peaches?"

Maggie said something, but Conner's laughter drowned it out. "You're the greatest, Bells."

She stood, hovering over Bellamy, who didn't understand what was happening until it was too late. Conner scooped her into her arms, kissed her on the cheek, and jumped into the steaming pool.

Chapter Twenty-nine

Conner blew her breath out in a cloud of frustration and chucked her pen across the room.

"Hey! No one warned me of projectiles in here."

She shot her head up but relaxed her shoulders when she saw Emi. "Sorry, babe. I didn't think anyone would be here for another half hour or so."

Emi folded herself next to Conner on a small couch, the leather cracked and worn. "I had to run an errand on Melrose, and for once traffic was super light. No point in going home just to turn around. Why are you here early?"

Conner played with the frayed edges of her notebook, wishing she still had the pen in her hands. Not that it was helping in the slightest. For any number of people, she would have bullshitted an answer, but this was Emi, who still knew her very well despite everything, and she would find out the truth in half an hour anyway.

"I've been trying to come up with something to give Kit, and I hoped a change of scenery would help."

Emi's face fell, and Conner looked away, unable to stand the disappointment. "Oh, shit. You really don't have anything for an album?"

"I have songs! I can write songs day and night. But they're not good enough, and there are no links. Remember why I chose *Broken Promises*? It has a theme! A dark and angry theme, sure, but a theme nonetheless. The songs have continuity. I don't want to just throw a dozen random songs together and call it an album. I can be better than that, and my band is better than that."

"Some might say it's our band."

Conner grunted, daring to catch Emi's dark gaze. "You know what I mean."

"Oh, I know what you mean," she replied with a harsh chuckle. "But never mind. Will you let me see your songs?"

Conner closed her fingers around the edges of her notebook. She glanced down, noticing with a distant part of her mind that she needed a manicure.

"It's me, Con. You know I can help. I wrote a song with you before, remember, and look where that led."

"Six months of sex followed by a lot of yelling?"

Emi coughed several times, and Conner didn't bother to hide her laughter. "I meant our lead single. But sure, that too, although if I remember correctly, the sex had plenty of loud noises as well."

Conner shifted, resisting the urge to tug at the collar of her T-shirt as the temperature ticked up. This was starting to feel too familiar. She bit the inside of her cheek, focusing on the notebook in her hands. "In that case, you probably don't want to hear these songs anyway. Some were written, uh, like two years ago?"

"Two years? Has it been that long?"

Not a soft tone. Soft tones were dangerous. "It doesn't feel that long to you? We released an album, toured the entire country, I filmed a movie and a half, and now we're in festival season."

"Conner." Oh, shit. Quicksand ahead. "It feels like yesterday to me."

The notebook fell to one side as she turned to face her head-on. Her eyes were so soft. "Emi, you need to move on, okay? I did. It was fun for a while, but we both know it ended for a reason."

"I'm just saying we wrote a great song together once." She shifted closer. Conner's pulse hammered at her like a tornado siren. "We can do it again. I'm right here."

Sometimes Conner watched news reports of damage and death after hurricane landings and wondered why so many people didn't heed evacuation warnings. She saw videos on social media of people filming tornadoes on their front porches while debris flew past and wondered why they didn't get their asses to safety.

And sometimes she understood those people entirely, such as when she ignored all alarm bells in her head and plunged forward without protective gear. What was the lesser of two evils: traveling a treacherous path with her ex, or risking the wrath of Kit and Maggie? At least Bellamy was usually lost in her own head enough to miss arguments.

She stood abruptly, digging for her tablet in her backpack next to the sofa. "Here are a few that are finished. Don't say I didn't warn you."

Conner pretended to flip through social media on her phone for the next ten minutes while Emi browsed the selection. Except for a few throat clearings and hmms, she didn't indicate her reception.

"Well," she finally said, and Conner almost choked on the water she was sipping. "They're all great songs, as if I expected anything less. When did you write the one about stop saying sorry?"

"On tour. The first part of the tour."

"And it's about...?"

Conner nodded.

"I figured. What about this one?"

She held out the tablet, forcing Conner to lean close. Too close. "Oh, I wrote that, um, a little longer ago."

"Like around the time we split up?"

"Something like that."

She exhaled sharply, tucking a lock of hair behind her ear. "Jesus, Conner, were you really that angry at me? This is brutal."

"At the time, yes. This is why I didn't want to show you."

She tried to tug the tablet away but only managed to close her fingers around Emi's. *Don't look up. Do not look up.* She looked up, and Emi's gaze locked onto hers, too sad and soft for her to handle.

Bad idea, bad idea, bad idea...

Yet when Emi closed the distance between them and their lips met, Conner didn't do anything but fall back, bringing Emi with her. Her hands curled around Emi's tight butt while she ran her fingers through Conner's hair. For a moment, as they made out, everything was okay. It was nice and familiar, and Emi clearly wanted her so badly. Wanted her enough for both of them. Why couldn't that be enough?

But she couldn't. "No..."

Emi broke their kiss, though she remained so close their breath mingled. "No?"

"I'm sorry, but no. I don't want this. I don't want..."

"What the fuck?"

Maggie strode through the doorway, a veritable ball of fire, followed closely by Kit, who had gone the opposite route with an ice-cold expression, and Bellamy in the rear, appearing more disappointed than upset.

"This isn't what it looks like," Conner said as they scrambled to disentangle themselves. She tried to fix her hair but only left it messier than ever.

Maggie's scowl could have cut a diamond. "What else could it possibly be?"

"A mistake." Emi stood and brushed at her jeans, avoiding Conner's stare. "Let it go."

Maggie and Bellamy exchanged a glance, but when Maggie swelled up again with another diatribe on their stupidity, Kit shook their head. "Drop it. No, I said, drop it. They're adults. They know they made a mistake. Let's move on."

Conner didn't care much for being told what she knew, even when it was true, but she snatched her notebook and followed the group to the table in the middle of the room that their label had so thoughtfully allocated for their meetings. Stupid notebook. If the damn thing had better songs, she wouldn't be in this mess.

Kit spread their hands out when everyone was settled. Conner sat between them and Bellamy, not trusting herself next to either of her other bandmates. "So? What do you have?"

A headache that's growing by the second. "Well, I have some ideas." She waited, and they waited, and when it became clear they were going to win, she sighed. "It's just not quite, you know, there yet."

Kit shook their head. "What's not there yet? What ideas? Spill, Conner."

Conner tapped a staccato beat on the table, better than any of the songs she had written so far. "The album, okay? It's not there. Or here. Or anywhere near complete. In fact, it doesn't exist at all. Happy?"

"Oh yeah, just thrilled." Kit threw their hands in the air, standing up to pace back and forth. "This is great, Conner. Just fucking fantastic. The label's going to love this."

"We've made the label more money than any other artist they have! We won a Grammy, a VMA, a People's Choice, and a Kids' Choice awards. We had a sold-out tour. *Broken Promises* was a top-five album. The label can chill."

Kit ticked off their words on their flailing hands. "Won. Had. Was. Go back to school and take a grammar lesson, sweetheart. Those are past-tense words. *Broken Promises* was released almost two years ago."

"You can make your point without being an asshole, Kit."

"Thank you," Conner told Emi.

"Don't thank me too much. They're not wrong, Con. We need an album soon. Your songs—"

"Those songs are not going on any album even if they're the last songs I ever write."

"They're not—"

"They're my songs, and I'm not recording them!" Conner winced when she slammed her hand on the table. The fracture she'd suffered by punching Harrison hadn't completely healed, probably hindered by the fact that she'd insisted on playing during their recent gigs.

"Here we go. Your songs, your album, your band." Maggie rolled her eyes.

Conner couldn't stop her mouth from falling open in dismay. Maggie had been treating her like shit for months, and she was sick of it. A decade of friendship, as close as sisters, was circling the drain because…she had been there for Maggie when she needed her? It didn't make sense.

"Maggie. Look at me, damn it. What did I do?" Maggie leaned back, folding her arms and avoiding eye contact. Conner made a fist in frustration, regretting it as pain shot up her forearm. "I was a good friend, and you know it. Why are you punishing me?"

"You're making a correlation that doesn't exist. The fact is, we need material for an album, and you aren't delivering."

Conner held her hands out, palms up. "Do you have a song, Mags? What about you, Bellamy? Emi? Even you, Kit? Does anyone have anything to offer besides complaints?"

"We could hire—" Kit began at the same time Maggie said, "As if you would ever—"

"We're not hiring songwriters. I'm not singing someone else's songs. I might as well give up the guitar and go back to being some manufactured pop artist. We're successful because we're real. The songs I write, the songs I play, the songs I sing, they're all my story. Mine."

She realized her mistake as soon as she said it, but Maggie beat her to it. "Mine, mine, mine. It's always about you, isn't it, Conner?"

"That's not true and—"

"It's your band, and they're your songs, and you're the only one who matters. Not like the rest of us have bills to pay. Not like Emi is perfectly capable of writing good songs. Not like Bellamy is a great composer. Not like I created this band with you. If we ever record a second album, we should probably release it under Conner Cody and Friends."

Conner's temper snapped. "Hestia Rising wouldn't exist without me. *My* manager found Kit. *My* money paid for our EPs. *My* contacts got us the best producers and label. *My* name put butts in seats. So, yeah. It's my band."

Kit chuckled and muttered something under their breath.

"What was that?"

"Nothing."

"Go on. Tell me what's so funny. I'd love a laugh right now."

"Okay. You asked for it. This band, and all the potential it has, is going to fall apart because you can't get over your ego or your libido."

Conner all but snarled. She was so tired of everyone. But she sure as hell wasn't going to be insulted or slut-shamed. "Fuck you, Kit. For the record, she came on to me, and I—"

"Gee, thanks, Conner. Throw me under the bus."

She returned Emi's glower. "It's the truth, isn't it?"

Maggie stood. "None of this ever would have happened if you hadn't encouraged her in the first place. All you two had together was sex dressed up in a relationship's clothing." Both Emi and Conner protested, but she plowed on. "I can't take this anymore. Lately it's constant drama with you, Conner, and I give up."

"Maggie! Wait! You can't…" Conner swallowed, willing her to turn around and look at her. "You're my best friend."

Maggie continued her march toward the door. "So you say. A true friend wouldn't let her own issues get in everyone else's way."

"Sounds like projection to me. Do you hear me? Sounds like—" She stopped as the door behind Maggie swung shut. When Kit headed for the door, too, she rounded on them. "Where are you going?"

"To figure out what to tell the label. No point in holding a meeting about an album that doesn't exist."

Conner's stomach threatened to revolt, competing with her head as to which part of her body took her down first. Right now, she'd welcome it. Her hands trembled on the table until she forced them to still. She thought of Meli with her gorgeous smile and eternal cheer and considered hopping a flight to Vancouver, where she was filming, just for one of her hugs.

She flinched when Emi spoke. "I should go, too. Apparently I'm only a convenient distraction for you."

"You're being ridiculous."

"No, you are. Maggie was out of line, but she wasn't wrong. How would you feel if someone else took credit for all your hard work over the last several years? We're a band, Conner, a team. Not your lackeys. Every band has a star, and I'm fine if it's you, but we work just as hard, and all you do when you insist on controlling every last detail is hold us back."

"I don't need a band. I could be a rock star all on my own."

Emi's smile was as bitter as baker's chocolate. "I know. If that's what you want, then do us a favor and leave us out of it. We'll all be fine, Mags and Bells and I. Even Kit. We'll be fine without you, and you can keep trying to hide that you're miserable and lonely."

She left. Only Bellamy remained, picking at her nails. Conner looked down at her hands splayed across the table. Talented hands, capable of playing any number of instruments and writing songs that people loved. Beautiful hands, almost always moisturized and manicured to perfection.

Hands that choked the life out of every relationship that crossed her path.

"Are you going to leave, too?" she asked.

Bellamy shrugged. "Probably. Doesn't seem like there's much point in staying now, is there?"

"I guess not."

At the door, Bellamy paused and pivoted on the heel of her Chucks. "Did our band just break up?"

Freezing ice ran down Conner's spine. "I don't know."

Chapter Thirty

Conner jerked out of her doze when something vibrated against the sand next to her. She squinted as her sister's face came into focus on the screen of her phone.

"Hey, girl."

"Hi, Conner. How are you?"

"I'm, uh, I'm okay." The sun made her faculties dull and sluggish. She struggled to clear her head.

"You sure? Did I wake you up?"

"No. I'm just watching the sunset on the beach. What's up?"

Sadie sighed. "That sounds amazing. Well, I was wondering if you could do me a favor."

"Anything. Shoot."

"Asher and I are going to a charity benefit next Saturday."

"How much do you want? I'll have my finance guy send a wire."

Sadie chuckled. "That's very generous, but I don't want your money. Actually, if you really want to donate, that would be wonderful, but that's not the favor. The girls were going to stay with my mother, but she sprained her ankle. What do you think about keeping them Saturday night?"

Conner froze. "Here? At my house? With me? All night?" Her voice belonged to someone else, squeaky like a prepubescent boy.

"That's the idea, but if you don't want to or aren't ready—"

"No! I mean, yes! I mean—I want to. I'm ready. I'll order pizza, and we'll swim in the pool, but not right after we eat, and we can play *Mario Kart* in the theater. I have a room all ready—unless, will they want their own rooms? Because I can do that, too. And for breakfast I'll have my chef—"

"Conner, relax!" Sadie laughed. "You don't need to do anything crazy. The girls will be ecstatic just to be with you."

"I'm excited, too."

When they hung up, she stretched out again, grinning. Finally something was going right.

❖

Conner spent the week in New York City walking the runway. She didn't walk as often as she used to, but her contract with Tom Ford stipulated a certain number of appearances, and she wanted them to keep making her signature perfume.

Professionally, everything went fine. She strutted up and down the runway with her best blank expression, pouting her way through endless photo shoots. Her days started early, with appearances on the morning news shows, passed quickly on the runway until her feet ached, and ended with tapings of late-night talk shows, followed by long dinners with people in the industry.

Vittoria was in attendance, of course, walking in some of the same shows, Lola beaming from the front row of every crowd. Conner ignored both of them, going so far as to simply turn on her heel and walk away in sullen silence when Vittoria had the nerve to approach her backstage the first day.

"How can you stand it?" another model asked at lunch one day. "They both watch you constantly when you're not looking. It's creepy."

"I don't care if they use a voodoo doll of me as a double-sided dildo as long as they leave me alone."

Her companion spat La Croix all over Conner's edamame and kale.

Personally, her heart was in none of it, including and especially the all-night parties until everyone passed out, but she was Conner fucking Cody. It was what she did. People questioned when she didn't attend, and she was expected to be taciturn anyway. Besides, the liquor numbed the mess that was her private life.

She hadn't spoken to Harlow in months, although she kept finding excuses to put off formally ending their contract. When her agent questioned why Conner was suddenly going directly through her for the first time in years instead of making Harlow take care of things, she told her that she was getting her fee either way. The band, too, remained incommunicado, which was good, as Conner couldn't compose even a note or lyrics these days.

On Wednesday she found some free time and snuck into the matinee of *Six*, hiding her pink-tipped locks under a Stanford baseball cap stolen from Lindsey while watching with rapt envy as the actors dominated the stage, singing their hearts out. Theater was in her blood. Abuelita had toured the country as Anita in *West Side Story*, and Gran had acquired both Tonys and Oliviers during her legendary career, carrying on a tradition that went all the way back to Conner's great-great-grandparents, who had worked with Lady Gregory in Dublin over a century ago. Even Camila had played Laurey in *Oklahoma!*

Afterward, as she dressed in her hotel room for yet another outing, her phone vibrated. Grinning, she answered but turned it facedown.

"Conner? Are you there? Why is it all black?"

"Because I'm getting dressed and figured you didn't want a show... again." Meli was silent for so long Conner wondered if the connection had dropped. "Was I wrong?"

Meli's laugh carried an edge of hysteria. "No, of course not. I only— you just caught me by surprise."

"Kind of like the last time you got a show, unless you've forgotten."

"I definitely haven't forgotten that." A shiver rippled across Conner's frame as she imagined a husky quality in Meli's voice. "What are you getting dressed for so late?"

"A party."

"Don't you ever sleep?"

She snorted. "You know the answer to that."

"I do, and that's why I ask. You need sleep, Conner. It's not healthy, the way you function."

"I'm fine. Worrying gets you nowhere."

Meli blew a raspberry. "Worrying gets me to say something to you that hopefully gets you to take better care of yourself, so it's not useless. It's only because I care about you and want to keep you around for a long time."

Conner paused her makeup routine to lean on the counter, eyes closed against the burn of sudden wetness. No one had ever told her they wanted her to stay around. She'd operated on the mantra of "live fast, die young" for so long that she had assumed it would eventually come to fruition. Not that she desired an early death, but it just seemed a fitting end. She had already lost some of her peers.

Meli was saying her name. "What?" Conner asked belatedly.

"I asked if you're okay. You went really quiet. I'm not trying to nag, Conner, honestly, so I'll let it go. You're a grown woman, and obviously you can do as you please. I didn't mean—"

"No."

"No, what?"

"No, don't let it go. It's...it's nice to have someone worry about me. Hey. What are you doing tonight?"

"Nothing, I think? I'm sitting in your kitchen eating this amazing veggie lasagna that your chef made for me. You didn't have to ask her to work while I'm house-sitting, you know. I can cook."

Conner grinned. "You can cook very well, but it's what she gets paid for. Just enjoy it, babe."

"Believe me, I am. Eriq is ridiculously jealous." Meli laughed, and the sound warmed Conner to her toes. "Why did you ask about tonight?"

"Well..." She sang the word, dragging it out. "What if I don't go out tonight, and we chat for a while instead?"

"I would *love* that, but I don't want you to feel like you have to change for me. Actually, you should go have fun. I'm not your parent, and I didn't mean to make you feel bad for wanting to go out."

She carried on in that vein for a while, and during the time she rambled, Conner washed her face, changed into loungewear, and curled up on her bed.

She rested her phone on the pillow opposite her and turned the camera back on, obviously catching Meli off-guard as she stopped halfway through a sentence and blinked.

"Hi."

"Hi," Meli replied with a smile so soft that Conner's heart betrayed her with an extra beat.

As they chatted, she allowed her imagination to travel to a dimension where this was an everyday activity, where Meli's pretty head always lay on the pillow opposite hers and they ended each day with these long talks... among other things.

"Conner?"

"Yeah?"

"Do you want to hang up so you can go to sleep? I'm sure you have better things to do than listen to me go on and on about my family drama."

Conner's eyelids fluttered open. She hadn't realized they had closed. "No. Don't stop. It's my favorite thing."

"Talking about family drama?"

"Your voice."

The voice in question caught. "My voice is your favorite thing?"

Conner nodded before catching herself. "About you. Your voice is my favorite thing about you."

Her expression shifted, leaving Conner with the impression that she'd let her down somehow. "That's sweet," she said, her words not matching her tone or her face.

"Seriously, though, you should try voice acting. I think you could be really good at it, and it's fun." She wasn't just blowing smoke to cover herself. Meli's voice reflected her personality, dulcet and clear.

"Maybe I will. So anyway, they're all insisting on coming, the whole big clan, and I'm responsible for finding a place for everyone to stay. Abuela wants everyone in the same place, but my dad is still holding a grudge against the Holiday Inn, and my sister-in-law is insisting on a Hilton because she has points, but my youngest brother says he can't afford that, and all the kids want is a pool even though the beach is right there."

"They can stay at my house." Conner realized what she'd said a moment later, and she schooled her expression to avoid the skeptical surprise written all over Meli's.

"That's really kind of you to offer, but I couldn't ask you to do that. My family is a lot, and I know how you like your privacy. Don't worry. I'll find a hotel. Or hotels. Honestly, it's great they want to visit, but it's so much easier for me to go there. I should just tell my parents—"

"Meli! It's totally fine. Seriously. *Mi casa es su casa*, you know? My house is your house."

Meli's smile was the sole highlight of her week.

It all started with a last-minute decision to postpone her flight home from the red-eye to early morning. After one final jaunt down the runway Friday evening, she headed to the afterparty, where she snagged a bottle of rum and a Spanish model in one go. By the time both were spent, it was time to leave, and Conner was in no shape for a six-hour flight. She dragged herself to the JFK airport anyway, watched the sun rise while she forced frittata and fruit into her stomach, and slept the rest of the way across the continent. Her hangover kept her awake yet bleary while her assistant crept through an hour of traffic, but once she was safely inside her beloved house, she popped two gummies and collapsed on her couch, partaking in the rare urge to binge-watch TV.

It wasn't until she wandered into the kitchen, looking for a snack, that she heard her phone vibrate against the quartz. She jumped and answered without looking at the screen.

"Oh, thank God. I was starting to think you were dead. Where are you?"

"I'm…in my house. Um, who is this?"

Dead silence, and for a minute, Conner thought she was so high she was hallucinating the phone call. "It's Sadie. Your sister."

"Sadie…oh, hi!" She laughed. "What's up?"

"Conner, what time is it?"

"Uh, it's…six, almost six. You know your phone has a clock, right?" She giggled again.

A frustrated noise came through the phone's speaker. "Come to the front door."

"Why?"

"Because I'm standing outside it."

Conner did a double-take when she opened the door. "Damn, girl, you look hot!" The tight silhouette of her navy dress flattered her curves, and the boatneck added a classy element. Then she did a triple take. "You don't think so?"

Sadie's frown deepened as they moved into the foyer. "I do, and so does my husband. Do you know why I'm dressed like this on a Saturday evening? On *this* Saturday evening?"

"You have a hot date, and you need me to pull strings to get you into somewhere really nice?"

Conner's grin faded. Sadie looked pissed. Really, really pissed. She remembered the time she had broken some gawdy vase her mother had loved when she was eight. The grip on Conner's arm as she was dragged sobbing to her room was probably the closest Camila had ever come to physical abuse.

"What the hell is wrong with you?" Sadie peered at her, narrowing her eyes. "Are you—are you high? Oh my God, you're high! You're supposed to be babysitting my children and you're *high*?"

Oh, fucking fuckity fuck. It was Saturday night. Sadie and Asher were going to a charity gala, and the girls were supposed to spend the night with Conner. She had fucked up. She had really, really fucked up. Top three fuck-ups of her life for sure, and her teenage antics had set that bar high.

Time for damage control. "I'm sorry. I'm so sorry. It was a very long week, and I'm jet-lagged and all out of sorts. But it's fine. I'm fine. Give me ten minutes to take a shower. I'll chug some caffeine, and I'll be fine. Are the girls in the car?"

It was, in fact, not fine, no matter how many times she repeated it. "The girls are at a friend's house. I called her when you didn't show up or answer your phone, and thankfully she was available."

The chill enveloping Conner propelled her toward sobriety in a hurry. "I really am so, so sorry, Sadie. I'll make it up to them. I swear."

"No, you won't."

"I will. I promise. They can spend the entire weekend with me next week! I'll pick them up from school on Friday, and—"

"No, Conner." Sadie took a deep breath and broke eye contact. A fist squeezed Conner's heart. "You're not going to because you're not going to see them."

Conner's mouth worked several times before she could speak, and when she did, she didn't recognize her tremulous voice. "For...for how long?"

"I don't know. Maybe—I don't know."

"Can I see you?"

The longer Sadie took to answer, the worse Conner felt. "I don't know that either."

Conner dug deep into her acting prowess and forced a smile, small yet hopeful. "How can I rebuild your trust if I don't see you?"

Sadie's head jerked up, and fire flared in her eyes. "You don't, Conner. Don't you get it at all? How could I ever possibly trust you with my children?"

"I would *never* get high around the girls! I can't believe you think that!"

"You're a drug addict. It's not like your judgment can be trusted."

"I'm not—" She forced herself to take a deep breath. "I'm not who I used to be. I don't do anything that isn't legal in the state of California."

"The first time I met you, you practically had cocaine dripping from your nose. Then you tell me that you quit, no rehab or anything, just stopped, but you still use marijuana. And I'm supposed to believe that?"

"You're supposed to believe it because it's the truth!"

Sadie shook her head. "I can't take that chance. Not with my daughters."

She turned to leave, and for a moment, Conner almost let her go. Let her and the girls walk out of her life. She had made it twenty-three years without a sister or nieces, and while they weren't always great years, she had done all right. Maybe Conner wasn't meant to have family, and maybe she was better off without them. Once again, she was learning that family always let her down. Or maybe she always let them down. Maybe Sadie was right, and she was a ticking time bomb who reeled from one bad decision to the next. Maybe the girls would be better off without her.

Then she pictured Sarah's shy smile when she mastered a guitar chord. Felt Hannah's arms as she squeezed tightly in one of her frequent hugs. And she recalled what it was like every time Sadie gave her advice, or supported her career, or listened to her troubles. What it meant to have a sister.

"Wait!" At the door, Sadie paused, although she didn't turn around. "Sadie, you're my sister. You can't do this to me, please."

Sadie's voice wasn't entirely steady. "I'm your father's bastard child that he's never met. It doesn't have to be more than that."

Conner reeled from a punch she never saw coming. "Y-you don't mean that. We're sisters, Sadie. We are. I tracked you down when I found out about you, and you came when I was sick. Because that's what sisters do, right?"

Sadie shook her head. "Sisters don't crush their nieces. Sisters don't break their promises." She advanced with each sentence, and Conner retreated, more from her words than her presence. "I wouldn't have thought twice of having my brother watch them. In fact, I should have gone with my instincts and asked him in the first place. But Asher said to give you a chance, and the girls wanted it so badly."

Conner's back hit the wall with a thump. The world didn't contain enough edibles to dull this hurt. She stared at Sadie, whose fury radiated off her in nearly visible waves. Conner had disappointed people all her life—her parents, her grandparents, her band, her label, men and conservatives all over the globe. Why did this one hurt so much more?

"I feel like you've been waiting for me to screw up since day one," she said slowly.

Sadie looked away, pursing her lips. "Maybe I was." The admission was another jab to the gut. "I didn't want you to, but you can never be too careful with your kids. If you ever have your own—"

Conner scoffed. "I can't even be an aunt, apparently. What kind of fucking mother would I be?"

"Conner..."

"Stop. You don't get to berate me for ten minutes then try to soothe my feelings."

"Excuse me? Why the hell are you mad at me? You're the one who screwed up, not me."

Conner bit down on her temper. "I'm not mad at you. It's just—please don't do this. Please don't take them away from me. I'm begging you. I can't—the idea—I can't handle the thought of not having you and your family in my life. Please, Sadie. I will do anything to make this right."

"You can't buy your way out of this like you do every other problem in your life. Fixing yourself is going to take more than that. I—I need to go."

Conner was hot on her heels. Her breath came so hard and fast that her chest hurt. "You can't do this! Please, Sadie, please don't do this. How can you toss me aside so easily?"

Sadie didn't speak until she was at the door of her car. The shadow from the house covered her face. "You really must be high if you think this is easy for me. I...never mind. I have to go."

Conner stood in her driveway, hands against the hood of Sadie's SUV, begging in broken, ragged sobs for Sadie to stop. But she didn't. She backed up, even as Conner followed her all the way into the street, heedless of her neighbors, and drove away, taking Conner's crushed heart with her.

Chapter Thirty-one

The waves crashed around Conner's feet, although she barely registered the increasing wetness of her leggings.

Water was one of the most powerful forces on the planet. It could wipe out entire cities, reshape mountains, and carve out canyons. It sustained life or took it away.

Could the Pacific erase all her mistakes? Could it stop her from being one colossal fuckup? For someone who was so successful on the surface, who commanded starring roles and immense salaries with the snap of her finger, whose legions of fans loyally ensured box office and tour triumph, she only seemed to succeed in pushing everyone away otherwise.

Those who weren't worshippers at the throne of "CoCo," as her fans called her, thought she was an irresponsible, partying slut who, thanks to Lola, treated women like disposable garbage. Her manager thought she was a child. Her label thought she was a one-pump chump incapable of writing a second album. Her best friends thought she was a selfish narcissist. Her parents thought she was at best a nuisance, at worst an embarrassment. And her sister thought she was a drug addict who was nothing but a danger to her nieces.

And the worst part, if Conner allowed herself to be honest, was that she believed all the same things.

The sun had long departed by the time she trudged indoors, shivering and half covered in salty brine. Despite that fact, she simply undressed, leaving her clothes in a damp pile on the floor, and lay on top of her bed naked, waiting for sleep that never came.

For two days she moped, barely eating or drinking. Her agent called repeatedly; she turned off her phone. What was the point of working? For the first time, life was meaningless without someone to share it with. Finally unable to stand herself any longer, she grabbed the first jeans and sneakers she found, shoved her hair into a beanie, and took off in her SUV.

Some people would think that this was rock bottom for Conner. She was miserable and had alienated nearly every important person in her life. It was only a matter of time before Lindsey and Meli figured out she was a cancer, and then she would be truly alone.

However, she'd already hit rock bottom in her life, an event she'd memorialized in a song but refused to talk about otherwise. At eighteen, her cocaine addiction at its height, she'd rejected every meaningful relationship in her life. Even she and Maggie hadn't been on speaking terms. The producers of her TV show had told her not to bother showing up if she hadn't cleaned up her act by the time the next season went into production, no matter how high their ratings were.

She was at a nightclub with the usual crew, other young Hollywood notables with too much money and too little supervision, when everything took a turn. One minute she was dancing, and the next, she was frozen in the parking lot behind the club as one of her good friends overdosed. Conner never did heroin; even as an addict, she had limits. But she didn't stop her friends, and that night, they had gone too far. Making matters worse, some asshole took a picture, one she couldn't scrub from the internet despite years of suing. The image of someone convulsing to death with herself off to the side, mouth agape and eyes haunted, was seared into her brain.

Conner's descent into addiction had been steep; she'd gotten drunk for the first time at thirteen, high at fourteen, and started playing with ecstasy by fifteen. Within six months she was doing cocaine regularly, mixing it with pills so she could still work. To this day she was baffled that she also didn't end up dead, or at the very least been blacklisted.

But it had ended that night. She hadn't touched illegal drugs since. Within months, she was clean, had landed the role of teenage superhero Lyss, and was dating Bree Mathews. Although, against all advice, she did still use THC to relax, she had no problem limiting it to that.

Just like she told Sadie, not that she listened or believed her.

Conner drove mindlessly, making random turns every time she encountered traffic. Her mind raced as if she were on uppers, bringing up rebuttal after rebuttal against Sadie's accusations. Plotting ways to get back in her good graces and formulating plans to fix her shit, only to dismiss them just as quickly.

She ended up on Mulholland Drive, where she parked illegally and stared at the lights of Los Angeles spread out before her. La-La-Land. Tinseltown. The City of Angels. For her, it had always been the city of excess. No one said no, so long as one was rich, famous, or beautiful. She had always been able to get into clubs no matter her age, obtain drinks no matter how intoxicated, score drugs no matter how illegal.

She yanked off her hat and mussed her hair with an aggravated groan. It was so easy to blame everyone else. Her parents for being objectively awful. Every other adult during her minority for forgetting she was a child. The media for jumping over every single indiscretion no matter how inconsequential. But...

She groaned again, dropping her head onto the steering wheel, only to jump when the horn honked. A light came on at a nearby house, and with a sigh, she shifted into reverse. The last thing she needed was another ticket, although it would be ironic if the ticket that finally got her license suspended was for sitting still, not moving as fast as possible.

When she ended up on Sunset Boulevard in West Hollywood, she wasn't surprised. She'd practically lived on the Strip during her teenage years, partying it up until that one fateful night. The fodder she'd provided for the tabloids and entertainment blogs had extended their lives by several years, bestowing upon her a reputation she still couldn't shake.

Conner scowled as she parked in a random lot and began to walk with her hands shoved in her pockets. Even her own goddamn sister believed her reputation over Conner's own words. She swallowed a scream in her throat, not wanting to draw attention to herself. A tsunami of memories assaulted her with each step, and something else came with it—longing.

Her addiction hadn't reared its head much in the last several years. It had been hard at first, obviously, but Conner was stubborn, and when she decided to quit, she did just that. Once she gained some distance from the habit, and the people associated with it, rarely did she look in the rearview mirror. Many thought she was playing with fire by not going completely sober, but she had no problem sticking to alcohol and weed, regardless of what happened in her pool house.

But now...now she recalled with crystal clarity the sweet, sweet release of oblivion. When she was up, nothing but time or another drug could bring her down. Not her parents' lack of caring, not her empty condo, not her increasingly uncomfortable relationship with the much older Britt, not the stress of carrying an entire television show on her shoulders.

She wiped at the sweat on her forehead.

It would be so easy. The easiest thing in the world probably. Just because she no longer hung around with that crowd didn't mean it was out of reach. In Hollywood, *nothing* was out of reach. One phone call, a quick transaction, and she'd be back in oblivion. After all, if she was going to be indicted anyway, she might as well get something out of the accusations.

Her hands flexed.

She could do it. If her band didn't want her, she'd sell out arenas on her own. If her manager didn't want her, she'd top box offices with mere cameos. Her fans were loyalty personified and didn't care what, or who, she did in her spare time as long as she kept producing. And her sister...

Her sister was already gone. Sadie had made it clear that she wouldn't trust Conner regardless, so screw her. So what if she never got to see Sarah win a Grammy? Or cheer Hannah to a World Cup victory? For Conner didn't doubt that *her* nieces would excel at whatever they wanted.

The girls. Her girls. Her girls she would probably never see again because she was a screw-up. Like Simba and Mufasa, everything her light touched got fucked up. She bit her lip so hard it split.

Conner stuttered to a stop at an intersection. When she pulled out her phone, her hand trembled. For a long time she stared at the light, watching it flip from green to yellow to red and back to green again. With the red reflecting on her face, she sucked in a deep breath and hit the call button.

EVER AFTER

Chapter Thirty-two

The streetlights strobed across Conner's face. She squinted with every flash.

"Are you going to tell me what's going on?" A beat passed. "If you're shaking your head, I can't see you."

"No."

"Fine. But at some point, you have to tell me why you called me for the first time in nearly a year, in the middle of the night no less, to pick you up from WeHo."

Conner shifted but left her head resting against the window. "Can I stay at your house tonight?"

The car slowed to a stop at a red light, and when it turned green, they didn't move. Conner lifted her head. "Um, are—"

"Are you okay? Did somebody hurt you? Are you going to hurt yourself? Do we need to go to the hospital?"

"What? No. None of those."

"I've known you for a decade, and you've never wanted to be anywhere but your own house, so this is weird."

"I just don't want to be alone." Conner curled into the window again.

The rest of the drive to Santa Monica passed quietly. For once, traffic was nonexistent. When they pulled into the garage, neither of them opened their door, and they sat in silence.

"Will you at least tell me why you called me, out of everyone?"

Only then did Conner make eye contact. The bags under Harlow's eyes and the messiness of her hair twisted up in a claw clip suggested that Conner's call had pulled her out of bed, which was likely, given the late hour. Or was it early at this point?

"Because I knew you would come."

Her reply was short and simple yet said so much. Harlow clearly softened as much as she ever did, though her brows remained furrowed.

Eventually she shook her head. "I can't have this conversation without sleep. Come inside."

Left alone in Harlow's guest room once Conner convinced Harlow she wasn't a danger to herself, Conner got into bed and curled on her side. Her hands still shook when she thought about how close she had come to tumbling down the slope of drug addiction again. If Harlow hadn't answered...

But she *had* answered, and more importantly, she had shown up although she owed Conner nothing. After Harlow, Conner couldn't think of another option. Her assistant was on vacation, Lindsey was on the East Coast in the middle of a three-game road trip, and she couldn't bear the idea of letting Meli down. She persisted in believing Conner was a good person, probably the only one left on the planet who thought so, and Conner would rather die than ruin that image.

When she'd played Princess Eilonwy as a teenager, her character had reached a crossroads at the end of the final movie: travel to the idyllic Summer Country or stay in the land of Prydain with the one she loved. She felt as if she was at a similar fork in her life: continue as she had been, looking out for only herself because no one else would, or risk letting people in, assuming she managed to repair enough relationships to have people to let in.

The memory of the Prydain series tugged the corners of her mouth down. She and Hannah had been reading them together chapter by chapter but were only in book two. Was she reading it on her own, or would she never find out the fate of the Black Cauldron?

A discouraged sigh blew her hair out of her face as she resigned herself to yet another sleepless night. But pure exhaustion finally caught up to her, or perhaps it was the security of knowing that someone out there cared enough to answer the phone, and she slipped into a deep, dreamless sleep.

Conner woke disoriented, and for a horrible moment she thought she had gone off the deep end the night before after all. Then her brain fog lifted, and she realized that the warm, soft bed she inhabited was in Harlow's guest room. She sat up, rubbing her eyes as she looked around. Like Harlow herself, the room was all cool grays and whites, with shuttered windows and framed pictures that appeared to be stock photos. The last time Conner had been in New York City, she had come across an anonymous artist she really liked at a gallery in Chelsea. Would Harlow appreciate a gift of artwork?

But first she should probably figure out if Harlow wanted anything to do with her after today. She wasn't well versed in the art of apologizing, but she was pretty sure it would take more than a desperate midnight phone call.

And speaking of Harlow...she viewed being asleep during daylight hours as a waste of time, and the sun was well beyond the horizon. Conner must have slept late, an occasion almost as rare as her apologies.

She shuffled downstairs, squinting through all the natural light. Harlow's home was as sterile as always, so spotless and impersonal it could have doubled as a model home for some new suburb. Not that she didn't like the place. She just thought it could use an extra touch.

Harlow sat at the bar in her kitchen with a mug of coffee and her tablet. She didn't even glance up, simply pointing at her French press coffeemaker. Conner made her coffee and assembled a plate with toast, avocado, and a banana from the spread on the countertop, all in silence. Then she couldn't stand it anymore.

"Are you going to say anything? Because if not, I'm going to call a driver to take me to my car."

Harlow put down her tablet. "You didn't want to talk last night, so how am I supposed to know you're ready now?"

"Okay. I kinda deserved that."

"Almost as much as I deserve an explanation, and since I didn't plan my day around babysitting you…"

Conner drained her coffee. She'd missed many things about Harlow, but her acerbic tongue wasn't one of them. Still, Harlow was right, so with a deep breath, she began.

She told her everything. Everything. All that had happened in the last two years, even parts Harlow already knew. The high of releasing the album, the constant worry over the band's sustained success, and her fear of trusting her bandmates. The memories that her former lover Britt Boyd had dredged up and how that had led to her poor choices with Lola and Vittoria. Lola's goddamn song that had more truth in it than she wanted to admit, though wrapped in a package of delusion. Punching Harrison Fisher for harassing Meli, not that she regretted that in the least. Her regrettable actions that led to her estrangement with her sister and her concern that Sadie wasn't even Seth's daughter. And all that prefaced last night's phone call, terrified that she would traverse a dark path again if left alone.

Harlow absorbed everything impassively, merely sipping her coffee until Conner finished. She shook her head. "I've said many times that you're one of the most talented people I know, but I never realized that included a talent for screwing everything up."

"I've missed your backhanded compliments." Conner bit her lip before releasing it when Harlow frowned. Just like old times. Then she blurted out, "I've missed *you*. I miss your guidance and your sarcasm and the way you pretend that you can't stand me. I was a jackass, and I'm sorry. Please be my manager again."

Harlow observed her for a moment before suddenly walking out of the room. She returned before Conner decided whether to follow and tossed a sheath of papers her way. It took her a second to recognize their contract.

"If you recall, we renewed your contract for a three-year term right before your album came out," Harlow said, "so there's still a year left. However, as long as we mutually agree to terminate, there shouldn't be a problem."

Conner's heart sank straight to her bare feet. She hadn't realized until that very moment that Harlow felt like as much of a sister to her as Sadie did, and the loss cut almost as keenly. But what had she told her all those months ago? *Grow up, Conner.* Part of that process was accepting the consequences of her actions even when they hurt.

She straightened her shoulders and nodded. "If that's what you want. Show me where to sign."

Harlow produced a thinner group of papers, marked with tabs, and a pen. "We have a key-person clause, so we should be protected anyway, but I want to cover my bases just in case."

Conner's pen trailed off halfway through her last name. Close enough. "We what? Why does that matter?"

"A key person clause allows—"

"I've been signing these contracts since I was fifteen. I know the clause. What does it matter in this instance?"

"Ah." Harlow leaned back in her chair, and for a moment, Conner swore she would smirk. "I'm establishing my own agency and taking some of my clients with me, as well as two other managers, three admin assistants, and an intern. I'd like you to come with me, if you want to resume our working relationship. In fact, you'd be our marquee signing, and our first." A satisfied glance rippled across her face. "Didn't I mention that?"

Conner didn't try to hide her grin, although she had to resist throwing her pen at Harlow. "You asshole. Was this punishment, thinking I'd lost you for good?"

"Somewhat."

"Did you enjoy it?"

"Very much."

"Wonderful. Now that you've had your fun, I'd love to come with you. But—" Harlow raised an eyebrow, and Conner matched her. "I want you to handle everything for me. Lawyer, agent, publicist—all of those fools. I want you to take care of it. I don't care if you keep who I currently have or hire new people, but I want to deal with only you. Obviously, we'll discuss raising your cut."

"Obviously."

"I can think of a few people to bring on board, too. One, for sure." Meli had been talking about finding management now that she was getting more regular work. Surely Harlow could cut her a deal for Conner's sake. Then they could share their management, their work, their dreams, their lives—

She stopped that line of thought in its tracks and dragged herself back to reality. "When is this happening? I need new work like yesterday."

"It'll take some time, but as long as I don't file the termination agreement, I'm still your manager, and it just so happens I might have the perfect role for you. It's a period piece with Oscar bait written all over it."

"As if I care about that."

Harlow sniffed. "Oh, please. There's not an actor on this planet who hasn't practiced their acceptance speech. You're already drooling."

"I can think of one person who doesn't care." Curves for days, wild curls, enormous brown eyes, the cutest gap in her teeth, and utterly unconcerned with fame and awards. Conner suppressed a sigh. "What's the role?"

"An English spy during World War Two, but it's a different take, and I think you'll really enjoy the ending. How's your French?"

"*Merveilleux.*" *Wonderful.*

"How's your accent?"

"*Rouille.*" *Rusty.*

"You better brush up. It's English-speaking, of course, but some scenes are in French. You also need to be able to sing like a 1940s nightclub act and swing dance."

"I can do all that. No problem. There has to be a catch."

Harlow smiled. "Always. The director is a man you've been wanting to work with for ages…whose son you punched out in front of a crowd."

A rock dropped through Conner's abdomen and took her stomach with it, but she rallied. "I regret a lot of things, but not that. I'll just have to be so good he overlooks it."

"I'll see what I can do." Harlow crossed one leg over the other. "Now, regarding my new firm, I have two conditions. Have you taken any illegal drugs, or abused any prescription medication, since Maggie and I babysat you through withdrawal?"

Taken aback, Conner shook her head. "Not a single one. Just small amounts of THC."

"What about last night?"

"I was tempted," she said slowly. "More than I have ever been since I quit. If I hadn't called you, I don't know what I would have done."

"Okay. You will have a clause in your contract that should you ever go down that road again, our working relationship will be terminated immediately. Furthermore, if you ever get tempted like that again, you're going straight to rehab. This point is nonnegotiable."

"Agreed," Conner replied, although it was clear Harlow didn't need that reassurance.

"Second, and just as important…" She furrowed her brow, studying

Conner in a way that made her feel far too exposed. Then she sighed in the most un-Harlow-like manner. "I want you to go home, take a week, and think about the life that you want. In all the time I've known you, I've always wondered if you really want to act and play music or if you just do it because you're expected to. Hold on. Let me finish."

She stood and began pacing. Harlow? Pacing? Harlow Thompson, her ice-queen manager, *pacing*? Conner looked up, expecting to see the world ending.

"I meant what I said earlier. You are extraordinarily talented, and you deserve every success. But sometimes you're so fucking miserable I want to tear up every single contract you've ever signed, exile you from this godforsaken city, and find a place where you can just live your life. I can't think of an easy way to say this so I just will: there's not a role you can win or a song you can compose that will get your parents' attention or love. If that's what drives you, give it up."

Conner gulped. "I didn't know you cared so much," she said, her voice shaky.

Harlow ceased her pacing and gave her a much more familiar look of disdain. "Either you're attempting a joke, you're putting up your walls again, or we really do need to reconsider our relationship."

She refused to allow her chin to wobble, standing to meet Harlow. "You're right. You know I—well, you're like—we're not just manager and client, we both know that, and I really value our friendship. Even if you scare me sometimes."

Harlow's lips broadened in the most genuine smile she'd ever given Conner, and a lovely one it was, too. "I know, Conner. I do, too, and I prefer to keep you scared. So you know I'm being serious when I tell you to think it over. And Conner?"

This look was much more on brand. "It's not a request."

Contrary to popular belief, Conner could be obedient when she chose to be, and this time, she was. For six of the required seven days, she stayed home, considering her life.

Her earliest memories were on set. She had started acting as a baby, if one could call it that at that age, and she'd never stopped. Most of her firsts took place on a set, if not on film—first steps, first word, first kiss. She didn't remember much before the age of five, and by that point she didn't know any life but acting.

Music had always been in her life. Whether it was Seth's band, the various hangers-on that accompanied any rock star, or one of her parents' elaborate parties, her house was rarely quiet, and she absorbed the noise like a cotton ball. Her inclusion in a manufactured girl group had been less of a choice than an order by her manager, but it had unleashed something inside her that wouldn't be settled until she formed Hestia Rising.

Yet none of that answered Harlow's question. She needed to figure out where habit ended and desire began. After six days of trying to decide what she would do if she didn't act or make music, she gave in and called for reinforcements.

Meli arrived with a giant bowl of pozole, her trademark bright smile, and a deliciously tight hug that lasted so long Conner failed to resist the urge to smell her hair. Even her shampoo was alluring.

"All right, spill."

Conner almost choked on her spoon, and not just because the soup was spicy. "What?" How did Meli know she'd screwed everything up?

"You've been avoiding me since you went to New York. Usually we talk every day, but lately I can barely get a text out of you. Then a week of nothing, and suddenly you call me to come over. What's going on?"

Conner took another bite, savoring the taste and the time it took her to swallow. With no intention of revealing her misdeeds to the most important person in her life, she had to walk with care. "I'm trying to decide if I really want to be an actor and a musician, and I need your help figuring it out."

"Oh!" Meli's shoulders lost their tension, and she beamed. "Oh, that's so much better than I imagined."

"What did you imagine?"

"Um, well, really nothing in particular, but I did wonder—I mean, it's none of my business if you are, honestly, I'd be happy for you. It's only—you kinda did this last time? When you and—you went really quiet for a while. Obviously your personal life is your own, but—"

"Meli?" Conner smothered a grin. "What are you talking about?"

"I thought maybe you got back together with, um, Vittoria? When you were in New York?"

Conner recoiled. "Vittoria? No. God, no. I didn't even talk to her. Why would you think that?"

"Just a thought. Are you—is there someone?"

Yes. "Nope. Single and—" *Miserable. Lonely. Wanting you.* "Well, just single."

"That's good! I mean, it's not—not that it's good that you are single, but it's not bad to be that way, you know?"

Conner laughed. "I think I do."

"Anyway, what led you to question your livelihood? You were born to do this."

"That's precisely it. I was born into this life. Has it ever been my choice? And to answer your question specifically, Harlow told me to think it over."

"Harlow! I haven't seen her in forever. How is she? Tell her I said hi, please." Then she screwed up her pretty face. "That's an odd question for a manager to ask, isn't it? You would obviously know better than I, since you've been doing this for so long...although I guess that's the issue?"

Meli often ended her rambles on a higher-pitched, interrogatory note, whether she was asking a question or not. It should have been annoying. It should have reminded Conner of the vocally fried Valley-girl stereotype she loathed (probably because she had a hint of vocal fry herself, especially when tired). It should have turned her off.

It did not.

"Well, you know..." Conner struggled for words. "We've known each other for a really long time, Harlow and I. We're not just colleagues."

"That's awesome. I wish I had that relationship." She laughed, and Conner's pulse throbbed in response. "Heck. I wish I had a manager."

Conner took a sudden breath but held her tongue, not wanting to speak out of turn. Instead, she simply said, "You will someday."

They moved to the den, where Meli had the bright idea to list pros and cons. Sprawled on a chaise, Conner reeled off all the celebrity trappings that she disliked—lack of privacy, long hours, paparazzi, endless schmoozing and politicking, required appearances, fake people, unrealistic body expectations, the pressure to constantly produce something new. On and on she went, unleashing frustrations she didn't even know she carried. Meli let her vent, rarely speaking beyond murmurs of sympathy.

After she'd exhausted herself, Meli reached over and gently held her hand, rubbing her thumb over the back. Every neuron in Conner's body focused on the contact.

"That's a lot, Conner. Can you think of pros now?"

She tried to pull her focus away from their joined hands. "The fans. Fans are usually fantastic."

"Usually?"

"It's aggravating when they think they know me because of a few interviews and social media posts."

Meli giggled. "I was probably just like that when we first met."

Conner shook her head and looked up until their gazes met. "No. I always felt like you saw the real me."

Meli smiled and squeezed her hand.

Conner hurried to continue before she dwelled on what she'd just revealed. "But mostly the fans are great. Sometimes...sometimes I feel like my fans are the only people on the planet who love me."

"Oh, Conner." Her voice carried so much emotion. Too much. "That's not true."

"It can be true. Sometimes."

Meli let go of her hand, and she missed the contact immediately until Meli cupped her face, pulling her close until Conner couldn't look away.

"Then I will just have to do my best to make sure you feel loved every day from now on."

Nope. Nope. Nope. She couldn't handle this. Her bottom lip quivered as the old urge to self-destruct reared its head. She had to push her away; it would hurt both of them, but better now, better to get it out of the way before it got too hard. Their friendship would never last anyway, and what sort of friendship was it when Conner constantly lusted after her?

But this was *Meli*. Conner would cut off her right hand before deliberately hurting her. It would be like kicking a puppy. The dearest, sweetest, most beautiful puppy in the world. A perfect puppy, even if she would never be Conner's. She meant what she'd said; Meli *saw* Conner, in a way that even Maggie had never managed. If she intended to start over and rebuild her life, a layer of honesty with the person she cared about most was the best-possible foundation. Maybe, just maybe, it would be all right.

And then the words tumbled out, uncontrollable verbal vomit. Everything she had said and done to people in her life, excepting nothing besides Maggie's abortion and Harlow's business plans. Those stories weren't hers to tell. Through it all Meli sat clearly stunned, showing only bewilderment.

When Conner finished, it was so quiet she swore she could hear the earth rotate. She slid to the edge of the chaise, elbows on her knees as she buried her face in her hands. "I didn't mean to blurt all of that out," she mumbled weakly.

She heard a rustle, and then Meli was pulling her hands away as she knelt in front of her. Her wide, brown eyes shone as bright as the stars. "Sweetie, that's too much for anyone to keep to themselves. So you—okay, you made some mistakes. A lot. And you hurt people you cared about. A lot. Well, that sounds bad. What I'm trying to say is, um…you feel awful about it, right? That's obvious. You're trying. That's all anyone can do. Nothing is broken for good, not even Sadie. You just have to start fresh and rebuild trust. And Conner? I promise you that you will never, ever be alone in this. I know you. I know your heart. You're a good person, even when you don't believe it. You'll get through this, and I'll be right there with you."

Conner hung suspended in time as something inside her broke wide open, something she wouldn't dare name, dwell on, or even look at too long. She might scare it away. She might accept it.

Meli leaned back, a smile splitting her face. "Remember, you're Conner freaking Cody. You can do anything. For what it's worth, from the outside looking in, I believe one hundred percent that includes acting and making music. I've seen you do both, and it looks as natural and as necessary as breathing."

❖

Meli didn't leave that night. They talked for hours longer, veering from earnest discussions about her career, serious conversations regarding how Conner would straighten up, honest confessions about her drug habit, and how Meli dealt with her nerves to enthusiastic plans for the Velasco family visit and mirthful teasing as they swapped their most embarrassing stories. Conner hadn't felt that light or happy since...ever, perhaps. Maybe it could all turn out okay after all.

She pressed Meli to stay the night when it grew late, not that she required much persuasion, but Conner couldn't sleep. She walked down to the beach and stared at the moon.

Meli was right. As much as she hated the extraneous activities, she lived and breathed acting and playing music. Performing was in her blood, but that didn't have to be a bad thing. Sure, she'd give it all up if the people who mattered in her life required she sacrifice it. But her utopia always had a camera and a microphone.

Despite the late hour, she texted Harlow.

I'm in.

Chapter Thirty-three

"It's six o'clock in the morning, and yesterday I flew across a continent and an ocean. Why the hell did you wake me up?" Conner squinted at her grandmother through bleary eyes.

Gran remained unbothered. "You came to me for help, so help you shall receive. We have a month to get you into shape."

Conner rolled over, burying her face into her pillow. "I exercise every day, and I eat right ninety percent of the time. I'm in perfect shape."

Either Gran couldn't make out her muffled words, or she didn't care. Probably the latter. "I've arranged, on very little notice, singing lessons, dancing lessons, a dialect coach, and a French tutor—at your request. You begin in an hour. I shan't climb these stairs again."

"You shouldn't be climbing five flights of stairs anyway. Send one of your staff next time."

"There won't be a next time, Conner. Up. Now."

She grumbled but got out of bed anyway. What she said was true; Conner *had* called a week ago to tell Gran she was coming to visit for a month and needed help preparing for an audition. Besides, she was trying to leave her petulant, self-absorbed persona in the past, even if six in the morning was a ridiculous hour she avoided whenever possible.

Freshly cut melon, juicy berries, hardboiled eggs, and a bowl of porridge awaited her downstairs. She wrinkled her nose at the porridge.

"You loved it when you were small," said Gran as she cracked the top of an egg.

"I don't recall that."

"You did. It's good for you. Eat."

She did as she was told...sort of, forcing down half a bowl before Gran relented. Conner vowed to have a word with the kitchen staff. She wanted whole-wheat toast, a nice spinach omelet, or perhaps a mushroom hash. Not porridge.

Gran was true to her word. At seven on the dot, a drill sergeant in the disguise of a dignified, elderly lady appeared, very sweet outside of their lessons and completely terrifying during them. Obviously Conner knew how to sing, but 1940s big band inhabited a different plane than indie rock music. After her voice lessons, she jumped into French with a tutor who went from delight at her fluency to despair at her accent in about ten seconds. Their lessons involved so much discussion of food that she wished she'd eaten more of the morning's porridge.

"Do you always put this much effort into your auditions?" Gran asked over their lunch of smoked salmon and roasted vegetables, much more to Conner's taste.

She chewed a piece of cauliflower as slowly as she could, trying to figure out how to answer. "Not usually."

"I suspected as much. What makes this one different?"

"It's a good role. Substantial. A strong woman whose journey isn't driven by a man." She chased down a carrot. "I've been trying to determine what accent she should have."

The narrowing of Gran's green eyes told Conner her change of subject hadn't gone unnoticed, but she let it go. "Where is she from?"

"It doesn't specify. She's the bastard daughter of an earl—"

"Then she'll have a local accent. You must determine where she grew up."

"But she was acknowledged by the earl, raised in the same household as her half siblings, and educated alongside them. I'm thinking she can code-switch. Obviously she would've had to be posh at school, but she lets it slip when she's around her mother who's from like East Anglia or something like that."

Gran nodded. "Good, good."

"Any tips on maintaining the accent?" Gran had mastered an RP British accent so long ago that Conner sometimes forgot she was Irish, especially when they met outside of Belfast. This wouldn't be Conner's first role that required an accent, but somehow this part had become intrinsically linked to getting her life back on track. It was imperative that she nail every single aspect.

"Practice until you begin dreaming in it."

Her afternoon sessions were as demanding as the morning. The dialect coach drilled her on every single vowel sound until she'd forgotten her own accent. Then came dancing.

Conner hadn't danced since she was a teenager and hadn't taken any sort of lessons since childhood. She had to screw up every single bit of determination inside her to get past her inhibitions against dancing in front of anyone, and a full week passed before she found some enjoyment in the lessons.

When she wasn't practicing, she alternated between long strolls in nearby Hyde Park or walking down to St. James's Park, and working. Harlow, picking up as if they'd never left off, kept her busy with requests for interviews and potential auditions and had also sent along a box full of glossy photographs of Lyss that needed to be signed for various purposes. She attempted to compose, but her muse remained as elusive as ever.

She suspected the muse was currently in California, or at least that's where her thoughts kept drifting, as if pulled by the tides. Meli hadn't left her side after her unintended confession and was now watching her house, as had become their routine, although both knew Conner's staff had it well in hand. They picked up their former habit of good morning/good night texts, and the time zone difference meant each always had a message waiting when she woke up. Even though they chatted daily, Conner wondered what Meli was doing. What was she eating? What was she wearing? How were her auditions faring? Did the commercial she booked go well? What was she thinking? If she was she thinking about her? Did she miss her? Did she miss Conner as much as Conner missed her?

And, when she couldn't stop herself, if she was dating.

When she ventured too far down that path, she veered away and usually landed on another source of pain: her sister. Conner had given her space before first trying to call and then sending her a few texts begging for forgiveness, but Sadie remained irascible, and Conner left off, not wanting to upset her further. She hadn't been removed from Sarah's social media accounts, so she took what she could get, soaking up every glimpse, promising herself it wouldn't always be like this. Her chest hurt too much if she let herself consider that this might be the extent of their relationship forever.

For a fortnight she remained under the radar of the British press until she stopped for a tea one afternoon. Later that night, she cursed at her phone when her publicist sent her a screenshot that had captured her offering a half-smile to the barista as she picked up her drink.

Gran peered over the edge of her newspaper as they sat in what she called the drawing room. "Hmm?"

Conner shook her head and let her phone drop to her lap. "Gran, do you ever regret becoming famous?"

"Can't say that I do. It's part and parcel of the job, darling girl. You know that."

"Yeah, I just…Christ, Gran, I just want to be left alone sometimes, you know? I want privacy. I want to go out for a fucking drink and not get my picture plastered all over the internet."

Gran folded her paper, then her hands, and Conner geared up for the incoming lecture. "Perhaps they would lose interest if you didn't give them quite so much to discuss."

"I don't"—she said before turning down the heat—"*always* give them ammo. Sometimes it's just that I exist."

"Is that why you've stayed so close while you've been here? I haven't seen you this much since you were a toddler."

"I guess. I came—wait. What do you mean? Did we visit a lot when I was little?"

A look of perplexion dawned across Gran's wrinkled visage. "I wouldn't call it a visit, more that you arrived and didn't leave. Don't you recall?"

Something tightened in Conner's gut. "Clearly not."

"Oh, you were two or three, thereabouts, out of nappies to be sure. Your parents brought you for a visit, and they decided they wanted a holiday before Seth went on tour. So off they went to Bangkok or Singapore, somewhere in Southeast Asia, and left you here without so much as a by-your-leave. A month had passed by the time they finally rang me back to say that your mother had decided to join him on tour, no doubt to keep him from shacking up with someone else. It took only a few times for me to hear that she would come get you 'soon' before I realized she wouldn't."

Huh. So she'd been abandoned after all. She'd have guessed it would hurt more, but maybe she'd finally numbed herself to her parents' callous neglect.

She blinked, aware Gran was watching her. "Why don't I remember this?"

"I don't know. You were very young. But you seemed content enough. You asked for them a few times, and then you stopped. I put you in the larger bedroom on the third floor and installed a nanny in the smaller, and there you—"

"Ducks."

"Hmm?"

"I remember a duck nightlight. I liked to watch it. Did you decorate my room with ducks?"

Gran flicked her hand. "Perhaps. I hired someone, I'm sure."

Conner caught herself chewing her bottom lip. "How long?"

"Before they came back for you? About two years."

"Two years?!" Conner's jaw dropped. "They just left their kid for two years? What the fuck, Gran? Why didn't you, I don't know, drag them back home?"

"You can't force people to do as you please, Conner. At any rate, you were already on that show your mother pushed you into, and after several months with me you were due back in Los Angeles to film. I was preparing to revive *Mourning Becomes Electra*, so your other grandmother kept you." She sniffed. "You came back to me speaking perfect Spanish. Of course I enrolled you in French right away."

Conner rolled her eyes. "So glad I helped you put one over on each other. Are you ever going to tell me the story between you two?"

"There doesn't have to be a story. Sometimes people simply don't get on."

Conner didn't believe her, but she let it go. "So that's it? You took turns babysitting for two years?"

"If that's how you want to look at it. Seth's tour finished, but then he went with your mother on location as she filmed a Bond movie. You were nearly ready for primary school, and your grandmother finally must have raised hell with that daughter of hers, because they showed up one day and whisked you away. As I recollect, you wailed like a banshee."

Conner frowned. Why didn't she remember any of this? Of course she remembered both of her grandparents' homes, and spending the night, but she should have been able to recognize the difference between living somewhere and visiting. Was upheaval such a natural part of her young life that she didn't notice a change, or had it been so traumatic that she repressed the memories into some dark, cobwebby corner of her mind?

"Conner." A delicate, blue-veined hand lifted her chin. "Let it go, lass. If it hadn't been us, it would've been nannies, just like the rest of your childhood. You're an award-winning actress and musician. I reckon you got the best of your parents, after all."

She pressed a kiss to the back of her grandmother's hand before standing. "Thanks, Gran. I think I'll go up now."

"Ta." Gran lifted her glass of sherry and returned to her paper.

After pouring a glass of Macallan as old as she was, Conner headed for the stairs, only to pause in the doorway. "Gran, why did my parents marry?"

Gran's lips thinned. "Your mother refused to have a bastard child, not that it stopped her from creating the child out of wedlock. She said it would hurt her reputation. I've always believed she got pregnant on purpose to keep Seth around."

Conner had to stop herself from blowing a raspberry. Fat lot of good that did Camila in the end.

On her way up, she took a long look at the larger room on the third floor. No ducks remained, replaced by a lurid floral wallpaper. No trace of Conner endured as well, neither corporeal nor spiritual.

Lounging on the terrace outside her current bedroom, she sipped her Scotch and contemplated the evening's revelations. So her parents didn't want her. Not exactly news. Her grandparents, though not perfect themselves, had stepped up, and she was truly grateful for them. Gran and Abuelita criticized her plenty, but they also threw occasional praise her way, which was far more affection than Camila or Seth ever demonstrated.

Suddenly overwhelmed by the need for someone who liked her, even if not in the manner she wished, she scrolled to her favorites on her phone.

Meli's beaming face popped up so quickly that Conner nearly dropped her drink. Gran would've been furious if she broke the crystal.

"I was just going to text to see if you were free!"

Conner grinned. "We must have a psychic connection."

"We have something," Meli said, and Conner ordered herself not to read anything into that remark. "How are your lessons?"

"Good. Nothing I haven't done before, so it's just a matter of taking the skills I have in a different direction. My teachers are hardcore, though. Wouldn't be out of place in a Russian gulag."

Meli's smile illuminated the London darkness surrounding Conner. "It's really awesome how hard you're working to get this role. I try to prep as best I can, but this is a whole other level."

"I really want it. It's a good role—it's meaty and challenging, it has the best ending...I won't spoil it, but it's so good, and she's an adult! I swear I'm never playing a teenager again."

"It's those youthful good looks of yours."

She winked. Meli fucking *winked*. She had never done that before, although Conner winked at her plenty, enjoying the squirming she provoked. Now she was the one discomfited, she was the one being teased, she was the one confronted with sexy confidence.

The worst part—the best part—was she really, really liked it.

She scrambled for something to say before she revealed herself. "It's also privilege, you know?" She received a blank stare in response. "The ability to prep like this. Not everyone can take off for a month and pay for personal coaching."

Meli slowly nodded. "That's true. I definitely couldn't." She held up her hand, stopping Conner before she started. "I know you would, and I love you for it."

Conner nearly stopped breathing.

"Isn't it enough that I practically live at your house?"

At that she did stop breathing, just for a moment, as she pictured waking up to Meli, watching her cook, eating meals together, running lines with each other, playing music for her, falling asleep with her. Sharing a life.

"Don't worry! I'm just kidding. I know how much you value your privacy, and I would never take advantage of you. In fact, I can totally get my family to stay at a hotel. It's probably for the best anyway. We could never intrude on you like that. They'll drive you completely crazy. God knows they drive *me* crazy enough as it is, and I'm one of them. I mean, it was really generous of you, but it was totally stupid of me to think—"

Conner belatedly realized that Meli had misinterpreted her silence. "Meli! Chill out. You know I love having you at my house." She swallowed. "And I'm really looking forward to meeting them. Tell me what you have planned."

She settled back, relishing her adorable rambling. With anyone else, she would have lost patience long ago, but everything Meli did charmed her. God, she was fucked.

"You look like an entirely different person."

"That's the point. I'm not Conner fucking Cody, rock star slash tabloid darling. I'm Cecilia bloody Hargreave, Cambridge scholar by day, nightclub singer by night, and soon to be spy. Both badasses, but otherwise very different."

"Take that ego into the audition, and you'll nail it," Harlow said. "Good luck."

"I don't need luck, but thanks anyway."

After Harlow hung up, Conner studied herself in the mirror. A demure, shoulder-length, light-brown wig covered her shaggy hair, no bright purple tips in sight, and her makeup artist had paired that feature with bright red lipstick while emphasizing the natural arch of her eyebrows. A navy polka-dotted wrap dress with posh white gloves completed the look. She carried a garment bag with a stunning red cocktail dress to change into to represent the duality of the character and her ability to morph as the situation demanded.

Like most actors, Conner was her own worst critic, but she usually had a good feel for an audition. Sometimes she knew she'd blown it, sometimes she knew she'd rocked it, and sometimes she knew she'd done well but wasn't who they were looking for.

She aced it. She knocked their socks off. She cooked with gas, to use era-appropriate slang. Whatever cliché she came up with was accurate because she blew the casting director's mind with her two scenes, and she strutted away knowing she'd get a callback.

She did, and she rocked it again with a stunning rendition of Glenn Miller's "I Know Why (And So Do You)" before tearing up the makeshift dance floor during Benny Goodman's version of "Sing, Sing, Sing" with a talented dancer who swung her with abandon.

"That was excellent, Conner," the casting director said. "Do you mind waiting for a few minutes?"

She took a seat with a bottle of water, chatting with her dance partner. The casting director reappeared only a few minutes later, beckoning her with a finger.

"Mr. Fisher would like to speak with you."

The director waited in a small office. A large man, he dropped no clues. After a few complimentary words about her audition, he leaned back.

"I understand you punched my son."

Oof. So they were going to do this now. No point in denying it. "That's true."

"Would you do it again?"

She froze, caught between the truth and her desire for this part. A devil on her shoulder urged her to lie. It would hurt no one, while the truth could hurt only her. Another devil on her other shoulder (Conner had no delusions that she had an angel) pressed for the truth. Was any role worth sacrificing her integrity?

Meli's frightened face floated before her eyes, and she lifted her chin. "Yes, I would. He put his hands on a friend of mine, and she didn't want them."

"I see." He steepled his fingers under his chin, and for several long moments they both were silent. "Reputation is a funny thing, Ms. Cody. While one hears many things about your personal life, not all complimentary, your professional reputation is sterling. What I hear about my son is not always flattering, but it appears that is deserved."

How was she supposed to reply? Was she expected to respond at all?

He tossed a pen onto the desk, startling her. "Your auditions were miles beyond anyone else's. You brought Cecilia to life. There is no one else but you for her. Congratulations, Ms. Cody. I look forward to working with you."

She stood, shaking his outstretched hand. "Call me Conner, Mr. Fisher. Thank you very much. You won't be disappointed."

Her smile outshone the sun beating down on Los Angeles. The role was hers, all hers. Conner had won many roles in her career, some more desired than others, but none that she had worked harder for, and none had come at a better time.

She couldn't wait to tell Meli.

Chapter Thirty-four

Harlow glared at Conner over the rim of her glasses. "Remove your feet now."

"How did I make it so long without you ordering me around?" Conner slid her boots off Harlow's desk even as she teased her. "Complete chaos."

Harlow narrowed her eyes but said nothing as she continued to work on her tablet. Conner read a book on her phone until Harlow cleared her throat.

"I'm just getting to the good part. The main character is drunk and has called her ex to come get her." Conner's mind drifted as she thought of the person she wanted most when she was down, before shrugging the idea away. Never going to happen. "If they ever make this series into movies, I better be first in line. I could play a soccer star."

"Fit that into your schedule, and I'll make it happen." Harlow slid the tablet across the table.

Conner scrolled through the calendar, letting out a low whistle. She was glad to be back at work, but once again, her free time was ghosting her for the next several months. Some last-minute ADR, then a press tour for her final run as a superhero before the various premieres, plus a festival and an endorsement campaign. She was supposed to have a little time at the end of the year, before filming for her new movie began in January, but Harlow had blocked that out as well.

"What's this for?"

"Recording your next album. Didn't you agree on an every-other-year schedule? I assumed you'd record it then and go on tour as soon as you finished filming."

"Yes, that was the agreement," she replied slowly. "But we can't record what I haven't written."

Harlow paused, eyebrows climbing her forehead. "You haven't? That's unusual. You're always scribbling something."

"I have some songs, but it just hasn't been happening for me."

"Have you considered hiring a professional songwriter?"

Conner recoiled, outrage rising. "I certainly have not. I'm not singing someone else's music."

"You're not going to be singing anything if you don't record another album."

"I'm gonna write it," she muttered under her breath. "I just need more time. You wouldn't understand creativity if it bit you in the ass."

"I can hear you," Harlow said without looking up. Conner stuck her tongue out. "Saw that, too. Very mature."

"How do you do that? You're a freak."

"Takes one to know one, doesn't it?"

Conner grinned, leaning forward. "Why don't you clear that desk off and find out?"

"Never going to happen, but I doubt you're suffering from lack of attention."

Actually...she wasn't suffering, but she hadn't hooked up in months. For the most part, she hadn't been in the mood. When she had an itch to scratch, she only had eyes for one person, and her trusty box of toys sufficed, although she felt guilty for getting off to thoughts of someone who was and always would be just a friend. She needed to get her mind on something—or someone—else. Maybe she should give Lindsey a call.

"Conner?"

Her head shot up, aware she'd been silent for several minutes. "Sorry, what?"

Harlow looked at her for a moment as if considering what to say, which was so unlike her that dread pooled in Conner's gut. "I've been holding on to this because I wasn't sure how you would take it, but I don't think it's my call to make."

"Okay..."

"I got an email from Carly Boyd. She's—"

"Britt Boyd's daughter. I remember Carly."

Carly Boyd had been a gangly tween when Conner was hanging around the Boyd house, all braces and awkward limbs. Her adulation of Conner had been apparent even through the height of Conner's teenage self-absorption, only concerned with impressing the much older Britt, but their interactions were largely limited to greetings and the occasional chat while she was waiting for Carly's mother. Britt had a son, too, a few years younger than Carly, but he'd always been glued to his video games.

Conner cleared her throat. "What does she want?"

"She included a letter for you. I haven't read it." She hesitated. "Do you want my advice?"

"Sure."

"Be very careful, Conner. You dropped a bomb on her mother's reputation on national television and detonated her parents' marriage. I don't see what good could come of talking to anyone in that family."

She bit hard on the inside of her cheek. She didn't regret blowing up Britt Boyd, but she'd never considered the collateral damage. Maybe she could help the girl. After all, she knew what it was like to have her parents' indiscretions blasted from every corner.

"Forward it to me. I should at least read it. I know what I'm doing, Harlow. Send me the email."

Conner,

I don't know if you remember me, but my mother is Britt Boyd. I know you remember her.

I've wanted to reach out for months, even though I'm not really sure why. I was angry at you for a long time after your interview with Larissa Lamont. I blamed you for everything— Dad moving out, my brother quitting all his sports, me having to transfer to a different college. It was just easier to blame you than admit that my mother is who she is.

But she is. I don't know why. I don't know if you were the only one. I'm not sure if I want to know. But you were a victim, so I wanted to tell you that I'm sorry. Sorry for blaming you, and sorry for Mom doing what she did to you.

I'm in therapy, and I'm learning more about what grooming is. I was a kid at the time, so I never noticed anything wrong. I just thought it was really cool that THE Conner Cody was always around. I used to brag to my friends that I knew you.

Anyway, I just wanted you to know.

Carly Boyd

Harlow watched her carefully as Conner closed her phone with a frown. "Are you okay?"

"What? Oh. I'm fine. I guess I never thought about Britt's actions affecting anyone but me."

"Maybe it will help you get some closure."

"I thought I had closure. But maybe I can help someone else get it."

Later that night as she curled up with a book, Conner kept thinking about the email. With a sigh, she pulled it up and typed a quick response before she could talk herself out of it.

Time for her to start cleaning up her messes.

They ended up meeting for lunch. Though awkward and even uncomfortable, she answered all of Carly's questions as best she could and got the impression that the woman was able to make more sense of it all.

And Harlow had been right—it did help Conner get closure and rid herself of lingering guilt that she hadn't known she carried.

She sat alone for a little while after Carly left, struck by the sad realization that under other circumstances, the two of them could have been friends. Meli's roommate Eriq, who had waited on them at Conner's request and was the reason she chose that restaurant, interrupted her ruminations.

"Good lunch?"

She smiled as he hovered over her. "Necessary lunch. But yes, good overall."

"So...not a date, then?"

"Definitely not."

A corner of his mouth curled up in a knowing smirk. "Excellent."

"What does that mean? Eriq! What does that mean? I'm going to reduce your tip!"

Thumping bass set the pace for Conner's heartbeat. She peered through the door to the artists' lounge at the masses of humanity crammed into Golden Gate Park in San Francisco before ducking back inside to avoid causing a scene. Some might have called that response arrogance, but she just called it reality.

Her presence at the Outside Lands festival had caused enough of a stir already. Hestia Rising hadn't been invited, but Conner had, a request from an old colleague to guest for a few songs. She'd thought nothing of it, merely repaying a favor they'd frequently asked of others while on tour, but Kit thought otherwise. After a bitter disagreement, she turned to Harlow, who advised her to go, engaging Kit in an argument of her own.

Conner was her own woman. She didn't need her band in order to sing a few songs for someone else. The band that had remained suspiciously mute during the dispute as well as the months since their quarrel. She needed to figure out how to make that right, but her gut told her not to crawl back until she had something to give them, so off to the festival she went, hoping the weekend would provide her muse with sustenance.

Because, the life-giving joy of making music aside, she really, really missed her friends.

But for now, she intended to enjoy her time. She wasn't performing until the second day, so she spent most of her time in the lounge, occasionally slipping out to catch a few choice acts from one side of the stage.

It was during one of these ventures outside the relative safety of the lounge that her weekend took a turn. She'd been watching the set of an emerging pop star, campier than her tastes usually ran but entertaining nonetheless, and was heading back when a voice halted her mid-stride.

"Well, well, well. Conner fucking Cody. I just can't escape you, can I?"

Conner turned around with the speed of someone facing a firing squad, and nearly as much dread. "What the hell do you want?"

Lola smirked at her. She was as pretty as ever, although Conner suspected that the heavy makeup around her eyes hid bags and wrinkles. "I just want to catch up. It's been a minute."

"Not nearly long enough. I have nothing to say to you."

"So hostile. Don't you get tired of being grouchy all the time? You're going to get frown lines on that gorgeous face of yours."

"Don't you get tired of bothering me? Go find someone else to bother, like my sloppy seconds."

Lola laughed and moved closer. Conner tensed. "Jealous? She said you would be, but don't worry. She's around. She also said—and I'm sure you know this—that you're welcome to join us any time you want."

"Here's the thing." Conner lowered her voice, regretting it when Lola leaned in even more. "I've had both of you separately. I have no desire to have it again, much less together."

"That's a shame." She put on an exaggerated pout. It wasn't a great look on her. "I know we had a good time together. I still remember the sounds you made when you came…"

Conner brushed her hair out of her face and shook her head, flinging the tresses right back into her eyes. "I'm so done with this conversation and with you. Go away, Lola."

She marched toward the lounge. The last thing she needed was someone's cell phone blasting pictures of the two of them all over social media.

Unfortunately, Lola could take neither hints nor outright instructions and followed. "I'm just messing with you, Conner. That's all in the past. We had our fun, and now it's over. What I really want from you is work."

Conner narrowed her eyes. Lola made her brain hurt. "You want a job? From me? Are you on something?"

"I don't need a job," came the cool retort. "I want to work *with* you. The tour was a success. We should take that to the next level and do a song together."

Conner's sardonic chuckle quickly morphed into full-blown laughter. What Lola lacked in tact and subtlety she certainly made up for in audacity. "Okay, I'll indulge you. Why in the world would I ever work with you after you released a song trashing me?"

"Trash is a little harsh," Lola said with a scoff, tossing her long, dark hair.

"It was bullshit, and you know it."

"It was...exaggerated, yes, but every songwriter uses artistic license. As if you never have."

Her blood pressure wouldn't survive another interaction with Lola. "All my songs are entirely true, but it's good to hear you finally admit that you made it up."

Lola reddened. "I didn't make it up. You came to *my* room, fucked me, and then completely ignored me."

"We agreed that it was one night only. I don't know how many times I have to remind you of that fact. Also, I didn't ignore you afterward. I just didn't give you what you wanted. Even if your story was true, which it isn't, why would you want to work with me again?"

Lola fidgeted, suddenly evading her gaze. "It's just business, Conner."

"It's just—oh. I get it." She began laughing again. Karma could be glorious sometimes. "You need me. You're a fraud, you've got nothing, and your one real hit was based on lies. It's a damn shame that you're not a good person, because you're actually talented. Later, and by that I mean never again, Lola."

She walked away, but that didn't stop Lola from shouting at her back. "I've done it once, and I'll do it again, Conner Cody! You're not invincible."

She turned, intending to tell Lola to fuck off, but nearly ran into Vittoria, who emerged as if from thin air. Great. An already annoying encounter made even worse.

"Hello, *mia luna*."

My moon. The old nickname, once so sweet, felt like an anchor around her neck, dragging her back to a place she didn't want to be. A person she didn't want to be. She took Vittoria in, recognizing that she faced a beautiful woman, but her stomach remained calm, her chest unbothered, her arousal dormant. Vittoria's body was as alluring as a siren, which she now understood had always been the paramount draw, but she remained unaffected.

"Your girlfriend is literally right there." She gestured at Lola, whose clenched mouth radiated anger, although it was unclear if it was at Conner, Vittoria, or both.

Vittoria lifted one apathetic shoulder. "She understands how it is."

"You two deserve each other, you know that? Have at it. Just leave me out of it."

Vittoria's long fingers encircled her wrist. Conner took a long look at the grasp before turning her glare onto her ex-girlfriend. "It's been a year, Conner. You had your fun. Let's move on."

"Yes, let's. I'll move on to my home, you'll move on back to Italy, and we'll never see each other again."

"Do you want to be wooed? Is that it? We belong together, Conner. Admit it."

Conner's temper exploded into the stratosphere. "No, goddamn it! Why don't any of you people understand that? You don't want me; none of you want *me*. Lola wants me to further her career, and you want me to fulfill some power-couple fantasy and Britt wanted...well, I don't really know what she wanted, but it wasn't *me*. I just want to be left alone, for fuck's sake."

Outrage laid claim to Vittoria's face. "You would compare me to her? I would never do what she did!"

"You mean you would never talk down to me? You would never try to persuade me that I want something when I say that I don't? Go fuck yourself, Vittoria. I broke up with you a year ago because I didn't want to be with you, and I still don't want to be with you."

Only her harsh breathing broke the silence. She looked down at her hands, surprised to find them trembling.

"Listen, you were an important part of my life for several years, and I don't regret the time we spent together." Mostly. "But it's over. It's been over for a long time. You need to accept that fact, please."

For perhaps the first time ever, Vittoria appeared genuinely hurt. The corners of her mouth tucked downward, and her forehead softened. "You really don't want to be with me?"

Conner forced a smile. "I know it's hard to believe that anyone would turn you down, but no, I don't. And maybe I'm wrong, but I don't believe you really want to be with me, either. I think you want to be with someone who fits a role that you desire. It's not me. It's what I represent. We don't love each other, Vittoria. We never have."

Vittoria took so long to reply that Conner hoped her rejection had finally sunk in. Behind them, Lola watched, her face an interesting shade of crimson.

Vittoria spoke, shattering Conner's illusions. "You'll regret this, Conner Cody. You'll regret it very much, but I won't be here when you do."

Conner was done. No point in furthering this conversation.

"Good-bye, Vittoria."

What promised to be a doozy of an argument between Lola and Vittoria fired up before Conner had even left. Good riddance. They could have each other. As she ducked into the nearby tent, something collided against her side. "What the—"

Two young women, eyes wide and cheeks pink, blurted out apologies as they scurried away, a trail of giggles in their wake. Conner frowned, trying to figure out where they'd been and if they could have overheard the conversation, but eventually she gave up.

She never figured out where they'd been, but they'd definitely overheard.

Her phone was going off like a cluster bomb by the time she returned to the artists' lounge. The two girls had posted a live play-by-play of the entire interaction almost down to the exact words.

Harlow: Conner, what is happening?
Meli: Um. You're blowing up on socials rn.
Lindsey: DUDE! Blast 'em!
Kit: We really need to talk.

She ignored them all and indulged in a rare scroll through her social media accounts, once again handled by Harlow's intern, thank goodness. The reactions almost entirely lambasted Lola for admitting she'd bent the truth for her song and Vittoria for her callous treatment of Lola and disregard for Conner's wishes. Only a few people had an issue with Conner, and as most appeared to be pearl-clutching conservatives, she probably offended them simply by existing. A surprising number railed against the two girls who'd eavesdropped on their conversation, arguing for privacy and consent, with which Conner wholeheartedly agreed even if she appeared to be coming out on top for once.

Harlow asked if she wanted the posts taken down, but Conner decided to let the situation slide. After all, she was getting some halfway decent press for the first time in months. The fact that Lola and Vittoria were getting shit from all sides didn't hurt, either, although she almost felt bad for Lola for getting dumped in such a public and insensitive manner.

Lola texted her that evening, pleading with her to speak out in her defense. Conner replied once before blocking her number, done with her forever.

I told you not to fuck with me, babe.

The next day, she cavorted onstage and thrilled the crowd with a few songs, taunting them with loose jeans that clung to her hips with the faintest of hopes, teasing glimpses of the Tom Ford logo on the waistband of her underwear. She returned to her hotel immediately afterward. The festival would last another day, but she was finished, exhausted by the drama. Her hotel room had a welcome shower and bed, and then she was changing her flight to the next one available. LA had her home, her car, her beach, her guitar.

And Meli.

Chapter Thirty-Five

Conner lay in her bed, flat on her back and as rigid as a cadaver, hands fixed at her sides as she barely dared to breathe. In all the uncomfortable scenarios she'd imagined this week would bring, she had never given thought to this particular one.

When she'd offered her house to Meli's family, she'd only wished to make Meli happy. While a houseful of strangers for a few days was the exact opposite of fun for her, she figured it couldn't be too bad.

So far it hadn't been, although her alarm grew with every person who streamed through her door. Her house was packed to the rafters with Meli's family. Every room was full, including the pool house, and some of the older kids were camped out in the living room.

That led her to her current predicament. Everything had been fine until they'd finished dinner. Conner and Meli had cleaned up (pizza didn't exceed Conner's limited domestic capabilities), and then Meli announced she was leaving for her apartment.

"Leaving?" Her mother, a short woman inclined to very tight hugs, put her hands on her hips. "To go where?"

"Home, Mami. Where else would I go?"

"But we came here to see you, and I'm making chilaquiles for breakfast. You said your apartment is an hour away."

"I'll be back first thing in the morning. I promise I won't miss your chilaquiles!"

"Just stay here. You have room, don't you, Conner?"

An entire family of beseeching brown eyes turned to her, accompanied by a chorus of pleas and persuasion and general comments she couldn't really make out. Meli's abuela, her maternal grandmother, tiny and wrinkled yet clearly in charge, put the situation to rest by declaring that they were grown women who could certainly handle sharing a bed.

"I would offer to share, but I'm afraid my CPAP machine would keep you up all night, my girl. Now, you, help me up the stairs." She pointed one gnarled hand at Meli's uncle, who jumped as if his pants had caught fire.

Somehow amidst all the ruckus of getting over a dozen people settled, Meli and Conner found themselves in her room, standing on opposite sides of her bed.

"I'll just go home once everyone is asleep," Meli said at the same time Conner said, "I can sleep in the theater."

"You're not sleeping in there! Chairs aren't for sleeping."

"They recline. And you act like I haven't done that before." Conner shrugged. "But your mother would be really upset if you didn't stay."

"You think I never snuck out and back in during high school?" Meli winked, and images of all the trouble they could have gotten up to as teenagers flooded Conner's mind before sense asserted itself. Meli had likely been passing around a bottle of Boone's Farm, while Conner was doing lines of cocaine and washing down pills with shots of tequila. Not quite the same level.

"I mean, it's a pretty big bed." Meli gestured.

"King-sized."

"We could just…"

"Yeah. If you don't…"

"We've done it before."

They held each other's gaze for a moment before bursting into nervous giggles. Conner scouted for extra pajamas while Meli turned down the bed.

"I feel like a kid at a sleepover. Any moment now my mother's going to bang on the door and tell us to be quiet and go to sleep."

"I never had a sleepover." Conner couldn't stifle a smirk. "Well, I've had plenty of sleepovers, but I don't think we're talking about the same thing."

Meli threw a pillow at her, Conner lobbed the pajamas back, and for a moment it really felt like someone might tell them off for being too loud. Thank goodness for soundproofing.

Then they lay down on opposite sides of the bed, and all their light-hearted joviality fled, leaving Conner with only an uncomfortable awareness of their proximity. They chatted softly for a while until Meli's breathing deepened and evened out, but sleep was a remote stranger to Conner.

It was all too much. Too easy for her to imagine that this was their life, hosting family get-togethers and retreating to the sanctuary of their shared bedroom every night. In her fantasy, Sadie's family joined them, the kids playing in the pool together while Asher pretended to know how to grill and Sadie gossiped with Meli's sister. She let her thoughts wander down that path, dreaming of pulling Meli close so they could decompress, laughing at her brother's antics and complaining about her mother's fussing. Then maybe she'd make a few suggestive remarks, initiate a few ardent caresses.

Meli would pretend to object at first with her parents right below but give in all too eagerly, sliding her palms up Conner's—

Her eyelids flew open, and she stared at the dark ceiling, straining to make out the gently circling fan blades. Anything to distract her from the persistent throbbing between her legs and the pounding of her pulse in her neck. She would not do this. She could not do this, not with the woman in question a few feet away.

Conner smothered a groan before slipping out of bed as quietly as she could. Inside her bathroom, she locked the door before flipping on the light, welcoming the harsh glare. She stared back at herself in the mirror, desperate and flushed with arousal. *Stop it. Be an adult and get control of yourself.*

Meli in her bed.

Meli in her clothes.

Meli out of her clothes.

She let out a frustrated growl and dropped her head to the vanity. It was wrong, so wrong, but if she didn't do something about it, she'd never sleep. When she slipped her hand into her shorts, her sigh of relief segued into a whimper at how wet she was. Her fingers circled her clit several times before dipping into herself and spreading the wetness around. She clenched the countertop with her free hand, then bit down hard to swallow a moan as her fingers went to work, urging herself to a quick climax that insisted on hovering just out of reach.

"Come on," she begged under her breath. She had fucked too many women to count, hot, gorgeous, stunning women who played her body like a fiddle. She should be able to pick any one of them and sprint to the finish line on those memories.

Her knees were on the verge of collapse as she rubbed herself so quickly she half expected smoke to rise. Her elusive climax taunted her until she nearly sobbed, and finally the dam of her resolve broke.

Meli's fingers sliding over her clit, Meli's tongue on her neck, Meli's hand squeezing her breasts, Meli, Meli, Meli. She bit down on her free hand to stifle the name she moaned as she finally jerked to completion, riding out her orgasm against the bathroom sink.

Her panting breath bounced off the tile floors. She took her time composing herself before washing her hands. Wild eyes and a reddened chest greeted her in the mirror. She flicked off the light, opened the door, and—

Nearly shrieked as she faced a figure standing in the middle of her bedroom.

"Fuck me!" She clapped a hand over her mouth, more out of embarrassment that she had been doing just that and less out of concern that someone would hear.

"I'm sorry! I saw the light, and you were in there for a while, and well—I'm not going to pry into your bathroom habits, but I heard a noise and thought maybe you were crying? Which is stupid, I know, but—"

"I'm fine, Meli. I just, um, couldn't sleep."

"You poor thing. You never sleep well. I have an idea. Come here."

Meli climbed back into bed and lifted the covers, waiting for Conner, who hesitated before following. She laid her head on her pillow as Meli nudged her.

"Nuh-uh. Slide toward me."

She allowed Meli to tug her hip until she was in the middle of the bed on her side. Then—oh God—Meli pressed against her back, spooning Conner with an arm draped over her waist.

"Is this better?"

Conner could feel Meli's heartbeat, curiously fast. Could Meli feel her trembling in return? She didn't trust her voice above a whisper.

"It's perfect."

Conner woke early the next morning with a warm pressure against her back. She took a deep breath. Her delay in falling asleep aside, she'd slept hard and wasn't sure either of them had moved, except Meli's arm had slipped from her waist. She refused to miss it.

She was in her pool before sunrise. Back and forth she swam, clearing her head with each lap. She could handle this. She had to work during most of their visit, her days packed with ADR, photoshoots, and interviews. She just needed to make it through a few dinners, drop some gummies at night so she fell asleep before her libido could betray her, and get Harlow to book something for the one free day she had.

Except that would hurt Meli's feelings. Damn it.

Her muscles protested, and she climbed out, nearly jumping back in when she came face to face with Meli's mother.

"Mrs. Velasco! You scared me."

"I'm sorry, Conner. I finally figured out your fancy coffeemaker and came out to catch the sunrise." She hefted a steaming mug.

Conner dried her ears with her towel. "I get better sunsets out here, but it's still nice at sunrise."

"Join me, please."

Though clearly a request, Conner felt compelled to oblige and took a seat facing the ocean next to her after grabbing a bottle of cranberry juice.

"This is so peaceful," Mrs. Velasco said after several quiet minutes.

Conner hummed an agreement. A private oceanfront view had been at the top of her list when she bought her house, and even though she didn't get to appreciate it as often as she liked, it never failed to soothe her. A stretch of rocky sand lay between her house and the Pacific, the waves reflecting the pinks and oranges of the sunrise behind them.

"You have such a lovely home, and it's so generous of you to let us stay here."

Conner shrugged. "What's the point of having empty rooms if no one ever sleeps in them? Anyway, Meli's a good friend. I'm happy to help her out."

Mrs. Velasco regarded her for a moment before smiling. "She's very lucky to have you."

"I'm the lucky one."

She quickly schooled her expression, afraid she'd given herself away, but Mrs. Velasco's smile merely broadened, traces of her daughter's megawatt grin appearing. "I won't argue with that. I have to tell you I didn't believe you were actually friends until you called her while she was home. I thought you had hired her to housesit."

They shared a laugh and swapped stories while they finished their beverages. Then, without much idea of how it occurred, she found herself directed into her own kitchen, chopping tomatoes and onions. If Abuelita could have seen her now…

The next few days passed in exquisite torture. After working all day, Conner came home to a houseful of people who greeted her with enthusiasm infused with varying degrees of starstruck awe. She helped prepare dinner under the watchful eye of family matriarchs and didn't accidentally poison a single person.

And then came the nights. Swapping bathroom times and passing each other in stages of half-dress. Quiet, sleepy conversations followed by cuddling until they fell asleep, a gentle insistence on Meli's part, who was convinced that it helped Conner sleep.

And the really awful, terrible, wonderful, amazing part was—she was absolutely right.

As she crawled toward Malibu through the endless LA traffic after a long day of press, she couldn't decide what was worse: feeling Meli pressed against her all night long without being able to do anything about it (she refused to give in to any urges again), or the knowledge that in a couple of days, she'd be all alone again. Lindsey was back in North Carolina for a funeral, but even if she had been available, Conner had no urge to call her. She didn't want any warm body, regardless of how sexy. She didn't even want a close friend with a proven track record of getting her off.

She wanted Meli. She wanted her, and she couldn't have her, and it was just so unfair. Meli was straight. Meli was one of her best friends. Conner couldn't want her, and yet…she did.

They left Malibu early the next morning, arriving at Venice Beach after loading up with breakfast burritos at Conner's favorite taco shop. Both she and Meli had tried to talk her family into going to other beaches, but they insisted on the popular tourist spot. Half of them immediately went to fish, the kids took off for the sea, and the rest set up shop on the sand.

"I'm glad you were able to come with us today." Meli poked Conner's bare leg with her toe.

Conner reclined on her elbows, fully stretched out on a towel. "I am, too."

"Really? Only I figured that you were fed up with all these people around. I know my family can be a lot, especially when you're so used to your privacy. If you want us to leave you alone…"

"I don't." Conner smiled at her, taking advantage of her mirrored sunglasses to admire her curves in a vibrant red swimsuit. "But I appreciate you thinking of me."

Meli's cheeks began to match her bathing suit. "Of course. I'm always—what are friends for?"

Friends were for many things, but not ogling, so Conner averted her gaze, promising herself that she'd leave the image of Meli in a swimsuit on the beach where it belonged. Not in her bed later that night.

By lunchtime Conner found herself more relaxed than she'd been in months. Years, maybe. Though the beach had quickly filled, no one recognized her, and she was able to lounge in the sun and wade in the ocean to her heart's content. She didn't often partake of her beach at home except for occasional runs on the sand.

She enjoyed getting to know Meli's family, too. The elder generations conversed in Spanish almost exclusively, whereas the younger ones were comfortable switching back and forth but chose English when left alone. She had rarely been immersed in Hispanic culture like this, from the language to the food to the traditions. In fact, she wasn't sure she'd spoken Spanish at all since Abuelita died, and she sometimes struggled to keep up with the conversations.

Conner frowned. Abuelita would have loved this. She'd always pushed her to get more in touch with her heritage, but Conner had always been so busy and, frankly, hadn't cared all that much until it was too late.

"I love your accent, Conner," Meli's aunt said, interrupting her thoughts.

Meli nodded. "Me too! It's so se—um, musical."

"My accent?" she repeated. "Oh! My Spanish accent."

"Did your mother teach you? You wouldn't have learned that in school."

"Ah, no. She actually speaks very little. My grandmother taught me when I was young and made sure I kept it up."

Mrs. Velasco twisted her mouth. "She doesn't? Weren't both of your grandparents from Argentina?"

She always marveled about the things strangers knew about her life. "Yes, but…to be honest, I don't know why."

"It's never too late for her to learn. You could teach her, couldn't you?"

"Abuela, you're a big fan of Isabela Morales, right?"

Conner smiled at Meli, grateful for the redirect from her least-favorite subject.

Meli's grandmother leaned forward from her chair under an enormous umbrella. "Yes, I am. She was one of the first big Latina stars, you know. I cried myself dry from her performance in *The Roses Have Thorns*. In fact, while I'm here, I would like to pay my respects."

"Um, yeah. We can do that. Whenever you want."

"We'll go now. You there, help me up."

Meli laughed. "Abuela, we're about to eat lunch. Let's go after, okay?"

Her grandmother harrumphed. "If we must. Take me back to Conner's house after that so I can nap. You kids wear me out."

Mrs. Velasco began distributing what appeared to be an endless supply of tortas with cold chicken cutlets, accompanied by bags of chips.

Meli handed Conner a sandwich, half smiling in an apologetic manner. "I know you're used to better and healthier fare, but she insisted. Ow! Mami, what was that for?"

Mrs. Velasco brandished a wooden spoon, both its origin and true purpose unknown. "Don't be ungrateful, Melina."

"This is fine. Don't worry. Thank you, Mrs. Velasco."

"See? Conner has manners. You could learn a few things from her."

Oh, the things Conner could teach Meli…

"Quit making me look bad, Conner."

Meli elbowed her, and Conner snatched the bag of Cheetos from her paper plate and tossed it at Meli's cousin. They played keep-away for a few minutes, laughing as Meli huffed, until Conner finally took pity on her and presented her with the chips with an exaggerated bow. With an indignant sniff belied by the twitch of her lips, Meli tried to turn away, but Conner hooked an arm around her shoulders and tugged her back, laughing as she kissed her cheek before she could think better of it.

Meli smiled at her, all bashful and pink suddenly, and Conner's heart beat a rhythm that would have sent cardiologists into a panic.

Conner led the way through the sprawling cemetery, hands shoved in the pockets of her shorts.

Meli guided her grandmother. "This way, Abuela. It's just past this next row."

Conner stopped, spinning on the heel of her sandals. "How do you know where her grave is?"

"I, uh, I bring flowers when you're gone? I know you bring them once a week, so it seemed important to you. They're not as nice as your bouquets, of course, but I've gotten pretty good at finding deals, and I always buy something pretty even if it's small. I hope I didn't overstep. I only wanted…"

Conner stared as she rambled, floored by the way Meli cared for her. Her affection would always be platonic, but it was affection nonetheless, and Conner's eyes pricked at the idea of anyone doing something for her without expecting credit or gratitude. She might never have known if they hadn't made this trip.

Meli's grandmother looped her arm through Conner's as Meli sped ahead, clearly embarrassed for some reason. "So thoughtful, isn't she, our Melina?"

"More than anyone I've ever met."

"Hmm, and so pretty, too, don't you think?"

Conner shot her a look, trying to determine how guileless that knowing smile actually was. "Of course."

"It's very curious that she doesn't date. Young and beautiful and single in a town like this. I'm sure she has people lined up at her door."

Conner chanced another glance at the emphasis on "people." This tiny, wrinkled woman was too sharp for her own good—or Conner's. "She dates…I'm sure she does."

"Maybe so. My daughter-in-law doesn't tell me as much as she should."

As she went on, proving that rambling ran in the family, Conner's mind spun like a Ferris wheel. Meli dated, didn't she? As much as Conner didn't like to think about it, Meli's grandmother was right. Certainly Meli got asked out. How could anyone resist those curves, those doe eyes, that charming little gap between her front teeth, how well she listened, how tightly she hugged, how hard she worked…

At the grave, while her grandmother said a rosary, Meli took Conner's hand and squeezed, flashing her a smile. At risk of being overcome by longing and despair, Conner forced thoughts of her dating situation out of her mind. She had Meli's friendship, and that had to be enough.

Chapter Thirty-six

Conner frowned at her phone; the gate guard had just informed her Jamal was there. She wasn't expecting him, not with Meli's family still in town. Shrugging, she texted her permission and leaned toward Meli's ear.

"I'll be right back. Jamal is here for some reason."

Meli twisted her neck to look up, frowning. "Is Maggie okay?"

"I'm sure she is. He would have called otherwise."

Conner's heart sped up as she hurried to the front door. Surely Maggie was fine, but perhaps Jamal was bringing her over so they could mend their rift. That was just the sort of thoughtful thing he would do.

That was not the case.

She took one look at the thunder on his face and realized this wasn't a social call or a chance to make amends.

"How could you keep this a secret from me?"

Oh, shit. She knew exactly what *this* was, and dread didn't begin to cover the feeling that spread across her like a pox. As Jamal stepped into her space, aggression wafting off him like too much garlic, she looked over her shoulder where her guests were gathered at the back of her house.

"I have company. Let's go in here."

She led him to the small room she used as an office. He started up again before the door shut.

"What the fuck, Conner? I thought we were friends."

She stalled, trying to control her own feelings. "Are you planning to tell me what you're talking about?"

"Don't play stupid. You know what Maggie did. You *helped* her." The accusation slapped Conner across her face.

"I drove her. I supported my friend in her decision. *Her* decision. I didn't talk her into it."

"You sure as hell didn't try to talk her out of it, did you?"

She took a calming breath. It didn't work. "I repeat: it was always *her* decision. I wouldn't change that."

"So the goddamn father just gets to stay in the fucking dark, is that it?" She wanted to let him know she had urged Maggie to tell him but thought better of it. "What would you have done if she had?"

"I would have—" Anguish twisted his normally handsome features. "I deserved to have a say."

"No, you didn't." His head snapped up, but she plowed on. In for a penny, as her Gran said. "It's her body, her decision, and I will support that opinion until the day I die."

He glared at her, thick eyebrows nearly meeting in the middle. She lifted her chin, meeting his stare. Very few people intimidated her, and she refused to allow anyone to see it when she was. Let him glower all he wanted. If that helped him, she could absorb it.

Finally he shook his head. His hands curled into fists. "I don't know how to deal with this. She's such a fucking—"

"You better shut your goddamn mouth when you're talking about her." This time she lashed him across the face with the razor blade of her words. "Maggie is my best friend. I'm sorry this happened, and I'm sorry that it hurts you. I really am. I'm your friend, too, and I'm here for you if you need me, but don't make me choose because you won't like the outcome. Maggie is my *best* friend. Don't you dare disrespect her."

Even as she spoke, she wondered at the truth of her words. Did best friends go silent for months? At what point did a friend cross the line into former friend territory? Her chest tightened.

Jamal paced across the small space. Despite her words, her heart went out to him. Regardless of his feelings about the abortion itself, he was obviously immensely hurt that Maggie had kept this from him for a year.

She had to strain to hear him say, "She was the love of my life, and now…"

"And now?"

He stopped, lifting his head at her challenge. "I don't know. How the fuck am I supposed to deal with this betrayal?"

"You either do, or you don't. I don't want you to break Maggie's heart, and make no mistake, you would, but I also won't allow you to hold this over her."

"You won't allow me?"

He scoffed as he moved into her space, and Conner squared her shoulders. She was Conner fucking Cody, a whole-ass Disney princess. She backed down from no man.

"Jamal, you better find a way to deal with this anger before you talk to her. I don't like this side of you." She put her hands on his shoulders, waiting until he met her gaze. "This sucks. It really, really does, and nothing anyone says will make you feel better. The fact that she told you means she's probably moving on, finally. You don't have to be in the same place as her, and honestly you don't have to forgive her. But if you can't, do both of yourselves a favor and just go. Right now you're being a giant dick, and since I very unfortunately once saw you naked, I know that you're not."

He scowled at her one last time before his shoulders slumped. "It was cold, okay?"

They talked for a little while longer, and although Jamal hugged her for a long time when he left, she had no idea what would happen between him and Maggie. She pulled up her phone and stared at Maggie's name for a long time, her thumbs itching to call her. But she'd sent her too many unanswered texts over the last few months. Maggie would reach out if she wanted Conner. That was all there was to it, and just like her advice to Jamal, she had to find a way to deal with it.

"Everything okay?" Meli asked when she reappeared.

She forced a smile. "Sure. He just needed to ask me about something."

Meli's gaze seemed to pierce her façade, and she was right. Meli pulled her into the dining room and took Conner's face in her soft hands, staring into her soul before gently running her thumbs up between Conner's eyebrows and across her forehead.

"There." Her voice, low and sweet, merely added to the spell she was weaving over Conner. "Can't have the most famous face in Hollywood get wrinkles. Is that better?"

"Maybe once more?" Conner's voice belonged to someone else.

She repeated the massage, resting her thumbs on Conner's cheekbones. A moment passed, then a year. Conner was very aware, all of a sudden, that she'd parted her legs as she leaned against the heavy, dark table she didn't remember buying, and Meli stood between them. She took a deep, steadying breath. Meli broke their shared gaze to glance at Conner's heaving chest, and she lingered—Conner swore she lingered—on Conner's mouth before lifting her gaze again.

She could no longer deny the pull between them any more than she could deny the tides that went in and out on her beach, and she lowered her head, a stray lock of hair falling into her face. Consequences be damned.

"Melina! Con—oh, there you two are! Mami wants to say grace so the kids can eat."

Meli's older brother Samuel, clearly clueless of what he'd interrupted, draped one arm over his sister and the other over Conner and steered them outside. Neither of them spoke of the moment that night. Perhaps it hadn't been a moment at all, as dreamlike and incomplete as it had seemed. Perhaps Conner had simply, finally fallen too far.

❖

"Care to dance?"

Samuel extended his hand, all roguish dimple and bravado. He had a certain charm, and even a certified lesbian such as Conner could see the attraction, though it failed to move her. He shared his sister's confidence, but whereas Meli's was quiet and self-aware (at least until she got flustered, one of Conner's favorite Meli modes), his was playful and swaggering, borderline arrogant. Conner recognized this trait all too well.

She demurred and declined several appeals before he gave up, spinning his eldest sister around Conner's deck. They'd opted for a cookout on their last night in California, making enough food to feed half of Orange County, and while they refused to let her buy any of it, they had allowed Conner to open her liquor cabinet. Pitchers of margaritas and sangria covered the kitchen island alongside bottles of beer and her most expensive mezcal.

She sipped on a glass of sangria, observing the festivities. Jumping in and out of the pool, the kids screamed as only kids could. Meli's father and uncle stood around a grill Conner hadn't known she owned, flipping carnitas, while the rest of the adults danced to music or took turns on kitchen duty. Meli had invited her roommates and a few other friends, so they had a true crowd.

"Why don't you dance?" Meli plopped down next to her, slightly out of breath from dancing with her cousin, and helped herself to Conner's drink.

Pretending to be annoyed, Conner reclaimed her glass and ignored the question, but Meli persisted.

"Maggie told me you used to go out dancing all the time, and, well… you were all over the internet, Conner. What did they call you?" Conner stiffened. Not that. "The 'Dancing Queen,' that was it!"

Conner downed the remainder of her drink in one gulp and set it on the table harder than she intended. Meli's eyes widened. "Never mind. It's none of my business. You don't—"

"Levi's was the most sought-after ad campaign in ages. Two years of commercials celebrating a huge milestone for an iconic brand. The exposure was unmatched, the paycheck outrageous…and it was mine."

"I remember those! The ones where you were in the attic with a lady, I assume she was supposed to be your grandma, and when you put on a pair of her jeans, you were transported to a different time period in every commercial, and you danced."

She'd danced her ass off. Conner had learned so many classic moves, she'd lost count. "Jailhouse Rock" and "Achy Breaky Heart." The twist and the moonwalk, the macarena and the dougie. "Thriller" and "Single Ladies."

"I was partying so much back then. In Hollywood, when you're rich or famous, you can get away with pretty much anything. I was welcomed into clubs as soon as puberty hit. They loved the publicity, too, so they'd make such a fuss about protecting your privacy while you were inside but make sure the paps waited for you outside." She flattened her lips, remembering all the times her bleary-eyed face was splashed across screens. "The 'Dancing Queen' ad dropped during the Super Bowl. I was seventeen, dancing across TV screens by day and through every club in LA or New York by night. The headlines wrote themselves. I don't know which one came up with that moniker, but it sure fucking stuck."

Another screwed-up child actor. *America's little sweetheart gone bad. Conner Cody won't make it out of her teens. Out-of-control actress trashes another Hollywood club. Can anyone reel in Conner Cody?* They had been so fucking eager for her downfall, salivating for it as much as they panted for her eighteenth birthday.

"I didn't realize you hated it so much. I'm sorry."

"Don't apologize for someone else's transgressions," she said harshly. "When I got sober, it reminded me so much of who I'd been that I didn't want any part of it. I haven't danced since then."

"Can I make an observation or a suggestion or a little of both?"

"Pick one, but nothing more." She smiled.

"I'll try to limit myself. So, sometimes you seem like you care an awful lot about what people think of you, and I think it gives power to them? Like, you're letting things that some losers wrote about you years ago hold you back from something it sounds like you used to enjoy." Conner opened her mouth, but Meli plowed on. "I'm not trying to diminish anything. I remember all the horrible crap they said about you. I, um, I used to believe some of it. Before I knew you. Obviously not anymore. Anyway, my point is, you're Conner freaking Cody. You shouldn't let a bunch of assholes dictate your life."

She was right. Of course she was right. Harlow had given her similar advice before, though with more measured words. Besides, it wasn't like any tabloids were hanging around. She'd won an injunction against paparazzi using drones over her house, so she was even safe from that.

"I guess once wouldn't hurt."

Meli grinned. "Perfect. Let me pick out a—"

"If you're standing, does that mean you reconsidered?"

Samuel reappeared out of nowhere, hand extended and a twinkle in his eye. What the hell? Conner accepted it, letting out a whoop when he spun her around.

"Maestro! A song, please." He gestured toward his sister, who scowled at them. Conner guessed Melina didn't care for his over-the-top mannerisms, but they made her laugh. He grinned at her, waggling his eyebrows. "Now, Señorita Cody, let me teach you about cumbia."

She quickly mastered the basic eight-count step, and they were doing spins and cross-body turns by the second song. Samuel led with confidence and flair. Conner couldn't remember the last time she'd had so much fun or felt so loose. When "Amor Prohibido" came on, she couldn't help singing along.

"Hey! You know Selena?"

She fixed him with her most withering stare, completely at odds with their quick, light steps. "I'm a Latina musician. Of course I know the Tejano Madonna."

She lost herself in the song, pouring all she had into the lyrics and melody of forbidden love. When it ended and silence filled its place, she returned to reality. Meli stared at her with a fierce, blazing expression. Conner blinked as cheers filled her ears, the entire family applauding her impromptu performance. She'd accepted accolades from crowds of all sizes, always cool and gracious, but the intimacy bowled her over, and she ducked her head into Samuel's broad shoulder. When she looked up again, she noticed that Meli's gaze and countenance had shifted, firing daggers of irritation laced with something akin to jealousy at her brother.

"Don't you think you've bothered her enough?" she said, all but stepping between them. "She's not going to sleep with you."

Samuel blew a raspberry toward his sister. "No offense to Conner, but I wasn't asking." He winked, and Conner couldn't help but laugh.

"Come on, Meli..." Conner chased her, tugging her hands until she relented. "What was that all about?"

Meli tossed her head. The golden highlights in her hair caught the light. "Nothing. I just didn't know you were going to spend all night with my brother."

"Technically I'll be spending all night with you, in my bed, unless your plans have changed."

"I didn't mean—that's not what—God, Conner!" Her giggles were infectious, although Conner managed to restrain herself to a grin. She loved winding Meli up. "You know what I meant."

"Let's say I do. Maybe I'm spending all night with your brother because no one else asked me to dance." She poked Meli in her soft belly, rewarded with another giggle.

"Maybe I was waiting for you to ask me."

Oh. The challenge coiled in her belly before shifting to arousal, journeying southward. She swallowed through a dry throat. "Then would you like to dance with me?" She held out her hand with a flourish despite feeling rather silly.

Meli didn't hesitate, and if a spark jumped when their skin met, only Conner saw it. "Yes, I would. How do you want to dance? I can do cumbia and two-step."

Conner wrinkled her nose. "We're not going to two-step, cowgirl."

"Fine, fancy-pants. Pick something that's not from Texas."

An idea that straddled the border between great and terrible perked up, and Conner had never met a bad idea she didn't like. "Abuelita didn't only teach me Spanish, you know. We're Argentine. How would you like to learn how to tango?"

She cued up "La Cumparsita" on the speakers and led Meli to the center of the deck. They had a curious audience, but as soon as they locked eyes, they were alone.

Known as the forbidden dance, the Argentine tango is sensual and passionate, a dance of seduction rather than provocative sexuality. Conner held Meli in a close embrace, their breasts brushing against each other, and although she only demonstrated the basic movements, the intimacy wove a spell over them from the first motion. Every step in sync, every breath in unison, they moved as one. The dance was temptation, foreplay, and conquest all wrapped up together. Conner was stripped bare, not of clothing but of her defenses, vulnerable and ready to be flayed. She was sure her feelings were exposed to the world, and she didn't care.

Meli was alight once more, just as she'd been when Conner was singing. The brightness in her eyes rivaled the stars above, and through it all she never wavered, never stumbled or laughed or did anything but surrender to Conner and the enchantment that tied them together. As Conner's hips moved, so did Meli's, mirroring the act of sex, desire dripping down their bodies.

The song ended, but they didn't. Their hands remained clasped; one trembled, or perhaps both. Conner gripped Meli's waist to the point of bruising and pulled her so close that the proximity inhibited further dancing, but she no longer realized they had been. Time held its breath, and they spoke only with their eyes.

"Am I the only one who needs to jump in the pool after that? Me next, what do you say, Conner?"

They stared, stunned at the abrupt shattering of their world. Shards of glass pierced Conner as Meli backed away, dropping her hand as if it burned.

"Fuck all the way off, Samuel."

They ignored his aggrieved protest. Meli avoided Conner's gaze and left her behind, but only for a second. Conner pursued her into the kitchen, cornering her in the pantry.

"What are you looking for?"

Meli jumped and whirled around. "I—um—I need, uh…napkins!"

"They're on the table outside. What's going on?"

Conner moved closer, trying to figure out what she'd done, and Meli backed up. Her eyebrows drew together as her eyes widened, and she looked almost…afraid? She couldn't be. But the fright melted away as quickly as the idea crossed Conner's mind, replaced by something soft and curious.

She murmured words too quiet to make out. Conner was drawn by an invisible magnetic force, leaning toward her with one hand on a shelf. "What?"

"I don't know. He just…he annoys me so much."

"Is that really it?" Conner's voice was too low, too soft, and entirely out of her control. She lifted a hand to push some of Meli's curls back, leaving it tangled in the wild tendrils.

Meli's eyes tracked the movement of her fingers. She swallowed. "Conner…"

Conner's heart threatened to jump out of her body. Her hand trailed down the gentle curve of Meli's jaw, coming to a rest under her chin. She lifted it ever so slightly, and when their gazes connected, she was lost. Their breath merged, chests rising and falling as one. She opened her mouth to ask permission, but when Meli's lips parted as well, she took the invitation and bent her head.

Raucous laughter spilled into the house. Meli's mother and aunt walked past, chattering rapidly in Spanish, but neither noticed them in the half shadow. They took the moment with them, stolen at the very cusp, and Conner wanted to press charges.

She pulled back, consumed by anxiety that climbed her spine like an insidious vine. Her greatest wish had almost happened. Could she risk losing Meli, or, worse, hurting her, by what could be nothing more than lustful curiosity? Meli wouldn't be the first woman Conner had inspired to momentary slips on the Kinsey scale. But Meli would not—could not—be a fling, an experiment, an itch. She was far too precious, and Conner's feelings were far too complex for anything so plebian as that.

"N-napkins are on the table." No number of acting classes could keep the throaty quiver out of her voice.

A blush crept up Meli's neck before she cleared her throat, although only nonsensical mutters emerged, and then she was gone. Conner followed in a more circumspect manner several minutes later, and by the time she returned outside, the pantry might as well have been a portal to Middle Earth, so remote and fanciful. She resumed her dances with any partner that happened to come along, although Meli wasn't one of them and the tango never returned.

She danced and teased, laughed and chatted, and soon she was able to tuck away her confusion and revel in the joy of the evening. She smiled so much it hurt.

God, did it hurt.

Chapter Thirty-seven

Emi

Before tonight, Emi was certain she knew a few absolutes about Conner Cody, which included her dislike of her birthday and her refusal to dance. In all the years they'd known each other, she had never wavered on either, regardless of entreaties.

And yet...here they were.

She hadn't been able to hide her skepticism when she got the call. "Have you ever known Conner to celebrate her birthday?"

"No, but last year she was in Germany, and the year before she was on tour." Melina paused. "Besides, I think she needs this. She needs her friends. She misses you, Emi, you and Bellamy and Maggie. You're her best friends."

Some best friend. Emi still carried residual anger over Conner's callous treatment of her so-called bandmates. It was one thing to know she was controlling, another to suspect she viewed the band as her own, but something else entirely for her to so blatantly dismiss them. If Conner wanted a solo career, she could have it. She might have more talent than Emi, Maggie, and Bellamy put together, but that didn't mean they didn't contribute. And Emi would die on the hill that she was the better guitar player.

"Have you talked to Bellamy or Maggie yet?"

"Bellamy said she would come." Typical. She could carry any melody in the world, but a grudge? Not a chance. "I haven't called Maggie yet. Um, I was kinda hoping maybe you would? To be honest, she intimidates me a little." She cleared her throat, confidence emerging in her voice when she continued. "But I'll call her if you don't want to. She needs to be there. Conner will be so hurt if she isn't."

The jury was still out on whether Conner would appreciate this little surprise party, but Emi agreed. If it was going to happen, Maggie needed to be there, even if something had been off between them for months. In the end, Melina was the one to convince her.

To Emi's surprise, Conner appeared pleased about the party, if shocked by some of the invitees. Namely, her bandmates—if there was still a band. But Emi didn't want to dwell on that.

"Happy birthday, Conner," Maggie said quietly as the three of them walked up together.

Conner turned away from the group she'd been chatting with, and her mouth fell open. She stared for a long moment. Emi shifted her weight from side to side after handing over a bottle of her favorite mezcal. Only Bellamy gave Conner a loose hug.

She eventually got her voice to work. "Thanks for coming. I'm... surprised."

"Yeah, us, too. But who can say no to a cinnamon roll?" Maggie nodded toward Melina just as her laughter rang out. She stood with Lindsey and some other WNBA stars, judging by their height.

Conner followed her gaze, and her face softened ever so slightly. "Nope. Can't say no to her." When she yanked her attention back, one corner of her mouth tugged up in that half-grin that used to drive Emi wild. "Why do you think I'm here? Seriously, though, I'm really glad you came."

"Happy birthday, Conner," Emi said. "But this doesn't change anything."

Conner's lips thinned, and her chin dropped as she gave a jerky nod. "Right. I understand. I should go say hi."

Emi watched her go, admitting against her will that she looked good. Not as haggard or miserable as the last time she saw her. Not as tired as, well, ever. Still traces of melancholy, but that was Conner.

Like many others her age, Emi had fallen in lust with Conner the moment she walked onto the screen in *On the Bay*. When Maggie mentioned that she knew Conner during a class they shared at UCLA, Emi thought she was full of crap. Plenty of people in LA "knew" celebrities. They served them at coffee shops or worked as an extra on a film or paid for backstage passes.

Then Maggie said they were forming a band, and everything changed. Emi was a goner from the instant Conner swung around in a chair, lounging with an ankle resting on her knee. Always indolent, always cool, always intense—a combination that shouldn't have existed but that she nurtured to perfection. Conner's gray-green eyes gleamed as she offered that half-smirk for the first time, and Emi knew she'd been clocked.

Dating was a mistake that both had realized early on but refused to admit. Emi had wanted her so badly for so long. At first it was glorious, sex half the night that had her seeing new colors, and deep conversations the other half. The intensity that made up the attraction leaked into other aspects of their lives, however, and no matter how hard she tried, Conner never quite let her in, never fully lowered her defenses, never completely committed to the relationship, although she was always the pinnacle of faithful.

The latter was Emi's mistake.

"Why did you have to say that?" Bellamy interrupted her reminiscence.

"Because she's right." Maggie scowled. "We all know we're here for Melina because she's literal sunshine. Conner still owes us an apology."

"You've been upset with her since last summer. What happened between you two?"

Maggie glared at her. "Nothing happened, and it's none of your business."

Emi persisted. "Well, which is it?"

Maggie just shook her head. She could be as closed off as the birthday girl. No wonder they were best friends...or had been, anyway.

"Where's Jamal?" Bellamy asked.

"Not here, obviously. God, do you two ever shut up?"

She stalked toward the bar, where she quickly downed a shot of something amber. Emi ground her teeth to keep from calling her out on her rudeness. It was fine to be upset with Conner, but the rest of them hadn't done anything.

"Do you ever wonder if something happened between Jamal and Conner?"

Emi's bark of laughter surprised everyone standing nearby. "Hell, no. Conner is as gay as the sun is bright. She'd rather go celibate than touch a man."

"I don't know. Something's weird with all three of them. Remember how Jamal and Maggie used to be glued together? That stopped at the same time she started acting mad at Conner. I'm just saying."

"Well, don't say. The last thing I need in my life is more Conner drama."

Bellamy eyed her with suspicion. "You're not still—"

"Absolutely not," Emi said as firmly as she could. "That's over, and it's going to stay that way."

Melina had done a good job with the party. Nearly everyone that Emi considered a friend of Conner was there, from her fellow actress Bree Mathews to Harlow to half the female professional athletes in LA. The same DJ Conner had been using for a while pumped disco hits one after the other, fitting for the 1970s theme Melina had chosen. Tight bell-bottoms, feathered hair, and boldly colored minidresses dominated. Even the food was era-appropriate, with quiche, Jello molds, cheese logs, a fondue fountain, and an enormous chocolate layer cake that took up a table of its own.

Emi settled in with Bree, some fringe director, and a group of pro surfers discussing the next time LA would host the Olympics. She harbored a hidden dream of Hestia Rising being asked to participate in the opening ceremony of the Games, assuming the band still existed at that point.

On that note, she grabbed a fresh beer and set off to find the birthday girl. Although it wasn't exactly the appropriate time, maybe Conner would be in a good enough mood to talk about the issues surrounding the band. They couldn't exist in a holding pattern forever. As much as she hated to think about it, if the band was at an end, they just needed to get it over with. She didn't want to be a studio musician forever.

A chorus of cheers and wolf whistles drew her attention. In the middle of a crowd, Lindsey had Conner bent over backward, kissing her soundly. Emi paused mid-stride. Their arrangement had predated her relationship with Conner, and she was fully aware they'd picked back up afterward, but they'd never been prone to public pronouncements of affection. Kissing in the middle of a birthday party seemed more suited for a romance than for friends who occasionally slept together.

When they parted, Conner's wide-eyed expression suggested shock, but she didn't say a word as Lindsey grabbed her hand and dragged her toward the house.

A low whistle sounded next to her ear. "Somebody's getting birthday sex." Maggie exchanged an amused look with her.

"Yeah. I wouldn't go in—oof!"

Melina rebounded off Emi after crashing into her. "Oh, gosh. I'm so sorry! I totally didn't see you there. I'm such an idiot. My mom is always telling me to get my head out of the clouds, which I guess is funny because it's dark, and I don't even think there are clouds tonight, ha ha."

"It's fine." Emi took a step back. Melina's wild eyes unnerved her, and her rambling was more frenzied than normal. "Where are you headed in such a rush?"

"Um, nowhere. Well, no. I mean, I wanted a drink? Yeah, a drink. And obviously I can't go—I mean I could go in there—" Maggie ducked, narrowly missing losing her head to Melina's flailing arm that Emi was pretty sure was supposed to mean the house. "But why would I when there's a bar right over there? So I'm going to go. Over there. For a drink. Yeah."

Emi looked at Melina, then at Maggie, before glancing at Melina again. "That was weird."

"Weirder than usual for sure."

"Do you think she's weird?"

"Not like strange, but too nice and bubbly to be normal. Very likable, though."

Emi nodded, still watching Melina, who had ended up nowhere near the bar and appeared deep in conversation with Bellamy, by the pool. "Yeah.

She's easy to like. Don't you think it's interesting how she and Conner have hit it off? They couldn't be more different."

Maggie snorted. "You got that right. Little Miss Sunshine and Queen of the Mood Swings. But maybe she's good for Conner. Her obvious crush aside."

Emi nearly got whiplash. "Obvious crush? I thought Melina was straight!"

"Girl, chill. She is. I was talking about Conner. It's kind of funny."

"Oh." Nothing like feeling like an idiot in front of your friends.

Maggie stared at her, eyes thinned to slits. "Are we going to have any more drama between you?"

"God, no. I'm serious, Mags. It's in the past."

"Thank goodness for that. I'd quit the band before I sat through that mess again."

Emi made a face. "Gee, thanks."

"What? It was a disaster class."

"What was a disaster?"

Conner popped up between them, hands shoved in her pockets.

"You and Emi together," Maggie replied without missing a beat. Emi gave her a dirty look.

Conner's eyebrows skyrocketed, and she cleared her throat. "And on my birthday, no less. I think disaster is a bit much. I prefer two friends who ran their course."

She offered Emi a smile, and for a moment they simply were just that, two friends who ran their course. No childish games, no harsh argument, no hurt feelings, no threats to the future of the band.

Thoughts of the band fired up memories of their last conversation, and deciding in that instance that she didn't want to bring it up tonight after all, Emi searched for a change of subject.

"Where's Lindsey?"

"I think she left. Why?"

"No reason." Behind Conner's back, Emi pulled a face at Maggie. Even Conner wasn't capable of that much of a quickie.

Later, after they sang an incredibly dirty version of "Happy Birthday" and served the cake, which Emi discovered was made with Guinness and Bailey's in a nod to Conner's Irish heritage, the party hit its stride and started to feel more like a Conner Cody party. The drinks flowed, the music pumped, and the pool house did pool-house things.

"The revenue argument is bullshit," said a soccer player Emi struggled to place, Bryce something or other. "You have to account for the decades of lack of support, the disparity in funding from the youth level up, the uneven marketing…do I need to go on?"

"But at some point, you have to stand on your own." She barely knew the producer who had retorted, but she instantly disliked him. "It's basic economics, babe."

Conner sent him a withering glare. There went his invitation to her next party. "It's basic misogyny, *babe*."

"Besides, US Soccer is a nonprofit. It's obligated to support all teams equally."

"Especially the teams that win," Emi said. The soccer player held up her hand for a high-five, which she met gladly.

The producer's face darkened, and he departed, muttering something about a beer. The remaining group laughed and segued into a lively discussion about the double standards of the entertainment industry. Emi was bantering with a keyboardist who had toured with them when a distinctive glissando interrupted her.

The DJ had been playing disco music all night to go with the seventies theme: Donna Summer, Bee Gees, KC and the Sunshine Band, and, of course, ABBA. Which was all well and good, but "Dancing Queen" was strictly forbidden. Conner never would have allowed it, which meant Melina either didn't know or had royally screwed up. Emi tensed, waiting for her temperamental friend to blow up. Nothing ruined a party like a Conner Cody tantrum.

Sure enough, Conner had noticed as well, and her shoulders hunched. Melina danced up, a grin stretched across her cherubic face, and held out her hand.

"Dance with me, Conner. Please?"

Across the table, Maggie lifted her head, as she, too, anticipated the frosty retort Melina was about to receive.

"You danced with me a couple of weeks ago right here, and it was fun, right?"

Doctors said cotton buds weren't supposed to go in ears, but Emi really wished for one right now, because no way in the world had she just heard what she thought she heard. Either her ears were blocked, or she had been drugged and was hallucinating. Conner Cody didn't dance. Ever.

Then the moment deviated even further from the norm, going from strange to truly bizarre, for after Melina leaned into her to murmur something Emi couldn't hear, Conner smiled, took her hand, and followed her to the makeshift dance area. Emi was severely tempted to capture the dance on her phone, but that would break another of Conner's cardinal rules—no phones at her parties—and a night could hold only so many surprises. They looked good together, Conner long and lean in obscenely tight bell-bottoms and a Fleetwood Mac T-shirt, Melina all curves in a red floral minidress.

"Well, I never," Bellamy said softly in her Georgia twang.

"For the last time, that's not a replacement for 'I can't even,' Bells." Maggie joined them, resting her chin on her hand as they watched the pair dance. A number of attendees danced as well, and Conner's laugh floated over to them. "Isn't that interesting? The things Conner will do to get a woman to sleep with her."

Emi shook her head. "No, she won't. Conner doesn't need to do that. Believe me, I would know. This is...different, somehow."

She felt an odd sense of loss as they observed this new version of Conner. She had moved on months ago and felt confident she was over their relationship, but at that moment she knew, watching her dance with Melina, that she never would have been the one for Conner. Maybe not Melina, but someone else, eventually, would prompt Conner to do things she'd never done before.

It hit her like a thunderbolt. "She's happy."

Bellamy's mouth hung open. "Huh. Look at that. Good for her!"

Eventually the novelty wore off, and they returned to their conversations. Bellamy joined the dancers, but Maggie soon departed, carrying her own cloud of woe with her. Emi had tried to get her to open up, but she was more closed off than a bank vault. Emi supposed it was too much to ask for all of the band to be happy at once, a finite resource, passed from person to person instead of spreading the wealth.

For her part, she set her eyes on the cute Aussie DJ. She suspected Conner had slept with her before, but that was more common than not at these parties. Emi didn't care, and she knew Conner wouldn't either. She deserved a little of her own happiness, if for only a night.

Chapter Thirty-eight

Conner stretched to her full length on her sofa, resting her head against a pillow. With a fruit smoothie at her side, she relaxed and opened her book, ready to delve into the world of Neve Blackthorne for the third time.

(And what a world it was! Conner wished such a woman actually existed in Hollywood.)

But she kept getting distracted, thinking back to the party Meli had coaxed her into allowing. She hated her birthday, associating it with all the years it had passed by without a word from her parents. Meli was persuasive, however, and then…Maggie, Emi, and Bellamy arrived. They didn't chat as much as she wanted, and she couldn't bring herself to broach the subject they desperately needed to discuss, but still. They were there.

She wrenched herself away from her reminiscence and returned to her novel. She'd just reached "Mind the door," steeling herself against the cruelty to follow, when her phone vibrated. Huffing in annoyance, she reached to switch on Do Not Disturb mode but froze when she saw the name and face on her screen.

The call ended before she could bring herself to answer, and she scrambled to call back. Something had to be wrong.

"Aunt Conner?"

"Sarah?"

Her niece's voice was small and hushed. "Can you come get me?"

Conner was already on her feet. "Of course. Where are you? What's going on? Where are your parents?"

"I was staying the night with Audrey and Bella. We snuck out to go to a party with Audrey's brother."

Conner sighed and closed her eyes. "Are you safe? Are you scared? Did someone touch you? I swear to God, I will kill—"

"Nothing like that. Bella and Audrey left with Bella's boyfriend, but I wasn't comfortable going with them. Please come get me."

"I'm on my way, kid. Drop me a pin with your location. Where are you right now? Like an apartment or a park or—"

"A house. I'm in the bathroom."

"Stay there, lock the door, and don't let anyone in no matter what they say. Okay? Do you want to stay on the phone until I get there?"

She did, although long stretches of silence accompanied Conner as she broke several traffic laws, making it to Sylmar in just over half an hour. She pulled to the curb in a neighborhood of Spanish-style homes, several houses down from where a party had clearly spilled outside. The bars on most windows made her leery of leaving her Porsche, but she had no choice. Tugging a slouchy beanie over her hair and slipping on a fake pair of glasses she kept in her car, she strode down the sidewalk at a clipped pace, following the sound of a thumping beat and texting Sarah that she'd arrived.

A cloud of marijuana smoke, cheap alcohol, and poor decisions met her at the door. Most people didn't give her a second glance, although she did have to sidestep a couple of teenage boys with bad acne and worse haircuts. Sarah met her at the foot of the stairs, throwing her arms around her.

They trudged through a sea of disposable red cups and half-empty bags of chips. Conner wrestled with her conscience, unsure of the protocol in this situation. No one had ever expected her to be the adult. Ultimately she decided against calling the police, not wanting to risk Sarah or herself getting caught up in the consequences. As they left, a squeal of "Oh my God, that looks like—" followed them.

Sarah didn't say anything until Conner turned north on the Five. "Where are you going?"

"I'm taking you home."

"No! You can't—Aunt Conner, they'll kill me for sneaking out."

"Do you want to go back to your friend's house?"

"They're not there."

"So where am I going?"

"Can't I stay with you tonight? I can go home in the morning."

Sadie would kill her. Sadie would probably kill her for even having Sarah in her car. But Conner was pretty sure she was already dead to her sister, so what was the harm in digging her grave a little deeper? Sarah was safe. That's what mattered.

As she turned around, Conner contemplated her role in the evening. Was she supposed to lecture Sarah on making better choices? Hypocrisy at its finest, considering what Conner had done at age fourteen. But neither did she want her niece to follow in her footsteps.

"You know, any friend who would leave you in a situation like that isn't really your friend," she finally said.

Sarah chewed on her fingernail. "All they care about are their stupid boyfriends. I thought if I went to the party with them, they'd still want to hang out with me."

"Why didn't you go with them when they left?"

"They'd been drinking."

Conner wasn't the person best suited for this conversation. "I'm glad you called me instead."

Sarah didn't reply for several miles, still worrying her fingernail. "I didn't know if you would answer."

Conner's head jerked to look at her niece. "What? I always answer your calls."

"Yeah, but Mom said you wouldn't be around anymore and wouldn't let me talk to you. I was going to text, but…I thought you might not like us anymore."

Conner let out a slow, measured breath, counting to three so she wouldn't say something stupid. "Of course I like you and your sister and your parents. Your mom and I…it has nothing to do with you. We just had a disagreement."

"It's not fair. When Hannah and I argue, Mom makes us hug. Can't you just do that?"

"I wish."

Both were yawning by the time Conner rolled into her garage. Sarah went to the bathroom while Conner gave up on her room-temperature smoothie, pouring it down the drain.

"Um, Aunt Conner?" Sarah shuffled forward, her face pale. She mumbled something Conner couldn't understand.

"What?"

"I think I started my period."

"Shit. Well, they're sneaky sometimes. Do you use pads, or are tampons okay? I assume you're not a cup user."

"I…this is my first time."

Oh, fuck me. This was a punishment, right? This was what Conner deserved for being a shitty person. Then she glanced at Sarah again. If it was some sort of divine punishment for Conner, she sure as hell wasn't going to let it affect her innocent niece.

"Okay." She took a second to reset and modulate her voice. She would treat this as a role, one of a competent parental figure. "You know what feels great when you're on your period? A really hot bath. Why don't you take one, and while you're doing that, I'll get fresh clothes and…supplies delivered."

As soon as Sarah was situated in the jetted tub in Conner's bathroom, Conner called for backup. Then, after glancing back and forth between the bathroom door and her phone for several minutes, she dialed, letting out a sigh so heavy it shook her shoulders.

Naturally, Sadie didn't answer. Conner didn't bother leaving a voicemail that would be ignored, calling a second time, then a third. Finally she sent a text, asking Sadie to call her as soon as she could.

Conner allowed herself a moment to revel in the moment, Pyrrhic though it would be by the next morning. Sarah would never trust her again once she learned of her betrayal. But they had tonight, and maybe when she was old enough to make her own decisions, Sarah would remember her as a good aunt.

Being a semi-responsible adult really sucked sometimes.

"Oh, thank God." She met Meli at the door, nearly snatching the shopping bag from her hands. "You are literally the best."

"You're so silly. Now can you tell me what's going on? You were very vague and frantic on the phone."

Conner brought her up to speed at a clipped pace that Meli herself usually exercised before dashing upstairs. She paused before knocking.

"Hey, Sarah? I have some clothes and, um, stuff for you. Do you know how to use pads?"

Please say yes. Please say yes.

"Yeah. They showed us at school, and Mom went over it, too."

Conner let out her breath in a relieved sigh. "Good. Just take your time, and I'll be downstairs, all right? Call if you need anything else."

Sarah shuffled down the stairs not much later. Pale, she looked embarrassed. Meli wrapped a comforting arm around her, rubbing her back and murmuring words of reassurance. Conner wished such actions came that naturally to her.

"How do you feel?"

"My stomach hurts, and my back, too. Is it always going to be like this?"

Conner and Meli exchanged a glance of commiseration.

"Unfortunately, yes. Every month since I was thirteen."

Meli nodded. "I was eleven. It's not always so bad, but mostly, yeah."

"This sucks." Sarah spoke with such vehemence that Conner choked on a laugh.

"You said it, kid. Why don't you get some sleep? Hopefully you'll feel better tomorrow."

Sarah surprised her by throwing her arms around her, squeezing tightly. She froze for a second before returning the hug, startled to realize how much Sarah had grown since they last saw each other. Her braces were gone, and her hair was longer, too. She was in high school now, attending parties with beer and boyfriends. What else had Conner missed? How tall was Hannah now?

"Thank you for coming to get me, Aunt Conner." Her voice was muffled against Conner's shoulder. "And for the stuff."

"Any time, babe. I mean it."

They watched her trudge back upstairs. Conner dropped to the sofa in a heap, expelling the air from her lungs with a whoosh.

Meli sat next to her, that same comforting arm Conner had been slightly jealous of now wrapped around her shoulders. "Oh, sweetie. It's a lot, huh?"

"I miss them so much it's painful. I tried to call Sadie, I swear. Three times. She's going to kill me tomorrow, and after that, Sarah will, too. I should have taken her straight home, right? Did I just kidnap my niece?"

Meli chuckled. "I don't think so. It's late, and the important thing is that she's safe. She called *you*, Conner. That's a big deal. She'll remember that you came to pick her up, not that you took her home afterward. Sadie might be angry, sure, but she'll focus on the important part, too."

Conner's chin dropped to her chest. "I wish I shared your optimism. My family isn't like yours."

"No, I guess not, but…um, I don't know if this helps, but my family really wants to adopt you. My abuela thinks you're sweet, which is true, and my mother says you're so polite, which is—"

"Not true."

"Oh, please." She elbowed Conner in the ribs. "You're nicer than you admit."

Conner turned to face her, allowing a half-grin. "I disagree. We both know I'm bad. Very, very bad."

As she'd predicted, a blush crept up Meli's face. She was so easy to fluster, and doing just that remained one of Conner's favorite things in life. "I didn't—you're so—I mean—you're not—oh, go to bed, Conner."

Conner laughed as she stood, grateful for the playful moment. "Are you staying?"

Meli's expression softened, and not for the first time, Conner wished she had some sort of legend to the map of Meli's face. She could read the fondness and amusement often there, but sometimes, like now, she sensed something more that she just couldn't decipher.

She didn't have the energy to dwell on that puzzle tonight, so she draped an arm over Meli's shoulders and headed upstairs.

Chapter Thirty-Nine

The vibration of her phone woke Conner from a dead sleep. She fumbled on her nightstand until she located the offending object.

"Hello?" she muttered without opening her eyes.

"Conner? What's wrong?"

She shot up in bed. "Sadie?"

"You called me late last night. Three times. What's going on?"

Conner steeled herself. "Don't get mad."

"Conner, if you don't—"

"Sarah's at my house."

A pause, lasting simultaneously five seconds and five hours, and then, "Have you lost your mind? Now you've graduated to kidnapping? What in the world—"

"Sadie."

"Was she ever even at her friend's house, or was that some sort of cover story you two cooked up? I can't believe—"

"Sadie."

"—behind my back! I knew you were unreliable, but this is a new low, even for—"

"Sadie, damn it, will you let me explain?" She heard a gasp, then silence. "Listen. Sarah called me. She and her friends went to a party, and she didn't want to be there."

"They went to a party?"

"Yes. I should have taken her to your house right away, but she was afraid you'd be angry."

"She's right. That girl isn't going to see the light of day for months."

"I'm not going to tell you how to parent, but—"

"You're absolutely right about that."

Conner gritted her teeth. "Just maybe consider that she let her friends talk her into it, and then she did the right thing by calling an adult?"

"She should have called me or her father."

"Sure, she should have, but come on. You didn't do anything dumb as a teenager? I might have set the bar, but I'm sure you weren't perfect. Or maybe you were. What do I know?"

The line grew quiet. Had Sadie hung up? "I'm on my way," she finally said.

Conner's heart constricted, both at the hope of seeing her sister and the fear that she might never see her nieces again. "Sure, of course, but...she's asleep, and—and—I'm completely sober. I swear. I haven't had anything at all, and Meli has been here all night, so...if you don't trust me, you know you can trust her. I can bring Sarah home right after breakfast. Please, Sadie."

After a rustle, Conner heard muffled background noises, presumably Sadie conferring with Asher. She found herself whispering "please" over and over, just as she used to as a kid when she really wanted a role. Seeing Sarah tonight and hearing Sadie's voice had been a soothing balm of aloe for her bruised heart. She'd take what she could get.

She nearly jumped out of her skin when Sadie spoke again. "As soon as she's awake."

"I swear. Thank you, Sadie, I—"

"I'll see you in a few hours."

The call ended. Conner stared at the display. Five a.m. She would never go back to sleep, so she threw on a sports bra and shorts and headed to the basement for a workout, pushing herself until she couldn't think about the morning to come.

Conner took Sarah out for breakfast at a nearby diner. After they finished their veggie omelets—Sarah had amused her by copying her order and regretting it, judging by her face—they climbed back into the Porsche, and Conner drove slower than ever before.

"How's high school?"

"Fine, I guess. My classes aren't too bad, except for algebra. It sucks."

"Algebra does suck."

"My friends are all obsessed with boys, too."

In her peripheral vision, Conner could see Sarah peering at her from under her long eyelashes. This was no throwaway comment. "That happens. Is there a person that you might like?"

Sarah shook her head slowly. "No-o. I think I might be weird."

"You can't be weird, kid. You're my niece. Cool is in your blood."

"Yeah, but you like lots of people, right? You *like* like them, like Melina."

"I don't—" Sarah eyed her with raised eyebrows, and she gave up the charade. "Yes. I have *like* liked a lot of people."

"How do you know?"

"That I like someone?"

"Yeah, but also, um…how did you know you were gay or whatever?"

For a moment, Conner contemplated if she could jump out of the car without injuring anyone. In lieu of that, she forced herself to be an adult and took a deep breath. "Well. As far as being a lesbian, I never felt any pull towards boys. I have male friends that I care about, but I've never been attracted to them. But girls, well, I've always liked girls."

"Like you want to kiss them and stuff?"

"For me, yes, but you don't have to be sexually attracted to someone to like them in a romantic sense. When you really like someone, they're your favorite person in the entire world. You always want to be around them, you can't stop thinking about them, and you feel like there's no one else in the world like them. It's like taking your best friend and multiplying by ten. Your heart races, and you can't breathe, and everything is better when you're with them." She sighed at the familiar tug at her heart before glancing at Sarah. "Does that make sense?"

She shrugged. "I guess so."

"Do you think you might not be straight?" Conner treaded with the care of one traversing a minefield.

"I don't know. I've never felt like that about anyone."

"You could be ace or demi, or maybe you just haven't met the right person yet." She tousled Sarah's hair. "I know this is easier said than done, but try not to worry about it. You'll figure it out. All you need to be is you." She flicked on her blinker and exited the highway. "Sarah?"

She didn't respond until they stopped at a red light, turning to look at Conner accusingly. "Where are we going?"

Conner bit her bottom lip before forcing herself to stop. "I'm taking you home."

"WHAT? You can't! Then Mom and Dad will know about the party, and I'll be in so much trouble!"

Conner squeezed her eyes shut. She really, really hated this. "They already do. I had to call them, Sarah! They're your parents. They deserved to know where you were."

"They're going to call Bella and Audrey's parents, so they'll never talk to me again!"

"That wouldn't be a bad thing. They left you alone at a random party. They're not good friends."

"Whatever. I wish I'd never called you. I wish I'd never met you!"

She turned back to her window with a huff, crossing her arms. With something in her stomach that weighed about a ton, Conner drove several blocks in silence before switching on some music. Half a verse played before Sarah turned it off with another huff.

Despite the hurt radiating through every facet of her being, Conner rolled her eyes. Teenagers.

The instant they pulled up to the house, Sadie stepped out the front door. Her lips were so thin they nearly disappeared, and her arms were clamped across her chest. Sarah slammed the door of the Porsche, and Conner almost snapped at her before thinking better of it. She was just lashing out.

Sadie pointed at her daughter. "Inside. Now."

Sarah made a show of stomping to the door, pausing just before she entered the house. Tears filled her eyes. "I thought you were so cool, but you're not cool at all. I hate you!"

Conner took a step back, stunned. She'd done the right thing, but at what cost?

"She didn't mean that." Conner jerked at the words. Sadie watched her, her expression revealing nothing. "Kids say that when they're hurt. She's fourteen and moody."

"She's also PMSing."

"She's *what*?"

She probably should have let Sarah tell Sadie, but the damage was already done. "She started her period last night. I gave her pads and fresh clothes. She said she knew what to do."

"Great. So my oldest daughter started her period without her mother around."

"You can't blame biology on me. She wouldn't have been home anyway." Sadie didn't budge. "Can we talk, please?"

They surveyed each other in silence. Conner fought against the urge to plead her case, knowing it would be a waste of words until Sadie was ready to listen. But if telepathy existed, she was trying her hardest.

Sadie bobbed her head exactly once and sat on the steps, jerking her chin to indicate Conner could do the same. Conner took a deep breath before beginning.

"I never knew what to do with kids. I never had a chance to be one myself, and I don't want any of my own. When you wanted me to meet them, I was terrified. But, God, Sadie, I adore those girls. They're the most important people in my life. I would never do anything to hurt them."

"You did, though."

"I know. I fucked up, and I can't tell you how awful I feel about it. But you have to believe me that it was an honest mistake. I was so exhausted, and—you know what? I'm not going to justify it. I screwed up, and I'm so, so sorry. I'll never do it again."

"How do I know that? How do I trust you?"

"We start over, and you give me another chance. Please, Sadie. I've changed. You just need to let me show you."

Sadie stared at her for a long moment. "How have you changed?"

The question caught Conner off-guard, and she took a second to get herself together. "For one, I cut down on my commitments. Harlow and I had a long talk, and I'm not going to run myself ragged any longer. I'll still be busy because that's the nature of this business, but only when I want to be."

"That's good. So you and Harlow are back together?"

Conner smiled. "Yep. She set some conditions, which I'm following."

"What about the drugs?"

She stifled the instinct to defend herself. Once an addict, always an addict. But not a user, an important distinction. "I still take edibles every so often, but that's it. They help me relax, and they aren't illegal. You know, it really hurt when you didn't believe me that I no longer do hard drugs."

Sadie opened her mouth, shut it, then opened it again. "I'll admit that was unfair of me."

Score one for Conner. Still lopsided, but at least she was on the board. She decided to press her advantage. "I've really missed you, too. My life has been kinda shitty for the past year, and while much of that is my fault, I really needed my sister. In case you haven't noticed, sometimes I'm an idiot, and I need someone to look up to."

Her voice had begun to waver, so she paused. When Sadie replied, her voice was unsteady, too.

"Hard to look up to me when I'm shorter than you."

She chanced a look at her. Sadie still gazed at the lawn in front of them, but the tightness around her mouth had evaporated. Conner's insides danced a jig.

"My mother took Hannah out to brunch. They should be back soon. Do you want to stay so you can say hello? You can tell me why you're such an idiot while you wait."

Conner stopped trying to hide her grin and let it out in full bloom. "I'd blame genetics, but you share half of mine, and your head seems to be screwed on straight. One more thing about me that's not straight, I guess."

Sadie made a noise that was almost a chuckle. "I guess so. Listen, Conner…" She stood, and Conner followed, allowing her gaze to land on her sister. "If you mess up one more time…"

She held her hands up. "No third chances. I understand."

"Good. Come inside. I have to ground my daughter for the next four years."

❖

When Hannah arrived, she squealed loud enough to be heard on Huntington Beach and leapt into Conner's arms, squeezing with astonishing strength for an eight-year-old before saying in an accusing tone, "You missed a lot of my games." With Sadie's nod of permission, Conner promised she'd come to the next one.

She spent the morning with Sadie, Asher, and Hannah. Sarah refused to come out of her room or speak to Conner, and nothing anyone said could sway her, even when Hannah offered her favorite stuffy and was highly offended by the rejection. Conner was less offended and more wounded, although she couldn't think of another option.

She didn't expect to repair their relationships within a few hours, and though Hannah accepted her return with the easy forgiveness of a child, Asher and Sadie remain stilted. Still, they were obviously trying, which was all Conner could ask.

However, Asher and Sadie both gave her hugs when she left shortly before lunch. Then Hannah, who'd rarely let Conner out of arm's reach all morning, threw her arms around Conner's midsection and looked up with wide green eyes.

"Are you going to come back?"

"Yes. I promise. Soon?" She glanced beseechingly at Sadie, who nodded.

"Good. I love you, Aunt Conner."

Conner stood immobilized as if cursed, barely able to breathe. No one, save her adoring but impersonal fans, had ever said they loved her. If someone had, she probably wouldn't have believed them, anyway. What was love? Was it her parents, torturing each other with pointed barbs and blatant affairs? Or her Irish grandparents, who rarely said two words to each other? What about Vittoria, who viewed her as a prize to be both won and shared? Even Maggie, who knew her better than anyone yet blamed her for Maggie's own choices?

"Now you say 'I love you, too,'" Hannah said helpfully.

"Hannah." Sadie's voice was hushed, less warning than curiosity.

Everyone was looking at her, waiting. Hannah, this child, this earnest niece of hers who shared Conner's blood and Conner's eyes, loved her and asked nothing but her love in return. Did she love her? Did she love all of them? Was that what this feeling inside her was, this deep well of joy from a simple hug?

"I love you, too, kid." She patted her back, and if her eyes burned, no one knew it but her.

Afterward, she practically flew to NoHo. She had to tell Meli about her day. She never considered not sharing. Besides, Meli deserved to know the outcome of the reunion after helping her out last night.

She practically spun Meli in a circle after waltzing into her apartment.

Then, facing each other on the narrow couch, she told her everything that had happened, sparing only the detail about Hannah's good-bye and her own reaction. She didn't want Meli to think she was pathetic.

"I knew it would work out!" As always, Meli was nothing short of enthusiastic. "It was only a matter of time. No one can resist you."

Conner shrugged. "I can think of a few people."

Meli smiled, her eyes gleaming. Conner would *not* read anything into this. "I can't." She reached up, cupping Conner's cheek with a tentative hand and stealing her breath at the same time. "Look at you, so happy. You're so beautiful when you're happy. So irresistible."

"Am I?"

Her voice had dropped to a rasp.

Meli matched her. "You know you are."

Then she tugged Conner's chin toward her, stretched up, and kissed her.

Chapter Forty

They were kissing.
Conner was kissing Meli.
Meli had kissed her.
They were *kissing*.
Conner couldn't wrap her mind around it. She had yearned, dreamed, fantasized about this moment for longer than she wanted to admit, yet now that it was here, she had no idea what to do.
They broke apart. Did Meli's expression, as if she'd been plucked from Earth and dropped on another planet, mirror her own?
"Wha…why…what?" She was fairly certain the English language contained other words, not to mention the other languages she spoke, but they eluded her.
Meli's chest rose and fell in deep, rapid breaths. "I—I wanted to. I've wanted to for…a while."
Conner nodded, blinked, then surged forward to capture Meli's lips again. She swallowed Meli's surprised gasp, delighting in the sweetness. She was soft, so soft. Conner pressed against her and loosely grasped Meli's curls in one hand, the other wrapped around her back. If this was a dream, she never wanted to wake up. If it was a coma, she never wanted to be revived. If she was dead, she'd found her heaven.
She still couldn't comprehend what was happening, so she stopped thinking at all and gave herself over to the moment. The honey of Meli's taste, the floral of her scent, the pillowy softness of her skin, the—her tongue, oh God, her tongue flicking ever so hesitantly against Conner's lips. A whimper rose from Conner's throat. Their kisses ratcheted up in intensity, tongues massaging each other, hands roaming to find every inch of exposed skin, heavy breathing beginning to fill the thankfully empty apartment.
Conner could have kissed Meli forever, luxuriating in the perfection of her mouth, but so much else remained to explore, and this heaven could end

at any moment. She trailed her lips to Meli's jaw, working her way up to her ear. Meli moaned and tilted her head back, tempting Conner with her neck. Conner didn't resist, immediately latching on and sucking hard. She wanted to leave a mark. She wanted everyone to know.

Meli's strangled gasp spurred them on. Conner nipped with her teeth before sucking again, desperate for some sort of reminder that this had actually happened. Meli yanked Conner's flannel shirt off her shoulders, and Conner nearly tore it the rest of the way off.

Then Meli's hand slipped under Conner's T-shirt, brushing her bare skin, and Conner had to collect every single bit of her will to pull away.

Oh, but she had left Meli a glorious mess. At some point she'd ended up nearly on top of her, so Meli lay half-prone against the arm of the couch. Her chest heaved, and her perfect lips, swollen beyond their usual fullness, were parted in anticipation, beckoning. And that mark Conner was so desperate to leave was already halfway there, calling her name.

She grasped for whatever tendrils of sense remained buried beneath layers of yearning and arousal. "Meli...what's happening?"

"We...I thought we were making out."

"Right, and I'm not opposed to that, obviously, but you said you were straight? I'm confused."

Meli pushed herself up, which gave Conner time to regain her wits. She ran a hand through her hair, reminding herself that stopping had been the right choice. It helped if she didn't look at Meli, but her gaze kept returning like a compass to true north.

"I'm confused, too. So, um, I've been wondering lately if maybe I'm not?" Conner's heart paused its beat. In fact, her entire body stiffened. Meli picked up a throw pillow and twisted it into an unrecognizable shape. "I—I meant what I said. I wanted to kiss you. I've wanted to do that for, I don't know, just a while, I think. I wanted to take your shirt off, and I—" She took a deep breath. "I wanted to keep going. I do want, I mean. I want to keep going."

"Keep...going? To what?"

"To, um, to my bedroom?" She looked up, landing on Conner's shell-shocked gaze, and swallowed hard. "To my bed."

Conner shook her head. She was either dreaming, drugged, dead, or in some alternate universe. She let her gaze roam Meli once more. With her dilated pupils, fast breathing, and eyes that constantly darted down to Conner's lips and chest, she was clearly aroused. But mangling the pillow and biting her lip said she was nervous.

Meli must have taken her silence as hesitation, for she rambled on. "Bellamy told me, you see, about how you helped her figure out her sexuality. And I thought—I think—I am, I'm attracted to you, and you're such a good friend to me, that maybe this would be something we could, um, explore? Together?"

A heavily loaded pause, just one beat, then, "No."

Surprised disappointment clouded Meli's lovely features. "No?"

Conner couldn't quite believe herself, either. The word had come out on its own accord. Yet she, too, was disappointed. Sex with Bellamy truly had been one friend helping another. Puzzled by her lack of interest when sleeping with men, Bellamy had decided to give women a shot. Although both of them had enjoyed themselves physically, she didn't find what she was seeking, and after some soul searching had realized she was asexual. Nothing had changed between her and Conner.

So that's what Meli wanted, was it? Just a night of no-strings sex, a warm body she could trust? Sure, she'd admitted she was attracted to Conner, but so were two-thirds of the rest of the world. Conner couldn't help paying attention to the dark voice inside her, pointing out that once again she wasn't the end game. She was the casual partner, the notch on the bedpost, the trophy, the dress rehearsal. No one wanted her for *her*; they wanted her name, her fame, her body, her face, her bank account.

Then she looked up again and faltered. Maybe Meli didn't want her in the same way she wanted Meli, but she was interested. She'd come on to Conner, after all. She hadn't chosen someone else. She was trusting Conner with something potentially life-altering. Conner couldn't allow someone to take advantage of her at such a vulnerable moment, someone who would take what they wanted with no care for her feelings. The sapphic community had its fair share of such people, unfortunately.

Conner ignored the fact that doing this would probably destroy her.

"No, not today. Not right now." She took Meli's hand in hers, warm and soft. Her heart gave an extra pump. "This is a big deal, and I want you to be sure you've thought it through."

Meli lowered her chin and her voice. "I have thought it through. I've thought about it so much. It's something—I want this, Conner."

This. She wanted *this,* not Conner. But Conner was part of it. Her head swirled, while her heart continued its traitorous staccato beat. "That's good. I just need a few days to wrap my head around it all. Not that I haven't thought about it, because I definitely have." That admission earned smiles from both. "But just give me a little time to, you know, prepare and all that. Besides, I have to go to Toronto tomorrow, and this isn't something to be rushed."

"Rushed? How long do you need?" Meli asked with a nervous chuckle.

"Twenty-four hours." Her chuckle died instantly. "If you want a proper experience. And trust me, you do."

"I do."

"Trust me, or want a proper experience?" She swallowed her own nervous laugh.

"Yes."

She was clearly sincere, but the tension overcame them, and they dissolved into giggles.

"I'll be back a week from tomorrow."

"I have to be on set Monday and Tuesday." Conner must have asked a question with her eyes, because Meli added, "I got the role on that Netflix comedy."

"That's awesome, babe!"

"Thanks."

Conner briefly examined her cuticles. Finally, she glanced up. "So, Wednesday?"

Meli's throat worked, but there was no mistaking flare of desire in her eyes. "Wednesday."

Conner had always loved Toronto. The diversity and culture made it a fun place to visit and topped the list on the unlikely chance she ever bailed on Hollywood. But she forgot this trip before it ever started. She faked her way through several days of press but couldn't have recalled what she said with a gun to her head. Then she headed to a convention for three days. Cons weren't her favorite events, crowded with fanatics as they were, but she usually relished dressing in her costume and wandering around in rare anonymity, though it never lasted. This time she was too distracted to enjoy even that experience, but Harlow said she just came across as slightly bored, which fit her reputation.

Meli wasn't straight. Meli had made out with her. Meli wanted to have sex with her.

She simply couldn't comprehend the turn of events. Suspecting that Meli was attracted to her was completely different than confirming that possibility. She argued with herself over the merits of confessing her feelings to Meli and seeing where that led, but that path seemed dangerous. If Meli didn't reciprocate, she might explore her sexuality with someone else or, worse, ruin their friendship altogether. Conner couldn't handle either of those things, therefore...

She was going to have sex.

With Meli.

On Wednesday.

By the time she returned from Toronto, she was wound tighter than a former prom queen's dress at her high school reunion. She was desperate to talk about the situation with Maggie, but none of her bandmates had spoken to her since her birthday party, and she couldn't handle a difficult discussion right now. She ended up booking a massage, but even her experienced masseuse couldn't resolve her tension.

When Wednesday arrived, though, something inside her shifted. The nerves remained, but anticipation overshadowed them. After all, she'd been longing for this for a long time. While their liaison wasn't taking the exact form she desired, she would still experience being with Meli, and Conner had learned to take what she could get.

When Meli arrived, she was flushed, almost breathless. They faced each other in Conner's foyer, waiting for some invisible signal.

"Do you want something to drink?" Conner gestured in the direction of the kitchen.

Meli licked her lips, and Conner had to stop herself from groaning at the sight. "Yes. Water would be nice."

In the kitchen, as Conner watched her sip a glass of water, she couldn't stand it any longer. She stepped up behind her, her hands on Meli's arms. Meli tensed, lowering the glass to the countertop with a shaking hand.

Conner bent her head to Meli's neck. First, she pressed feather-light kisses down her neck and onto her shoulder. Every time Meli sighed, a volt shot through Conner. Then she repeated the actions on the other side, even winding Meli's curls in her hand and languidly exploring the back of her neck. Only when she saw some of the rigidity slide from Meli did she stop.

"Still thirsty?"

Meli shook her head, and Conner bit down on a grin, for she saw only hunger in Meli's expression.

Their hands clasped, Conner led her upstairs, glancing back every so often. The slightest hint of fear, and this was all over. But every time, Meli smiled, seeming nervous yet excited.

Finally, she stopped in the middle of her bedroom, dropped Meli's hand, and leaned down to kiss her again. They slowly explored each other. Conner let Meli set the pace, waiting for her to open her mouth, to use her hands. Their mouths fit so well together. How would their bodies match?

When their kisses became demanding and hands turned insistent, Conner knew they were ready to move on. She broke apart with a final nip at Meli's bottom lip, pleased with the craving she saw in Meli's darkened eyes.

They'd already checked that both were free of any diseases, but they still needed to discuss a few items before they jumped into this.

"Is there anywhere you don't like to be touched? Anywhere you don't want to be licked?" Meli shook her head. "Nowhere? Because I'm going to touch you now. All over."

"No-nowhere. But I…um…I don't know what you like. You know, grooming-wise, so I—"

Conner held up her hands. "Hold on. What I like? I don't care where other women choose to shave or not. I have my own preferences for myself, but what you do with your body is your business."

"Oh."

"You're gorgeous regardless. You know that, right?" She relaxed, leaning against the dresser, her legs crossed at the ankle. "Now I want you to take off your clothes. Can you do that for me?"

Meli's eyes flared with lust as she gulped, then nodded. Conner had half expected nervous babble, but Meli was surprisingly quiet. So far. Conner would have to be sure to check in with her at frequent intervals.

"I need some help with my zipper," said Meli with a certain shyness.

"I can take care of that." Conner crossed the distance between them with purposeful strides, drawing one finger across Meli's stomach as she moved behind her. Finding the zipper on Meli's yellow sundress, she lowered it at an infinitesimal pace, letting her knuckles brush Meli's spine as she unzipped it before pressing a kiss to each inch of uncovered skin. After she finished, she stared at the uncovered strap of Meli's bra for a long moment, then forced herself to return to her previous position against the dresser.

Whether intentional or not, Meli's unhurried strip put Conner on edge. She was riveted to every movement, finding it harder to breathe as more and more skin appeared. When the dress hit the floor, Conner bit her lip so hard she nearly drew blood.

"Fuck," she murmured.

Conner loved lingerie, her one consistent concession to her femininity. She lived for the look in a lover's eyes when she revealed something sexy, and she reveled in seeing it on someone else. Meli had chosen a matching set, all white lace and not much else. Her generous breasts strained against the flimsy material, nipples already pressing against their confines, and the cut of her panties flattered her wide hips.

Conner became aware her lips had parted, and she quickly pressed them shut, circling one finger in the air for Meli to continue.

Meli hesitated, never looking away. She slipped first one, then the other strap off her shoulders. When her fingers moved to the place where the cups joined between her breasts, Conner had to grip the wood of her dresser to keep her knees from buckling. Oh, God. Her bra had a front clasp. How had Meli known all of Conner's favorite things? For a second she suspected Meli had quizzed her friends, and then she stopped thinking at all.

The instant Meli released the clasps, her breasts spilled out, dropping the bra to the floor. Round and full, slightly paler than the rest of her skin and topped with dark nipples, they were magnificent and begged to be worshipped. Conner wanted to drop to her knees like a subject to her queen.

When Meli was fully nude, Conner simply drank her in without a word. She simultaneously wanted to stare forever and to jump ahead to the next stage. Meli fidgeted, which caught Conner's attention.

"Do you know how beautiful you are? I'm serious. Your hair is glorious, your eyes are gorgeous, and I can't get enough of your smile. Your body, God, Meli, your body is amazing. Your laugh is my favorite thing in the world, and you're so sweet I want—" She suddenly realized she was veering into dangerous waters and scrambled to right her course. "You have to believe me. You're stunning."

"Conner…" She ducked her head. "When do I get to see you?"

Every so often Meli had these spurts of boldness that always caught Conner off guard. She worked hard to keep her composure.

"Soon enough."

Conner held her gaze while she took her rings off her fingers, one by one, laying them on the dresser behind her with audible clinks. Then she sauntered over to her once more.

"Hey." She lifted Meli's chin. "If you're uncomfortable at any point, speak up, okay?" She nodded, and Conner smiled. "Words, babe. Sex is an ongoing conversation."

"I will. I trust you."

Conner released her chin and ran her thumb up one of Meli's cheeks, repeating the motion on the other side. She moved her hands across Meli's shoulders and belly, up and down her legs, everywhere but the places she most wanted to touch. She gloried in her discoveries: a spray of freckles on her lower back, a scar on her elbow, the ripple of stretch marks on her thighs. Again and again she skimmed her curves, luxuriating in the soft sensations until Meli was nearly panting.

"Conner, please…" Conner waited for her to say it. "Will you touch me?"

The devil on Conner's shoulder wanted to ask where, but the truth was she was nearly as desperate. Anticipation only worked with a payoff.

"Okay." Meli began to move, but Conner held her firm. "Nuh-uh. You're gonna stay right here."

"Standing? I don't know if I can…"

"Trust me. You will. Now look up." Resting her chin on Meli's shoulder, she guided her until both were gazing into the mirror on Conner's dresser. They looked good together, and Conner's stomach twisted. "Look how fucking beautiful you are, babe. Now watch."

She snaked her arm around Meli's stomach and cupped one of her breasts. The instant she rolled one puckered nipple between her fingers, Meli threw her head back, very nearly taking Conner out, and moaned. The sound traveled straight to Conner's already throbbing pussy.

Soon she was gently massaging both breasts, delighted that Meli was both sensitive and vocal in her appreciation. Time to up the ante.

"The most important part of sex, after consent and communication," she said, enjoying the shivers she provoked whenever her breath grazed Meli's ear, "is paying attention. Watch her face, listen to the sounds she makes. Clearly you like this."

She brushed her thumbs over Meli's nipples again, earning a contented sigh.

"But what about this?" This time she squeezed and was rewarded with a sharp intake of breath. "Oh, yes, you like that. More?" She pinched one nipple, releasing it as soon as Meli quietly grunted, and soothed it with a gentle stroke. "Nope, too much. See?"

"Mmm." Meli closed her eyes as Conner continued.

Conner enjoyed breasts like any good lesbian did, but at heart she was an ass woman, and she'd been lusting after Meli's for a long time. Deciding she'd waited long enough, she let one hand drift down the planes of her back until she took a handful of Meli's rear.

"You have such a luscious ass," she said, squeezing hard. "Delectable."

"You don't think it's too big?"

"The only thing it's too much of is perfection. I could devour it." Meli laughed, and Conner squeezed again, although she enjoyed the laugh. Sex should be fun. "You think I'm kidding."

"You're—you're not?"

She'd save that discussion for another time. Then she faltered, realizing there wouldn't be another time. Conner shook her head. *Focus.*

Meli was flushed and panting, nipples tightly furled, eyes dark. She was ready.

She brushed a handful of curls out of her way and began kissing the crook of Meli's neck again. She tasted so sweet. Conner couldn't help but wonder how she tasted elsewhere.

She planned to find out.

Meli groaned. "God, you're good at seduction."

Conner chuckled against her skin. "Is that what I'm doing? I thought it was just foreplay."

"That makes—ah—more sense." Meli gasped as Conner returned to her breasts. "You don't need to seduce me. I'm yours."

The words immobilized Conner, words she was reading far too much into. Everyone knew not to trust sentiments expressed during sex. Meli just meant she was putty in Conner's hands.

Her hands slid down until they rested on Meli's hips. Waiting until Meli met her gaze in the mirror, she skimmed a single finger across Meli's pussy, astonished by how wet she was.

"Do you like penetration?" When she didn't get an answer, she continued to run one finger back and forth, just brushing the surface. "Meli?"

"Yes, Conner, please!"

On her next swipe, she parted Meli's lips, still abstaining from entering her. Bit by bit she caressed harder and harder, until on one pass she deliberately put pressure against Meli's swollen clit.

Meli shook all over as she cried out. Conner wrapped her free hand around her waist to keep her standing. Before she could recover, Conner slid one finger inside her.

She fucked Meli with steady, deep strokes, using her thumb to lavish attention on Meli's clit, soon adding a second finger. The position was far from the most comfortable, but seeing Meli come apart in the mirror only heightened her arousal.

Meli was so fucking gorgeous. Conner had to remind herself to keep going, because all she wanted to do was watch. Meli was getting close. Her head dropped back against Conner's shoulder as she cried out again and again. When she clenched her own breasts, Conner nearly came.

"Do you remember that first night you stayed here in the summer, and I got out of bed?" The confession poured out unbidden. She might ruin everything, but Conner couldn't help herself. "I was so turned on just by being next to you that I had to touch myself until I came, standing up facing the vanity mirror, just like this. I imagined how you would feel, how you would sound, how you would taste. And you know what? You're so much better."

"Conner!" Meli's walls trembled around her fingers, and her eyes flew open to reveal her dilated pupils.

"Now look in the mirror, and watch yourself come for me, my beautiful girl."

She did, with a loud, guttural wail. Conner was relentless, fucking her so hard it was as if she was trying to bring both of them to orgasm through Meli, and she nearly succeeded. When Meli tightened around her fingers, Conner's pussy throbbed so hard she nearly lost her balance. Thankfully she didn't, for Meli's knees had buckled entirely, and only Conner kept them standing.

She laved her clit one more time, and Meli's entire body shuddered as she gave a weak cry.

"I can't, I can't. Oh, God, please. It's too much."

Conner eased out of her. Meli's little whimper when they parted almost finished her off. Afraid she'd fall to the floor, she half carried Meli to her bed, where both collapsed.

Conner curled up on her side, watching Meli catch her breath and regain her senses. To her shock, tears dripped down Meli's face.

"Babe? Did I hurt you? Was it awful?" She scrambled to her knees, cradling Meli's precious face in her hands.

Meli shook her head, brushing her cheeks with the back of one shaking hand. "No, not awful. I don't know why—I'm so stupid. Conner, that was so amazing. You're so...I can't even...please kiss me."

Without waiting for a response, Meli yanked her down and kissed her thoroughly. If their previous kisses had been exploratory, this one was urgent, demanding, and all Conner could do was give in.

She was, she finally allowed herself to realize, in far too deep.

Chapter Forty-one

Conner rolled onto her back, trying to catch her breath. "Shit, babe. Who taught you to kiss like that? I'm going to send them a gift."
　　Meli giggled. "Do you normally ask about other lovers during sex?"
　　"Why not? I'm secure in myself and my skills."
　　"You should be." Her sigh was pure pleasure.
　　Conner grinned at the ceiling and attempted to school her expression into something less smug before facing Meli again. She was unsuccessful but didn't really care. If she jumped off the roof right now, she could outfly Peter Pan. Happy thoughts, indeed. "Enjoyed that, did you?"
　　"Wasn't it obvious?"
　　"I had an inkling." She traced patterns on Meli's stomach, which rippled under her teasing touch. "Do you want to find out what else you enjoy?"
　　"Oh." Her eyes grew wide. "You weren't exaggerating about twenty-four hours, were you?"
　　"Exaggerating? I was being conservative."
　　She shifted onto her side, leaning in to kiss Meli once more. She could live forever with only these kisses as sustenance. They made out in a languid fashion, tongues caressing the other, all soft moans and contented sighs.
　　Meli toyed with the hem of Conner's tank top. "You're still dressed."
　　Conner pushed herself up on one arm. "Is that a problem?"
　　"I mean, it feels kind of uneven." She squirmed, her shyness equal parts charming and amusing. "I wouldn't mind if you took off your clothes."
　　"All you had to do was ask."
　　She climbed off the bed and wasted no time shedding her shirt and leggings. Conner had never been one to make a show of stripping. Down to her bra and underwear, she stood in place, letting Meli get a good look.
　　And look she did. Even though she had seen Conner in bikinis on multiple occasions and completely topless one memorable night, she took her time, perusing Conner's body from feet to tits. If the makeouts and

orgasm hadn't been enough evidence of her attraction to women, the blatant admiration of her body sealed it.

"Do you need a picture?"

She expected a blush but received a slow shaking of her head instead.

"I won't forget."

"Do you want something else you won't forget?" She straddled one of Meli's thick thighs, grinding against it just once.

Meli sucked in her breath. "You feel wet."

"Oh, I'm soaked." Licking her lips, she dragged her middle finger through Meli's folds again, smirking when she twitched. Holding her gaze, she brought the finger to her mouth and sucked it clean, unable to restrain a moan. Just as good as she'd imagined.

A strangled squeak escaped Meli. She was zeroed in on Conner's mouth. Conner's smirk broadened into a grin. "Have you ever tasted yourself?" A slow shake. "Do you want to?" An even slower nod.

She dipped her finger into Meli again, gathering plenty of her moisture, but instead of bringing it to Meli's mouth, she brought it to her own, painting her lips with the sweet, tangy gloss. Then she leaned in, giving Meli a long, soft kiss.

Meli's mouth remained in a surprised *O* when they parted. "That's... interesting."

"Interesting good or interesting bad?"

"Not bad, just interesting. Better than men's...you know."

Conner recoiled, curling her upper lip in disgust. "Gross. I don't know, thank God."

"Sorry. Guess I ruined the mood, huh?"

Conner stroked a hand up and down Meli's stomach before idly playing with one nipple. "Look at you. Nothing could ruin the mood."

Before she could reply, Conner leaned down to capture Meli's breast in her mouth. They groaned in unison. She'd been waiting for this since the moment her bra dropped to the floor. She gave equal attention to each breast, sucking and nipping, waiting until Meli writhed beneath her before moving lower.

She licked her way down Meli's stomach, nudging her legs apart and shifting until she made herself at home between them. Her heart pounded with eager anticipation. She loved the reactions she received when she ate out a woman. Conner had every intention of making Meli launch off this bed and going back for seconds.

But first, some teasing. An appetizer. She squeezed Meli's thighs, pushing them apart until she reached resistance. Her mouth watered at the feast in front of her. She glanced up and winked at Meli's wide-eyed expression, noting how rapidly her chest heaved. Conner dragged her tongue up one crease between her thigh and pussy, then down the other. She pressed a kiss to her mons and left love bites all over her inner thighs. She nudged Meli's clit with her nose as she breathed in her unique scent. Then she repeated the process.

By the time Meli was ready, she was panting audibly, whimpering every time Conner's mouth came close to the prize. Conner looked up again. Could she make Meli beg? But her clear impatience was more than enough.

Conner grinned, bent her head, and thoroughly licked up Meli's pussy. Meli crashed to the bed with a choked cry. Conner took her time, exploring every inch of her folds except her clit. She drove her tongue inside as far as she could before licking up and down again. Unable to resist, she let one of her hands drift south until she cupped one of Meli's generous butt cheeks, letting a finger slip in between them. Meli's breath caught, and Conner filed that reaction away for later before remembering there wouldn't be a later.

Disappointment crashed into her before she refocused on her task, doubling her efforts. When Meli clutched the duvet, she upped the ante and flicked her clit with the tip of her tongue.

"Fu-uck." The curse sounded like it came from deep within, and Conner was doubly gratified since Meli rarely swore.

Teasing flew out the window. Conner chased Meli's orgasm like a woman possessed. Meli began to thrust her hips off the bed, so Conner wrapped her arms around each thigh to hold her in place. She licked and sucked at a measured, deliberate pace, fast enough to climb toward climax but not so fast she lost her rhythm.

When Meli's gasps gave way to unintelligible cries, Conner latched onto her clit and sucked hard, flicking her tongue back and forth as quickly as she could. With a final keening cry, Meli lurched her hips as she came into Conner's mouth.

Conner took a little time to soak up the glorious sight of post-orgasmic Meli. Greedily she noted how proudly her nipples stood at attention, traced the contours of the flush that started on her chest and crept up her neck, memorized her slack-jawed expression. Through it all she continued to lap gently, just enough to never let her fully recover.

Once Meli caught her breath, Conner went back for another helping.

Meli's head shot up. "Again? I don't think I can—ohhh, fuck, oh God. You're amazing."

Conner smirked but didn't revel in the compliment, instead doing her best to live up to it. This time, in addition to her oral attention on Meli's sensitive, swollen clit, she slid a finger inside, massaging her velvety walls in sync with her licks.

Meli's fingers flexed against the duvet until one hand reached down to clutch at Conner's sweaty locks. Her own neglected body, already humming with delayed arousal, gave an extra throb. As with all aspects of her life, Conner liked to be in control during sex, but she fucking loved making a woman so desperate she tried to hold her in place. As if she were going anywhere.

Successive orgasms sometimes took their time, her partner hovering on the edge for what felt like forever before finally plunging off the cliff. But this one was a rocket. When Conner added a second finger, curling and stroking, Meli nearly sobbed.

Conner flicked her gaze up, noting the tension in Meli's torso. "Breathe, babe. It's so much better when you breathe." Obediently, she took in a deep breath that ended in a ragged gasp, and Conner was rewarded with the telltale fluttering of her walls.

She was so very, very close. She just needed something to tip her over. Conner moved her free hand farther south, and though she was careful not to penetrate, she pressed the tip of her finger against Meli's rim.

With a glass-shattering scream, Meli all but levitated off the bed, crashing down with a second wail. One of her feet kicked out, and only then did Conner disengage, although Meli's death grip on her head kept her from going far.

Stunned and soaked, Conner lay between her legs, flexing her jaw and trying to catch her breath. She'd given a lot of women orgasms, but none so memorable as this. She wanted to do it again, and again and again, until Meli understood—until both of them understood—the depth of her feelings. She wanted to make Meli come every night and day. Wanted to worship her like she deserved. Wanted it all.

Meli gave a shaky little laugh, one arm over her face, and Conner relaxed, grinning as she rested her head against Meli's leg.

"I think you're trying to kill me, Conner." Her voice carried a slight rasp, and Conner thought she might die, too.

"The French refer to orgasms as the little death, so that might be accurate. *La petit mort.*"

"It's very sexy when you speak French. Say something else."

"It's very sexy when you come all over my face." Conner repeated the phrase in French and, showing off, in Italian, too.

Meli laughed again, clearly both exhausted and delighted, and pushed herself up on her elbows. "You're such—oh my God, did I—I thought—is that…is that from me?"

She stared first at Conner's wet, shiny face and then at the pool of liquid on the duvet, eyes widening in obvious mortification before she flung herself back down with a groan.

"Hey, hey." Conner scrambled to her knees and pulled Meli's hands from her face. "Meli, look at me. Yes, that was you, and it's the sexiest fucking thing a woman can do. Don't you dare be embarrassed."

"I didn't even know I could…do that."

"You've never?" Meli shook her head. "Well, some women do, some don't." Conner laced their fingers together and made sure she held Meli's gaze before she made a show of licking her lips. "Babe, I would drink this off the fucking floor. You're delicious."

Meli groaned, attempting to pull her hands away, but Conner held fast. She straddled her hips, unable to keep herself from rocking back and forth. Meli shuddered when she made contact and tried to twist away.

"I can't, Conner. Not again, not yet. Oh God, please."

Conner took pity on her and rolled off, curling on her side with her head propped on her arm. She didn't want to waste one second of being able to touch and look and kiss.

Meli sighed and laughed simultaneously. "You should have told me lesbian sex is a marathon sport."

"Is it safe to say you've satisfied your curiosity about your attraction to women?" If she hadn't, Conner would be totally confused.

Meli broke eye contact, staring at the ceiling as she fidgeted. Something unpleasant awoke inside Conner. "I mean, I think it's obvious that I've enjoyed this. *Really* enjoyed it. But I don't know if satisfied is the right word." She peered at Conner from under her eyelashes, a bashful smile blooming. "I, uh, I haven't touched you yet."

"You don't have to."

"I want to try."

Her arousal, which had dimmed momentarily, roared back to life. She had barely withstood fucking Meli and would almost certainly explode the moment Meli reciprocated. Oh, well. No better way to go out.

Still, she hesitated. She already had the memory of how Meli tasted and what she looked like when she climaxed to torture her. How much worse would it get if she added the experience of Meli touching her or—she nearly came at the thought—licking her? A tendril of regret worked its way up, but she squashed it. She had agreed to help Meli explore her sexuality. No matter the cost.

She leaned forward to kiss her, but when Meli paused, she grinned. "Do you want me to wash my face?" Meli ducked her head but nodded, and Conner chuckled.

When she returned from rinsing her face, Meli was sitting up, knees tucked under her, radiating with nervous energy. Conner approached until her legs hit the bed. She cupped Meli's angelic face in her hands, intending to kiss her, but when Meli covered her hands with her own, they paused.

The Hollywood Reporter had once called her a jill of many trades but a master of facial expressions. Her livelihood in movies meant she had to understand how to convey any emotion with her eyes, her eyebrows, her forehead, her nose, her mouth. She'd even spent time with psychologists to study the science behind various emotions.

That made it all the more frustrating that she couldn't read Meli's. A hint of excitement in her dilated pupils, yes. Affection in her gentle smile, sure. An overlay of earnestness, certainly. But fear or concern, perhaps, in the creases of her forehead. And something else that she couldn't identify deep in the brown of her eyes. Something that Conner's brain insisted was vital even as its identity remained elusive.

She leaned in tentatively despite their earlier intimacy, as if any rush would scare Meli away. When their lips met, it was not yet with passion but rather unhurried tenderness. Conner felt their kiss down to the soles of her feet. Had she ever kissed anyone like this, simply for the sake of kissing? Letting her lips say things she couldn't vocalize?

Fear of her own feelings struck her with the precision of lightning, so intense that she broke the kiss and jerked back. She couldn't have this emotion. She couldn't. She was falling, and nothing but scars lay at the bottom.

"What's wrong?"

"Nothing. I just..."

She kissed Meli again, surprising both of them with her ferocity. She didn't want to think, only to do. This was for Meli, not her, and she couldn't lose sight of that fact.

Thankfully Meli was a quick learner and met her eagerly. Their tongues slid against each other, and when Conner thought about that tongue sliding other places on her body, her lust flared again. She'd been worked up since their first kiss over a week ago and on edge since the moment she touched Meli earlier that day.

Meli chose that moment to skim her hands over Conner's shoulders, and she immediately knew she wouldn't last long. The sheer enormity of having sex with Meli was enough to tip her over. When Meli brushed against her bare stomach, she shuddered.

Meli pulled back, her lips swollen into a perfect pout. "Is this okay?" Conner nodded. "You told me to use my words."

Conner couldn't help but laugh. She'd never laughed this much during sex, and somehow that response enhanced the experience. "It's more than okay."

"Can I touch you?"

"Meli, you can do whatever you want with me. You could slap me across the face, and I'd ask for more." At her startled expression, Conner quickly added, "I'm not into that, for the record, but you get the idea."

"Oh, good. I'm not sure what to do as it is, but slapping is nowhere near my repertoire."

Conner captured her hands and pressed kisses to each palm. "Think of what you like and start there. I'll guide you. I'm not shy."

"No, you're not. Can, um..." She cleared her throat. "Can you take the rest of your clothes off?"

"I could." She pulled Meli's hands to her breasts. "Or you could do it for me."

Meli gulped. Moving excruciatingly slowly, she raised her hands to the straps of Conner's bra and slid them off her shoulders one by one. Conner obligingly pulled her arms free. Then she pivoted so Meli could access the clasp. She fumbled with it for a minute, fingers trembling against Conner's back, but just as Conner was about to ask if she was ready for this, the clasp released. The bra fell to the floor, and she turned back around.

Meli stared at her with evident awe, her mouth falling open just enough to reveal the gap between her front teeth. She didn't even seem aware that her hands reached out, but when they met Conner's hardened nipples, both gasped.

She massaged Conner's breasts with breathless wonder. "They're so... perfect."

"They should be. I paid good money for them."

Her joke earned a distracted half-smile, but as Meli continued to explore, the smile slipped away, and her brow furrowed. All she was missing was the tongue sticking out of the corner of her mouth. It was adorable.

While Meli focused on her breasts, she also explored the rest of Conner's body with maddening deliberation. The juncture between Conner's thighs ached from prolonged arousal, and she was surprised she wasn't dripping down her leg.

Meli's hands smoothed the planes of Conner's back, working their way down, and when she reached Conner's ass, she cupped her cheeks and pulled until Conner nearly fell on the bed. Then she captured one of Conner's nipples in her mouth.

The sudden move caught Conner by so much surprise her knees buckled. A moan tore from her throat as her head dropped back. Meli might have been new to this kind of sex, but she was proving an avid student. She switched to Conner's other breast, placing a tender kiss on her nipple before laving it with her tongue.

"Shit, babe. You don't do things by halves, do you?"

Meli's thumb took the place of her mouth. Conner missed it immediately. "Is it good?"

"Amazing." She tucked errant curls behind Meli's ear, though they immediately escaped again.

Meli's gaze traveled lower, and she stared briefly at Conner's underwear before taking a deep breath and tugging them down her hips. Conner stood before her fully nude, and when Meli didn't make another move, Conner decided to take charge, guiding her onto her back and climbing on top.

Meli sucked in her breath as their breasts met. Their mouths found each other, but soon Meli pulled away, making her way down Conner's neck. Conner couldn't stop her hips from thrusting, seeking traction against Meli's thigh.

"I want to make you feel good, Conner."

Conner could have orgasmed just from those words. She forced herself to calm. "You're doing great."

"I just—I don't know—"

"It's okay. Let me."

She rolled onto her back and took Meli's hand in hers. Hardly believing this was actually happening, she led her to her pussy. The instant she made contact, Conner let out a deep groan. She definitely wouldn't last. Watching Meli watch her, she wasn't sure which of them was more fascinated, but as she guided Meli's fingers, her eyes fell shut, and she gave herself over to the sensations. Soon she released her grip, reaching up to tweak her own nipple as Meli ran her fingers up and down.

"You're so wet," Meli whispered.

Conner didn't respond, already focused on chasing her orgasm, but her pleased sigh when Meli slid one finger deep inside her abruptly switched to a loud yelp.

Meli snatched her hand away as if burned. "That didn't sound like it felt good."

Conner squeezed her eyes shut, grimacing against the sharp sting inside her vagina. "It didn't. Let me see your hand." She tapped one of Meli's long nails, which she really should have paid more attention to before it invaded her. "Fingernails and penetration don't really mix. It can work if you're more experienced, but maybe we save that for later?"

Meli buried her face in her hands. "Oh my gosh, I'm so sorry. This is humiliating."

"Not at all. Please don't be embarrassed. I should have checked. Hey." She pried Meli's hands away and lifted her chin. "I can come without internal stimuli, or I have toys we can play with. Trust me. I'm more than ready to continue if you are." She lowered her voice. "I was already halfway there anyway."

Meli gulped. "You were?"

"Still am. You're so sexy, and you're making me feel great."

The intensity of Meli's gaze made Conner shiver. "You're the sexy one."

Conner shifted onto her side so they faced each other, throwing one leg over Meli's hip. She guided her hand to her pussy again, but Meli quickly took charge, stroking her neglected clit.

Meli's touches were uncertain at first, likely afraid she'd scratch her again, but she obviously gained confidence as Conner's heavy breathing filled the room. Conner had had more experienced and skilled lovers, but this was *Meli*, and that fact more than made up the difference. At some point reality would kick in and she would wake up, but for now she was happy to continue dreaming.

Conner's pelvis rocked in motion with Meli's strokes. Her mouth sought Meli's, desperate to connect in as many ways as possible. Their kisses grew frantic and sloppy as both chased her climax. Meli alternated between circling Conner's clit and stroking it with light pressure, and Meli's other hand held Conner close by the back of her neck, a combination that worked astonishingly well. She clenched Meli's ass, her fingers digging in so hard she was going to leave marks.

"Fuck, babe. Don't stop."

"Is it good?" Meli's voice was low and husky and the absolute sexiest sound in the entire world.

"So good." She was going to come. Meli was making her come. She was having sex with Meli and they were giving each other orgasms and oh God she was so close she could taste it. "A little bit—fuck—harder."

Meli pressed against her clit on her next stroke, and a shock wave struck Conner. She thrashed against Meli's hand, holding her wrist in place as she rode out her orgasm. With one final cry, she claimed Meli's lips, moaning deeply against her as she shuddered.

Conner collapsed onto her back. Only her panting broke the silence. The leg she'd curled around Meli's hips slowly slipped off, the sweat on their skin helping it along. She blinked at the ceiling fan as she caught her breath. If she had her way, more orgasms would follow, but although it had been wonderful, she was struck by sadness that this particular one, this very first time Meli had touched her and brought her immense pleasure, was over. There would never be another first time between them.

After today, there would never be another at all.

As if to delay the inevitable, she pulled Meli halfway on top of her and captured her lips again and again. The fire in her belly, though diminished, began to stoke once more.

Meli giggled against her mouth. "Do you want more already?"

"I want you." The confession slipped out on its own, and Conner hurried before Meli could grasp the truth in it. "You called this a marathon, but I think it's more of a triathlon. Do you want to find out what it's like to make each other come at the same time?"

Meli's whiskey-colored eyes darkened, and she gulped, which was the answer Conner needed.

Conner lost track of the number of times they brought each other to the crest of pleasure. Even pausing for dinner—eggplant moussaka they ate sitting on the kitchen table, wrapped in robes, before Conner had Meli for dessert on top of the island—didn't stop them, and it was late in the night before they curled up with each other in the middle of her bed, exhausted.

When Conner woke, the sun was high in the sky. She stretched experimentally, humming with pleasure at the soreness across every muscle. She'd had sex with Meli, incredible sex, because Meli wasn't straight.

A rustle of sheets interrupted her thoughts. When she looked over, Meli was propped on one arm, watching her with a curious expression.

"Watching me sleep?" The rust in her voice ruined her attempt at teasing.

Meli nodded. "Just for a few minutes. You pout when you sleep, you know. A sexy little pout."

Conner caught her breath. She hadn't been sure what she would wake up to, but this was promising. "Sexy, huh?"

"You're always sexy, and you know it. The fact that you know you're sexy just adds to the, um, sexiness."

Conner smirked. "Say 'sexy' again. I don't think I quite comprehend."

"Shut up. Your ego doesn't need more stroking."

She shoved Conner's shoulder, but Conner grabbed her arm, pulling her close until their mouths collided. Meli didn't resist at all, sighing into her mouth when Conner prodded her lips with her tongue.

"I can think of somewhere else you could stroke."

She attempted to follow up her suggestion with another kiss, but Meli hesitated.

"Actually, I was thinking…um." She ducked her head before glancing up again with a coy smile. "I want to go down on you."

Conner was a dead woman.

Chapter Forty-two

Conner jumped to her feet and watched, hands on her head, as Lindsey charged down the court after stealing the ball. When she finished in a graceful layup, Conner pumped her fist in the air and resumed her seat.

The tickets had cost a fortune, but Conner was courtside for every game of these WNBA finals, shuttling back and forth between LA and Seattle. They were tied at two games apiece, and Lindsey had just given the Sparks the lead in the decisive game five.

"I didn't realize you were such a basketball fan." Sadie observed Conner from the seat next to her.

"I'm a casual fan. At this point I'm cheering for my friends more than anything."

"Nothing says casual like a jersey and baseball cap. Even your hair is purple."

"Only the tips!" Conner adjusted the hat that sat backward over her shaggy locks and grinned.

She glanced at Sadie out of the corner of her eye, secretly thrilled that she had agreed to attend. The thawing of their relationship so far had been on Sadie's terms and Sadie's turf, so this was a big step. Not to mention a very public one, also a big step considering Sadie's reservations about Conner's fame.

She had dragged Harlow to one game, and Teddy Maguire had accompanied her to the other three (to the delight of their fans, who persisted in shipping them despite her sexuality), but she had dropped him without a thought when Sadie expressed interest.

Sarah would have loved it, but she still wasn't speaking to Conner, and Sadie wouldn't have allowed her to attend anyway. Nor was Conner willing to expose either of her nieces to that much publicity.

She peeked at her phone. The person she really wanted to bring was on location and overdue for a check-in text. Meli easily could have looked at the score on her phone, but she persisted in asking Conner, and Conner was more than willing to continue the charade.

They had talked plenty since their sexual encounter, but they also hadn't talked at all. Whether real or imagined, flirtatious overtones sprinkled every sentence, some more overt than others, but they hadn't discussed the sex, Meli's sexual identity, or any change in their relationship. Conner hated dancing around the issue, but she didn't feel like it was her place to bring it up.

"You know, at some point, you have to tell her."

"Huh?"

Sadie pointed at her phone. "You keep looking at your phone like it holds the secrets to the universe, and when Melina texts, you're more excited than when Lindsey scores. I've seen you two together. Tell her that you have feelings for her."

Conner sputtered, but to her shame, no actual words emerged. Sadie laughed, and Conner finally found her voice. "That's not true."

"Oh, really? Which part?"

"The part about the...you know."

"The phone? Your face? Or how much you looove her?"

Conner glanced around them, but no one seemed interested. She could barely hear Sadie over the crowd as it was. Still, she leaned in. "You sound just like your teenager."

"So? Even Hannah knows you like her. What's the worst that could happen?"

The end of their friendship? Meli's realization that Conner wasn't worth the effort? The utter crushing of her heart? Or worst of all, the utter crushing of *Meli's* heart when Conner inevitably did something stupid?

"Conner." She looked up again. Sadie slipped an arm over her shoulders and pulled her close. "You're not perfect, but neither is she, and you deserve just as much love as anyone else. I might be hard on you, but I see how much you love my kids, even if you can't say it. You are very capable of love."

The crowd roared at something, but Conner might as well have been on another planet. An odd lump lodged in her throat. Even if everything Sadie said was true—and besides the kids, Conner had her doubts—it didn't change the fact that either of them could get very hurt.

"When you and Asher got together, was it hard?"

Sadie shook her head with a fond smile. "Not really. He's so even-keeled and secure. He made it easy to fall in love, and besides my children, he's the best thing in my life."

Conner nodded. At that moment, her phone vibrated, and she couldn't quite keep her face neutral, even knowing Sadie watched her closely. After she'd updated Meli on the score (Sparks up by five with eight minutes to go), she made a face at her sister.

"Not one word."

They didn't broach the subject for the rest of the night, although it was never far from Conner's mind, even as the game went into overtime. Still, she pushed it to one side to cheer Lindsey on and was genuinely ecstatic when they won.

Later, as they pulled up to the club hosting the Sparks' victory party, Conner turned to Sadie and sucked up her courage. "Um, you know what you said about the girls? About how I, you know…well, with you, I, um—it's the same."

Sadie smiled and leaned in for a hug. "I know. I love you, too, Conner."

"Conner!"

She raised her hands, a bottle of Krug champagne in each, acknowledging the cheers as she entered Lindsey's Brentwood condo. The victory party had been a night to remember—or not, for Conner and many others, as it had also been a night to overindulge—but this end-of-season party promised to be a more low-key affair.

She admired the condo, all high ceilings and natural light, even if she no longer spent time in the primary bedroom, Plus, she liked most of the Sparks players, so she was looking forward to the evening. Something relatively chill was just what she needed after the year she'd had, especially as they approached the holiday season. Her final starring role as Lyss premiered on Christmas, which meant press tours and red carpets, and in February she headed to the UK to film her coveted role as amateur spy Cecilia Hargreave.

But the biggest draw of the evening was that Meli was invited.

Conner tried to play it off as she relaxed on the rooftop deck with a glass of sparkling water, mindful that she intended to drive home later. She was Conner fucking Cody, coolness personified. One of the few players she wasn't familiar with plopped down next to her and wasted no time making her interest clear, touching Conner's knee, shoulder, and hair.

"Mm-hmm." Conner made a half-hearted attempt to stay a level above rude disinterest, but the woman's inane chatter was making it a mountainous task.

"I know, right? So then I told him, do you even know…"

The fine hair on the back of her neck stood at attention, and Conner knew, as surely as she knew her own name, that Meli had arrived. She nearly gave herself an injury as she whipped around.

Meli stood in the doorway to the deck, a goddess among mortals. No director could have framed the scene better. The setting sun illuminated her perfectly, from the wild tendrils of hair that captured the golden light to the curves hugged so deliciously by her purple fit-and-flare dress. Conner was consistently impressed by Meli's style; no matter what she wore, her clothing always perfectly accentuated her figure.

She rose to greet her, only to be stopped by a tight hand on her wrist. She looked down at the offending appendage as if it were an alien.

"I'm not done with you yet," her companion said with a beguiling pout.

"Perhaps not, but I'm done with you."

She left the woman and her outrage behind. Meli noticed her at the same time, and their gazes locked like missiles. Only a few yards separated them, but the deck seemed a mile long. Conner's heart danced a tango that rivaled the one she and Meli had shared.

Right before they met, Lindsey cut in line. Conner's glare sent daggers at her unsuspecting back. Didn't she know Conner couldn't breathe until she shared the same air as Meli?

"I really wanted to come, but I didn't get back until today. You looked awesome when I got to watch, though! Congratulations!"

Meli threw her arms around Lindsey's neck. Conner wasn't jealous of that neck. Not at all.

"Thanks! I'm glad you could make it tonight. Help yourself to anything you like. There are drinks up here and in the kitchen, kabobs on the grill, and all kinds of dips downstairs." Conner cleared her throat. When Lindsey glanced over her shoulder, her grin broadened into something mischievous and knowing. "Look who it is, my own personal cheerleader."

"Short skirt not included."

"Wouldn't that be a sight?" Meli's eyes held a wicked gleam.

Conner licked her lips as the moisture in her body fled south. "I could arrange that."

"I'm just gonna go..." Lindsey departed, ignored by both of them.

"Hey, girl."

"Hey, yourself."

"You look great."

Meli beamed. "Thanks. You look good, too, but you always do."

Silence reigned for a few moments, and then they spoke at the same time.

"Do you want to maybe—"

"Do you think we could—"

They laughed before Conner indicated for her to proceed.

"I was going to ask if you wanted to sit down somewhere. We could, you know, talk."

Conner nodded. "Downstairs? I think fewer people are there."

They settled in the corner of Lindsey's sectional sofa and turned toward each other to the exclusion of anyone else. Conner rested her arm on the back of the couch, unable to resist drawing her fingers across Meli's exposed shoulder.

She shivered. "If you keep doing that, I won't be able to talk."

Conner persisted. "Do you want to talk?"

"Yes...no...I don't know."

At that she stopped. As much fun as it was to tease her, Conner didn't want to prolong any lingering confusion Meli might have been carrying. Besides, she wanted to talk, too. It was a strange sensation, to desire conversation as much as sex.

"How was the shoot?"

They chatted for a while. Conner wasn't aware either of them had been moving closer, but when their knees brushed, she suddenly realized she could smell Meli's flowery perfume and make out the gold flecks in her eyes. She followed Meli's gaze as it fell to their knees, then drifted back up.

"Conner...I can't stop thinking about you."

She heard the confession, barely a whisper, so clearly it could have been piped directly into her ear. Willing to do anything to reduce Meli's anxiety, she opted to keep it light.

She leaned in so they wouldn't be overheard, all but sitting on Meli's lap. "In a Conner-rocked-my-world, good kind of way, or an I'm-freaking-out, bad kind of way?"

Meli took a deep breath. "The first."

Jesus, Mary, and all the saints. This woman really would be the death of her. She turned Meli's hand over, palm up, and stroked the soft skin on her wrist. Meli's pulse was racing. "Do you—"

"Yes."

Conner had intended to ask if she wanted to leave, but clearly there was no time for that. She rose and pulled Meli with her in one fluid motion.

Bedrooms were too obvious, bathrooms too much in demand. They found the kitchen empty, but nearby laughter propelled her into the hallway that connected with the garage, serving as a laundry room, and Conner stumbled upon inspiration.

She yanked the door to the pantry open and dragged Meli inside, pressing her against the door as soon as it shut. Then they were on each other, mouths devouring each other with more desperation than precision.

"Want you," Conner mumbled when they came up for air. "Want you so bad."

She seized Meli's neck, biting down like a possessed vampire, and Meli cried out, her head hitting the door with a thud.

"Shhh." Conner pulled her deeper into the cramped alcove, laughing quietly. "Do you want everyone to know we're in here?"

Meli kissed her again, repaying the favor by taking Conner's lower lip between her teeth and tugging, and suddenly Conner was the one trying to stifle her moans. She pressed her against a shelf without a single care for comfort and nudged her knee between Meli's legs, pressing upward at the juncture between her thighs until Meli let out a gasp that morphed into a groan.

Meli rocked against her with abandon. Conner shifted so that she also straddled Meli's thigh while still providing the pressure Meli needed, and suddenly it was a race. They rocked against each other in sharp, frantic motions, taking what they needed from the other without any other concerns. Meli grasped for purchase on a shelf, and something fell with a dull thump.

They were making too much noise but paid it little mind. All Conner cared about was Meli—her orgasm, her obvious desire for Conner, her happiness. Her. Because if she thought too much about the fact that this was happening again, that Meli might want her just as much, she would drown.

"God, Meli," she managed to say. "You're so fucking—"

"Perfect. You're perfect. Oh my God, don't stop. Don't ever stop." Meli punctuated her demand by sucking on Conner's neck.

She didn't intend to do so. The seam of her jeans pressed just so against her clit, and she was so close, she could taste her orgasm in the back of her throat. Then Meli let out a surprised cry, thrusting against her several more times before stilling with a groan, and Conner was jolted into her own orgasm with a deep sigh.

They came down with soft pants, holding each other close. Conner peppered Meli's neck with kisses, flexing her thigh against her just for the reaction, rewarded with a shudder.

"I can't believe we just did that." Meli giggled.

"I can't believe we're still standing here when we could find somewhere private so I can make you scream."

Meli's laughter broke off, and Conner felt more than saw her gulp. Then she said, "Take me home, Conner."

"My house, or—"

"Yours. Take me home."

Conner trembled as she led them out, sneaking past the party guests without a word. Lindsey would understand, not that she was ever likely to get an explanation. Conner didn't kiss and tell, and Meli was far more precious than anyone else she'd ever kissed.

She opened up the Porsche as much as she could, encountering limited traffic for once. They didn't speak, for they didn't need words, not yet. About halfway there, she reached out tentatively to grasp Meli's knee, only for her to squeeze Conner's hand in between her own, keeping it clasped until the car purred into the garage.

They were all over each other the instant they walked inside. Conner backed her against a wall, and Meli pushed back until they stumbled into a console table. Meli nibbled her earlobe, and Conner clenched her ass until her knuckles hurt. When they crashed into the stairs, Meli fell back with a loud exhale.

Conner took a moment to admire her, splayed out in disarray, before she dropped to her knees and lifted Meli's dress enough to lower her head underneath. She didn't bother to remove Meli's dainty pink panties, merely shoving them to the side so she could take a long, thorough lick.

"Conner, oh God, how are you so good at that?" Meli's head dropped to the stairs with a thud, and Conner paused long enough to make sure she was okay before she dove back in.

She was relentless, chasing her climax like it would sustain life. The sheer debauchery of it all, taking Meli on a staircase fully clothed because they couldn't wait one more second, made her pulse throb between her legs. She blindly reached up with one hand until she grasped one of Meli's breasts and squeezed until she cried out with pleasure. When Meli clenched Conner's hair like a lifeline, she knew she was close, and she focused on her clit, sucking hard and driving the tip of her tongue back and forth.

Meli's back arched when she came, and she practically lifted Conner off the stairs as her hips bucked. Conner held firm, not that either of Meli's hands gripping her head would have let her move, and licked up every drop of Meli's essence.

When she was finally released, she leaned back on her heels, trying to catch her breath while Meli returned to herself. She could have come from the sight alone, for Meli was so obviously, thoroughly fucked. Desire warred with apprehension inside her. With every kiss, every tender touch, every explosive climax, she fell deeper and deeper, and soon she would have no way out.

They should stop. At the very least they should clarify what this was, and if Meli was merely seeking a friends-with-benefits situation while she explored her sexuality, then Conner needed to come up with a reason—and the willingness—to end it.

Meli chose that moment, ducking her head with a demure flutter of her eyelashes, to inform Conner that she had trimmed her fingernails. "And I filed them, too, because, um, people online said that trimming could leave rough edges and it's more, er...enjoyable if you file. So I wondered if maybe we could try again?"

"You want to finger me?" Conner barely sounded like herself, so throaty and desperate.

Meli's blush was in full bloom, but she maintained their eye contact as she nodded.

Holy shit. If Conner hadn't already been on her knees, she would have dropped to them. Meli had planned this. She had thought ahead and done research, for fuck's sake. She wanted this, maybe as much as Conner did. The enormity of the realization sent her heart into overdrive.

She rose, pulling Meli to her feet. They undressed each other in deliberate measures, breaking the contact of their mouths only when required. Conner's shirt, Meli's dress, Conner's jeans...by the time both were naked, they'd ended up in the theater room, simply because it was nearest.

Conner pushed Meli into one of the cushy leather seats and straddled her. She brushed Meli's hair away from her face before gently cupping her cheeks.

"Look at you," she said in a low voice. "Exquisite."

Meli tilted her head up for a kiss. Their tongues met, each caressing the other. They kissed slowly, deeply, lingering as if this was all that mattered in the world. At that moment, it was.

"Conner?" Meli said once they parted.

"Yeah, babe?"

"Show me how?"

Conner paused. Her heart threatened to thunder right out of her chest. Lifting her hand, she extended her index and middle fingers.

"Suck."

Meli was the picture of obedience, and Conner's arousal grew with every pass of her tongue. She could have watched the scene unfold forever, drunk on the power dynamics, but more important things lay ahead. She trailed her wet fingers down Meli's torso, swirling around a nipple and enjoying the twitches of her belly as she went.

Conner instructed as she demonstrated. "I like to start with one, but most women have a number."

"What is yours?"

Her eagerness stole Conner's breath right out of her lungs. "Two. Three if I'm feeling rough."

The catch in, and subsequent speeding up of, Meli's breath spurred Conner on. She began fucking her faster. "It's not just in and out. Do you want another?"

"Yes, oh, yes..."

"You want to stroke her." *Me.* "Caress her." *Me.* "And when you're ready, turn your hand palm up, curl your fingers just a bit, and feel for that area right around...there." She licked her lips when Meli moaned. "You like that?"

"You know...I do...but I want...to try."

She tugged Conner's wrist, and though Conner initially resisted, she gave in, impatient for her turn. Conner squeezed her hand before releasing it.

"Get your fingers ready." She lifted them to her mouth, but Conner shook her head. She motioned toward Conner's mouth, but Conner declined again, nodding downward. With raised eyebrows, Meli caught on and complied, replacing where Conner's fingers had just been so pleasantly busy with her own.

She was so hot fucking herself that Conner was almost content just to watch. Maybe another time…and this time she didn't shut down the idea of later.

When Meli pulled her glistening fingers out, Conner was already panting with excitement. She positioned them right above Meli's waist and sank at an aching crawl. When she was completely full, everything crystallized into perfect clarity.

She had thought sex with Meli would be glorious, and it was. The sight of her wide eyes as she took her first taste of Conner was seared into Conner's mind for the rest of this life and the next. But it just kept getting better. She couldn't imagine ever getting bored or tired.

They sighed in unison, and then she began to move. She rotated her hips slowly at first, letting both of them get used to it. Meli was no passive partner, rocking her wrist in time with Conner and flexing her fingers.

"You feel amazing," she said, awe dripping from every word.

Conner moaned her agreement. She felt fucking amazing. She scrambled for Meli's hand until they intertwined their fingers. She wanted to bring Meli off at the same time but didn't want to interrupt their rhythm.

"Fuck, Meli." She fell forward until their foreheads met. "You feel so good. So—fucking—good."

They shared the same air, panting and moaning into each other. All of Conner's muscles began to tighten, every nerve sending the same message. Meli's fingers continued their exploration, massaging Conner's walls until she arched her back and cried out. Meli took that opportunity to capture one of Conner's breasts in her mouth. Conner added multitasking to the growing list of things at which Meli was proving to be very good.

She trembled on the verge of overstimulation. The right touch, the right stroke, the right lick, and it would all be over.

Or, as it turned out, the right word. Meli released her nipple after one hard suck that jolted her entire body. Then she looked up and said, with the veneration usually reserved for deities, "Conner…"

Shouting her exaltation to the heavens, Conner soared, leaving her body a writhing, sweaty, rapturous mess. When she returned to herself, she was shuddering, on the verge of sobbing, collapsed in Meli's arms. Vulnerable.

She wanted to say so much. Wanted to say it all. But she couldn't, not then, not while still high on climax. But later, much later, after they'd finally made their way to Conner's bedroom with a detour to the shower, she watched Meli sleep peacefully and admitted Sadie had been right.

She had to tell her.

Chapter Forty-three

Conner threw another rejected outfit onto her bed to join the half dozen others and groaned. What did one wear for the most important confession of her life? *Get a grip, Conner.*

She leaned on her dresser and glared at herself in the mirror. The outfit wasn't the problem. She was merely procrastinating, reluctant to have this necessary but also most terrifying conversation of her life.

She drew herself to her full height. She needed to remember who she was. Conner fucking Cody would survive this, even if she didn't want to. Being rejected was still preferable to not knowing at all. They had to be honest with each other, and Meli had to remain in her life one way or another.

In the end, she chose her standard attire: ripped jeans, a green tartan button-up over a black V-neck, and, of course, her trusty Doc Martens and faux leather jacket.

Like any good performer, she rehearsed on the drive over, but everything she came up with sounded canned and meaningless. She thought back to every romantic scene she'd ever filmed, but nothing fit telling one of your best friends, who was probably no longer straight but hadn't officially declared a change of sexuality, who you had already slept with, who had turned you down once, that you wanted more.

Add to that the fact that Conner had never once made a declaration of feelings, nor had she felt this deeply for any prior girlfriend, and by the time she pulled up in NoHo, her heart was racing like she'd just run the LA marathon.

With everything to lose, she knocked on the door of Meli's apartment. Eriq answered, and his normally genial expression and blinding-white smile melted into confusion.

"Hi, Eriq. Is Meli here?"

His forehead wrinkled like a pug's. "No…she's out. To be honest, I thought she was with you."

"With me? Why?"

"She said she was going on a date, and when she referred to them as 'her,' I just assumed..."

His mouth kept moving, but Conner didn't hear anything over the ringing in her ears. She stepped backward with a grunt as the force of his words crashed into her.

Meli was on a date. With a person who used she/her pronouns. Less than a week after they had slept together again.

She muttered something about forgetting what day it was and stumbled down the stairs. She might as well have teleported home for all that she was aware of the drive.

When she got home, she bypassed the house and trudged onto the beach, where she dropped in a heap just above the high-tide line. The truth that had been chasing her for months, that she'd been hiding from with all her might, washed over her like the waves at her feet.

She was in love with Meli.

She was crazy, desperately, irrevocably in love with Meli. She had been in love with Meli for a long time, even if she couldn't pinpoint when it had happened. Was it when they tangoed, or when Meli held her after Abuelita died? Or way back when they kissed for the very first time? Did love happen at once like that, or did it bloom from a seed into something glorious? However it happened, she was in love for the first time, and she didn't know what to do.

She couldn't be angry at Meli. She'd been up-front with what she asked of Conner, and even if she had sent a few mixed signals, that was during the heat of the moment. Meli was a precious cinnamon roll and deserved every good thing in life. If that was her mysterious date or some other person in the future, Conner would learn to deal with it.

The sun went down as she wrestled with the enormity of her epiphany. For Conner after falling in love would never be the same person as Conner before falling in love, just as life after meeting Meli was never the same as life before meeting Meli.

She loved Meli.

Fuck.

She sat on the beach, slowly becoming one with the sand, until something wet smacked her head. She looked up, catching another drop on her face. Of course she was going to get rained on. Hollywood never missed an opportunity for a good cliché.

Thunder echoed in the distance, so she pushed herself to her feet, made a half-hearted effort to remove sand from her skin, and began to plod back to the house.

Then she paused, cocking her head. After a minute she heard a noise again, a distinct meow.

Conner could never say what made her seek it out, but she followed the sound to a shrub on her property line. There, crouched underneath the leaves, was a small calico cat. It stared at Conner and meowed again.

"Oh. Where do you belong?" She glanced at her neighbor's house, wondering if it lived there.

The cat trotted off a few feet away, meowing again. Feeling ridiculous, Conner followed anyway with a shrug. They repeated the exercise several more times until the cat led her to a final shrub, larger than the rest, and lay down underneath it.

Conner crouched, unsure what the prize at the end of this journey was supposed to be, and then she rocked back on her heels. Three tiny, fluffy kittens with pointy tails swarmed their mother, feeding with greedy squeaks. The mother cat looked up at Conner and meowed again.

She took a step back. "Oh, no, you don't." Thunder rumbled again, closer this time. When lightning flashed across the sky, Conner sighed. "Fine. But it's only for one night, understand? Tomorrow you go to a shelter."

The cat chirped an agreement and laid her head down. At least, Conner thought it was an agreement. She backed away, one hand out as if to stop them from following, until she could see them no longer.

In her house, she shed her jacket, not willing to let it get wet, and searched for a container. What did cats travel in? Even the biggest dishes from the kitchen were out of the question. Her laundry hamper was too bulky. Finally she struck gold in a closet she'd never paid attention to, where she upended a box of toilet-paper rolls and grabbed a few towels.

The cats remained where she had left them, and a surprising hint of relief crept up her neck. But how to get them in the box? She tried setting it down and asking them to hop in. Nothing. She put it on its side and tried to shoo them in. Nothing. As the sprinkles grew into proper rain, she made a decision.

"Don't freak out, don't freak out, don't freak out," she whispered, unsure if she was telling the cats or herself.

Conner scooped up one kitten and placed it in the box. It squeaked a protest, and the mama cat looked alarmed, but when neither moved, she grabbed the other two. As soon as they were in the box, the mom followed, licking one kitten on its head. Conner covered the box with a towel and trotted back to the house, hoping none of them made a desperate lunge for freedom.

Back in the house with her precious cargo intact, Conner dripped onto her kitchen floor as she tried to decide what to do. A bathroom. Surely they couldn't harm anything in there. She settled them in the powder room nearest the kitchen with a bed of towels, a bowl of water, and a can of tuna she found in the pantry. For litter she dumped some sand from outside into the same box and hoped it worked.

"So you aren't gonna, like, chew through the door or anything, right?" she asked, leaning against said door.

The kittens curled around their mother, who purred away on the towel bed like she belonged there. Conner felt an odd sense of pride as she watched them. She might not have saved their lives or anything, but she at least had given them a comfortable place for the night. She wasn't completely useless, although her struggles to find anything in her own house didn't speak in her favor.

Once she left them, the distraction wore off, and the reason she'd been on the beach in the first place roared back into the forefront of her mind.

She was in love.

With Meli.

Who didn't love her back.

Conner plopped onto the sofa in her den and ran her hands through her hair. Unfortunately she couldn't brush her racing thoughts away as easily.

Falling in love with a straight girl was practically a rite of passage for sapphics, one she thought she'd dodged. Falling for a friend, another trope. Falling in love for the first time when she'd never thought she wanted, needed, or understood love was staggering enough. Falling in love for the first time, with Meli, one of her closest friends who was also bicurious, was simply too much. Surely someone had made a movie or written a song about this.

A song…

Conner glanced at her neglected notebooks, organized in a neat stack on a coffee table by her housekeeper. She reached for one slowly, hesitantly, afraid to scare it away, and then she began to write.

For the next three weeks, Conner composed, barely leaving time for eating, drinking, or sleeping, and briefly showering. A terse text to Harlow cleared her schedule. Sadie got one perfunctory response that she would call (and explain) later. Everyone else was ignored.

Except for Meli.

She had called Conner during her feline adventure, but Conner hadn't seen the missed call until the following day. She avoided her until guilt won out, sending a vague message that she was busy with something for the band. Meli sent a few follow-up texts, but Conner couldn't bring herself to reply again.

That didn't mean she wasn't thinking about her.

On the contrary, all she did was think of Meli. When she wrote, she thought of Meli. When she composed, she thought of Meli. When she played, she thought of Meli. When she sang, she thought of Meli. When she recorded, she thought of Meli.

During the rare moments she dreamed, she dreamed of Meli.

The music poured from her fingertips. She couldn't have stopped the flood if she tried, not that she wanted to. Every time she thought she might be done, another song used her as a conduit to write itself. Lyrics covered the den, notes littered the kitchen, melodies decorated the stairways.

Connor was so lost in the fog she didn't even realize what was happening until a track ended one day as she sat in her small basement studio. For the first time in weeks, her fingers didn't twitch with the urge to change a lyric or tweak the mix levels. No voices in her head demanded to write a new song. Like the Western Front, all was quiet.

She tapped her laptop, smiling when she fell into a familiar rhythm. A ghost of an itch to go over the songs one more time niggled, but she laid it to rest. All creators had to know when to stop meddling.

She decided to give it a day. After ordering a pizza, she luxuriated in a long, hot shower. All four cats waited when she emerged from the bathroom.

She'd been so caught up in the maelstrom of composing that she'd forgotten about the shelter, and by the time she had a chance to think about it, she couldn't bring herself to get rid of them. Her assistant took them to a vet, and Conner named them Stevie (the mother, obviously), Linda, Alanis, and Sheryl.

"Those are the worst cat names I've ever heard," her assistant had said. "I'm not calling them that at the vet."

"They're my musical heroes. What else was I going to name them?" Conner replied, in the middle of a song and distracted. "Just make sure they don't have diseases."

She knelt in her bathrobe and gave Linda, sleek and gray, a good scratch. She'd never intended to own pets, much less become a cat mom of four, but so far it seemed to be working out. They were good company and ridiculously cute to boot. She started to wonder what Meli would think of them before shutting down that train of thought.

She missed her with a ferocity that had been absent before she realized she was in love, but she wasn't ready to face her. Conner in love felt like a stranger, and until she figured out how to exist with that knowledge, she didn't trust herself around Meli.

With a stomach full of melted cheese and tomatoes, she fell into bed for a long, dreamless sleep. In the morning she fired up her laptop again and listened to every song once more. When they were done, she grinned.

Hestia Rising had a new album.

She loaded the songs onto four USB drives, booked three flights, and left the next day.

Chapter Forty-four

Conner stood outside the split-level home in Bellevue, Washington, for a long minute before squaring her shoulders and striding forward. Soon after she rang the doorbell, the door swung open to reveal a petite woman with a luminous smile.

"Conner! I haven't seen you in so long!" She swept Conner into a hug, the strength of which belied her small stature, before holding her at arm's length.

"You don't eat enough. Come, come. Dinner's almost ready. You remember how much you love my butter chicken. Savtaj, look who's here!"

"I didn't mean to—"

"Allia, I was—Conner! Why, this is a pleasant surprise." Mr. Bhandari peered at his wife. "Did I know she was coming?"

"No. I—"

Mrs. Bhandari fluttered her hands impatiently. "It doesn't matter. You know you're always welcome here."

"Dear, I don't expect she's here to see us."

"Of course she's not, but that doesn't mean I can't be welcoming. Emira!" Conner jumped when she bellowed. "You have a guest! Savtaj, don't be rude. Take Conner's bag."

"It's okay. I can—"

Mr. Bhandari relieved her of her backpack with a knowing smile while the light tread of feet announced Emi's arrival from upstairs.

Her eyebrows knit together. "Conner? What are you doing here?"

Conner straightened. "I was hoping we could talk."

An excited squeak escaped Mrs. Bhandari, and Emi cast a warning glance. "Sure. Do you want to—"

"Absolutely not. Dinner first! Emira, set the table."

❖

The moon was high in the sky before they escaped Mrs. Bhandari's clutches, full of butter chicken, hara bhara kabab, and naan. Emi suggested a local bar, and they took a rideshare in near silence.

Ensconced in a dark corner, Conner tugged her beanie over her hair, which had grown too long to completely hide. She kept her head down as she ordered a naked and famous.

"So, how's your visit?"

Emi traced the rim of her glass. "Fine. Conner, what are you doing here?"

So much for pleasantries, but she probably deserved that. She took a deep breath. "I came to tell you I'm an asshole."

A surprised snort of laughter escaped Emi. "Way to jump right into it. But you're not wrong, not completely, anyway."

"Thanks," Conner said dryly before leaning forward. "I am, though, and I'm not saying it to be like, this is who I am, take it or leave it. I'm saying it because I acknowledge it, and I'm trying to be better. I'm sorry, Emi."

Emi fidgeted with her napkin. "I'm sorry, too."

Those three words derailed Conner's carefully planned speech. "You are? For what?"

"For cheating on you."

"Oh. That." Conner leaned back, absorbing the unexpected words. "You know I'm not still mad, right? I got over it a long time ago."

"I know."

"But since you brought it up…why did you do it? Especially right after you said…well, you know."

Emi exhaled, finally meeting Conner's gaze.

"Honestly? To get your attention. It was stupid. I knew it was stupid. It's just…this isn't an excuse, okay? Just an explanation. Dating you was both amazing and crushing because I got to be with you, but I never felt like I had all of you. There was always a distance between us, no matter what I did. Part of me wondered if you even cared. I didn't want to hurt you, but I did anyway, and I'm sorry."

Conner absorbed that in silence, nodding. She couldn't deny the truth of what Emi said, even if it didn't justify cheating.

"My turn for a question?"

"Sure."

"Why did you hook up with me?"

Oof. Right to the jugular, no soft punches to warm up. Well, if she was turning over a new leaf, she might as well start with the truth. "Vittoria had dumped me again, and I was lonely. You wanted me so much, and I was attracted to you, so I thought maybe it could work."

To Conner's relief, Emi didn't appear upset. She merely nodded. "I kinda figured. I hoped it might turn into something, but then…"

Then Emi had told her she loved her, and Conner had panicked. She didn't even recall her response, only that in no way did she say or imply that she felt the same way. Emi had cheated a week later.

"We fucked that one up, didn't we?"

"Yeah."

Conner caught the waitress's glance and signaled for another round. "That's not all I want to apologize for. The shit I said to the band that day was so far out of line. I didn't mean it, not really. Maybe I could do it without you—" Emi snorted, but Conner plowed on. "But it wouldn't be as good and not nearly as much fun. The band breaking up would suck, but losing you as a friend would break my heart. I'm really sorry."

Emi regarded her for so long that Conner began to feel exposed. She tapped on the table, quickly recognizing the melody of one of her new songs. And on that note...

She pulled a USB drive out of her pocket and slid it across the sticky table. "This is a demo for our new album, if you want it to be. All I ask is that you listen to it and meet me back in LA in four days."

One corner of Emi's mouth tugged up. "You know, for a second I thought I was dreaming, but it's good to know you haven't changed entirely."

"What do you mean?"

"You apologized twice, which is unheard of, but you also expect everyone to jump when you say."

"We can reschedule. I just wanted—"

"Conner, chill. I'm just giving you crap. I'll be there, and I can't wait to listen. I'm sure it's great."

"It's pretty good, but I know the four of us could make it even better."

Emi grinned. "I like this Conner. Still full of herself but willing to accept she's not perfect."

Conner laughed. She'd missed their banter more than she'd realized. "What can I say, I'm a work in progress. So, friends again?"

Emi reached across the table and squeezed her hand. "Best friends."

Their waitress chose that moment to approach. "I'm sorry, but you're Conner Cody and Emi Bhandari, aren't you?"

They released their hands immediately. Conner let out a tiny sigh of resignation before nodding. "In the flesh."

The waitress all but danced a jig, wiggling with glee. "Oh my God, I'm such a huge fan! Listen, you can totally say no, but it's karaoke night. Do you think maybe you could do one song?"

Conner was prepared to decline, but she glanced at Emi, who raised her eyebrows and shoulders. They had a quick, silent conversation, and Conner gave in. It wouldn't hurt.

"One," she muttered to Emi as they made their way to the miniscule stage. "One, and then we leave."

❖

They closed down the bar. They sang duets, backed each other up on solos, and brought up members of their audience, which grew to capacity in the blink of an eye and forced the bouncers to turn people away. Conner unleashed her inner pop diva, forever putting the debate to rest on just how good her voice actually was, even if she didn't go all out without warming up. She bought a round for everyone, which morphed into covering the entire bar tab for the rest of the night. She was so drunk by the time she signed the receipt that she couldn't recall how much she'd spent, but she was pretty sure the figure had a comma. She ended the night sliding across the bar on her knees, half stripped and drinking straight from a bottle of tequila.

It was the most fun she'd had in a very long time.

Back at Emi's parents' house, they passed out until the next day was half gone. Conner woke up just in time to make her next flight, for Emi was merely the first stop on the Conner Cody Apology Tour.

Upon landing in Georgia, Conner went straight to her hotel from the airport, still recovering from their epic night. Social media had blown up with videos of the pair of them cavorting to retro hits, and someone had managed to capture a grainy picture of them holding hands across the table, which people were dissecting to death. She appreciated her fans to the point that she buried her intense dislike of their nickname for her, but they overanalyzed everything.

She wondered if Meli saw the picture. She wondered if Meli cared.

The following morning she stopped at a bakery before heading to Bellamy's father's home in a small town outside Savannah. He greeted her at the door with a puzzled smile.

"Conner? Is that you? Is something wrong, darlin'?"

She slipped through the door he held open. "Does something have to be wrong for me to visit my favorite Southerner?"

"I thought that was me. Or Lindsey."

Conner looked up at the familiar drawl and grinned. "Neither, sorry. You're a close second, though."

"How are you doing, Con?"

"Good. A little tired."

"Long nights will do that to you." Mischief lurked in her dimples.

"I see you've been online."

"You know you can't blink without making headlines." Bellamy nodded at the box in Conner's hands. "I assume those aren't for me?"

"Actually, there are two mint truffles with your name on them. Everything else, of course, is for first place over here. Sugar-free, of course."

Mr. McCubbin rubbed his hands together. "You spoil me. Now gimme the box, and you girls go talk. I know you ain't here for me."

She surrendered the treats and followed Bellamy to the back porch. Georgia was cooler than Malibu but certainly milder than Seattle, and the sun warmed them.

"The place looks good, and it doesn't smell as much of cigarettes anymore."

"Dad finally let me pay for a cleaning service. I tried to convince him to move somewhere else, but he won't budge." She offered a tight smile.

Conner would have swapped the mansions in which she grew up for Bellamy's father's single-wide mobile home in a heartbeat, if it came with the same love he showered on her, but she knew not to bring up the subject. Bellamy had her own issues from her childhood. No need to compare.

"And his health? Everything okay?"

"Yep. He's watching his diet and taking his insulin. I can't thank you enough for paying for his healthcare all those years, Conner."

"I'll do it again, if you need me to."

Bellamy shook her head. "I've got it, but thanks. So you didn't come out to the trailer park for no reason. What's up?"

"I came to apologize, because I treated you and the rest of the band like crap. I'm sorry for not letting you make any decisions and acting like I own the band. And I came to give you this." She held out another USB drive. "This could be our next album, if you want it to be."

Bellamy took the proffered drive, turning it over in her fingers. "Wow. I wasn't expecting this."

"Which part?"

"Any of it. Do you mean it, or are you just saying it so we'll record this album with you?"

Conner winced at the sting, but she deserved it. "I mean all of it. If the three of you don't want to record this album, or—" She gulped. "Or if you don't want to record any albums, then we won't. It's just a demo, okay? A concept of an album. Hestia Rising could make it into something amazing, but only if you want to. I want my friends back. The album, and the band, are secondary to that."

Bellamy leaned back, stretching her feet out on the roughhewn wooden steps. "Let me ask you a question, Conner. Why didn't you apologize before writing and recording an entire demo?"

Someone's dog barked. A car backfired. Two people yelled back and forth before laughing. Conner's attention drifted from distraction to distraction as she tried to figure out how to answer that. Her stomach twisted into knots.

"I guess I thought you would know that I meant it if I had some songs. I know you've been waiting on our next album for a while."

Bellamy sighed. "Okay." She took Conner's shoulders and turned both of them until they were looking directly at each other. "I know I'm not the smartest person out there."

"You're not dumb, Bells."

"I'm not saying that, but we both know I don't always pick up on unspoken cues. The world would be easier for people like me if everyone just said what they meant, but that's not the issue right now. You didn't need to wait until you had something else to offer besides an apology. Sometimes you're infuriating, but you can also be a really good friend. You've been there for me in a lot of ways. I wish you knew that you're worth more than your bank account or your connections or your talent."

"I—I realize that." Her voice sounded small.

"Good. But since you went to the trouble of bringing it all the way to me, I can't wait to listen."

"And then if you could—" Conner remembered Emi's comment and changed tactics. "When are you coming back to LA?"

"Tomorrow, actually, so if you're planning on staying…"

"I'm not. That's great. I'd like it if the band could meet the day after you get back, if you're free."

"I can make that happen."

"Cool. So are we friends again?"

Bellamy grinned. "We never stopped being friends, Conner. I'm glad you can see it now."

They hugged tightly. Conner spent the morning with Bellamy and her father. After lunch, they treated her to something called a Blizzard from a place called Dairy Queen, which was a surprisingly tasty ice cream-adjacent experience. Then it was back to LA, where she really hoped she could go a week without getting on another plane.

Conner swung by Kit's condo first, but they weren't home, so she left the USB drive and a note with their roommate and headed to Maggie's. She'd left her until last on purpose, knowing this would be the most difficult conversation with the most potential repercussions.

Maggie didn't look surprised to see her. Conner suspected Emi had sent advance warning but didn't comment. Jamal wasn't there, but she didn't comment on that either.

"Do you want something to drink? I have lemonade."

"That would be great."

She sat across from Maggie in her living room, wondering when they had become strangers. Maggie had been one of the few people in her life that she could count on from the moment they met, and now it felt like they barely knew each other. Maggie didn't know anything about Meli, and Conner had no idea what was happening with Jamal.

She had planned to handle this situation just as she had with the others. But what came out of her mouth surprised her.

"Why are you so angry at me?"

Maggie's shoulders twitched. She shuddered, and suddenly she began sobbing violently into her hands. It took Conner a long, dumbfounded minute to react. She hated crying, whether she or others did it, and felt helpless at the sight. Still, she wrapped Maggie in her arms, silently squeezing tight.

Her shirt was soaked by the time Maggie cried herself out with what seemed like a year's worth of tears. Even after she stopped, Maggie didn't move away, hiccupping and sniffling into Conner's shoulder, so she stayed in place, rubbing her back.

"Do you want to talk about it?"

"Not really, but I think we should."

That response didn't give Conner much direction, so she decided to start at the beginning and narrow it down from there. "Do you regret it?"

Maggie shook her head as she finally pulled back, using the heel of her hand to wipe her eyes. "No. It's not that. It was the right decision. But I betrayed Jamal, and I just kept making it worse. You tried to tell me, and I was mad that I didn't listen, and somehow that became your fault. It was really unfair of me. Then you gave me an actual reason to be upset with you, and I focused on it. I'm sorry, Conner."

"Wow. I don't know what to say. I came here to apologize, but instead you're apologizing to me."

"You can still do that." They shared a shaky laugh. "But before you do…I've been talking to a therapist, and she thinks I directed my anger at you because I knew you wouldn't give up on me. Something about how we hurt the ones we care about the most."

"Next time you decide to do that, can you clue me in first? I can handle it, but a warning would have been nice."

They laughed again, and Maggie promised.

Conner didn't want to break their tenuous truce, but she ventured forth anyway. "Can I ask about Jamal?"

Maggie's entire demeanor shifted, bringing a cloud over the room. "You can ask, but I don't have an answer. He's taking some space. I don't know what's going to happen."

Conner wanted to know more, including the extent of her betrayal of Jamal, but it wasn't for her to know. Maggie surprised her once more.

"He told me you stood up for me when he confronted you, even though you and I weren't even talking. That's real best-friend shit."

"Kind of like coming to a birthday party when you're not talking?"

"Yeah. Kinda like that."

They grinned at each other.

"Are we talking now?"

"I guess that depends on your apology."

"Right." Conner cleared her throat. "I came here to say that I'm a giant dick, and I'm trying not to be. I know that I act like the band is my own personal plaything, but I don't think that, honestly. I'm sorry for everything I said that diminished your role. I, um, I wrote a new album. Or songs for a new album." She placed the final USB drive on the coffee table. "If you want it. I've given all of you and Kit a copy, and I booked the studio for tomorrow to discuss your thoughts."

Maggie looked from Conner to the drive and back. "Giant dick is a pretty good way of putting it. I love the band, and I want to perform with you three for the rest of our lives, but we can't do that if you act like a diva. You're not Stevie Nicks or Daisy Jones, Conner. You don't have to be some tortured artist."

"I don't—"

"Yes, you do. You have this idea of who you're supposed to be, and you're constantly worried about living up to that image instead of just being you. You're actually pretty cool even when you aren't trying to be. Stop worrying about what people think of you."

Conner found it hard to breathe around an odd lump in her throat, and her eyes pricked. Three days out of California and suddenly she had allergies. She turned her head so she could brush at her eyes with her sleeve.

"I'm trying. I might have control issues."

"Wow, I get an apology and an acknowledgment of your control issues all in one day? Who are you, and what did you do with my best friend?"

Conner's smile stretched until it hurt. "She went on a grand apology tour and is so jet-lagged she has no idea what she's saying. So you're still my best friend?"

Maggie inclined her head with a knowing grin. "We're not just best friends. We're sisters."

Sisters. She was really starting to like that word.

Despite her exhaustion, Conner tossed and turned for half the night. The apologies had gone well, and she had her friends back. Now, their potential second album. *Dark Streets* had been as personal as they came, revealing some of the darkest periods of her life, but this one, which she was calling *ForM*, was intensely vulnerable in an entirely different manner. She had nothing left in her. If they didn't like it, she didn't know what she'd do.

The next day, she listened to the demo over and over, but all it did was increase her nerves and make her think about Meli, neither of which helped matters. Meli had texted while she was in Washington, begging to talk, and Conner had promised to call her after the band was settled. For the first time ever, she dreaded it. How could she go back to just being friends after falling in love? What if the date Meli had gone on had become something, and Conner had to pretend to be happy for her? She didn't think even her tremendous thespian skills were up to that.

Keyed up and restless, she arrived early at the studio, surprised to see their vehicles in the parking lot already. Murmurs filtered out of the room, but everyone fell silent when she entered. Spontaneous combustion sounded wonderful right now.

She couldn't read their faces. "So, did you like it, or…?"

They looked at each other. "Who wants to go first?" Emi asked.

"I will." Maggie crossed her arms, muscles flexing, and Conner almost crossed herself to save her nerves. "I'm not going to mince words, Conner: it's fucking incredible."

"You really like it?"

Emi's jaw dropped. "Are you kidding? You rose to a whole new level with this one. It's phenomenal."

"Yeah, Con. You evoked emotions I didn't know I had. Or you had, for that matter. I cried, and then I listened to it on repeat," Bellamy said.

They began to talk over each other, hands gesturing, voices rising.

"How did you come up with the arrangement on the second track? I can't get that bass line out of my head."

"What about the bridge on track five? You went fucking feral on that!"

"And the last one? God, talk about heartbreak."

"I'm confused, though." Bellamy raised her hand like a schoolchild until all eyes were on her. "It's a fantastic album, but it's not finished."

"Of course it's not. That's where the three of you come in. I have ideas, obviously, tons of ideas, but I figured we could work on the songs together."

Bellamy shook her head with vigor. "Not that. You tell a story with this album. It's a great story, but it doesn't have an ending. This is about you being in love with Melina, right?" She glanced at Emi's and Maggie's stunned expressions. "Isn't it?"

"I, um, well…yeah, it is."

"Oh my God." Maggie began to chortle. "I can't believe that you, Conner Cody, first of her name, queen of infatuations and defender of one-night stands, ruler of sapphics throughout the realm, have fallen for a straight girl."

Emi held up one hand. "Hold on. If it's about Melina, then track nine would imply that she's not entirely straight. Conner, your powers of seduction never cease to amaze me."

"It's not like that! It's complicated."

"Does she know?" Bellamy asked quietly.

Conner shook her head.

"Then Bellamy's right. You have to tell her. We can't put out an album about someone without giving her a heads up."

"That's not what I meant. She doesn't know you're in love with her, does she?"

Miserably, Conner shook her head again.

Her bandmates shared a glance, then said as one, "Go."

"Go now." Emi shooed her.

Maggie nodded. "We'll handle Kit when they get here."

"Now? But—"

Bellamy turned her around and walked her to the door. "Go tell her. Make a grand declaration or something."

Still she hesitated. She wasn't ready. She didn't know what to say. She'd tried this once, and it had backfired in her face.

A small piece of plastic slipped into her hand. She stared at the USB drive before looking up at Emi, who was smiling.

"You already have your grand declaration. Go get your woman, Conner."

Chapter Forty-Five

Conner didn't leave room to talk herself out of it. She kept the pedal to the floor all the way to Meli's apartment and practiced her speech the entire way. No matter what she came up with, she sounded like an idiot, which she hoped somehow came across as charming.

Too soon she pulled up to the nondescript building and stared up at the second floor, trepidation creeping through her veins. She had never thought of herself as a coward, but right now she'd rather jump off the Hollywood sign.

No backing out now. She took the stairs two at a time, and only after she knocked did she realize she hadn't looked for Meli's car in the parking lot. How very on-brand for her to assume everyone waited around for her. She turned around, seeking the navy Honda.

"Conner?"

Everything stopped, and warmth spread across Conner's chest despite her fear. Even in sweats with her hair spilling out of a messy bun, Meli's beauty made Conner ache. This was love.

Love.

The word lodged in her teeth, gluing them together like an overlarge bite of caramel. Meli repeated her name, this time with more concern than curiosity. Conner thrust the USB drive at her, forgetting everything she'd planned to say as dumb instinct took over.

"I wrote an album."

"Wha—you did? That's awesome! I knew you weren't ignoring me. Can I listen to it? Is that what this is? Oh, gosh. I'm so excited! Come on, come on. Let's get ice cream and play it!"

Conner didn't budge. Her boots weighed two tons apiece.

"Um, Conner? Are you okay? You look kinda green…are you sick?"

Conner shook her head and used every single bit of willpower to say something. Anything. "I wrote an album for you. Listen to it, and—and you'll understand. I have to go."

She practically dove down the stairs, leaving Meli's confused calls behind, and raced to her house like a woman possessed. Panic seized her. What had she done? She could have just said she had feelings for Meli and asked her out, like a normal person would. No, Instead, she'd barely been able to speak, all but throwing the tiny piece of plastic at Meli and expecting her to make sense of a dozen songs.

Conner mussed her hair and made a split decision. She couldn't stay here, not where she was too easily found, and the ghosts of sex with Meli taunted her from half a dozen rooms. She packed up her cats, tossed them and a bag into her G-Wagen, turned off her phone, and headed for Big Bear.

Conner curled up under a thick blanket on her sofa, chuckling as the kittens stared at the gas fireplace. Stevie purred next to her, entirely unconcerned about her offspring's fascination with fire. Conner was still getting used to life with cats, particularly life with litter boxes, but they were funny and surprisingly good companionship.

She was regretting her hasty trip as she stared at the empty refrigerator, when someone banged on her door. Three blurs of color flashed past, destined to hide under a bed.

The banging continued as she headed for the door, alarm growing with every step. No one knew she was here. She went out of her way to avoid her neighbors. She found her phone on a table next to her keys and turned it back on, bringing up the app for her video doorbell. Then she nearly dropped it.

Meli stood at her door, hands on her hips.

Conner jumped when she peered at the doorbell.

"Conner Cody, you open this door! I know you're here."

Jaw somewhere near the basement, Conner did as she was ordered. Meli swept in like a tempest, bringing a gust of icy wind and a never-before-seen temper. She spun on her heel and jabbed Conner in the chest with a finger. Conner stumbled back, more from shock than anything else. No one had ever poked her before.

"How dare you?"

"You didn't like the album?" The churning in her gut rivaled the North Sea on its worst day.

"That's not the—Conner, you can't do that! You can't just show up, hand me something like that, and run away without an explanation!" Her curls stretched in every direction, which, combined with her round eyes, gave her a slightly deranged look that still somehow managed to be sexy. "What does this mean?"

"Did you listen to it?"

"Did I listen to it? She wants to know if I *listened* to it." Conner risked a glance around. Who was she talking to? "I can't stop listening to it! I played it twice, and then I had to call Eriq at work so he could figure out how I could play it in my car, where, by the way, since I don't have a fancy car like you, I had to put my laptop on the passenger seat and play it from there, and then I listened to it all the way here."

Conner's head spun from trying to keep up with the world's longest sentence, but one thing stood out—Meli had played it on repeat. That had to mean something...didn't it? But she seemed angry about it.

And she wasn't done. "You have to tell me what it means. Right now, right here, you have to tell me. Because you said you wrote it for me, and the things you say in those songs—God, Conner, those *songs*."

She approached, and Conner tried to retreat, but the damn door betrayed her.

Meli turned beseeching as she looked up at Conner, eyebrows knitting together. The fist clenching Conner's heart relaxed just a bit. "You have to say it, all right? I need to hear you say it." She reached up to tuck a rogue lock of Conner's hair behind her ear with the gentle touch of an angel. "It's okay, sweetheart."

All Conner's defenses dissolved, because it would be okay. This was Meli, after all. They would get past this moment, and Conner would survive. Meli was right; it hadn't been fair to dump the album on her without an explanation. All she had to do was tell her how she felt, and it would be over.

She took a deep, shaky breath.

"I love you."

The world didn't end. Volcanos didn't erupt. Lightning didn't strike. Conner didn't keel over dead.

Instead, everything shifted. The world before telling Meli she loved her and the world after weren't the same. Saying it aloud, saying it to the object of her affection was entirely different than admitting it to herself. Now it was out, and it could never return to the studiously ignored recesses of Conner's mind.

Once it was out, she couldn't stop.

"I think I've been in love with you for a long time. I tried really hard not to be, I swear, but you're just so—so you. So wonderful. Loving you feels as easy as breathing. I don't know how I missed it for so long. I've never been in love, you know, and except for my nieces, I've never said those words to anyone."

"I—"

"But it won't change a thing, okay? I promise. I—I can handle this. I want you to trust me on that. I respect you, and I won't cross any boundaries. Your friendship is too important to me. The album was stupid, right? I think I just needed to get it out, and now that's over. I won't release it."

"You can't—"

"Also, this has nothing to do with us sleeping together. Obviously I enjoyed it. I really, really enjoyed it. But I fell for you a long time before that, and I understand what it was for you, so don't think I just got caught up in that. But if—"

"Conner, shut up!"

She did.

Meli inhaled as if to speak before pausing and cocking her head. "Is that what it's like when I go on and on?"

"Kinda, yeah."

"Huh. You don't get annoyed?"

Conner shook her head. "Nah. The whole love thing, you know? You're adorable when you ramble. And when you don't."

"Oh, okay." She took a sudden, deep breath. "Right. So, before you keep going, you're missing an important piece of information."

Conner waited. Her breath came in quick, shallow pants.

"The thing is…the part you're missing…what you need to know…" She wrung her hands, but when she looked up, fire blazed in her eyes. "I'm in love with you, too."

All the oxygen left Conner's lungs. Her hands scrambled against the solid wood of the door behind her, both reassuring her this moment was real and keeping her standing. She stared at Meli, searching her face for some clue that confirmed she was telling the truth.

She tried to speak but had to clear her throat twice before forcing words out. "Say—say that again."

"I'm in love with you, Conner."

A thousand questions roamed her very confused mind, but only one escaped. "How?"

A wide grin split Meli's cheeks as she threw her head back and laughed. The little gap between her front teeth had never been more attractive. "How? How could I not? How does anyone fall in love? It just happened."

"Are you sure?"

"Oh, Conner." She moved into her space, caressing one of Conner's cheeks with a soft hand. "I won't lie. This has been a confusing journey for me, but I've never been surer of anything than the fact that I love you. We have a lot to talk about, but can I please kiss you now?"

Conner blinked rapidly, willing her brain to catch up before abandoning the effort. She lunged forward, capturing Meli's lips in a long, searing kiss that left both of them breathless. She wanted more—she wanted it all—but Meli was right; they had a lot to discuss. Still, she kept returning for one more kiss half a dozen times.

"If we don't stop, we never will." Meli giggled against her lips.

"Sounds good to me." Conner kissed her again and again, afraid she'd wake up from this dream.

They walked backward, lost in each other, until the back of Meli's knees hit the arm of the couch and she toppled onto it with a breathless laugh, pulling Conner with her. Conner pushed herself up to gaze down at her, framing Meli's face with her hands. Astonished disbelief battled with joy in her heart.

"Say it again."

Meli's smile stretched even farther, a feat Conner didn't think was possible. "I love you."

"Again?"

"I love you." Meli giggled as Conner attacked her neck. "What about you?"

"I love you, too." She peppered any exposed skin she could find, from ears to hands, with kisses. "I love you, I love you, I love you."

She could have stayed there forever, but a small orange fluffball chose that moment to leap onto her back.

Meli's eyes bugged out. "Uh, Conner? There's a cat on your shoulder."

She turned her head. "Oh, that's Sheryl."

"Excuse me?"

She sat up, balancing the kitten, who squeaked in protest, with one hand. Once she stopped moving, Sheryl cuddled against her neck with outsized purrs.

"I have cats now."

"You have cats? In the plural? I haven't seen you for a month, and in that time you managed to write and record an entire album and adopt multiple cats?"

"It's a demo, not an album yet, but yes. Although you could say the cats adopted me. I found them on the beach one night after…" Her stomach plunged at the memory. She didn't want to think about Meli with another woman. "Do you want to meet them?"

Meli regarded her for a moment, clearly not missing that she'd left something unsaid, but then she smiled and nodded.

"Watch this."

She began to sing the chorus of Fleetwood Mac's "Dreams," something she'd done during her infrequent breaks while writing the album, and soon Stevie trotted in, meowing along.

"This is Stevie. Obviously she's the mother. You've met Sheryl, and the gray one over there is Linda. Alanis is around here somewhere, although she's completely black, so sometimes she blends in. I almost sat on her one day." Alanis chose that moment to launch herself out of hiding at Linda, and they began to battle with fierce squawks.

"You have *four* cats, and you named them after someone's aunts?"

"I named them after my musical heroes. No cat is going to live in my house without a proper understanding of the women who paved the way."

"And you trained them to come at a song?"

"They like to listen to me sing. I don't know if they can recognize a specific song, but I'm trying."

Meli sat up, crossing her legs underneath her. Stevie jumped up with an inquisitive meow, settling herself in Meli's lap, to the apparent delight of all involved.

"The night you found them: it was after what?"

So they were going to do this now. Conner described the night she'd gone to Meli's apartment, and although Meli tried to interrupt her, she then talked about making the demo and her apology tour across the US. Then, chronology be damned, she reversed, discussing her growing attraction and all the ways she'd tried to fight it, tried to hide it, tried to deny it.

She finished with a weary laugh. "And after all that, I fell in love anyway. I don't know where we go from here. Hell, I don't even know how to be in love."

"Sweetheart." Meli laced their fingers together. Conner wasn't sure whether to blame the endearment or the contact for the disruption to her heartbeat, but she didn't care. Her heart could stop altogether right now, and she'd die the happiest she'd ever been.

"I wish you'd give yourself more credit. Of course, you know how to be in love. We're here, aren't we? I didn't fall in love with you because of the way you posture or the image you work so hard to project, even though some of that's still ridiculously attractive. I love you because of the person I know behind all that. I didn't fall for Conner freaking Cody. I fell for Conner."

Conner leaned forward to kiss her again. Both cats left, seeming highly offended at the disturbance. When they parted, Meli sighed.

"You're so good at that. So I guess it's my turn for a story? The truth is, Conner, I think I fell in love with you the first time I ever saw you. Maybe not love, but something happened."

Conner's eyebrows skyrocketed. "When we shot the music video?"

"Yes, but not when we met. I saw you about ten minutes before that. You were walking across the set, all broody, with your hands shoved in the pockets of that jacket you live in, and I don't think I've breathed properly since. I breathe, obviously, but you know what I mean. Anyway, at first, I thought I was just starstruck because you're, well, you. But then I got to know you, and I've never been able to stop thinking about you. You're so intense, you know, like when you look at me or talk to me, it feels like no one else exists. And your eyes and your hair…"

"I do have those."

Meli tried to pull away, scrunching her nose and laughing, but she only succeeded in tugging Conner into her lap. "You know what I mean. And the way you're always leaning against things!"

"My bad posture turns you on?"

Meli dragged a hand down her face. "Everything you do turns me on. Don't you see? But the kicker was...Vittoria. When you got back with her, it—it hurt, even though I had no right to feel that way. So that's when I really started to figure out that I, you know—"

"That, as Sarah says, you like liked me?" Conner snickered.

Meli chuckled along with her. "Something like that. So finally, after talking to Bellamy, I got up the courage to talk to you, and, well, I didn't quite confess my feelings so much as I—"

"Propositioned me?"

"I did not!"

Her protest failed. "You very much did. You used me for my talented body."

"Conner! That wasn't it at all, and you—oh. You're teasing me. You're so bad!"

"I don't know about that. Judging from your screams, I was pretty damn good."

Meli groaned. It shouldn't have been a sexy sound, but Conner started thrumming from head to toe. "Is this what life with you is going to be like?"

Conner's breath caught at the same moment Meli's eyes took over her entire face as she realized what she'd said. "Is that what you want?" she asked softly, leaving the teasing behind.

Meli gulped. "Kind of? I mean, I'm not saying we should move in together tomorrow and combine our bank accounts or anything, but yeah, I want to see where this goes. Only if you do, obviously. I'm not going to assume—"

Conner caught her flailing hands, stilling them with her own. She brought them to her lips, pressing a tender kiss to each. "Babe, I just told you I'm in love with you. What else do you need?"

"I don't know." Conner would have given up her entire fortune to erase the anxiety written across Meli's face. "You date supermodels and professional athletes and rock stars and famous actresses. I'm just—"

"Gorgeous." Conner kissed her between every word. "Sexy. Amazing. Kind. Talented. Hard-working. Adorable."

"I have these love handles..."

Conner swatted her hands away from the offending hips and tugged Meli toward her, leaning back until Meli straddled her. "And I love them, so they're very appropriately named."

"I just don't know if I can live up to what you're used to."

"Meli, listen to me, please. On paper, maybe we don't make sense. But in my heart, we make total sense. You're one of the few things in my life I've ever been able to make sense of. Do you know what the difference is between you and any other woman? I never loved any of them. I never wrote an entire album about falling in love with them. I never wanted them around all the time. I'm in love with you, and that's what matters."

She pulled Meli's face to hers, coaxing her mouth open. They kissed until Meli lay fully on top of her, hips grinding into each other. She was beyond ready to make love to Meli slowly and thoroughly, but she pulled away before they removed any clothing.

"I'm different from other people you've dated, too."

"Because you're a woman, or because you're rich and famous?" Meli said with a teasing grin.

"Both, but mostly the famous part. You've already seen what it's like to be seen with me. It'll only get worse if we're together. Fans can be fucking relentless, and I hate the thought of subjecting you to that. If I'm seen with another woman, they'll say I'm cheating. If we aren't at an event together, they'll say we're broken up. If we're seen looking remotely unhappy together, they'll say we're fighting."

"Let them say what they want. We'll know the truth. You know I don't care about any of that."

Conner tightened her arms around Meli. Would she ever stop feeling like the luckiest person in the world, or would she spend the rest of her life questioning if this was all a dream? As long as she spent that life with Meli, she didn't really care about anything else.

Meli found Conner at her piano early the next morning but didn't speak right away, simply sitting next to her on the bench and resting her head on Conner's shoulder.

"Is that what I have to look forward to?" she asked softly once Conner finished her song. "Our life together, immortalized in song?"

Her voice carried a playful lilt through the roughness of sleep, so Conner relaxed. "Maybe sometimes, but not this one. This is just for us. And you always have the ultimate veto power. That goes for the album, too. You know that, right?"

"Don't be silly. It's brilliant, and I wouldn't dare keep it to myself."

Conner gazed at her, bursting with affection. It baffled her to think she'd denied this for so long, when now all she could picture was playing songs for Meli every day, spoiling her with everything she desired, and making love to her whenever they wanted. They'd done plenty of that the night before, leaving her with a delicious ache between her thighs and various other places.

She enjoyed the morning perhaps most of all, waking up next to Meli as she slept peacefully while four little balls of warmth scattered around told her the cats had joined them at some point after they fell asleep.

Overwhelmed with contentment, she couldn't help writing a song about it. Bellamy was right that the album needed an ending, but she'd find another song for that. This one belonged to just the two of them.

Meli shivered next to her, so Conner pulled her to a recliner, draping a blanket over them once Meli was snug on her lap.

One last nagging question popped into her head. "So, about that date you went on…"

She felt Meli's sigh against her chest. "Is this going to be a thing between us?"

"No, and you can tell me it's none of my business. Just curious, I guess."

"I've never been attracted to another woman before. I noticed that they're pretty, but I never felt that pull until I met you. But I've been attracted to men—" Conner pretended to gag, which prompted the giggles she sought. "So figuring out my sexuality has been difficult, and I felt like I needed to sort that out first. She was a woman I met on-set, and when she asked me out, it seemed like a good opportunity. She was nice and cute, and the date was fine, but I thought about you the entire time. I couldn't stand the thought of kissing anyone else, so I ended it early. When I got home, Eriq told me you had come by, and…you know the rest."

Conner preferred reality to all the scenarios she'd obsessed over regarding the mystery date. "Did you decide how you want to define your sexuality?"

She shrugged before snuggling into Conner once more. "Yes. No. I don't know. I guess I'm just Conner-sexual."

Conner didn't even bother trying to mask her smugness. "I like that. I like that a lot."

"You would."

Conner nuzzled her neck, pressing a kiss that was more tender than passionate. They cuddled in comfortable silence, watching the winter sunrise, until Conner squeezed her waist. "Look, babe. It's snowing."

Meli gasped in delight and rambled like a child about how pretty it was and how much she loved snow even though she hated being cold and pretty please could they make snow angels after breakfast?

"I've never made snow angels."

Meli gaped. "How is that possible? We are literally sitting in your house in the mountains."

"I don't know. Just never did."

"Oh, we're going to fix that. We'll make snow angels and a snowman and maybe even have a snowball fight!"

Conner shivered. "Sounds like I'll need to be warmed up after all of that. Like a long, hot bath…"

She raised her eyebrows at Meli, enjoying the way her eyes darkened. "I could get down with that." She looked pensive. "Do you realize we could've had this conversation like two years ago?"

"About snow?"

"About us."

Conner took her time considering that possibility before shaking her head. "No, I don't think we could have. We both needed to work through our feelings, and now we're right where we need to be. Besides, I asked you out once, and you turned me down."

Meli groaned and buried her head in Conner's shoulder, so her words came out muffled. "You're never going to let me live that down, are you?"

"If I have my way, I'll spend the rest of my life teasing you about it."

"The rest of your life, huh? Still as cocky as ever."

"Hey, just because I fell in love doesn't mean I changed completely."

"Good." Meli pressed a kiss to her lips. "Because I happen to love you exactly the way you are, arrogance and all."

"Say it again, one more time?"

"If I have my way, I'll spend the rest of my life saying it. I love you, Conner."

"I love you, too, Meli."

Chapter Forty-six

Their timing couldn't have been worse. Conner spent December jet-setting across three continents, working the red carpets and doing press as her final superhero movie premiered. In between, she and the band worked night and day to perfect their songs in time to record before she headed to England in February to film.

Once she accepted the loss of control, the ease with which the band worked together surprised her. She and Emi primarily handled the lyrics, but all four had input into the arrangements, and she was beyond pleased with the results. Her demo had been great, but they were elevating it into something truly special. Not feeling like all the responsibility rested on her shoulders removed a great deal of stress, as well.

But all that meant she had very little time for Meli, who had her own work obligations. They decided not to officially appear in public together for the time being, enjoying their little bubble. Instead, they lived for the snatches of time they could manage.

"I don't even know what time zone I'm in." Conner sighed as Meli scratched her scalp. "How long am I home this time?"

"Twelve hours and forty-nine minutes, give or take."

"Are you counting?"

"Every second. We have…eight hours and twelve minutes left. I guess this is what life with a superstar is like."

Conner opened her eyes at the warning bells in Meli's voice. "It won't always be like this. I promise."

"I know. I'm just being selfish and want you all to myself."

Though reluctant to move away from Meli's soothing scratches, Conner nevertheless rolled onto her knees and straddled Meli's lap, tugging on one ringlet. "You have me, babe. Forever."

They kissed, and while she was tempted to spend all eight hours making Meli come in as many positions as possible, Conner remained content to simply kiss her. Kissing was fun. With previous girlfriends, kissing was merely foreplay, a precursor to the main event. With Meli, kissing itself was an event. She was quite good at it.

And she was all Conner's.

"Come to England with me," she blurted out.

Meli blinked away the haze of a good make-out session. "I thought you spent Christmas in Ireland, not England, and besides, we talked about this. We're sticking to our plans."

"Not Christmas. In February, when I go to film. I know you can't spend the entire time with me, but come for just a while. We'll stay in Gran's house, and I'll show you London. Maybe we can even hop over to Belfast for a weekend. I don't want to go so long without seeing you." She caught herself biting her lip.

Meli shook her head in resignation, grinning. "You're a hard woman to say no to, Conner Cody."

"I was counting on that. Now, we're down to less than eight hours, and I have a few ideas for how to spend it."

Conner was headed to Belfast for Christmas, and Meli to Texas. Neither wanted to spend the holiday apart, but their plans had long been set. If Conner had her way—and she usually did—this would be their last Christmas apart. She would have blown off Belfast without a second thought, but Meli wouldn't hear of it. Besides, she planned to come out to her parents, and she wanted to do it alone, which Conner could respect.

"I think they already know," she told Conner on the phone one night.

They were at their respective homes, a suggestion from Meli to temper their urge to spend every single minute together. Despite being on her own for a decade, Conner felt it was the most grown-up decision she'd ever made.

"Why do you say that?"

"Because after they were here last summer, Mami told me that they would love me no matter what, and Abuela said that if she'd ever tangoed with someone the way you and I did, I wouldn't exist because she never would have married my abuelo."

Conner laughed, although the comment from Mrs. Velasco tugged at her heart. What was it like to have the unconditional love of a parent like that? Or any love from a parent, for that matter. Seth was his usual disinterested self, and Camila had been completely silent. She and Conner hadn't spoken since Abuelita's funeral, a new record for them. Conner missed Abuelita far more than whatever semblance of a relationship she and Camila ever had.

"I don't think they'll care about having a pansexual daughter, to be honest," Meli said. "They adore you. All they talk about is when I'm going to bring you home."

"Well, when are you?"

"Hmm. Maybe when you're very, very good."

Conner snorted. "Then they'll be waiting a long time."

"I don't agree." Conner prepared for a lecture on being nice to herself, which she was fond of doing, but Meli surprised her. "You were pretty good last night."

Conner's ears, libido, and nipples perked up at the suggestion curling around her words. "You think so? Wait until you see what I can do with just my voice."

Conner threw a party for New Year's Eve, but not the type of debauchery she normally hosted. (That was planned for later, before she left for England.) Instead, she invited only those she and Meli cared about the most: the band, Maggie's mother, Kit, Harlow, Lindsey, Eriq and Meli's other roommates, Jamal, and Sadie's family.

"Aunt Conner! Daddy said I could stay up until midnight!" Hannah launched herself at Conner as soon they followed Meli into the living room.

Conner took a few steps back, exhaling audibly. At eight, Hannah was unfortunately getting too big to hold, but Conner squeezed her hard before letting her go.

"You think you can make it that late?"

"Duh." Hannah rolled her eyes, so clearly imitating her older sister that Conner had to chuckle.

Sarah walked in with a friend, whose eyes swelled to a concerning size the moment she spotted Conner. With a noise reminiscent of an alarmed mouse, she sped over until they were nearly nose to chin.

"Oh. My. God. You really are Conner Cody! Can we take a selfie? That would literally make my entire life."

"Sure, babe."

Conner winked, and the teenager swooned so hard Conner was worried for her health before she recovered and brandished her cell phone like a weapon. They posed for two selfies before Sarah dragged her away with a scowl.

"Come on, Kaylen. That's Lindsey Schafer!"

Conner narrowed her eyes as she watched the girls gawp at Lindsey and whisper to each other. She glanced at Sadie. "Kaylen? Why does that name sound familiar? Wait. Is that the girl who didn't believe I'm Sarah's aunt? I thought she hated her!"

"That was middle-school Sarah. High-school Sarah and Kaylen are now friends."

"What happened to those other girls? The ones she snuck out with?" Conner's heart broke just a little when she realized she no longer knew what was going on in her niece's life. Sarah used to text her daily.

"She said, and I quote, 'Any friend who would leave me in a situation like that isn't really my friend.'" Sadie leveled a glance at Conner. "Sound familiar? I know my daughter, and there's not a chance in the world she came up with that."

"She listened to me?" Conner held a hand to her chest in alarm. "Did I impart wisdom to a child? Well, fuck me."

"If you could keep that last bit of wisdom to yourself, I'd be grateful," Asher said dryly, holding his hands over Hannah's ears.

Conner wandered over to the teenagers, resting a hand on each shoulder. "Hey, Linds? Come here. I want you to meet someone."

The two fangirled as expected, leading Conner and Lindsey to share an amused grin, and then all four of them posed for a picture together. Conner maneuvered until she was next to Sarah, draping an arm over her shoulder. Afterward, she tugged on Sarah's wrist. "I want to talk to you for a second."

Rebellion drifted across Sarah's face before she sullenly shrugged and followed Conner to the staircase, where they sat next to each other a few stairs up.

"Are you going to be angry with me forever?"

Sarah was quiet for so long Conner had nearly given up when she finally said, in a very small voice, "I thought you were my friend."

"I am, but sometimes even I have to be an adult." She nudged her, hoping for a laugh, but Sarah hadn't thawed. "I want you to feel like you can talk to me."

"So you can tell my parents on me?"

"So I can keep you safe. Trust me, I know what it's like when nobody cares about your safety. Look at me." When Sarah didn't comply, Conner's temper began to fray. "Damn it, Sarah. Can you try to meet me halfway here? Just look at me."

Sarah finally turned her head, and the hurt on her face was an arrow straight to Conner's heart.

"Do you know what I was doing at your age?" She shook her head. "Smoking weed every day. Popping whatever pills someone handed me. Drinking and dancing with people twice my age in clubs all night long. Having sex with randoms. I could have been drugged, I could have been raped, I could have gotten a disease. I could have died. And no one fucking cared."

Sarah's eyes widened, either at the story or at Conner's casual swear word.

"I am super proud of you for calling me that night. I don't care if you have a beer or party with your friends. You're a teenager; you're gonna do stuff like that. But you recognized that you were uncomfortable and unsafe, and you reached out. I'm so proud of you. I don't think I'm that mature even now." Sarah's mouth twitched. "But there are lines I can't cross, like keeping you for a night when your parents think you're elsewhere. I can't promise I'll always get it right. I'm still figuring this out."

"Being an aunt?"

"I meant being an adult, but yeah, that too." Sarah's mouth twitched again, and she looked away. "I can promise, though, that the decisions I make are because I love you, kid." She let that comment simmer for a moment before nudging Sarah again. "Do you still hate me?"

Sarah's mutter was barely audible over the laughter from the rest of the house. Conner could make out Meli's melodious peals. "I don't hate you."

"Do you like me?"

"You got me grounded. So not cool."

"I'd argue that *you* got you grounded, but whatever. I'll take half the blame. Could we maybe hang out sometime, if your mom lets us?"

Sarah cast a serious side-eye. "Are you still in trouble, too?"

Conner wiggled her hand. "Work in progress, which coincidentally should be the name of my autobiography, but it won't be."

"What will it be?"

"If I ever write one? Queen of the nepo babies, duh." A chuckle escaped Sarah, and Conner did a comically exaggerated double take. "Is that a laugh? Did Sarah Cohen actually laugh? I thought you forgot how to smile at all."

"Shut up, Aunt Conner."

The title warmed Conner to her nepotistic toes. She elbowed Sarah again, Sarah shouldered her in return, and with that they rejoined the crowd. Sarah still clung to her grudge in a way only a teenage girl could, but her grasp was tenuous, and Conner felt they were on their way back.

She found Meli on the loveseat and wedged herself in the middle, forcing Bellamy to squish to one side. Meli pressed a kiss to her temple as Conner hooked one leg over her knee.

"Did you work things out?"

She wiggled her hand just as she had to Sarah. "I think we'll get there. We established that she doesn't hate me, but she also said I'm not cool, which is clearly untrue."

Bellamy let out a bark of laughter while Meli kissed her again. "I think you're the coolest person I know."

"I think you're the nicest person I know."

"I think I'm going to barf." Bellamy's pained expression was a sight to behold.

In a nearby armchair, Emi rolled her eyes. "I am so not ready for wifed-up Conner."

They began to tease the couple, which Meli accepted with her usual good nature, but something about the comment didn't sit right with Conner. She filed it away until she could get Meli alone.

Though one of the countdowns to the ball dropping played on her TV, Conner also piped music through her state-of-the-art speaker system. She danced with Jamal, Maggie's eyes tracking their every move, before switching to salsa for Meli. She and Sadie both attempted to teach Asher to dance but fell over laughing at his complete lack of anything resembling rhythm. Even Hannah took a turn with her, letting Conner twirl her around until she grew too dizzy to stand.

With less than half an hour until midnight, Meli asked if anyone needed anything from the kitchen.

Conner spotted her chance and followed, catching her as she passed the pantry.

"Only you." She squeezed Meli's waist, nibbling on her neck.

"We have a houseful of guests, Conner, you—ah—can't do this. Mmm…behave."

Conner's heart gave an extra beat at her use of "we." She pressed a kiss behind Meli's ear, accidentally inhaling a curl, before turning her around. "I have a serious question, actually. Do you want to get married?"

Meli's round eyes dominated her face as she stepped back. "Conner, I love you, and obviously I want to explore life with you, but don't you think that's a little soon? I mean, we don't even live together officially, we haven't gone public as a couple—not that there's a specific order to any of this, because I guess most people wouldn't have sex, then say I love you, then start dating, unless they're in like a romance novel or a movie. I'm just trying to—"

"Babe, hold up. I probably should have phrased that differently. I mean, are you a person who wants to get married someday, to anyone? We haven't talked about it, and you should know that I've never seen the point."

Meli's shoulders dropped. "Oh. That makes so much more sense. I guess I never thought hard about it. As long as you and I know that we love each other and we're committed, that's enough for me. Besides, look at all the rings you wear. Where would a wedding band go?"

Conner searched her open face for signs that the joke was a cover-up for her real feelings and, finding none, pressed her against the pantry door and kissed her hard. Despite Meli's earlier protests, they lost themselves in the kisses until an exclamation interrupted them.

"My eyes! Is that what track eight is based on?"

Conner pulled apart with reluctance. "Kit, you couldn't handle what track eight is based on."

"Conner!" Meli swatted her gently, color creeping up her neck.
"Whatever works for you. Please don't ever leave her, Melina. You've inspired Conner to new greatness. Although a breakup album would be absolute fire..."
"Kit, watch your mouth."
Meli simply laughed and wrapped her arms around Conner's waist. "Sorry to burst your bubble, Kit, but you'll have to do without."
They lifted their hands in surrender. "Fine, fine. Sticking around will work, too. Having you as her muse is going to propel this band into the stratosphere. But, Conner, I have a bone to pick with you. You need to reconsider switching track ten into a major key."
"I'm not doing that."
"The tone doesn't fit the lyrics. That song celebrates falling in love and deserves to be played at weddings across the country no matter how often you wrinkle your nose at the thought."
"First, if anything's going to be played at weddings against my will, it's track twelve. Second, it's not just about falling in love. It's about the double-edged sword that is love and how it can kill you or give you life. The dissonance between the lyrics and the tonality is intentional. Also, assigning emotions to major and minor keys is a tired and unsophisticated trend, and this, my friend, is why you're our manager and not our producer."
Kit folded their arms. "Muse, what do you think?"
"Leave her out of it."
Meli looked between them. "I don't know what you're talking about."
"You remember track ten, right? Okay, so a key is a group of notes based on a scale that's either major or minor. People tend to think of major keys as happy and minor keys as sad, and sometimes artists pair a major key with a depressive theme or vice versa. Think...'Pumped Up Kicks' by Foster the People."
"Oh, I get it! But I love track ten. Don't change it."
Conner turned to Kit with a smirk. "The muse has spoken."
"What would you have done if she'd agreed with me?"
Conner squirmed but had an answer at the ready. "I would have said that her opinion is important, but the band has already discussed this issue and agrees with me."
A slow clap drew their attention. Lindsey wandered in, wearing an amused expression. "Look who's learned to be diplomatic."
"Don't be so hasty. Her first reaction was an outright no." Harlow followed, tilting an empty wineglass.
"Why are you always lurking?"
"I was very much not. The last thing I want to see or hear is you and Melina getting up to something in whatever space you can find, like that pantry you're leaning against."

Conner bent her head to Meli's ear and said, as quietly as possible, "We do like pantries, don't we?"

Apparently not quietly enough. Lindsey's eyes and mouth formed perfect *O*'s. "The pantry? I knew it was you! Oh, don't even give me that look, Conner Cody. Remember that party I had at the end of the season? You two disappeared, and the next day I found spilled flour with a handprint in it in my pantry."

Conner would have kept denying to preserve Meli's honor, but Meli gave it up with a groan, burying her face in Conner's shoulder. Over her head, Conner grinned.

Harlow held a hand to her temple. "Do you not have a single boundary?"

"No," came Meli's muffled reply, interrupting whatever Conner was going to say.

Everyone laughed, and she held Meli close, rubbing her back. Let them laugh. She had Meli; she had her band and her sister and her nieces. Let them laugh away.

Still, as Harlow brushed past her to refill her glass, Conner couldn't resist. "You just need to get laid, Harlow. Maybe that'll remove the stick from your ass. Hey, Kit's single."

Her two managers sized each other up and answered, in strident unison, "No."

As midnight approached, they gathered in the living room, glasses of champagne in hand. Asher carried a grumpy Hannah in from a guest room as she had demanded to be woken up. Assuring Meli she'd return by the countdown, Conner slipped next to Jamal.

"Talk to her." Jamal gave her a look, and she repeated herself. "You can't avoid her all night."

"I'm not."

"Yes, you are, you fucking coward. Friend to friend, dragging this out is only making it worse for both of you. Maggie's been drinking. Offer to drive her home."

He flicked his gaze at her again. "Are you going to be one of those people who tries to matchmake now that you're all coupled up?"

"Nope. I'm Maggie's best friend, and I want her to be happy. Talk. To. Her."

She left it at that and returned to Meli's side. As everyone counted down, she gazed around the room. She'd read that one should start the new year the way they wanted to spend it, and she could think of nothing better than this moment, except perhaps to add a platinum album and an Oscar-winning movie.

Maybe next year.

At midnight, she wrapped her arms around Meli and kissed her thoroughly, ignoring the catcalls as their kiss lingered. When they finally parted, she rested her forehead against Meli's.

"Happy New Year, babe. I love you."

"I love you, too, Conner."

"Say it again?"

Meli laughed and complied.

Most everyone stayed the night, and in the morning, they prepared a feast. Harlow baked luscious cinnamon rolls while Sadie cooked bacon and scrambled eggs. Lindsey and Bellamy joined forces for fluffy biscuits and a pan of sausage gravy that clogged Conner's arteries just by looking at it. Emi conscripted Sarah and Kaylen into cutting up a platter of fruit, and Meli made tortillas with an ease that made Conner learn that even domesticity could turn her on.

Meanwhile, Conner destroyed Asher in *Mario Kart* only to lose to Hannah for the first time, a defeat she wouldn't live down for six months until she reclaimed her title.

Breakfast ran long, but finally everyone headed home to nap off the long night and heavy food. After shutting the door, Conner pulled Meli to her and gave in to the urges she'd been resisting since the night before.

Their kisses started slowly, almost lazily, gradually growing demanding and ardent. Conner found her favorite part of Meli's body and squeezed, pulling her pelvis down to meet her own thrusting hips. She contemplated having Meli sit on her face right where they were before another idea struck her.

With some difficulty, she freed her mouth. "Babe, do you want to take this upstairs? I have something for you."

Meli wore the dazed look and swollen lips of someone thoroughly kissed. "I'll go wherever you want me to."

God, Conner loved this woman. She took her hand and pulled her up the stairs at a brisk pace, pausing on the second floor to flash her a filthy grin. "Have you ever been fucked by a strap-on?"

Heat raced up Meli's cheeks, and she shook her head. Ready to come just thinking about it, Conner jogged up the remaining stairs, only stopping when Meli tugged her arm at the top.

"Hey, Conner?" The wicked glance Meli threw her way nearly burned the clothing right off her.

"Have you?"

Epilogue

Five years later

Conner strummed her guitar, going through her chords to calm her fingers. She wasn't usually nervous when playing a cover song, but this wasn't just anyone's song.

It was her dad's.

She'd vowed from the very beginning that Hestia Rising would never play a Seth Cody song, no matter who begged. She had stuck to that vow for close to a decade, until the last person she ever expected to request it did just so.

When Kit first relayed that Seth's band had been selected for the Kennedy Center Honors, Conner had been glad for him in a vague sort of way. It was cool and all, the ultimate honor, but she couldn't summon any personal feelings on the matter. When Kit further relayed that the band had been asked to perform a tribute, she'd blown a raspberry, laughed, and forgotten about it.

Then Seth called.

"I hear congratulations are due," she said, turning on the speakerphone so she could finish notes for a song that would eventually be on Hestia Rising's fourth album.

"Yeah, yeah, thanks." He cleared his throat. "I suppose that's why I rang."

"Hmm?"

"They said you, er, don't want to perform."

She frowned, marking out a note and dropping it half a key. "Yeah. I figured you didn't care."

He coughed. "The thing is, I do care."

Conner jerked her head up and looked around until she remembered he was probably an ocean away. Or maybe an hour. Who knew? "You do?"

"I wouldn't have asked for you to perform if I didn't."

Conner's pen dropped to her notebook, then the couch, then the floor, where it rolled to parts unknown to be found by a delighted cat later. "You asked?"

"Aye. I did." He sighed. "Conner, I'm a shite father, always have been, but you're still my kid. That's my blood in your veins, my name on your birth certificate, and my talent every time you get onstage."

Conner came by many of her traits honestly, including her arrogance.

"I knew you were going to follow me from the moment you stole my wee guitar."

"You knew that was me?"

"Of course I did. It was a good choice for a first guitar, that Martin."

She worried her bottom lip before making a rash decision. "I don't have it anymore." He swore, but she plowed on. "Your granddaughter picked it out."

Dead silence.

"When I first began teaching her to play years ago, I let her pick, and she chose that one. It's not just me who shares your blood."

"Yes, well, that's, um—"

"She's good. Really good. She'll be famous one day."

"Right, well, ah—are you gonna play for me or not?"

Ten years ago, Conner would have been furious at his gruff dismissal of the topic. She would have pushed and picked until he declared that she needn't bother with the bloody Kennedy Center. In short, she would have done exactly as Camila always did.

But Conner was older, wiser, and happier now, and she understood love in a way she hadn't comprehended ten years ago. Seth was a shit father; that was true, but it didn't mean she had to be a shit daughter, too.

"Yeah, Seth. I'll be there."

So here she was in Washington, DC, preparing for a performance that made her more nervous than any arena she'd played in across the world. Meli was filming and couldn't attend, but she had her girls.

Kit made their usual fussy rounds and lingered with Conner. "You good?"

"Yeah." She didn't look up, running through a tricky portion of the song, which had a polyrhythm that was a bitch to get right.

"We can still back out—"

"We can't, and we're not." She lifted her gaze. "I'm fine, Kit. I swear."

They nodded and squeezed her shoulder. "Knock 'em dead, Con."

All too soon they were called to the stage. The foursome gathered in the wings for their routine, as comforting as it was encouraging. All eyes rested on Conner, and she met them with quiet confidence, leaving her nerves in the green room.

"Keep it tight," Maggie said.

"Keep it cool," Emi added.
"Keep it right," Bellamy said.
"And keep it real," Conner finished.

When the lights came on, Conner lifted her chin, finding Seth in the crowd instantly. She began with the notes he had made iconic long before she'd been born, and they played.

At the afterparty—nothing honoring Seth Cody would pass without a party—his bandmates sought out the group to thank them for their performance. The drummer ruffled Conner's hair before she ducked away out of annoyance.

"You always hated that." He chuckled. "I knew even when you were a wain that you'd follow in his footsteps. Always peeking around the corner, watching us until Seth spotted you and made you fetch us drinks."

She attempted to tame her hair back into shape. "I should have asked for tips."

"You did get tips, lass. Best musical education out there. Your mam was so jealous of the attention we gave you, but you didn't care. Soaked it up like a sponge."

Conner scoffed. "Sounds like her."

"She's likely raging now as it is. Sitting right next to Seth while he couldn't take his eyes off you."

Her head snapped up so quickly something in her neck cracked. "She's here?"

"Wise up, Conner. She wasn't going to miss this opportunity to be seen with him, and Seth is just dumb enough to let her. You should've caught on to that by now."

"Don't be a dicko." She smiled to take the sting out of the insult. Seth's bandmates had always treated her with affectionate amusement, and she returned the sentiment.

"Glad to see you're not all American. And speak of the devil himself."

Seth ambled up, hands shoved deep in the pockets of his rumpled tux. Camila was nowhere in sight. "Hey, kid. You did good."

"Yeah? I thought we were a little fast on the outro."

He shook his head, running a hand over the perennial stubble on his chin. "Nah. It was good. Where's that lady of yours?"

"She had to film, but she said to give you her love."

Because of course she did. Because she was Meli, and she'd charmed every single Cody from the moment they stepped foot in Belfast for the first time. Even Conner's bitter aunt adored her. No one could deny her honest face or the heart that saw only the good in everyone. The list of people Meli truly disliked was very short, consisting mostly of conservative politicians and people who disparaged Tex-Mex food. She was even on good terms with Vittoria.

The list also included Camila Morales.

"I heard Camila was here," Conner said as casually as she could manage.

Seth nodded, looking around. "Somewhere. Are you going to talk to her?"

"If I see her, sure. I'm not going out of my way. She knows my phone number."

Though they occasionally ran into one another at industry functions and held exchanges that were brief, polite, and devoid of substance, they'd actually spoken only once in six years, when Conner asked Camila to get Meli an audition. Camila had been shacked up with the director at the time, and Meli had lost sleep over her desire for the role.

"You owe me," Conner said when she called her mother. "You can protest all you want, but you know that you do. Just an audition. I don't want any favors when it comes to casting. She'll do the rest."

"What are you going to do when she discovers that all you have to offer is a bank account and strings to pull?"

Conner's instinct was to lash out, but she reeled herself in. For Camila didn't know love the way Conner did and probably never would. It was her own fault, but she pitied her.

"She knows exactly what I have to offer, and it's far more than that. Stuff you wouldn't understand or appreciate. It doesn't matter. Be a goddamn mother for once and do this because your daughter is asking, and you never have to hear from me again."

Meli had gotten the role, and Conner had held up her end of the bargain. She wasn't looking to break her streak tonight.

Seth brushed his hair away from his face. "You two give me heartburn."

"I think that's your diet." She shifted her weight from foot to foot.

He grunted. "So...you did good."

"You said that already."

"So I did. Well, I reckon I haven't done much as a dad, but I must have done something right, because you're as good a musician as I ever was. I was, you know, proud to see you play my song."

She inclined her head. "It was, you know, an honor."

"Smartarse."

"I learned from the best."

They grinned at each other. Conner could count on one hand the number of real father-daughter moments they'd shared in her thirty-one years, so this was truly surreal for her. With that in mind, she decided to press her luck.

"Seth, I have a question."

❖

Back home after her East Coast trip, Conner woke and stretched with an enormous yawn. She patted the empty space next to her with a sleepy frown. Conner nearly always woke up first, and she loved admiring Meli's peaceful expression before teasing her awake with soft kisses and gentle touches.

Still…the rare occasions that Meli rose before she did and didn't have to work usually meant one thing.

Conner padded downstairs and leaned against the refrigerator with a contented grin. Meli stood at the stove, flipping something in a pan. Two plates sat next to her with sliced avocado, turkey bacon, and sourdough toast, pats of melting butter on top.

She'd never believed this sort of contentment existed. For the first twenty-six years of her life, she'd thought only self-indulgence was her path to happiness, so she chased conquests, fame, and adulation. In return, she received only loneliness and self-loathing.

Now she lived for the moments when Meli picked her up at the airport, when the girls stayed the night and pigged out on junk food, when she and Meli floated in the pool to run lines with each other. Sure, she still enjoyed the thrill of a screaming crowd, the satisfaction of an award selected by her peers, and the triumph of winning a coveted role, but she lived for the smaller things in life. The fact that she enjoyed domesticity tickled her to no end. It turned out that love was calm, not the tempest of her relationship with Vittoria or perpetual drama of Seth and Camila.

With a few taps of her phone she sent music piping through the kitchen speakers and made her way to Meli, sliding her hands across the waist of her silk robe and kissing her neck.

Meli arched into her touch. "Mmm. Good morning, my love."

"It's always a good morning with you, Miss Series Regular."

"Flatterer."

"Truth-teller."

She swayed to the music but otherwise refrained from distracting Meli as she finished cooking. At the table she took a bite of her egg, over-medium just as she preferred, and offered Meli a lazy smile.

"Thank you for making breakfast. What did I do to deserve you?"

Meli beamed, a sight that still made Conner's heart sing "Bidi Bidi Bom Bom." "Loved me and spoiled me endlessly."

"I knew you only wanted me for my money."

Conner pointed a piece of bacon at her but moved too slowly to rescue it from Meli's mouth. They laughed together and finished their meal in genial conversation. After cleaning up—under Meli's tutelage, Conner had graduated from completely useless in the kitchen to one step above a nuisance—they migrated to the den. Conner sprawled across a couch, draping her feet over Meli's lap.

"Harlow wants us to confirm our schedule through the end of the year." Conner hummed an agreement, browsing her phone.

"I'm filming all week, while you—"

"Oh, that's right. Because you're a *series regular* now."

"Are you ever going to stop talking about that?"

"Let me check. Um, no. I'm not. Sue me for being proud that the love of my life just got promoted to series regular and gets to look hot in scrubs every week on TV."

"It's not that big a deal. My contract is only for this season, so who even knows what will happen next year. There might not even be a show! You know how brutal networks are these days. Anyway, it's nothing compared to—" A guilty smile spread across her face. "I know, I know. I broke the rule. No comparing accomplishments."

"You did. I'll have to punish you later."

Meli's pupils dilated at the suggestion, and for a moment Conner considered taking her right there, but then she continued, clearing her throat.

"Right. So. Anyway. Next weekend we have Sarah's show, then you have that convention, and we'll meet up in North Carolina for Lindsey's wedding." She rested her phone on her stomach. "I can't believe she's getting married."

"I can't believe *who* she's marrying."

Meli's gaze drifted to the ceiling with a dreamy smile. "Their story is incredible. After all that time…"

Ever greedy, Conner pulled Meli's attention back to her with a nudge of her toe. "It's great, but I like our story better. No years apart, no painful breakups, just you and me falling in love and living happily ever after. And cats."

Their gazes converged, and Conner marveled again at how lucky she was. Not just to fall for a beautiful woman, but *this* woman, who loved her right back, loved her deeply, and always indulged Conner's need for validation of their love without question or frustration.

"Say it again?" she asked softly.

Meli's smile deepened. "I love you, Conner."

"I love you, too."

Meli continued through their schedule, absently tracing the top of Conner's foot, before coming to an abrupt stop. "Conner Cody!"

Conner's head popped up at her tone. Uh-oh. "Yes, *mi reina*?"

"I am not your queen right now. What did you put on our calendar?! Conner, that is filthy!"

Conner pushed herself up to a sitting position, grinning. "You didn't think it was so filthy in Barcelona."

Meli's eyebrows launched. "That's not—we didn't—how do you even—"

"We did. I just flipped it around and added one thing."

Meli blinked rapidly, her mouth slightly ajar as she clearly tried to imagine the scenario that Conner had described in lurid detail. Finally she shook her head and fixed Conner with a beseeching look.

"Did you forget that we share this calendar with Harlow?"

"...yes."

"Delete it before she sees!"

Conner picked up her phone just in time to drop it when it vibrated. Harlow, right on cue. After a scolding that had Meli red-cheeked and squirming while Conner fired sardonic rejoinders right back and didn't bother to conceal her laughter, Conner erased the offending entry and tossed her phone aside.

"Yes, yes, yes. I'm sure the schedule is fine. It's always fine. I'll do whatever you and Harlow tell me to. Now, onto more important things..."

She yanked Meli toward her by her ankle and stretched out on top of her before tugging her phone out of her hand. Meli made a half-hearted grasp for it, already ceding her focus to the subtle motion of Conner's hips.

"But we didn't even get to Hannah's—"

"Hannah has the Concacaf Girls' U-15 Championship in Costa Rica. We cleared our schedules to attend the final, and if I can move a few things around, I'm going to the semifinal, too. See? I'm on top of it. Now, how about I show you what filthy really means?"

Meli tilted her head up in surrender as Conner discovered she was nude under her robe. A younger Conner would have wondered if five years with the same woman would get boring, but she and Meli delighted in each other every time like it was the first. If anything, their intimate knowledge of each other, body and soul, simply enhanced their lovemaking.

Even if it was sometimes filthy.

Conner paced back and forth, considering biting her nails for the first time in her life. Maggie watched her go, head swinging as if observing a tennis match.

"You need to relax. You're acting like you're the one performing."

"This is so much worse than when we're playing."

Maggie let out a bark of laughter. "Oh, I see. You're not in control. That's why you're bugging out."

"I've never bugged out in my life." Conner stopped marching and crossed her arms as she leaned against the wall. "I just really want this to go well for Sarah. It's her first show."

"Honey, she'll be fine. You've been teaching her for years, and she's great. You know I wouldn't just say that." Maggie punched her on the arm before looking around. "Where's Melina? She always chills you out."

"She's stuck in traffic. Fucking Los Angeles. And I am chill!"

Maggie snorted. "Said every chill person ever."

"Don't you have a husband to call or something?" Conner flipped her off.

As Maggie walked away to do just that, Meli rushed in, hair flying in every direction. "Did I miss it? Am I late? You should be proud of me. I broke the speed limit and everything."

Conner kissed her temple. "Just in time. She goes on in a few minutes."

They chatted about their days before Sarah emerged from the tiny dressing room, flanked by her parents and sister. She appeared to have left every bit of color in her face behind.

Meli gave her a big hug. "You look fantastic! I'm so excited!"

"I don't feel fantastic. I feel like I'm going to vomit."

"You'll be fine. You're ready for this." Asher squeezed her shoulders. "Your mom and I will be front and center. Kaylen is saving us seats."

"I'm going to video it in case you barf!" Hannah added with glee.

After a parting word of encouragement to Sarah, Sadie marched her youngest out with audible threats.

Sarah approached with a gulp. "Aunt Conner?"

"Look at me, babe. You're beyond ready. Besides, you and I share DNA, and I'm a fucking rock star. You got this. If you get nervous, I'll be right here."

She nodded. Meli hugged her again, and she was on.

Conner glowered at the stage. "I want to watch from the audience. This is bullshit."

Meli rubbed her arms. "We have a great view from here, and you know what would happen if you sat out there. She wants to do it on her own, which is really cool."

So Conner watched from the sidelines as five years of weekly lessons came to fruition when Sarah played her first solo show. The venue was tiny but well-known as a place that had launched a thousand careers. What no one else knew—and what Conner would never share—was that she'd made Harlow tip off a few A&R reps, who were also attending. Conner's interference would go no further than that, but just as she had with Meli, she couldn't resist nudging the opportunity in the right direction. Everyone else in Hollywood did it. Conner was only trying to level the playing field.

Sarah brought down the house in her own indie singer-songwriter way, and afterward everyone gathered at Conner and Meli's for a small party.

Conner tried to identify the feeling in her chest as she watched her friends and family mingle. Hannah, Kaylen, and Asher splashed in the pool. Sarah chatted earnestly with Kit. Maggie, Emi, and their partners laughed next to the bar, while Harlow and Meli shared a quiet conversation on the deck. She felt…good, in an almost painful way. Notes swirled in her head as she tried to put her emotions into words.

Her phone vibrated in her pocket, and she knew without looking who it was. After answering, she glanced at Sadie. "Ready?"

Sadie set her shoulders. "As I'll ever be."

"Big day for the Cohen family."

Sadie hummed an acknowledgment but was otherwise silent. In the living room, Conner turned to her.

"I don't think I've ever said this aloud, but I'm glad you're my sister, and I'm so thankful that you gave my stubborn ass a second and third chance."

"I am, too. No matter how this goes, I'll always be grateful to him for giving me a sister. Love you, Conner."

"Love you, too."

Leaving her alone in the room, Conner strode to the front door. Seth Cody stood on the other side, scuffing his shoes against the stoop. For the first time, she realized he looked old. He was in his seventies now, and though his rakish good looks lingered, the years of hard living had left their mark in his wrinkles and gray hair.

"Hi, Seth. Come in."

He followed, glancing around. "Place looks different."

"It's Meli. She makes everything better."

He grunted. At the door of the living room, Conner turned to him with a firm look. "Be nice, all right?"

"What else would I do?"

"I don't know. I'm just happy you agreed to meet her. Long overdue, but better late than never, I guess."

"Well, you haven't asked me for much, and I reckon I owe both of you this."

"Yeah, you do. Thanks…Dad."

After leaving Seth and Sadie alone, Conner headed back outside, where Harlow met her at the door.

"I just took a very interesting phone call."

"Anything I care about?"

"You might, if you care about the role of Eva Perón in the Broadway revival of *Evita*." She delivered this with a ghost of a smirk.

Time stood still. "I got the role?"

"You got the role."

"I got the role? I'm Eva?"

"I already said that. Conner, don't you dare hug me."

But she wasn't the one Conner wanted to hug. She beelined for Meli, sweeping her off her feet and spinning around as she chanted, "I got the role! I got the role!"

Meli swayed when Conner let her go, but her gaze never wavered. "You got it? *Evita?*"

"Pack your bags, *mi reina*. We're going to New York."

"You got the role!" Her scream nearly deafened their friends. "I'm so proud of you, my love! So, so proud." She punctuated each word with a kiss. "Your grandmothers would be proud of you, too."

"Wherever they ended up, I'm sure they're arguing over which of them can take credit for this."

Conner felt like a grin was permanently glued to her face. She was vaguely aware of others gathering around, drawn by the commotion, but, as always, she only had eyes for the love of her life.

"I couldn't have done it without you. I love you so much, Meli."

Meli's smile stretched from ear to ear, showcasing the gap between her front teeth. "Happiness looks so good on you, Conner. I love you, too."

"Say it again?"

"I love you."

Happiness did look good on her. Most things looked good on Conner Cody. But happiness felt even better than it looked. With a whoop, she scooped Meli up and jumped into the pool.

About the Author

Chelsey learned to read around age three and never looked back. Today she enjoys everything from historical nonfiction to contemporary mysteries and, of course, sapphic romance. Her writing journey began in the first grade and has ranged from fanfiction to sports journalism.

Chelsey lives in Texas with her two cats where she dreams of a future with real seasons. She has a bachelor's degree in history and an MBA. In her free time, she enjoys watching sports, traveling, photography, and the occasional video game.

Books Available From Bold Strokes Books

A Thousand Tiny Promises by Morgan Lee Miller. When estranged childhood friends Audrey and Reid reunite to fulfill their best friend's dying wish, the last thing they expect is a journey toward healing their broken friendship and discovering a newfound love for each other. (978-1-63679-630-7))

Behold My Heart by Ronica Black. Alora Anders is a highly successful artist who's losing her vision. Devastated, she hires Bodie Banks, a young struggling sculptor, as a live-in assistant. Can Alora open her mind and her heart to accept Bodie into her life? (978-1-63679-810-3)

Fearless Hearts by Radclyffe. One wounded woman, one determined to protect her—and a summertime of risk, danger, and desire. (978-1-63679-837-0)

Stranger in the Sand by Renee Roman. Grace Langley is haunted by guilt. Fagan Shaw wishes she could remember her past. Will finding each other bring the closure they're looking for in order to have a brighter future? (978-1-63679-802-8)

The Nursing Home Hoax by Shelley Thrasher and Ann Faulkner. In this fresh take for grown-ups on the classic Nancy Drew series, crime-solving duo Taylor and Marilee investigate suspicious activity at a small East Texas nursing home. (978-1-63679-806-6)

The Rise and Fall of Conner Cody by Chelsey Lynford. A successful yet lonely Hollywood starlet must decide if she can let go of old wounds and accept a chance at family, friendship, and the love of a lifetime. (978-1-63679-739-7)

A Conflict of Interest by Morgan Adams. Tensions rise when a one-night stand becomes a major conflict of interest between an up-and-coming senior associate and a dedicated cardiac surgeon. (978-1-63679-870-7)

A Magnificent Disturbance by Lee Lynch. These everyday dykes and their friends will stop at nothing to see the women's clinic thrive and, in the process, their ideals, their wounds, and a steadfast allegiance to one another make them heroes. (978-1-63679-031-2)

Big Corpse on Campus by Karis Walsh. When University Police Officer Cappy Flannery investigates what looks like a clear-cut suicide, she discovers that the case—and her feelings for librarian Jazz—are more complicated than she expected. (978-1-63679-852-3)

Charity Case by Jean Copeland. Bad girl Lindsay Chase came home to Connecticut for a fresh start, but an old, risky habit provides the chance to save the day for her new love, Ellie. (978-1-63679-593-5)

Moments to Treasure by Ali Vali. Levi Montbard and Yasmine Hassani have found a vast Templar treasure, but there is much more to the story—and what is left to be found. (978-1-63679-473-0)

The Stolen Girl by Cari Hunter. Detective Inspector Jo Shaw is determined to prove she's fit for work after an injury that almost killed her, but a new case brings her up against people who will do anything to preserve their own interests, putting Jo—and those closest to her—directly in the line of fire. (978-1-63679-822-6)

Discovering Gold by Sam Ledel. In 1920s Colorado, a single mother and a rowdy cowgirl must set aside their fears and initial reservations about one another if they want to find love in the mining town each of them calls home. (978-1-63679-786-1)

Dream a Little Dream by Melissa Brayden. Savanna can't believe it when Dr. Kyle Remington, the woman who left her feeling like a fool, shows up in Dreamer's Bay. Life is too complicated for second chances. Or is it? (978-1-63679-839-4)

Goodbye Hello by Heather K O'Malley. With so much time apart and the challenges of a long-distance relationship, Kelly and Teresa's second chance at love may end just as awkwardly as the first. (978-1-63679-790-8)

Emma by the Sea by Sarah G. Levine. A delightful modern-day romance inspired by *Emma*, one of Jane Austen's most beloved novels. (978-1-63679-879-0)

One Measure of Love by Annie McDonald. Vancouver's hit competitive cooking show *Recipe for Success* has begun filming its second season, and two talented young chefs are desperate for more than a winning dish. (978-1-63679-827-1)

The Smallest Day by J.M. Redmann. The first bullet missed—can Micky Knight stop the second bullet from finding its target? (978-1-63679-854-7)

To Please Her by Elena Abbott. A spilled coffee leads Sabrina into a world of erotic BDSM that may just land her the love of her life. (978-1-63679-849-3)

Two Weddings and a Funeral by Claudia Parr. Stella and Theo have spent the last thirteen years pretending they can be just friends, but surely "just friends" don't make out every chance they get. (978-1-63679-820-2)

Firecamp by Jaycie Morrison. Going their separate ways seemed inevitable for two people as different as Fallon and Nora, while meeting up again is strictly coincidental. (978-1-63679-753-3)

Coming Up Clutch by Anna Gram. College softball star Kelly "Razor" Mitchell hung up her cleats early, but when former crush, now coach Ashton Sharpe shows up on her doorstep seven years later, beautiful as ever, Razor hopes the longing in her gaze has nothing to do with softball. (978-1-63679-817-2)

Fixed Up by Aurora Rey. When electrician Jack Barrow and artist Ellie Lancaster get stuck on a job site during a blizzard, close quarters send all sorts of sparks flying. (978-1-63679-788-5)

Stranded by Ronica Black. Can Abigail and Whitley overcome their personal hang-ups and stubbornness to survive not only Alaska but a dangerous stalker as well? (978-1-63679-761-8)

BOLDSTROKESBOOKS.COM

Looking for your next great read?

Visit BOLDSTROKESBOOKS.COM
to browse our entire catalog of paperbacks, ebooks,
and audiobooks.

**Want the first word on what's new?
Visit our website for event info,
author interviews, and blogs.**

Subscribe to our free newsletter for sneak peeks,
new releases, plus first notice of promos
and daily bargains.

SIGN UP AT
BOLDSTROKESBOOKS.COM/signup

Bold Strokes Books is an award-winning publisher
committed to quality and diversity in LGBTQ fiction.